"JESUS!" CARPELLI YELLED. "THEY CAN HIT US WITH SLINGSHOTS"

Even without glasses, Carpelli could see the yellow flashes winking at him from the beach. There were splashes all around the ship, some in rows, while others fell in random patterns like handfuls of thrown pebbles. Suddenly the starboard recognition lights exploded, raining green, red, and yellow glass.

A great insect fluted, and then a hammer struck Carpelli's helmet, knocking it from his head, twisting his head as if he were in the grip of a crazed wrestler. The helmet rolled across the deck and thumped against the base of the lookout platform.

He felt something sticky on his temple, creeping down his cheek. He reached up. Blood.

Legs rubber, he staggered backward and crashed into the repeater. Then as horrified faces turned toward him, he slid slowly to the deck.

D1570653

THE SEVENTH CARRIER SERIES
by Peter Albano

THE SEVENTH CARRIER   (2056, $3.95)
The original novel of this exciting, best-selling series. Imprisoned
in an ice cave since 1941, the great carrier *Yonaga* finally breaks
free in 1983, her maddened crew of samurai determined to carry
out their orders to destroy Pearl Harbor.

THE SECOND VOYAGE OF THE SEVENTH CARRIER
                                                         (1774, $3.95)
The Red Chinese have launched a particle beam satellite system
into space, knocking out every modern weapons system on earth.
Not a jet or rocket can fly. Now the old carrier *Yonaga* is desperately needed because the Third World nations — with their armed
forces made of old World War II ships and planes — have suddenly become superpowers. Terrorism runs rampant. Only the
Yonaga can save America and the free world.

RETURN OF THE SEVENTH CARRIER   (2093, $3.95)
With the war technology of the former superpowers still crippled
by Red China's orbital defense system, a terrorist beast runs
rampant across the planet. Out-armed and outnumbered, the target of crack saboteurs and fanatical assassins, only the *Yonaga*
and its brave samurai crew stand between a Libyan madman and
his fiendish goal of global domination.

QUEST OF THE SEVENTH CARRIER   (2599, $3.95)
Power bases have shifted dramatically. Now a Libyan madman
has the upper hand, planning to crush his western enemies with
an army of millions of Arab fanatics. Only *Yonaga* and her indomitable samurai crew can save the besieged free world from the
devastating iron fist of the terrorist maniac. Bravely the behe-
moth leads a ragtag armada of rusty World War II warships
against impossible odds on a fiery sea of blood and death!

ATTACK OF THE SEVENTH CARRIER   (2842, $3.95)
The Libyan madman has seized bases in the Marianas and Western Caroline Islands. The free world seems doomed. Desperately,
Yonaga's air groups fight bloody air battles over Saipan and Tinian. An old World War II submarine, USS *Blackfin*, is added to
Yonaga's ancient fleet, and the enemy's impregnable bases are attacked with suicidal fury.

Available wherever paperbacks are sold, or order direct from the
publisher. Send cover price plus 50¢ per copy for mailing and
handling to Zebra Books, Dept. 3904, 475 Park Avenue South,
New York, N.Y. 10016. Residents of New York and Tennessee
must include sales tax. DO NOT SEND CASH. For a free Zebra/
Pinnacle catalog please write to the above address.

THE
YOUNG
DRAGONS

PETER ALBANO

ZEBRA BOOKS
KENSINGTON PUBLISHING CORP.

*Grateful acknowledgment is made for permission
to reprint lyrics from the following:*
*"BLUES IN THE NIGHT
(MY MAMA DONE TOLD ME)"*
(Johnny Mercer, Harold Arlen)
(c) 1941 WARNER BROS. INC. (Renewed)
All Rights Reserved. Used by Permission.
*"PRAISE THE LORD AND
PASS THE AMMUNITION"*
(Frank Loesser)
*COPYRIGHT (c) 1942
by FAMOUS MUSIC CORPORATION
COPYRIGHT (c) RENEWED 1969
by FAMOUS MUSIC CORPORATION*

ZEBRA BOOKS

are published by

Kensington Publishing Corp.
475 Park Avenue South
New York, NY 10016

Copyright © 1992 by Peter Albano

All rights reserved. No part of this book may be reproduced
in any form or by any means without the prior written con-
sent of the Publisher, excepting brief quotes used in reviews.

If you purchased this book without a cover you should be
aware that this book is stolen property. It was reported as
"unsold and destroyed" to the Publisher and neither the Author nor the Publisher has received any payment for this
"stripped book."

First printing: September, 1992

Printed in the United States of America

DEDICATION

For Dale O. Swanson, Max LeVine, Sidney J. Orlin, Nash Mistretta, Donald R. Ogren, Alfred G. Shaheen, J. Nives Quinn, Jr., Thomas P. Mercadante, Robert L. Kingsbury, John A. Thermos, Bernard L. Ervin, George H. Smith, Lowell C. Corbin; and all of the boys of the forties who heard the drummer, formed their ranks and never looked back.

They proved that evil cannot triumph if good men act.

ACKNOWLEDGMENTS

The author makes the following grateful acknowledgments to:

Master Mariner Donald Brandmeyer for his generous help with ship handling problems under wartime conditions;

Colonel Salvo Rizza, USA retired, who advised on infantry tactics. Colonel Rizza is one of the world's foremost artillery experts. His invention, the Rizza Fan, was used by NATO powers for many years;

Mary Annis, my wife, for her careful reading of the manuscript and her thoughtful suggestions;

Robert K. Rosencrance for giving so freely of his editorial skills in the preparation of the manuscript. I am also indebted to Mr. Rosencrance for suggestions concerning plot and character development.

"Come not between the dragon and his wrath."
William Shakespeare, King Lear

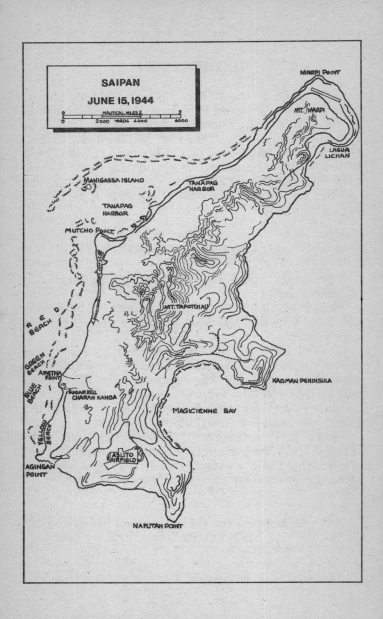

SAIPAN

JUNE 15, 1944

NAUTICAL MILES 2
0   2000 YARDS 4000   4000

MARPI POINT

MT. MARPI

LAGUA
LICHAN

MANIGASSA ISLAND

TANAPAG
HARBOR

TANAPAG
HARBOR

MUTCHO POINT

R E D
BEACH

GREEN
BEACH

AFETNA
POINT

BLUE
BEACH

SUGAR HILL
CHARAN KANOA

YELLOW
BEACH

AGINGAN
POINT

MT. TAPOTCHAU

KAGMAN PENINSULA

MAGICIENNE BAY

ASLITO
AIRFIELD

NAFUTAN POINT

One

Straddling the 145th meridian, the fifteen Marianas Islands stretch across the Western Pacific in a 425-mile arc, pointing northward at Japan's underside like a dagger. The ten northern islands are steep volcanic cones, barren and uninhabited. But the four southernmost— Guam, Rota, Tinian and Saipan—are blessed with plentiful rain and fertile soil that produces rich crops of sugarcane, rice, tobacco, coconuts, and corn.

Saipan is the largest of the Marianas. This rich fourteen-by-five-mile spit of weathered basalt, with an area of only seventy-one miles, is dominated by 1554-foot Mount Tapotchau. Thick with wild growth interspersed with stands of hardwood and casuarina, the mountain rises from the island's center like a green sentinel. To the north and east Saipan's spiny mountain backbone is broken by rolling hills and high plateaus, ending abruptly in narrow coastal flats where sheer cliffs drop hundreds of feet to rocky beaches. But to the south and west the mountain flattens into a long coastal plain, fringed by white beaches and protected by a great coral reef. Here are the patchwork farms, the towns of Garapan and Charan Kanoa and the flat land ideal for airstrips. And here, on these lovely beaches, men would find their rationale for dying in wholesale lots.

On the morning of June 15, 1944, the yellow sun filtered through a sky mackereled with a solid layer of high cumulus clouds, coloring both sea and sky with the pallor of a day-old corpse. Moving slowly across the flat, lifeless sea, the Americans came in their hundreds of ships: bulky transports ushered by scores of circling landing craft, swarming from their davits, Gray Marine engines snarling; pregnant landing ships, low in the water, laboring out their armored amphtracs like sluggish beetles; destroyers, cruisers and squat battleships blasting the beaches at such short ranges that fourteen and sixteen-inch shells sent seismic shocks through the rocky spines. And scurrying among the giants like nervous lackeys, scores of small craft — minesweepers, tugs, patrol craft, and submarine chasers — swept mines, cleared debris, and circled to seaward, sonar gear pinging the monotonous dirge of the submarine killer.

Shortly after dawn, four of the small vessels turned and moved away from the armada, approaching the reef cautiously like teenage boys entering a rival gang's territory. Flying incongruously gay banners at their yardarms, the tiny warships closed the reef in an irregular line, not stopping until each had found a passage in the coral barrier. Then, with engines idling, they lay to, marking channels.

The southernmost ship of the quartet was the PCS (Patrol Chaser Small) 2404. Wooden, 136-feet long, manned by three officers and fifty-nine men and top heavy with a forty-millimeter Bofors aft, four twenty-millimeter Orlikon machine guns amidships, and a three-inch fifty-caliber cannon on the forecastle, the small ship bore a giant white flag, broken by two vertical blue stripes, marked Blue Beach Two. Diesels rumbling at slow idle, the small patrol craft lay to only three hundred yards off Charon Kanoa. Her gun crews — bulky in kapok Mae West lifejackets and with helmets pushed to the back of their heads — squinted into the early morning light, searching for death's glistening wings.

High on the bridge, Quartermaster First Class Michael Carpelli leaned on the windscreen, eyes to binoculars, studying the pageant of invasion beginning to unfold all around him. Tall, with a redwood neck and shoulders like slabs of beef, the young quartermaster

8

was typically Latin: brown eyes, butched black hair, a Roman nose classic in form despite damaged cartilage, a full mouth scarred when a surfing accident drove an eyetooth through the upper lip, and strong, broad cheekbones stretched with olive skin.

Just to Carpelli's left, the ship's captain, Lieutenant Andrew Bennett, fidgeted restlessly. Short, pudgy with brown hair and quick hazel eyes, he was respected by his crew but distrusted by superiors. A twenty-six-year-old graduate of the Naval Academy, he was a unique officer, cynical and openly critical of decisions he considered witless and ill-advised, often spicing his criticisms with expletives that could stop a boatswain's mate in midstride. According to scuttlebutt, the top gold braid were determined Bennett would never see duty aboard a man-of-war. His assignment to the PCS had come immediately after the invasion of Tarawa, where, it was rumored, he had stormed at a staff meeting, criticizing planners who, by miscalculating tides, had doomed hundreds of marines to slaughter in the shallows fronting Betio. Fingering the voice tube that led to the pilothouse beneath his feet, Bennett silently cursed the vagaries of the gentle breeze making a sail of the vessel's high freeboard, while he shouted an incessant stream of commands — commands that started engines, stopped engines, and turned the small ship, in a continuous war to maintain station.

Behind Carpelli, the signalman, Dennis Warner, was kept busy at the gyro-repeater. Standing on the instrument's low platform and squinting through the crosshaired sighting device, he supplied tangents on Afetna, Agingan and Mucho points whenever Andrew Bennett shouted for them. To Michael's right, the gunnery and executive officer, Ensign Robert Bennington — the "ninety-day wonder" to the crew — stared idly through his binoculars, his pasty white face the color of vanilla pudding, his jaw twitching, his tongue dampening dry lips. Flanking Carpelli and standing on raised platforms next to the ship's two signaling searchlights, were two seamen lookouts: Jay Barton to port and Glenn Winters to starboard. Teenagers fresh from high school and boot camp and obviously frightened, the pair searched the sky with jerky movements. Far to the quartermaster's left, in a corner of the bridge, the seventh man in the bridge force, Malcolm Murphy — a married insurance salesman and old man of the crew at age twenty-eight — wore the grotesque kettle-shaped helmet of a "talker." On circuit with the radio shack, gun stations, magazines, depth charge racks, K guns and damage control parties, he alone was free of binoculars.

Thumbing the focusing knob of his Bausch & Lomb 7 x 50 glasses, Michael wondered about the lull. Not a shell had landed for nearly an hour. In fact, for the first time in two days, the air was free of dust and smoke. He sighed and leaned to the glasses. After glancing at the opening in the reef his vessel marked, he moved the glasses to the beach. Here he found a narrow strip of sandy soil dotted with low scrubby trees, the occasional palm groves or flame trees bloomed brilliantly. Behind the groves the land rose in layered escarpments, stepping upward until finally blending into the green tower of Mount Tapotchau.

Michael's mind pondered the enemy. They were always invisible. Thousands of dark-skinned men waited with tanks and artillery just a few hundred yards away, yet the island appeared deserted. Their observation posts must dot the mountain where men staring through range-finding binoculars marked the PCS on the grids of gunnery charts. He knew the PCS was a low priority target. The enemy would wait for the landing craft, guns zeroed in on the openings in the reef. They would not waste rounds or risk destruction of their precious artillery by firing on a patrol craft. He closed his eyes and tried to see the Japanese soldiers. But like all men facing battle he was incapable of visualizing his enemies or conceiving his death at their hands. Even in the long, bloody struggle north from Guadalcanal to New Britain, as a member of the crew of Subchaser

10

3028, he had never seen a live Japanese. Cadavers had floated around the ship and mountains of putrefying flesh had been bulldozed into craters, but never a live Japanese. "The only good Jap is a dead Jap," he had heard many times. He agreed.

Hatred was his constant companion. To a degree, it had begun immediately after Pearl Harbor, where Japanese had killed Americans without provocation. And they had gloated over heaps of American corpses in the Philippines. He had seen the pictures. But primal, consuming hatred came when he saw his first American dead at Guadalcanal—hundreds of bloated, dungaree-clad sailors floating quietly in vast schools after the cruisers *Quincy, Vincennes, Astoria,* and *Canberra* had been sunk in the disastrous battle off Savo Island. Cursing and sobbing while fighting maddened sharks with boat hooks, rifles and machine guns, the crew of the submarine chaser reclaimed the bodies, tenderly stretching them on the deck until the white, holystoned planking was covered by a solid carpet of dead boys. He remembered standing over them, tears streaking his cheeks, cursing God and promising revenge.

There Quartermaster Michael Carpelli had first seen the awesome power of the enemy's shells and torpedoes—weapons that had blown arms, legs and heads from some and eviscerated others. In the months that followed he had seen many more floating dead: swarms of camouflage-clad marines blown from destroyed landing craft, attacking islands the length of the slot—Russell, New Georgia, Vella Lavella, Treasury, Bougainville, and New Britain. And finally, as he had always known and expected, the turn of the submarine chaser came on December 30, 1943, off New Britain's Cape Gloucester, when she was obliterated by a 500-pound bomb. Blown into the water and miraculously the sole survivor, he had waved his fist at the sky, cursing and crying.

Carpelli shook his head, chased ghosts and stared with moist eyes through his glasses toward the sea.

11

Hundreds of landing craft swarmed from anchored transports and LSTs (Landing Ship Tanks) and moved toward the line of departure, where they followed one another in giant circles, waiting for the order to attack. The armored, tracked amphtracs could climb over the coral. But the LCVPs (Landing Craft Vehicle Personnel), LCMs (Landing Craft Mechanized), and LCTs (Landing Craft Tank) would be forced to use the four channels. His jaw hardened as he thought of the barges that would never survive the storm of fire the enemy would hurl at those narrow openings.

Suddenly, his stomach felt empty and sick. A new emotion he had first felt off Guadalcanal filled him with a strange dread. In fact, for a moment, he forgot his enemy and his hatred. Instead he damned the power that had thrown him into this arena, helpless to control his own destiny, to run from the steel storm about to explode or flee the strange sickness gnawing at his guts. Then he swallowed, felt a sour welling, and choked it down. Glancing furtively at the other men, he felt a flush of embarrassment, not realizing all men facing battle carried the same burden of dread.

Again Michael shook his head, took a deep breath and moved his glasses to the gun line. Studying first the *California* and then the *Tennessee* and *Pennsylvania* as the great battleships swung slowly to their anchors in a column parallel to the beach and about a thousand yards from it, he felt apprehension fade. The *California* was directly behind the 2404 with her twelve fourteen-inch guns level, seemingly trained on the PCS. Catching his breath, his eyes widened. He turned to Bennett. "Christ, Captain—the *California*'s going to fire through our rigging."

The lieutenant swung his binoculars and cursed. "The sugar mill."

Carpelli turned to the beach and found Mucho Point and the ruins of a factory incongruously marked by a single unscathed smokestack like a narrow tombstone. Suddenly, there was the shattering thunder of a hun-

12

dred kettle drums struck simultaneously, the shriek of express trains overhead. The quartermaster whirled, dropped his binoculars, and clapped his hands to his ears. The *California* was cloaked in brown smoke. Then the *Pennsylvania* and *Tennessee* became volcanoes, erupting tongues of orange flame followed by billowing saffron smoke.

"Jesus Christ," the captain roared, staring at the battleship, forgotten binoculars hanging at his waist. "We're on your side, you stupid assholes." He waved a fist.

Michael turned just in time to see twelve fourteen-inch shells weighing ten tons strike the sugar mill. The result was cataclysmic. A Vesuvian burst of flame, bricks, dust, iron girders and timbers leaped hundreds of feet skyward, followed by roiling black smoke. Then there were more great explosions, closer to the beach, as shells from the *Tennessee* and *Pennsylvania* flung boulders, dirt, and twisting trees into the sky like flaming cyclones.

The quartermaster returned his glasses to his eyes and stared at the thinning smoke. Then in disbelief he yelled, "Captain—the smokestack's still there."

"Well I'll be damned!"

Every man laughed—laughed too long and too hard. Bennington leaned over shaking, slapping his knees, making guttural sounds closer to sobs than laughter.

Michael felt disgust and turned away. Shifting his glasses to the sea, he saw four destroyers open fire, their incredible five-inch, thirty-eight-caliber cannons firing so fast the ships appeared to be burning. Then the cruisers *Indianapolis*, *Birmingham*, *Louisville* and *Montpelier* moved slowly to the gun line and opened fire. Now Michael heard uninterrupted ripping, rustling, and warbling overhead. Turning to the beach, he stood awed, hands to ears, watching torrents of shells churn the beach and smash into the surf flinging coral, towers of water, sand, brush, boulders, trees, and chunks of hillsides into the air. Quickly, the beach became dust and smoke, flickering snake-tongues of flame.

Andrew Bennett was possessed. Because of the drum-fire, his commands were almost impossible to hear. He screamed into the voice tube and gestured to the bridge force, shouting, "Uncover your ears! Uncover your ears." Reluctantly, Carpelli and the other men complied.

The quartermaster moved to the ship's log which was open on a small table next to the port signal light. He picked up a pencil:

15 June 1944: 0700. On station as before off Blue Beach Two. Vessel at General Quarters. Beach taken under fire by *California, Tennessee, Pennsylvania,* two heavy cruisers, two light cruisers and four destroyers.

Michael dropped the pencil and groaned as the *California* fired another broadside. Patiently, he waited as the minutes crawled by, eardrums overwhelmed by the bombardment. After an interminable thirty minutes, he heard the shout of *"Aircraft!"* over the thunderclaps. Jay Barton was pointing, screaming.

Michael raised his glasses and found them, barely visible in the far distance. Many crosses, high, in pairs, approaching from the west.

"Goddamn it! Where? Where?" Bennett boomed. "Bearing and elevation! Bearing and elevation!"

Scuttlebutt had it that Bennett was nearsighted and depended on his lookouts to put him on distant targets. Carpelli read the gyro and stepped close to the captain. "Many aircraft bearing two-six-zero true, zero-three-zero relative. Elevation angle twenty degrees, Captain."

"Very well," the lieutenant shouted, nodding and raising his binoculars. "I've got them."

The "six-ten," a squat, Army Signal Corps Radio (SCR), in a wooden crate pushed to the starboard side, suddenly came to life, squawking and hissing. But any intelligible transmissions were drowned by the cacophony of explosions.

Frantically, Bennett stormed at his executive officer. "Mr. Bennington, for Christ's sake — monitor the SCR."

Nodding numbly and glancing fearfully at the sky, the young ensign moved to the radio and crouched, ear to speaker, microphone in hand.

The lieutenant turned to the talker. "Murphy — all guns — many bandits bearing zero-three-zero relative, elevation angle — ah — twenty-five degrees." The talker repeated the command.

Michael knew the critical angle was fifty degrees; the bomb release point for horizontal bombers. He studied the distant planes. In the weak morning light they were dark crosses fleeting through mist and clouds. He strained for insignias, saw none, and knew that range was far more important to naval gunners than identity. In fact, he had seen a TBF Avenger and a F4F Wildcat shot down by American gunners in the Solomons. Quickly he cleaned his lenses, brought them back to his eyes, and propped his elbows on top of the windscreen. He saw square wing tips. Then squared-off elevators. He cursed. "Captain — they look like Grummans — F6Fs or TBFs or both. And some are flying in pairs."

The captain turned, eyes narrow. "I don't give a shit how they're flying or what they look like, Quartermaster Carpelli. What we need is what we don't have — air search radar — ranges." He turned to the talker. "Murphy: three-inch is to cut fuses for seven thousand-feet. Automatic weapons fire when in range — but only on my command."

Malcolm nodded, shouted into his microphone. The muzzle of the cannon moved swiftly skyward. Adjusting his binoculars, Carpelli felt a tightening in his throat and dry sand on his lips. No enemy planes he had ever seen had square wing tips or flew in pairs. In fact, the Japs usually flew in threes or multiples of three. He knew the captain was unsure. But, "When in doubt, open fire," was an adage born in the Solomons. The 2404 would be in range first and would fire first. Michael cursed under his breath, knowing the entire task force would follow their lead, adding thousands of weapons to the PCS's fire—and Americans would kill Americans.

At that moment the firing stopped, and twelve LCI-Rs (Landing Craft Infantry-Rocket), the close fire support group, moved toward the reef. Michael sighed with relief, shook his head and felt his eardrums pop with the same relief he had felt when descending a mountain in his youth, millenniums ago.

Suddenly, Bennington came erect, waving a finger skyward. "They're Vals, Vals, Captain. As gunnery officer, I recommend you commence firing."

"Vals?" Michael said incredulously. "The Aichi D3A has fixed landing gear, Mr. Bennington." He pointed. "These plans have retractable landing gear."

"That's right, Carpelli," the captain concurred. "No fixed landing gear."

Teeth clenched, the ensign stared through his binoculars. "But they're unidentified and almost in range. I suggest that it is our duty to commence firing, Captain."

The captain's knuckles were white against his black binoculars. He opened his mouth, closed it, squinted into his glasses and moved to the talker. "On my command, commence . . ."

With a burst of static, the six-ten came to life. The captain, gunnery officer and quartermaster all leaped to it, leaning. "Frog Town, Frog Town, this is Old Hickory. Friendly aircraft bearing two-six-zero true. Hold your fire. I repeat, friendly aircraft. Hold your fire."

The three men straightened. Michael felt a burning snake coil in his chest. He fixed Bennington with eyes as black as the bottom of a grave. The ensign averted his eyes, pushed on the front of his helmet, and swiped at his forehead with the back of his hand. "Nice going, Mr. Bennington," the quartermaster said evenly. "You almost killed some of our guys."

Shocked, Winters, Barton and Warner turned, staring at the quartermaster, not believing an enlisted man would dare talk to an officer with such obvious contempt.

"Belay that crap," the captain roared. And then to Murphy: "All stations. Friendly aircraft! Friendly aircraft! Hold your fire!" He turned to Michael. "And watch your mouth, Carpelli."

"Aye, aye, sir," the young Latin said firmly. "But he'd"—he nodded at a glaring Bennington—"kill our guys. I've seen it before at the 'Canal.'"

Wide-eyed, Winters, Barton, and Warner continued staring at Carpelli.

The retort was hot. "Remember this, I'm captain of this ship, Quartermaster Carpelli. I don't care who was right or wrong on the sighting; you'll show respect to your officers or you'll be 'Seaman Carpelli.'" And then to the ensign, harshly: "Mr. Bennington. Study your aircraft identification."

Red-faced as a man who had been slapped and obviously shaken by the rebuke in the presence of enlisted men, the ensign nodded, uttering a barely audible, "Aye, aye, sir."

"And something else—both of you. If you want a private war, have it somewhere else." The captain stabbed a finger at the island. "I don't want to interfere in your personal matters, but the United States Navy has a slight disagreement to settle with the Japanese Empire, first." He turned quickly to Warner, demanded bearings, and moved to the voice tube, grasping it with both hands.

Bennington whispered through lips skinned back from his teeth in a fierce snarl. "Someday . . . someday I'll settle with you, Quartermaster Carpelli."

"Anytime, Mr. Bennington," the quartermaster answered softly. "Anytime."

Winters and Barton stole glances, smiled at each other, and returned to their binoculars.

The quartermaster moved to the far side of the bridge, next to Jay Barton and the ship's log and as far from Bennington as the cramped space would permit.

He heard the pounding of dozens of forty-millimeter guns. Just outside the reef, the twelve LCIRs of the Close Fire Support Group had opened fire.

"Well boys, here comes the Fourth of July," the captain said in an obvious attempt to relieve tension. He failed.

One after another the decks of the small landing ships were splashed with flame, as hundreds of five-inch rockets blazed from their launchers. Roaring and hissing, they left parabolas of white smoke and sleeted into the beach, where they burst like cracking whips in carpets of flame, dust, and smoke.

"Wow," Carpelli heard Barton shout. "What a show."

Michael spoke to the teenager softly. "Just a show, Barton. The Japs are in caves or behind two feet of steel and concrete. All that shit's good for is clearing brush and giving reveille to the Jap infantry. The 'Gyrenes' need more big stuff, not firecrackers. That's why we aren't firing."

He moved to the log:

15 June 1944: 0730. On station as before off Blue Beach Two. Close Fire Support Group opened fire with 40 mm and 5 inch rockets.

There was a roar of radial engines. He turned, knowing it was time for air strikes. The distant crosses had become ten F6F Hellcats and twelve TBF Avengers, all painted blue and emblazoned with white stars. In pairs, the fighters began orbiting protectively, high over the island, while the TBFs, in a long column, approached the landing beaches.

Every man dropped his binoculars and stared at the aircraft. Gradually, the roar of the bombers' great Wright Cyclone engines drowned out the popping of forty-millimeter guns and the crack of rockets.

Suddenly, Winter's voice, high and shrill like a violin string scraped by an amateur's bow, jarred the bridge crew. "They're TBF Avengers, Captain."

18

"Very well, lookout," Bennett acknowledged, turning quickly, lips twisted by a slight smile, anger vanished. "That's true—the Grumman Avenger."

"But the Avenger is a torpedo bomber, Captain."

"I know, Winters. They're going to torpedo the fuckin' island and drown sixty thousand Japs." A tension relieving chuckle swept the bridge. And then in a fatherly tone, the captain added, "Nice work; stay alert. You have good eyes and are well trained." He nodded at Jay Barton. "Both of you; be sure to give bearings, elevation angles and try to estimate ranges."

"Aye, aye, sir," the teenagers chorused, heads high.

The captain raised his binoculars. "If you look carefully, you'll find bombs under their wings." The young lookouts stared and nodded.

The lieutenant turned to the ensign. "Mr. Bennington. Move your watch aft, next to the forty-millimeter talker. You can control the twenties and the forty there. We have two new gunners and all new gunners are trigger happy." He waved at the approaching TBFs. "Those Avengers are almost in range. Some asshole may open up." He tapped the windscreen with his knuckles. "The Japs'll be here soon enough—then they'll get more shooting than they want." He glanced skyward. "Do you read me?"

"Loud and clear, sir." The ensign turned, bounded to the ladder, and was gone.

"Quartermaster, man the six-ten."

"Aye, aye, Captain," Michael said, moving to the radio. Now he had the six-ten, log, and shared signaling duties with Warner. But he enjoyed responsibilities. Responsibilities kept him occupied. Earning his ratings on the subchaser where he had been the entire bridge force, he was a better signalman than Dennis Warner and knew more about navigation than any of the officers. In fact, Bennington's hostility began when the ensign realized the quartermaster could read the constellations like an expert astronomer and was a master at handling the sextant, chronometer, and the complex system of navigation the Navy called Hydrographic Office Method 214. The young quartermaster feared Bennington's stupidity. It made him a very dangerous man; his decisions could kill men. Michael glanced at his shipmates. The entire bridge force seemed to breathe easier with the ensign's departure. The quartermaster took a deep breath, expelled it through clenched teeth, and pushed Bennington from his mind.

Tilting his head back, Michael stared with the other men as the planes swung over the southern tip of the island. Suddenly, engine roaring, the lead plane pushed over, but not into the expected nose-down power dive. Instead, it descended gradually, almost a glide. Then another and another like children playing follow the leader, they swooped down on the beach. Carpelli had never seen TBFs used as glide bombers. "Dumb! Dumb! They're too big — too slow. Targets! Targets," he said to himself. Barton turned, but said nothing, only staring at the aircraft.

One after another the big planes labored the length of the beach like tired hawks, dropping bombs while their machine guns sprayed tracers and trailed brown smoke. A few tracers streaked up from the beach. Ignoring the enemy fire, the first half-dozen completed their runs and turned toward the anchorage, bombs exploding behind them in evenly spaced sticks. The remaining planes streamed over the enemy. Suddenly, a torrent of tracers sleeted skyward, tearing aluminum from one of the Grummans.

Michael Carpelli felt a familiar sinking in his chest. He heard Warner mutter, "Come on, you guys. Come on, you guys. Get out of there. For Christ's sake get out of there."

The Japs had the range. A plane staggered. Trailing flame and black smoke, it fell into a steep, curving dive, smashing into Mucho Point, exploding in a gout of flame followed by a column of black smoke. Carpelli cursed, gripping the windscreen until his fingers hurt,

20

and he felt the kapok of his Mae West push against the wooden barrier.

Silently, the bridge crew watched as the last three bombers made their runs. The first plane was over the sugar mill when its bombs were hit. Flashing in a vast, blinding detonation of over a ton of high explosives, the Avenger became a great, billowing black octopus with hundreds of black and white tentacles smoking to earth. Warner's voice: "Shit! Shit!"

The next plane completed its run unscathed, banked over the ships. Then the last plane swooped. Michael held his breath. A storm of tracers. Suddenly, the Grumman slewed off on one wing wobbling as if piloted by a drunk. Then, roaring at full throttle it curved downward, exploding against a hillside with violence rarely seen even in warfare.

Michael heard a youngster crying. Barton. Sobbing into a closed fist. No one looked at the teenager. The young quartermaster stared at the three pyres. Slowly, like the lives of the young men who had just died, the smoke melted into the wind and was gone.

"Consummate, motherfuckin', illiterate, blind bastards," the captain screamed. "What a stupid way to use TBFs. Whoever ordered that attack should be shot!"

Michael nodded. He was unable to swallow. He coughed. He finally spoke deep in his throat but not to anyone on the bridge. Instead his wide eyes were on the horizon and he seemed to be addressing someone in another place and another time. "Posthumous Purple Hearts for all hands . . ." Curious eyes turned to the quartermaster. "And the Navy Cross—maybe a half-dozen or more." The voice became steel. "But their next of kin won't know they died stupidly, uselessly, and for nothing."

Silence. Bennett stared at the quartermaster through narrow lids and bit his lip. There was a softness in his voice. "No. Next of kin is never told about the stupid ones—the useless ones. They get the medals and the gold stars."

The roar of engines ended the exchange and brought five pairs of binoculars up. Fighters raced the length of the beach, strafing vengefully and firing rockets that leaped from their wings in great bursts of white smoke. Trailing fire and smoke, the missiles smashed into the island, making cracking, whiplash sounds. Then at tremendous speed the Grummans streaked over the beach, casually avoiding the antiaircraft fire, banked toward the sea and were gone. Not one was hit.

Again, Michael heard thunder from the gun line, and explosions raced across the tortured beach. He glanced at his watch: 0800. He rid his mind of the dead aviators.

"It's time. It's time," the captain said, staring at the line of departure.

Michael brought up his glasses. Eighteen amphtracs followed by dozens of landing barges had left the line of departure. Slowly, the great steel turtles wallowed toward the beach, kicking up plumes of spray. As they passed the LCIs and approached the reef, splashes appeared among them.

"Shorts, Captain—some of our stuff is falling short," Warner shouted over the din.

"Negative, Signalman. That fall of shot is Jap incoming mail."

Carpelli glanced at Warner and then the lookouts. All appeared stunned. He snorted grimly, knowing the young sailors were now aware of the enemy—the invisible enemy, the seemingly nonexistent enemy. But now he did exist, firing on planes and landing craft.

The first amphtracs reached the reef and began to crawl over. Large and small splashes leaped from the sea around them. One armored vehicle exploded. Then another. Michael spoke. "Christ. Six-inch, Captain. And four point sevens."

"Very well."

Two more amphtracs were hit. "And Captain, automatic weapons—probably forties and thirty-sevens and small bore."

22

"I see it. You have good eyes, Quartermaster." The captain's voice was calm.

Michael moved to the log. "Belay the log, it can wait," the lieutenant shouted. "Report the Jap artillery to the *Rocky Mount.*"

Michael picked up the microphone. "Old Hickory, Old Hickory, this is Grable Zero Four."

"Go ahead Grable Zero Four."

"Landing force taking fire from Jap artillery, various calibers up to six-inch. Also, receiving small caliber automatic weapons' fire."

Michael leaned close to the crate and heard the message repeated. He straightened and turned to Andrew Bennett. "Sent and receipted for, sir."

"Very well."

Both men turned to the reef. More amphtracs blew up. But at least twelve survivors were over the reef and in the lagoon swimming for the beach. Then a stream of barges cut across the PCS's bow, headed for the passage. More splashes.

The captain spoke. "Damn. More fire support, Old Hickory. More fire support."

Abruptly, the blasts from the gun line reached a new frenzy. The new counterbattery fire raised Michael Carpelli's spirits. But he knew enemy artillery, carefully sited and registered, using flashless powder and doubtless firing from reverse slopes, would be hard to find and destroy. In fact, some of the enemy's big guns were probably miles from the beach. They could even be on Tinian.

The call of "Aircraft!" came from both lookouts. "Bearing zero-eight-zero relative. Elevation angle thirty degrees," Barton shouted. The captain acknowledged.

In minutes almost a hundred fighters and dive bombers swooped and dived over the beach, strafing and bombing, adding their bullets, rockets and bombs to the torrents of shells pouring from the gun line.

The overwhelming decibels brought pain to Michael's ears. He groaned and hit his helmet with a fist.

23

"Noisy fuckin' war," Bennett screamed.

Michael nodded. He saw the first barges enter the passages greeted by splashes. Despite the bombardment, the Jap fire did not slacken. In fact, more splashes leapt from the reef, flinging spray and coral skyward. Here and there landing craft belched smoke, wallowing in their death throes. Burning fuel spread. Michael dropped his binoculars and pounded his palm with a fist, because he knew men were dying hideously in burning fuel. Soon dozens of heads bobbed in the waves. LCVPs with ramps down charged recklessly through the flames, moving to the heads. Then, frantic hands began pulling marines from the sea.

The first amphtracs were on the beach crawling for the brush, geysers of sand leaping all around. And barges were streaming through the main boat passage. Slackening, the fire from the gun line began to move up Tapotchau, and the fighters and bombers headed for the southern part of the island and the Aslito airstrip.

Carpelli knew the Japs must be popping out of their holes to unlimber their guns and cut the marines down like wheat. But spotter planes — two tiny Piper Cubs were at that moment circling low over the island — might pick up observation posts, even gun flashes and the massing of troops.

Michael heard Dennis Warner shout "No!" A Cub, caught in a typhoon of tracers, lost its wings. Instantly, as if it had been turned to lead by an alchemist, it plummeted into the inferno.

Michael felt a strange pressure against his ears and eyes, a numbness in his mind. Death was coming too fast and too massively. There was not time enough to mourn or even comprehend. He caught a flash in the corner of his glasses — horizontal flashes from a low hillside just back of the sugar mill. There were huge splashes in the nearest passage. An LCM was flung into the air, spewing infantry.

He leaned to the captain and shouted calmly, "Six-inch again — maybe bigger, Captain." He stabbed a finger, "Back of the sugar mill in those foothills."

Bennett nodded, adjusted his binoculars. He opened his mouth as if to speak, but was stopped by a tremendous blast. All three battleships had fired simultaneously. The foothills became a maelstrom of flame, smoke, and dust. And then, impossibly, one entire hill rose slowly into the sky with a cluster of palms still rooted.

The captain gestured. "Ammo dump — ammo dump —" The ship shuddered as if struck by a giant's fist. Warner staggered and caught himself on the binnacle. A screw popped from the windscreen and ricocheted from a searchlight like a spent bullet. Every man, including the captain, grabbed his ears. But the sound was not a sharp crack. Instead, a long rumbling roar washed over the ship and was gone like a passing freight train, rocking the PCS in its wake. A giant exclamation mark of dust and smoke rose thousands of feet over the island.

The quartermaster caught his breath and brought his glasses to the beach. More broadsides and detonations raged. Men were on the beach, scrambling from landing craft. Dozens of LCVPs and LCMs, crowded with marines, had grounded and dropped their ramps. Men raced onto the beach, small black dolls against the white sand. The sand spouted up in little geysers. Some dolls fell to the ground, wiggling and twisting. Others flung their arms out in a final defiance of death and fell like cordwood. But most raced inland and disappeared in the undergrowth. Quickly, the pristine white beach became a burning, bloody junkyard. Michael lowered his binoculars slowly, the cold blade of horror twisting in his guts.

Within twenty minutes he saw nearly a thousand landing craft ferry eight thousand marines to the beach. But the enemy artillery persisted despite the bombardment. In fact, when the fourth wave landed, the Jap barrage curtained the whole reef with spray.

But no price was too high. The young quartermaster

25

watched the growing carnage, fatigue pushing him beyond emotion. He became part of the bridge, a fixture like the gyro, binnacle or signaling searchlight. And the ironical "spectator" phenomenon of war set in: he became an observer, detached and uninvolved, watching, even chronicling the carnage, but not participating. While thousands died almost within a stone's throw, he stood quietly on the bridge of a ship, watching, waiting, and doing nothing except to show a huge banner.

"Showing that banner is better than showing your ass on that fuckin' beach," Warner shouted suddenly as if he had read Michael's mind. Michael nodded, knowing their thoughts were running in parallel channels.

All morning long the SCR squawked with demands for tanks, water, ammunition, and above all else, fire support. Michael knew the marines needed a broad beach wide enough to allow deployment. This would be done by using head-on infantry charges and the crushing advance of amphtracs and Sherman tanks which were beginning to pour from LCMs and LCTs.

By noon a shallow front nearly four miles long had been established and the young Latin had hopes for a change in duty — duty on the antisubmarine screen running a ping line away from the crushing noise and far to sea where the air was clean, free of smoke, cordite, and the smell of death. Michael hated and feared the smell of death. The hot tropical sun would soon decay thousands of corpses and the nauseating smell of rotting meat would drift out to sea and envelop the 2404.

Periodically the captain prodded, "Stay alert for aircraft. The Japs will be here. Don't forget, we're in range of Guam, Rota, Yap, Palau, Truk, Iwo Jima, and a shit-pot full of other bases. They'll be here."

But as the day wore on, they did not come. "Waiting for dusk, Captain," Michael shouted.

"Probably. They're hard to see at sunset and we're easy targets." Barton and Winters looked at each other and took new interest in the sky.

At 1500 hours the Landing Craft Control Team came

aboard. Displaced from their submarine chaser when one of its engines broke down, a lieutenant junior grade and two enlisted men were ferried to the PCS by a LCVP. Michael felt hopelessness. Now they were tied to the beach, perhaps for days or weeks.

Boyish, with a freckled nose, blond hair, and tired blue eyes, the control officer struggled to the bridge dressed in marine's combat fatigues, carrying a pack over his right shoulder and a Thompson submachine gun over his left. Similarly dressed and struggling with a SCR, his two enlisted men followed. Both were armed with M-1 carbines.

Bennett was at his sardonic best. "What's the artillery for, Lieutenant. Do you expect to repel boarders?"

The young officer's smile flashed white teeth. He saluted. "Orders, Captain. Orders."

Bennett extended a hand. "Welcome aboard." He introduced himself and the bridge crew.

"I'm Mark Ogren," the young officer said. And then gesturing to his enlisted men: "This is Radioman First Class Tom Stafford and Signalman Third Class Jeoffrey Winkler."

"Stack your SCR on top of our six-ten and your weapons in that corner," Andrew Bennett said. He nodded at Carpelli, "My quartermaster is an excellent signalman. Feel free to use him and Signalman Warner."

"Thank you, sir. But you know most of our work is done with the SCR." Ogren pointed at the radio which his men had already hooked up to the ship's circuits.

"Your call, Lieutenant?"

"Ready Teddy One, Captain."

"Your command?"

"It varies. I've taken casualties. But at this moment I have two LCMs loaded with water, two with small arms ammo, four with one-oh-five artillery shells, six LCTs with Shermans and two with a single gasoline tanker each." He waved. "They're at the line of departure."

"Gasoline! Shit! I wouldn't want to peddle gas in a neighborhood like this," the captain said. And then with

27

an edge of authority, "We'll continue laying to here, Mr. Ogren." He stabbed a finger at the reef. "We're marking Blue Beach Two and the passage. I'll attempt to honor your requests and move this vessel, but only within the parameters of my orders."

"Understood, Captain." Ogren twisted his head. "You're ideally sited, Captain. There should be no problem and hopefully the SC will have its engine repaired soon."

"Very well."

The landing officer's radio came to life. A tinny voice droned. "Ready Teddy One this is Ameche Six. Request four snails. Also, request Nancy Hanks one zero zero two three bonded."

Ogren nodded to Stafford. Quickly, the young signalman repeated the message and then turned, "Receipted for, sir."

Ogren spoke. "The beachmaster on Blue One requested four Shermans and gasoline, Captain." He turned to Stafford. "Send in Rooney One, Two, Three, Four and Kong Three."

Stafford spoke into the microphone. In a moment, Michael saw five LCTs leave the line of departure and head for the reef. Quickly, they became part of the huge traffic jam crowding the main boat channel. Michael waited for the great swirling flare of burning gasoline. It never came.

As the day wore on, the radios were alive with voices calling for men, artillery, tanks, and water. And the flood continued. But so did the enemy artillery, exacting its price.

In the middle of the afternoon, the breeze freshened and Bennett requested permission to anchor. With permission granted, the 2404 anchored only a hundred yards from the reef and perhaps two hundred yards from the beach. "They could hit us with slingshots," Carpelli heard Warner grumble.

Late in the afternoon the empty LCVP came alongside. But, looking down, Michael could see the barge was not empty. It carried a ghastly load, its bottom covered with at least twenty wounded marines stretched out on blankets, all bloody and wrapped with dirty bandages. They were very still — still as the dead or heavily sedated. As was usual in the wounded, shock had drained their faces of blood and left them pasty and white, their breathing was shallow. They were no longer fighting infantry; they were just high school boys on the edge of death. A gunnery sergeant with a bandaged head moved among them.

The coxswain's desperate voice came through cupped hands. "We need help — they'll die — can you take them?"

"We have no doctor," the captain answered through the loud hailer. "I'll send you my pharmacist's mate and we'll call the LSTs."

"Thank you, Captain."

Bennett turned to Murphy. "Pharmacist's Mate Kohler to the LCVP." And then to Michael, "Get on the light." He pointed at an LST. "The Two Zero Eight Four is closest. Call her. We have twenty wounded. Request permission to send them aboard."

Michael leaped to the light, threw the switch, aimed at the bridge of the LST through the peep sight and began to work the handle furiously. The LST responded instantly. The quartermaster turned to the captain. "Permission granted, Captain."

"Very well." And then through the loud hailer: "Coxswain, take your load to that LST." He pointed. "My pharmacist's mate is on his way." He stabbed a finger at the ship's waist.

Michael Carpelli saw the husky figure of Pharmacist's Mate Bryan Kohler leaning over the lifeline, lowering his kit carefully to the gunny. Then the pharmacist's mate jumped from the bumper, landing next to the coxswain catlike, in a crouch. As the coxswain gunned his engine, Kohler turned quickly, glancing at the bridge. Michael caught the gray eyes with his and waved. The salute was returned. Then, hastily,

29

lines were cast off, the barge backed away, and the pharmacist's mate was moving to the wounded.

Andrew Bennett turned to Michael Carpelli. "We'll get your buddy back or we'll go on strike." Raising his loud hailer, he bellowed after the LCVP, "Bring back our pharmacist's mate — he's my whole medical department." The coxswain turned his head and waved.

As the sun declined, more wounded were directed to the LST 2084 and six more nearby LSTs. Although the PCS was only two hundred yards from the beach, it was impossible to tell how the battle was progressing. Not a single live combatant was visible, only still figures on the cluttered, burning beach and a few floating corpses. But Lieutenant Mark Ogren had committed most of his units. Consequently, Michael knew the beachhead must be expanding. But Ogren was given more barges to control, and there was no sign of the subchaser. Dusk was approaching. They would remain close inshore all night. Michael felt a familiar sinking in his stomach. However, his spirits revived when the LCVP returned with Pharmacist's Mate Bryan Kohler, who waved and shouted, "Hey, Mate!" Carpelli waved and smiled.

His response was cut short by the captain who shouted while staring at the sky, "Stay on the ball. They'll be coming."

The six-ten rasped, "Flash Blue — many bogies."

The captain's voice, calm but loud: "They're in the vicinity." And then to the talker, "Short-haul the anchor chain. Stand by to get underway. Enemy aircraft in the vicinity."

Michael felt the ship vibrate as the windlass took up the slack in the anchor chain, bringing the PCS directly over the anchor. They were ready to get underway.

The radio spat, "Flash red. Many bandits."

The captain fired a barrage. To the talker: "Flash red. Stand by to commence firing. Heave in on the starboard anchor." To the pilot house: "All ahead slow. Come to three four zero." To the landing craft control officer: "You and your men to the boat deck."

"Aye, aye, sir." The lieutenant and his men grabbed their weapons and vanished down the ladder.

"Aircraft, bearing zero-nine-zero relative, elevation angle thirty degrees," Barton called shrilly.

"Very well!"

Michael focused his binoculars, found the expected three threes of three. He narrowed his eyes, saw fixed landing gear: Aichi D3A, Type 99 dive bomber. "Twenty-seven Vals, Captain."

"Twenty-seven! Ah, shit!" and then: "I have them, Quartermaster."

Michael was jarred by Winters' excited shout, "Aircraft, bearing two-zero-zero relative, elevation angle forty degrees." Every man swung his glasses.

"Very well." And then the captain said, "Christ, they've got us on an anvil." He dropped his glasses and turned to Murphy. "Three-inch is to cut fuses for six thousand feet. All other weapons commence firing when in range." And then as an afterthought: "Twenties are to use tracer control — forget those Mark Fourteen sights. They're no fuckin' good! Don't even turn them on."

Michael caught the new sightings and found twin-engine bombers flying in seven threes. But there was a glint of white wings and black cowlings high above the bombers. A great icy fist closed on his lungs, bringing shortness of breath and a pounding in his temples. The Zero, the Mitsubishi A6M, was there — lithe, quick, deadly, with two machine guns and two twenty-millimeter cannons. The Zero brought back the horror as nothing else could. He remembered the Brewster Buffaloes, P40s and F4F Wildcats of Guadalcanal's "Cactus" Air Force. How the Zero made the Americans look clumsy, casually shot them from the sky and cleared the way for their bombers. Now it was back, escorting a massive raid. But there was no place to hide. You can't dig a hole on a ship. Maybe he could jump over the side. Swim for shore. But how? When? Everyone would see him. And the beach was an inferno. He choked it down,

31

took several deep breaths, and relied on his hate. *They killed the SC,* he told himself. *Killed all the guys.* He felt a surge of venom rise and melt the icy fingers. He focused on the Mitsubishi twin-engined medium bombers and then spoke with a calmness that surprised himself. "Bettys, Captain. Twenty-one at seven thousand. And Zeros, too. High above the bombers."

"I have them, Quartermaster."

Warner turned to Michael. "Where the fuck are our fighters?"

Before Carpelli could answer, the captain interrupted bitterly, "Back in their ward rooms fuckin' the dog and pretending they're John Wayne." And then to the bridge force: "The screen will engage those Bettys first." He waved a hand to the east. "But those Vals are ours. They're coming over the island." Then to Malcolm Murphy: "All guns will engage the Vals to starboard. They should be in range in a minute."

Even in the weak light of dusk, Michael could see the approaching Aichi D3As clearly: huge Sakae engines, oversized canopies, underwing dive brakes, ludicrous fixed landing gear, and a single huge bomb slung beneath the fuselage. He shuddered.

Warner's voice: "The picket line's opened up, Captain." Far at sea, the five-inch, thirty-eight caliber cannons of half a dozen destroyers vomited yellow flames. But the medium bombers ignored the bursts, boring on toward the massed transports and LSTs. Now cruisers, battleships and transports all joined the barrage, cannon belching. In the gathering dusk, exploding shells burst in little winks of lights. In seconds, scores of white puffs surrounded the Bettys, cotton balls thrown by a capricious child.

Michael heard a cheer. A Betty trailed flame. Curved downward. Another exploded. Then a third lost a wing.

The captain waved a fist. "They've radar control and proximity fuses. All we have are our eyeballs and tight assholes."

The Vals were almost in range. Their brakes were

down and they were stacking up in a single line. Michael knew they were ready to dive.

"Three-inch, commence firing!"

The sharp report of the three-inch was the sound of a thousand whip-ends snapped against Michael's eardrums. He groaned as the merciless weapon went to rapid fire. Luckily, it fired over the starboard bow, muzzle pointed away from the bridge.

Now the leading Vals were over the beach. And all along the reef other patrol craft were firing. LSTs spouted flame. The *California, Tennessee* and *Pennsylvania* blazed with huge gouts of flames.

"All weapons commence firing!"

Instantly, the Bofors began its pounding and the starboard Orlikons ran wild, a stuttering glissando weaving through the percussion of cannon fire. Thousands of Roman candles glowed skyward.

Both young lookouts began shouting, "Fighters! Fighters!"

Even through the din, Michael could hear the cheering. The thinning clouds were raining Grumman F6F and Hellcats. He expelled his breath in a burst. He had seen the Grumman F6F many times. In fact, dozens had just strafed the beach. But he had never seen it fight the Zero. Although he knew the big Grumman had twice the horsepower of the Japanese fighter, as well as armor, self-sealing tanks and six fifty-caliber machine guns, he still felt despair; he expected to see the killer Zero shoot the skies clear.

The captain shouted, "Come on you motherfuckers—come on. You're late for the party."

Michael counted at least thirty blue fighters with huge white stars diving on the mottled green bombers, trailed by a swarm of Zeros. But the light Zero, without armor or self-sealing tanks, dived poorly. More big blue fighters arrowed toward the Vals like hawks swooping on pigeons.

"Cease fire! Cease fire!" Bennett roared at the talker. "Cease fire!"

33

The roar of guns was instantly replaced by the snarl of scores of radial engines straining at full military power. Within a minute, the Grummans proved why the F6F was considered the best carrier fighter in the Pacific. Plunging through the Japanese formations, the big planes ripped the Bettys and Vals with their fifty-caliber machine guns.

Michael added his voice to the cheers of the crew as the massacre began. Slow and lightly armed, the Bettys were target practice. And the Vals were helpless. They were shot from the sky like clay pigeons shredded by shotgun blasts. Some bombers, trailing yellow flame, arced gracefully into the sea. Others cartwheeled grotesquely, sloughing wings and chunks of aluminum. And the Hellcats in pairs, turned and twisted through the bombers with the precision of ballet dancers. "It's like shooting turkeys," he heard Warner shout.

Michael held his breath as the Zeros plunged into the melee, but the lithe little fighters had no more chance against the Hellcats than a man has trying to stop a tidal wave with a broom. And more Hellcats poured from the clouds, plunging through the Zeros, firing. A half-dozen white monoplanes exploded, lost wings, and added their flames to those of burning bombers. The sky became a crematorium. Michael waved a fist and cheered hoarsely.

"Top cover," Bennett shouted. "They kept their own top cover. Caught those fuckin' Nips on an anvil."

Warner shouted, "Those fuckin' Japs go off like cherry bombs."

"They don't have self-sealing tanks," the captain said. And then with his lips peeled back: "Burn, Japs, burn."

But the massive confusion worked in the enemy's favor. With the Japanese formations scattered, the Hellcats raced to all points of the compass, chasing targets. Suddenly, two low flying Vals skimmed over the island and vanished behind Tapotchau with four F6Fs in pursuit. Then, out of nowhere, an Aichi dropped low over the beach and veered toward the transports. Not a single Hellcat was in sight.

"Val headed for the anchorage — bearing zero-eight-zero relative — low," Michael shouted. "No Hellcats in pursuit."

Bennett screamed at Murphy, "All guns — Val at zero-eight-zero low. Commence firing!" The crashing of the three-inch and stuttering of machine guns was instantaneous.

Winters screamed, "He's headed for us!"

Only a thousand yards away, the camouflaged green bomber curved slightly, headed directly for the PCS. Calmly, Michael dropped his binoculars and stood erect. Glancing over his shoulder, he could see the LST 2084 close to the port side, perhaps a half-mile. The LST was the Jap's target.

The big radial Sakae was an expanding bull's-eye. With near zero deflection, tracers raced to meet it. The three-inch crashed again and again. But the enemy roared in, oblivious of the glowing hailstorm.

Scores of forty-millimeter began to self-destruct in white clouds behind the Jap. There were too many. Michael glanced at the transports. A half-dozen LSTs had opened fire. Tracers sleeted through the patrol craft's rigging. "Our own guys — they'll kill us," Warner screamed shrilly.

Bennett looked over his shoulder and punched the windscreen. "Kill him! Kill him!"

The Val belched smoke, suddenly trailing a brown ribbon like a skywriter beginning a new word. Cheers. His starboard wing dropped. As he passed overhead, Michael craned his neck and stared straight up, transfixed. He could see carrier stripes behind the canopy, and the plane was so close he could actually read squadron numbers on the tail fin and rudder. And the single bomb. Big. Nestled against the fuselage between the pants of the old-fashioned fixed landing gear.

Unable to track such a close, fast target, the three-inch was silent. but the starboard twenties and the forty were on full trigger. Then, passing to the port side, the

35

roar of the Sakae became a bark suddenly Dopplered down octaves, blasting through the sounds of the guns. The port machine guns began firing.

The plane rose sharply, belching clouds of black smoke. Cranked in a frenzy, the three-inch turned through 180 degrees and fired a quick round at a seventy degree elevation. Level with the bridge, the muzzle was only about twenty feet from Michael's head. Every man, including the captain, grabbed his ears, opened his mouth and reeled, as the blast knocked screws out of the windscreen, sent the bearing ring spinning off the gyro repeater, nearly tore Michael's helmet from his head, and ripped the tail from the plane.

In a stall and burning, the Val was almost motionless, seemingly supported by a spiderweb of tracers. The guns raved. It could not be killed enough. Then the weight of its engine pulled it like a pendulum and sent it into a twisting power dive. Flaming, it crashed into the sea midway between the patrol craft and the LST, its grave marked by a tower of water, shattered Plexiglas, and a rain of torn aluminum. Burning gasoline spread. Cheers.

"Cease fire! Cease fire! Well done! Well done! Stay alert—there may be more of 'em. And watch out for Hellcats," Bennett shouted.

Michael felt Dennis Warner's hand on his back, pounding. "We got him—got the motherfucker!"

Michael smiled. He felt the exhilaration that came with the kill. He had seen the invincible Zero completely outclassed and shot from the skies. But a strange foreboding gnawed at him. The resourceful Jap knew no fear and welcomed death. The quartermaster looked up, turning his head restlessly. The dark sky was clear and nearly cloudless, with a few early stars beginning to burn through the blue blanket.

Something moved fleetingly against Topatchau. He brought up his glasses and found it: an aircraft with twin radial engines, Plexiglas nose, long canopy like a greenhouse, dorsal machine-gun turret, bomb bay doors open and flaming assholes on the wings and fuse-lage. "Betty, bearing zero-six-zero, relative — low — coming fast. Between us and Topatchau."

The cheering stopped. Bennett brought up his glasses, cursed. Then he shouted at the talker, "Betty, bearing zero-six-zero, low — commence firing!"

But the sun had set. The plane was a poor target against the dark tower of the mountain. The gunners needed a silhouette. The crashing and stuttering began. Torrents of tracers arced. Alerted by the patrol craft's guns, firing began all along the reef, and tracers stormed from the transports like firebrands flung by volcanoes.

Carpelli could see the twin-engine Mitsu-bishi G4M skimming the water, streaking toward the transports. Then it was over the anchorage, challenging swarms of tracers, dropping its stick of bombs. Michael expected six blasts. The concussions came, drowning out everything. Five great blasts of five-hundred-pound bombs, towers of water marching in a straight line through the LSTs. Then the sixth and unmistakable crash, flash and sound of tortured, ripping steel. The 2084 convulsed, seemed to leap from the sea, settled back rocking, wallowing, belching flame and smoke amidships.

"No! No! No!" Winters cried.

"Shit! Shit!" Michael groaned, punching the wind-screen. "The last plane — last bomb."

Suddenly, a great explosion ripped the LST, sending flaming debris flying for hundreds of yards. A bolt of flame followed by a black shroud of oil smoke shot sky-ward. Twisted metal, vehicles, and bodies rained into the sea.

"Gas and ammo — shit — the tank deck went," the cap-tain said, deep in his throat.

Warner choked. "All those wounded guys."

Michael raised his glasses. Heads were bobbing around the ship which had broken in half. But burning fuel spread across the sea, enveloped the heads. Some men flopped like seals, vainly trying to jump clear of the flaming fuel.

"Oh, fuck this station," Bennett shouted. Into the voice tube: "All ahead full. Steady up on the wreck." And then to the talker: "Fire and Rescue man both rails amidships."

The SCR rasped, "Grable Zero Four, this is Old Hickory. Maintain your station."

"Turn off the son-of-a-bitch," Bennett roared. "Don't acknowledge."

"Aye, aye, sir," Michael said, throwing a switch.

"The fuckin' SCR broke down," the captain said, glancing from man to man. Everyone nodded.

The quartermaster saw the red light of a reduced signaling searchlight blinking from the anchorage. It came from a massive gray superstructure beneath a mainmast crowded with antennas. The demands of the light were unmistakable: "P 2404" over and over.

"The *Rocky Mount* is calling, sir."

"Very well." The captain tugged at his chin. "I'll tell you when to 'King.' " He turned to the voice tube. "All ahead slow." They were entering the holocaust. "Stand by to pick up survivors."

Michael leaned over the windscreen. Over the rumble of the diesels he could hear the undulating wail of animals in pain. Flames billowed from the sea. He felt heat and choked on the heavy, oily smoke. The two halves of the doomed ship tilted toward each other, forming a "V." Screaming, men dribbled from the wreck, tumbling into the flames. More explosions roiled skyward like giant, glowing red balloons. Michael, unable to swallow, pounded the windscreen until his fists ached. Winters was crying. All the others stood in frozen silence.

"All stop!" the captain shouted as the bow of the PCS neared a flaming pool. "All back slow!"

Now Michael could see men swimming, floating on wreckage and rafts, and frantically paddling away from the flames. And the blinking red light persisted from the anchorage.

Bennett turned to Carpelli. "Give him a 'King.' "

"Aye, aye, sir." Michael leaped to the light, aimed carefully through the peep sight knowing the honeycombed reducer would only permit a weak, highly concentrated beam. He worked the lever, sending a crisp "K."

The expected order to return to station blinked back. The quartermaster sent his "Roger" and received the expected "AR" ending the transmission. He informed the captain.

"Very well."

The first survivors had been pulled to the deck. Michael could see crewmen standing on the ship's bumper, gripping the lifeline and reaching into the water, pulling in marines and sailors. One seaman grabbed a charred marine's hand, pulled hard. The hand and part of a forearm broke loose, slid from the bone. The marine tumbled back into the flames. Michael heard Barton wretch, and he tasted bile. Quickly, the waist of the ship was covered with men, some still in death, others writhing and screaming, clothes burned from their bodies. And moving among them, the tireless hulk of Pharmacist's Mate Bryan Kohler and three seaman assistants—bandaging, splinting, covering the dead with GI blankets.

There was the sound of Gray Marine engines as LCVPs with ramps down charged into the flames. Small and quick, the landing craft moved between burning pools as frantic crewmen pulled bodies from the water. Then there was a great roar and hissing and the two halves of the LST slid slowly beneath the surface. Huge bubbles of trapped air churned the sea while burning fuel spread across the grave.

"All back full," Bennett barked sharply into the voice tube, watching burning fuel close on both beams. And then to Murphy: "Tell radar to give me tangents on Mucho, Afetna and Agingan points." He turned to Carpelli. "Call the *Rocky Mount* and transmit the

39

following: 'Returning to station. SCR has broken down. Should be repaired soon. Have many wounded aboard. Request instructions.' "

As Michael transmitted, he felt an unusually warm raindrop on his right cheek. And then another on his left. They ran to his chin, followed by others. He glanced at the sky. The clouds were gone and the stars shone brightly. And there was the Southern Cross, four pulsing diamonds low on the horizon. But the beauty of the tropical skies erased none of the horror. Sleep was a memory. Maybe he should visit the flag bag. Solace in a bottle was hidden there.

But the captain would keep them at G.Q. all night. The flag bag was out. But he had his mind—his reveries. He had escaped in them before. All boys at war did.

After receiving his "Roger," the quartermaster brushed the drops from his cheeks with his sleeve and looked around. The bridge was manned by statues, staring wide-eyed at the sea, avoiding eye contact. Only Barton showed movement as he leaned over the windscreen, wretching and keening softly like an injured animal.

The sound sparked a memory, flickering back from the dark recesses. It was his mother. Yes, that was it. His mother crying softly, struggling with her anguish the day he told her he was leaving. Lord she loved him. Loved him as no one else ever could. Certainly more than Kristie or Lynn or Alma or any of the others. And he told Kristie that night, too.

He groped with his life jacket, and found his shirt pocket and the long tube of a Parker fountain pen. His mother had given it to him the day he left. It had taken two weeks of hard work in the Goodyear cafeteria to pay for the expensive pen. Beaming, she had watched him as he stared with delight at his first fountain pen. And then through tears, "Now you have no excuse not to write your mom."

And she cried. And Kristie cried, too. Was it two years before? Three? It seemed like a day and an eternity.

He had tried. Oh, Lord he had tried. "Mom! Mom! Please Mom, try to understand," he pleaded, standing close to his mother. "I'd be drafted anyway, and all the guys are gone—Ernie's in the Navy, Dale's in the Air Corps, Wally's in the Army—all gone." And then diffidently: "And I won't be killed automatically just because I joined the Navy."

Looking up, she had riveted her eyes to his, the intensity of the wide stare darkening brown to black while errant strands of blue-black hair traversed her forehead and wandered down her cheeks unnoticed. Glistening like varnish, a film of perspiration layered her flawless olive skin, setting the dangling hair in random patterns. Heartbreak and dread twisted her delicate features into a mockery of natural beauty. He wanted her to cry—cry a flood that would wash the look away. But she refused with a voice that lashed like a whip, "Why, Michael? Why? You're an honor student. You'll graduate in three years, start teaching, get out of this." She gestured at the squalor of their tiny housekeeping room.

With a rent of only six dollars a month, Maria Carpelli had rented a single room in a decaying Victorian home built in 1882. Six other rooms and the single bath were shared by other families. With doorways and window frames twisted by age and earthquakes, right angles no longer existed. The porch sloped uphill from right to left, the roof was supported by leaning posts. Warped siding had not felt a painter's brush in decades. Squalid on a street of dilapidated buildings, the dwelling squatted like a stricken septuagenarian patiently awaiting euthanasia.

Maria and Michael stood in the middle of a small area that was once the living room. It now contained two cots, a sink, ice box, and a two burner stove. A sofa, lumpy with distended springs, was pushed against one wall while a battered Kennedy radio faced it from the opposite wall. Michael knew his mother hated that room, the collapsing building, and the decaying neighborhood.

Time and again she had told him of her wasted youth. She, Maria Dante, once the most desirable girl in Brooklyn's Sicilian ghetto of Canarsee had become a *vagabondaggia,* living in a Los Angeles slum. Once her dark beauty had turned the heads of men; especially Alfredo Carpelli's. Against her parents' wishes, she had married that *bastardo* when she was sixteen and moved to Los Angeles where Alfredo went to work for his cousin, Pietro, as a barber. By the time Maria was nineteen, she lived on the west side of town, raising her infant son. By the age of twenty-four, she had a divorce: Alfredo's head had been turned by Pietro's manicurist. Then uneducated and unskilled, Maria's struggle began, raising her son on twenty-five dollars a month in alimony.

Mature far beyond his years, Michael was keenly aware of his mother's pride and love. He knew she was convinced his intelligence came from her side of the family, while, unfortunately, his good looks were found in a strong resemblance to his father. And he always worked, selling papers when in high school and sorting books in the city library when he entered junior college, deprived of the sports he loved. Maria glowed at Michael's grades — excellent marks despite his heavy load. He knew she expected him to become a teacher, to have a nice steady job. "No more depression for you, Michael," she said over and over.

But along came Hitler and those Japs and the boys began to leave. Then Michael saw fear begin to lurk in the black depths of his mother's eyes as the first casualty lists appeared in the papers. With no father or family, Michael's friends were everything to him. His mother knew them all and loved them like family. And they were all gone — the dearest, Max, with nothing to show for his brief lifetime except his name in the paper and a curt telegram to his mother.

Michael put his hands on Maria's slender shoulders.

42

She shrugged them off. His jaw twitched but he spoke with a controlled voice, "I told you on December seventh I wanted to join up."

"Max did and now he's on the bottom of the Pacific."

She had hit hard. He felt the loss of his dearest friend deeply. "Maybe that's why, Mom. We've been attacked, killed, for no . . ."

"No!" she interrupted. "Your grades are good, you'll be a teacher, live like a human being."

"I'd be drafted, anyway."

"But you haven't been. I'm a dependent . . ." She choked. The tears began.

"Please, Mom—I'm one-A. It's inevitable. And you'll get an allotment of fifty dollars a month. You can live."

She pushed him away, staring up with death in her eyes. "And when you're dead I'll get ten thousand dollars." She pushed a clenched fist against her mouth and groaned through her knuckles. "I don't want that monkey's paw."

"Don't, Mom. Only a small percentage of the men see . . ."

"Don't give me that percentage crap. What percent was Max?" More tears.

He held her. " I love you, Mom. Please, Mom. I'll be careful." He stroked her hair. "I probably won't even leave the states. Did you know that?"

Head against his shoulder, she spoke through the tears, gasping her words in short bursts. "And Kristie— you, you like her, don't you?"

"Why, of course, Mom. We go together," he agreed, smiling to himself, recognizing her ploy—the beautiful Kristie and the fierce attraction between them.

"You'll see her tonight?"

"Yes. Tonight."

"Does she know?"

"No, Mom."

She brushed stray stands of hair from her forehead and cheek with the back of a hand. "You'll have a hard time."

"I know, Mom. I know."

He would never forget that night. He had never seen
Kristie look lovelier. She was seventeen years old and in
the full bloom of her beauty. Her long blond hair fell
about her shoulders in a gossamer cloud like gold lace,
framing her perfectly ordered visage: wide-spaced blue
eyes as deep as a sunset sky, smooth brows, high molded
cheekbones, a straight nose with delicately chiseled nostrils, full pouting lips like the petals of a rose, lending
her mouth a maddening acquisitive quality. Since the
first moment he had met her at the Hollywood Palladium the year before, he had struggled for words to describe her. He had always been defeated. "Gorgeous,"
"magnificent," and a score of other adjectives that came
to mind were too commonplace. They could describe
Rita Hayworth, Betty Grable or Anita Louise, but not
Kristie. Finally, he concluded only metaphors supplied
by the poetic genius of a Shakespeare or a Byron could
do her justice.

As soon as he entered, she had pasted her trim, firm
body to his, kissing him fiercely and grinding with her
hips until his temples pounded, ears hummed and his
brain became a carousel. And he could not keep his
hands off of her, running his big palms over her back,
down her slender hips and over her hard sculpted buttocks, pulling her against his arousal.

She moaned, "Michael—Michael. Don't go—make
them draft you."

He spoke to the hard pulse in her neck. "It's too late.
I've signed up."

She pushed against his chest. "You never asked me—
not a word." There was petulance in her voice.

Throwing his head back, he pulled away, despairing
eyes moving over the large living room dark with mahogany: mahogany entry door, mahogany trim, mahogany paneling surrounding the natural stone
fireplace, mahogany doors leading to the dining room

44

where Michael knew one could find a solid mahogany buffet and dining room set.

Although Kristie's house was only three blocks from Michael's, it was a different universe to the young man. A rambling frame dwelling typical of thousands built during Los Angeles's building boom of the early twenties, it boasted a front porch as wide as the house and, in addition to the living room and dining room, it had three bedrooms and an enormous kitchen complete with a breakfast nook. All rooms were floored with varnished hardwood.

To Michael, Kristie's father, Desmond Wells — an engineer for the Lockheed Aircraft Company — was a wealthy man. He owned a beautifully furnished house, drove a 1937 Chevrolet Master Deluxe four-door sedan with radio and heater, ate meat other than hamburger and liver, dressed his only child like a renaissance princess, and owned three suits. And his wife, Brenda, had a real diamond ring and wore silk stockings. In fact, Michael's mother referred to Brenda Wells as "that rich bitch."

Wednesday night was "Bank Night" at the Home Theater and Brenda and Desmond made the weekly event a ritual. Even if one did not win the grand prize of three hundred dollars, everyone went home with a dish. The twenty-five-cent admission was a good investment.

Michael felt Kristie's hand pulling. Murmuring "Michael, Michael," she led him to an overstuffed sofa. While she pulled him down on the soft cushions, it was obvious her mind was not on her parents, prizes, or dishes. Holding the young man's hands on her lap, she spoke softly, moist eyes turned to his. "Why didn't you think of me? You'd leave me."

"Think of you?"

"Yes. Me."

He scratched his chin. "The British are losing North Africa and the war, the Russians have been pushed almost to Moscow and are losing their war, the Japs have conquered Malaya, the Philippines, the N.E.I., and

45

we're losing our war and I'm to think . . ."

"What are you going to do Michael, straighten out this whole world all by yourself?"

"Kristie, if enough of 'me' dodge it, this world of ours will be gone — lost. Ernie, Wally, Dale are in it . . ."

"And Max is dead!"

"Mom reminded me."

"And they'll kill you, too."

He knuckled his forehead. "Oh, Lord. Is that all you women think about?"

"Of course! Of course!"

"I should hide behind my mother's skirts."

"That's better than what Max got."

"I can't do that."

"You're a John Wayne."

"No. He's a draft dodger."

"He'll survive."

"I said I can't do that — won't do that. Anyway, I already told you, I've signed up. The decision's already made."

"When do you leave?"

"Next Monday."

"Four days — that's all we have — four days?"

"I'm afraid so, Kristie. Hitler, Tojo, and Mussolini don't wait for anyone."

"No! No!" Sighing, she lay back, pulling him onto her, lips covering his with a fierce hunger, mouth deep, wet, soft, and open for him to probe. Michael was shocked by the strength of his desire for her. His body moved to cover hers, a hot fist clenching in his groin, and he felt his heart pounding furiously in the cage of his ribs.

"When will your parents be home?" he managed hoarsely, pushing her into the cushions.

"It's Bank Night. Hours and hours."

He felt her hands on his back, clawing, moving down over the bunched hard muscles on each side of his spine. Then her tongue circled his lips, leaving fiery trails, chilling his skin and sending shudders down his spine.

46

Despite the shining innocence she radiated like a kitten or a beautiful child, she knew how to fan him, kindle the flame of sexual fury that always seethed for her. Quickly, the maddening tongue became a reptile, darting into his mouth, exploring his teeth, gums, finally finding his tongue. The flame became a bonfire. He kissed her savagely. Locked together, they breathed each other's breath, their tongues twisting together, kneading, pressing, so deep that they threatened to choke each other with their fervor.

Pushing her into the folds of the cushions with the weight of his body, he moved from her mouth, running the tip of his tongue over the satin of her cheek to her ear. His tongue darted inside. She squirmed and moaned. The tongue moved to her neck. He kissed her there hard and fumbled with her blouse, ripping off buttons. He tore at her brassiere, exposing her perfectly formed breasts. He felt her hands on the back of his head, pushing him down. Slowly he nibbled and kissed his way down her throat to a swollen breast and captured the pink areola with his lips. He ran his tongue over it, toying with the nipple. She twisted and cried out small animal-like sounds deep in her throat.

"You want me," she managed.

He was too choked with passion to answer. Instead, he kissed the valley between the hard upthrust mounds, capturing her other breast with his hungry lips. He ran a hand down over her tiny waist, the flare of her womanly hips, and over her marvelous buttocks. His hand found the hem of her skirt, snaked under. Slowly he slid the hand up her thigh. Her flesh was like hot velvet. He found the silk of her panties and began to pull them aside, seeking the prize as old as mankind. Trembling, she raised her hips and parted her knees.

Suddenly he was seized with a terrible thought and made an impossible decision that would torture him for the remainder of his life. He sat upright and turned away.

"What's wrong, Michael?" she asked plaintively.

47

His breath was short. He almost panted. "We've—we've never gone this far, Kristie."

"I know. I know. I—I want you Michael."

He straightened and threw back his shoulders. "You've told me a hundred times you had to be a virgin when you married. Promised your mother, your priest—took a pledge on the name of the Virgin Mary." He rubbed his head like a man tortured by a migraine. "You told me over and over. You said only whores do it before they marry."

"That's changed."

He felt the heat begin to change to anger. "Because I'm going away?"

"Maybe . . ."

"Fuck the departing heroes. Is that it?"

She came erect, obviously shocked. "That's a terrible word!"

"But it's true, isn't it? I'm leaving so it's easy for you. You'll be my whore because you think I might get it like Max."

She spoke softly, "Maybe it's because I love you, too, Michael. And, yes, of course, you're leaving and—and I may lose you without ever . . ." Hand over mouth she turned away. Her shoulders began to shake.

"Please," he said, pulling her to him, kissing the back of her neck tenderly. "I can wait, Kristie. Honest I can. And you and I will have it all when we marry."

"Of course, Michael. I'll wait for you, Michael."

"Promise?"

"Yes, Michael." She began straightening her skirt and buttoning her blouse.

Gently, he kissed the tears from her cheeks. She looked up at him and whispered in his ear, "I'll wait and wait and wait."

On the walk home the wind was from the north and the sky was a translucent sheet of dark blue ice. Flocks of fast-moving clouds scudded across the full moon like frightened sheep fleeing a predator. Michael wondered at his unbelievable decision. He had been offered something he wanted with every particle of his being, and he had refused it. His body still ached with desire, cried out for her, still radiated heat despite the cold wind. He must be mad. That was the only explanation. Insanity.

He laughed to himself. "No. No," he said to the glowing disc of the moon. "It was right. It was right because I love her."

He pushed his hands into his pockets and trudged toward home.

Two

Destroy the enemy on the beach.

> General Yoshitsugu Saito, June, 1944

> The year has taken
> With it many friends
> The vanished beyond count
> A forest of dead.

> Lieutenant Takeo Nakamura, June, 1944

Waiting. That was a soldier's curse. Always waiting. Lieutenant Takeo Nakamura hated it. Dressed in stained brown battle fatigues, his helmet circled by a white *hachi-machi* headband showing his determination to die for his Emperor, the young officer was high on Mount Tapot-chau, gripping his glasses, surveying the endless invasion fleet spread before him like toy boats on a vast blue *tatami* mat. Nonetheless, he felt secure, surrounded by the steel and concrete of his bunker.

With walls over two meters thick and pierced by six gun ports, the structure squatted on an escarpment protected by coconut logs and rocks, hidden by brush. But the low-ceilinged structure was crowded with sweating, filthy men suffering from malnutrition and diarrhea; it was hot and damp and rained chips of concrete and cement dust whenever an American shell landed nearby. A slop bucket added to Nakamura's misery, filling the small space with the smell of stale urine and raw feces. Throughout his short lifetime, Takeo had enjoyed the Japanese addiction to the daily bath, and the frustration of filth was almost as bad as the lack of food.

He sighed. For the first time in three days the Americans had stopped firing. An unusual quiet had descended on the island — a quiet broken only by the beelike drone of a small American spotter aircraft overhead. Occasionally, he could hear the shouts of noncoms bawling orders to two hundred soldiers of a reserve infantry company concealed in a ravine just fifty meters to the south and slightly up-slope from the blockhouse.

Almost two meters tall, Lieutenant Takeo Nakamura was a giant for a Japanese. Although food had been short for over a month, Takeo's shoulders were still broad, hinting at the power developed by a lifetime of hauling lobster pots and fishing gear from the sea. His face was well-ordered, with a broad intelligent brow, a wide flat nose that attested to violent encounters in the past, a strong jaw, and round brown eyes that gave him a rather unoriental appearance.

His eyes were Takeo's most impressive aspect. Intensely dark, they could take on an ominous, ruthless blackness when flashing anger, yet the soul of the aesthete could be found there, too. This ambiguity could be startling and disconcerting. When quiescent, he had the look of a man who loved poetry, and so he did — especially that of the modern poets Takuboku Ishikawa, Akiko Yosano, and Tōson Shimazaki. He was gifted with creativity and wrote his own clever haiku during lulls or even spontaneously when asked by his comrades. But, at the same time, when aroused by danger and the smell of battle, those arresting eyes could flash coldly with the chilling look of the implacable, merciless killer, the man who could unsheath the long blade at his side and decapitate a man with the nonchalance of a diner ordering a bowl of rice.

Four of his six companions were also young: Artilleryman Captain Tamon Yoshikawa hunched over his grid chart while his spotter, Sergeant Hajime Tomonaga, stared through huge tripod-mounted, range-finding binoculars, studying the invasion fleet and quietly mumbling ranges and bearings; Signalman Sergeant

51

Masanori Hashimoto and his assistant, Corporal So-kichi Sorimachi, squatted before two radios and a brace of field telephones, sending and receiving a steady stream of messages.

The two remaining occupants of the bunker contrasted sharply with their companions. Both appeared to be very old men, although neither had yet reached the age of sixty. To Nakamura's left, short, bony with wisps of white hair escaping his helmet and hanging over his serrated forehead like a transparent *shoji,* hunched Lieutenant General Yoshitsugu Saito, staring through his binoculars. Though he was frail-shouldered and very thin, the general's stern jaw and demeanor still exuded the steely resolve of command. And, indeed, as commander of the 23,000 troops of the Northern Marianas Defense Force, his command was the most critical in the Japanese Empire. The capture of Saipan would give the enemy bases from which he could bomb the sacred home islands with his giant new B-29 bombers.

To Takeo Nakamura's right and also glued to a gun port, gazing through binoculars, stood a withered little man with a face so ruined with crosshatched lines and deep furrows that it resembled the relief map of a ravaged countryside. Incongruously, the little man was dressed in the blue uniform of an admiral of the fleet. He was Vice Admiral Chuichi Nagumo, and he shared command of Saipan's defenses with Saito. Both the general and the admiral were hunched by time and the rigors of command, bent like pines on an exposed ridge, too long punished by the wind.

Admiral Nagumo's entire persona emanated the quintessence of bitterness. A back-breaking burden seemed to have crushed him under its weight into a shape so singular that one was reminded of those crabs and crayfish who heave laboriously across the sandy floor of an aquarium. His eyes showed the torment even more than his curved spine. Set deep in the cages of bony sockets, they were underlined with dark plum-colored smears, as though they had been bruised by massive fists. And, indeed, the capricious gods had dealt cruel blows to the little man.

When he was the commander of Koku Kantai (The First Air Fleet), Nagumo's carriers had ravaged Pearl Harbor, Northwest Australia, the Netherlands East Indies, India, and Ceylon. His brilliant, smashing victories had brought great glory and prestige. He had even been mentioned as a possible successor to Admiral Isoroku Yamamoto as Commander-in-Chief of the Combined Fleet. But all that changed at Midway — Midway where he was caught between strikes by Douglas dive bombers, his wave-high CAP scattered to all points of the compass carelessly chasing torpedo bombers. And his own Aichis and Nakajimas crowded the decks of his carriers, loaded with fuel, bombs, and torpedos. There they were caught in a hail of two hundred twenty- and four hundred forty-kilogram bombs. In one morning he lost carriers *Kaga*, *Akagi*, *Soryu* and *Hiryu*, three thousand men, and most of his superb aircrews. This disaster was followed by Santa Cruz, where American fighters slaughtered his few surviving veteran aviators. Relieved of his sea command, he had been banished to Saipan, where he commanded a few patrol craft, barges and 6,690 sailors equipped to fight as infantry. The split command, fanned by the perennial feud between the army and navy, led to incessant bickering with General Saito, who was actually his junior. Everyone knew the two old men despised each other with a rancor that came with age like sour saké long forgotten in a cellar. But even Nakamura, who had acted as liaison between the two for three months, was not prepared for the stinging, unsamurailike exchange about to erupt.

"In the name of *Amaterasu*," — Amaterasu-O-Mi-Kami, the supreme sun goddess — "how do you defeat such people?" Nagumo spat. Shocked, every man turned, staring at the admiral in disbelief. Defeatism in the Imperial forces was unthinkable, violating the basic tenets of Bushido — the code of the samurai.

"What do you mean, Admiral?" Saito answered with

guarded hostility.

"I mean in the last three weeks, I have been bombarded by two battleships I sank at Pearl Harbor," the admiral retorted, voice rising. Embarrassed, every man returned to his duties except Saito, who glared at Nagumo, binoculars dangling. Nagumo continued caustically, "I mean I sank the *California* and the *Tennessee* at Pearl Harbor—but there they are!" Straightening, he gesticulated wildly toward the sea, shouting, "Out there—blowing us to pieces!"

Facing the admiral, Saito's hand instinctively crept to the hilt of his sword. Nagumo's stance was identical as he grasped the handle of his own curved killing blade. The other men stole sideways glances as the general answered, "We will defeat the white devils by killing their marines and sinking their ships." Unblinking and hard as gunmetal his narrow eyes searched the admiral's. "You heard the radio reports. The Combined Fleet is engaging their Task Force Fifty-Eight in the Philippine Sea. Already, there are reports of a great victory."

There were shouts of "Banzai!" from the other men.

Filled with venom, Nagumo's laugh silenced the shouts. "Victory! Ha! Do you remember the radio reports after Midway? Midway was a victory, too." He choked, gasping for breath like an overextended runner. "I only lost the war at Midway."

The exchange was unprecedented, especially in the presence of subordinates. Every man knew that normally such words could only be satisfied by overt apologies or blood. But these were not normal times. Short of food, medicine and ammunition, cut off by submarines that sank anything afloat without warning, shelled and bombarded incessantly and with a garrison of only 32,000 men facing a force that must exceed 100,000, the Japanese were forced to wait for the enemy to approach in his armored boats and barges crammed with infantry, tanks, and artillery.

Both men had lost face in the dispute. Despite the acrimony, they still recognized the preeminent importance of duty and honor. The moment for mutual accommodation had arrived. Returning to his binoculars, Nagumo's voice took on a conciliatory tone. "You know, General, those unwashed barbarians seem to know too much."

Accepting the overture, Saito softened his voice as he raised his binoculars, stooping to the gun port. "I do not understand, Admiral."

"Midway was an ambush."

"An ambush?"

"Yes. They not only placed their carriers for perfect interception, but attacked with their dive-bombers while we were rearming and refueling."

"It could have been coincidence or luck, Admiral. War is filled with both."

"True, General, and I felt the same way until Admiral Yamamoto was ambushed and murdered over Bougainville."

"You keep using the word ambush, Admiral."

"Yes, because I suspect they have broken our fleet code."

"Impossible, Admiral. Even if they could, it is changed continuously."

"I know, I know. But they know too much, General. They just know too much!"

A shout from Sergeant Tomonaga brought a halt to the conversation. Without taking his eyes from the rangefinder, he reported, "A change in their screen. Four small vessels are approaching the reef."

Both of the old men grunted. Captain Tamon Yoshikawa spoke with the soft voice of a Shinto priest. "We can destroy them all with a dozen rounds, General."

"No. They are not worth the ordnance. Anyway, we can not risk exposing our batteries for such trivial targets."

Nakamura studied the intruders. "They fly huge bunting — channel markers." Drawn by flashes, explosions and billowing clouds of smoke, his eyes moved to the gun line. "The battleships have opened fire," Nakamura said. And then, stunned: "The sugar mill is gone."

General Saito studied the inferno of flame and smoke

cloaking Mucho Point, and he turned to his artillery officer. "You had an observer posted there, Captain Yoshikawa?"

"Yes, sir. In the smokestack."

"Well, he is in the Yasakuni Shrine, now."

Nakamura eyed the flaming ruin that had been the most modern sugar facility in the western Pacific. "Sir — the stack is still standing."

"No! Impossible," the general said. And then to Yoshikawa, "Your man must live in the arms of the gods."

Tension-relieving laughter filled the blockhouse. Chuckling, Nakamura returned to his glasses. He counted three battleships, four cruisers, and four destroyers firing on the beach while behind them landing craft had begun wallowing in huge circles. Dozens of gray landing ships and transports had anchored. The lieutenant glanced at his watch and spoke casually like a man awaiting the opening curtain at a Kabuki theater. "It is almost zero-eight-hundred. Americans go to work at zero-eight-hundred."

"Yes. They are creatures of habit," Nagumo offered dourly. "Punctual and they dislike fighting at night."

General Saito moved his eyes to Captain Tamon Yoshikawa. "Captain, the disposition of your heavy artillery?"

Nakamura's eyes widened with surprise. They had been over this dozens of times. The old man was becoming forgetful. Coming to attention, Yoshikawa spoke in rapid-fire bursts as if he were approaching a fresh topic. "I have eight Whitworth-Armstrong six-inch guns, nine one-hundred-forty-millimeter, eight one-hundred-twenty-millimeter dual purpose and four two-hundred-millimeter mortars in protected emplacements or camouflaged on reverse slopes. All weapons are sited and registered on the reef."

The old man nodded, staring at the sea. "Alert your batteries. Their first mission will be the four passes in the reef," he said crisply. And then as if reciting something he had rehearsed many times, he added, "First priority targets are the landing craft. Your thirty-sevens and seventy-fives will engage surviving barges over open sights. Our infantry will deal with any marines reaching the beach."

"Yes, sir." Quickly, the captain squatted beside Sorimachi and Hasimoto, mumbling orders.

General Saito turned to Admiral Nagumo. "What is the status of your flotilla, Admiral?"

The admiral shrugged. "Four small patrol craft are still afloat—one in Magicienne Bay and three at Tinian Town."

"Your barges?"

"Twelve are still hidden in Tanapag Harbor."

"Good, Admiral. Good," the general said. And then, waving at the sea: "In a few days, when they move their heavy ships from the gun line, we will put those barges to good use."

Nakamura's eyes widened. "An attack, sir?"

The old general smiled. "A surprise for the Yankee savages, Lieutenant. We will show them what *Yamato damashii*"—Japanese spirit—"can do."

The mention of "Japanese spirit" brought a spark to Nakamura's eyes. "Please consider me, General," he said, fingering his *hachimachi* headband.

"You have great devotion to the emperor, Lieutenant. We shall see." The old man swung his glasses southward. "Aguijan—we can not make a gift of Aguijan. Who do we have there, Lieutenant Nakamura?"

"Lieutenant Goro Isobe, sir."

"How many men?"

"A company, General."

"Full strength?"

"No, sir—eighty-three men."

"Any heavy weapons?"

"No, General. Two Nambu Keikikanjus."

"Model Elevens?"

"Yes, sir."

"Light, Lieutenant. Light. Six-point-five-millimeter. How are they placed?"

"One commands the path and the other is in the triangular cave with a clear field of fire over the beach."

The old man nodded. "The two machine guns will have to do. We cannot send him more."

Nakamura turned his glasses toward Tinian, only two miles off the southern shore of Saipan. Adjusting his glasses, he could see miles past the low, flat island to the jutting, forbidding peak called Aguijan.

Suddenly, there was a roar of engines. The men at the embrasures leaned forward, craned their necks, and tried to look skyward. "American bombers," Nakamura shouted.

"Those are Grumman torpedo planes," Nagumo said.

Silently, the Japanese watched as a dozen of the big planes lumbered over the beach in shallow dives, braving a storm of antiaircraft fire.

"What are those fools doing?" Saito asked himself. "Glide bombing?"

"Throwing away lives," Nagumo answered. Then the bunker was filled with shouts of "Banzai!" as three of the slow planes were shot from the skies.

"Good shooting," Saito said, staring at the trio of funeral pyres.

"It was target practice," Nagumo offered.

Nakamura's exhilaration over the kills was arrested by the spotter's voice. "Twelve close bombardment vessels moving to the reef and the barges have broken their circles."

"Here they come! Here they come!"

Enveloped by saffron smoke and flickering dragon's tongues of flame, the ships of the gun line fired with renewed fury. Coral, trees, sand, boulders, chunks of concrete, and occasional bodies leaped from the beach defenses. Then the rain of exploding horror began rolling inland and up the slope.

Suddenly, General Saito turned to Nakamura, taking him by surprise. "A poem, Nakamura-san. That is what we need. You write brilliant haiku."

What a stroke, the young lieutenant thought. The

mind of the consummate samurai. With 100,000 Yankees poised to storm the beaches, sixteen-inch and fourteen-inch shells raining around them, bombers overhead, the unperturbed samurai asks for a poem. Yes. Perfect. Use this moment of exploding battle for contemplation. Even Admiral Nagumo nodded his approval, showing a resurgence of his old samurai spirit.

Smiling, the young lieutenant reached into his pocket and removed a slip of paper. All eyes were on the lieutenant while he shouted over the din:

> Let the world flame around me
> I care not
> Nor for my life
> For I am the sword of my emperor.

The old man sighed contentedly. "You have the heart of a warrior and the soul of a poet," Saito said. Swelling with pride, Takeo bowed.

" 'Sword of the emperor.' Excellent," Nagumo mused, beaming, his spirits obviously rising. And then fiercely and with new resolve: "We are all his swords. We shall sweep the seas clean of the round-eyed, unwashed barbarians." Raising a fist, his voice became a drumbeat. "And Emperor Meiji showed us how to live — how to die with his maxim, 'Death is light as a feather, duty is as heavy as a mountain.' "

The tiny bunker resounded with shouts of "banzai!" and *"Tenno heika banzai* (Long live the Emperor)!" But the barrage moved closer, putting an end to the shouting.

The bunker shuddered from a near miss. Nakamura sucked in his breath, gripped his binoculars with white knuckles, and focused on the approaching hail of exploding shells. More planes: diving, firing, dropping bombs. And the Americans had a new weapon: rockets leaped from their fighters in great clouds of white smoke. But he feared the naval fire the most. Those battleships could fire AP shells weighing a ton and demolish a blockhouse.

He groaned, overwhelmed by the thunder in his ears,

and began to lower his glasses as the terrifying sound of a dozen rushing motorcars filled the bunker. All pulled their heads down like frightened turtles as the howling terror ripped overhead, smashing into a hillside. Convulsing, the blockhouse rained chips of concrete and sand. A fine mist of cement sifted into their nostrils, made a dry well of Nakamura's throat.

"Random fire," Tamon Yoshikawa said quietly.

Nakamura heard screams. He moved to another port and stared up-slope, cursing the poor visibility of the embrasure. Not only had the company of infantry vanished, but the hill they had used for cover had disappeared, replaced by a smoking crater rimmed by bodies and pieces of bodies. Here and there a screaming wounded man flopped like an injured seal marooned on a beach. The young lieutenant tore his eyes from the horror and returned to the sea. Two dozen armored barges were approaching the reef.

General Saito turned to Yoshikawa, screaming, "All batteries commence firing — commence firing and continue firing at will."

The general was answered by more thunderclaps and stabbing lightning booming and flashing from the *California, Tennessee* and *Pennsylvania*. There was the roar of an approaching typhoon. Takeo began to lower his glasses. Then a flash followed by searing heat and a great shock wave like a killer tsunami struck the blockhouse, piercing Nakamura's eardrums with a hundred hot needles, sending him crashing against the concrete and then to the floor on all fours, helmet clattering. The tiny structure leapt as if it was trying to free itself from the island, and the room was filled with the dreaded sound of collapsing, crashing concrete, splattering Nakamura with a strange rain — solid with bits and pieces of sharp hail, yet soft and wet. A wounded animal began an unearthly keening.

White smoke brought tears to Takeo's eyes while the acrid stench of cordite seared his nose and throat. Automatically, he searched for the senior officers first. Apparently unharmed, the two old men were seated on the floor side by side, staring through stunned eyes. Tomonaga was seated behind his range-finder holding his ears, rocking and moaning. Helmetless, Captain Yoshikawa had been hurled to a corner, blood streaming from nose, eyes and ears, arm twisted grotesquely behind him. These were the lucky ones.

Sergeant Hashimoto's head, smashed by a huge chunk of concrete, had been driven into his radios and then into the floor. His skull had split like a ripe melon, and its reddish gray contents had splattered Nakamura's tunic. Buried under chunks of concrete, shattered radios and splintered tables, Sorimachi lay across his still comrade, chest crushed, leg twisted impossibly, his foot reversed and pressed to his chin. Screaming through a toothless, bloody mouth, his face was tight with shock. His eyes were sightless balls of glass.

Nakamura tore his eyes from Sergeant Hashimoto and the wounded men. Then, after feeling his arms and legs and finding no broken bones, he grasped a port and pulled himself erect. He tasted blood. He had bitten a hole in his tongue. Fresh blood dripped from a cut on his cheek. Gingerly he touched his nose: smashed. Blood was running off his chin. Rocking on his heels, he looked at the overhead, a strange torpor hazing his mind. A large-caliber shell had struck the rounded fort squarely, knocking out chunks of concrete but not smashing all the way through the thick protective works. If it had, they would have all been killed instantly.

Sorimachi's shrieks tore his heart, tore aside the protective curtain of numbness. Suddenly, he was going mad in a charnel house. "Stop! Stop!" Nakamura screamed.

Disciplined to the end, the dying soldier rolled his glassy eyes to Nakamura, gasping and wheezing spraying blood. Then, almost comically, Sorimachi blew a huge blood bubble like a child's balloon expanding from his lips. He sucked the bubble in, choked and wretched when it collapsed on his face and neck in a red pasty smear. Then, tearing it from his lips with a claw-like hand, the corporal screeched in an unbelievably strong voice, *"Tenno heika banzai!"* Immediately, he stiffened as if his spine had become a steel rod and then sagged like a rag doll, arms and legs twitching and trembling in the final spasms of death.

General Saito came to life, staggered unsteadily to his feet, shouting, "Sergeant Tomonaga, the medical kit — tend to Captain Yoshikawa!"

Shaking his head, the sergeant lurched like a drunk to a corner locker.

Pushing himself to his feet slowly, Admiral Nagumo's eyes were on Corporal Sorimachi's corpse. "He died with 'Long live the Emperor' on his lips. A magnificent death in the highest tradition of Bushido," he said softly. The old admiral looked upward, and reverently quoted the *Hagakure,* the handbook of the samurai. " 'It is a cleansing act to give one's life for the Mikado.' " His eyes returned to Sorimachi. "Truly, his karma glistens with the purity of the sun goddess, Amaterasu, and he will enter the Yasakuni Shrine and dwell there forever with the spirits of the countless heroes who have preceded him."

The somber, eloquent words meant nothing to Lieutenant Takeo Nakamura's numb brain. His guts were a vast void turning to ice water. Turning slowly to an embrasure, he stared to the south and found Aguijan. "Like home," he said softly to himself while running his hand down over the scabbard of his sword. "Oh, Tama Shima — beautiful Tama Shima, my home."

Takeo closed his eyes, saw his home: an island like an emerald jewel jutting from the Bungo Suido. His mind detached itself from reality, carried him back, out of the horror, the stench, the death. Then he was there. He was home. It was the day he told his parents of his decision to serve the Emperor. The day his father gave him the Nakamura sword. It had been the greatest day of his life. Every detail was vivid. It all came back, every gesture, every emotion.

The day Takeo Nakamura told his parents of his decision, the Bungo Suido had been gray and dark, low cumulus clouds scudding across the sky in ranks like waves of demented spirits. He remembered clutching the gunwale of his father's fishing boat while his eyes moved from the rugged coastline of Tama Shima to the narrow coastal flats and then finally upward over the precipitous face of Toriyama, soaring skyward like a green tower.

Throughout his lifetime, Takeo Nakamura had been awed by Toriyama. Seen from a distance, the mountain's numberless pines seemed to point upward to the old stone lighthouse like an army of peasants saluting their *diamyo*. And just below the lighthouse stood the island's lone Shinto shrine — the Ogawa Shrine, dedicated to the god of the sea, Watatsumi-no-Mikoto.

Takeo had always disliked the arduous climb of over two-hundred stone steps leading to the shrine. But every time he reached the red *torii* and stone lions guarding the entrance, he knew the view alone was worth the climb. Here there was a breathtaking panorama of swirling blue seas marking the blending of the swift currents of the Bungo Suido with the calm waters of the Inland Sea. And to the northeast the Suido melted into the mists of the Pacific while directly north mountainous Shikoku could be glimpsed when the west wind was strong.

The Greater East Asia War was a year old that gloomy, cold afternoon when Takeo, with a halibut across his shoulders, followed his father up the stone steps away from the quay and toward their home, hidden in the forest. Prodded by the cold despite heavy lined trousers, denim jumper, and rubber boots, his father, Yoshikazue Nakamura — a short, balding man with a face creased and tanned like old leather — led the way with long, impatient strides.

Halfway up the mountain, the pair left the steps, following a path into the forest. Here they found their home, a small wooden structure crafted to blend with the glade that sheltered it. After removing their shoes, the pair entered the building following a route past a workroom, toilet and finally the aromatic kitchen where Takeo's mother, Sumiko — short, plain, thin like her husband, with graying black hair pulled sharply back into a knot—turned from a steaming pot of rice. She bowed. Without breaking stride, her husband nodded and grunted. Then he pushed a paper *shoji* aside and disappeared into the next room.

Stopping, Takeo bowed to his mother, offering the halibut. "This is the best of the catch, *Okāsan.*"

Smiling, she took the fish. "You had a good day, Takeo?"

"No, *Okāsan.* The seas were choppy. Watatsumi-no-Mikoto has been displeased all month. The co-op will not pay us much."

"I will go to the shrine tomorrow morning. Perhaps the gods will answer," she said earnestly. Then, turning and placing the halibut on the chopping block, she added, "I have heated your bathwater."

"Thank you, *Okāsan,*" the young fisherman said, bowing. In a moment he had followed his father.

Entering the main room, Takeo stepped onto the wooden floor in the heart of the small house. Learned from centuries of catastrophic earthquakes, the construction of the Nakamuras' home was typical of all classes. Built entirely of wood and paper with structured pieces fitted perfectly into the uprights without the use of a single nail, the entire building was held down by a thatch roof. Typically, there was no varnish or paint to mar the prized natural color of wood. Straw *tatami* mats covered the floor.

Crossing the room to a small *shoji* shielded alcove where his personal possessions were kept, Takeo passed his sixteen-year-old brother, Toshi, who was sprawled on a soft cushion with his feet pressed close to the glowing coals of a glazed pottery heater. Toshi, still dressed in his black student's uniform, was engrossed in a textbook lighted by the room's lone oil lamp. Anxious for his bath, Takeo grasped his towel and left the house without saying a word to his brother.

Disdaining the community bath located at the island's tiny village, which was clustered about the quay and fisherman's cooperative, the Nakamuras enjoyed the unusual luxury of their own four foot iron cauldron bought the year before after a decade of sacrifice. The tub, filled with warm water heated by an oil burner, was sheltered by a wooden shed behind the house. After washing himself thoroughly from a basin, Takeo entered the tub and seated himself opposite his father, who sat expressionless, eyes closed. The two, relaxed by the warm water, discussed the day's fishing and planned for the morrow, deciding on a new location for a string of twelve octopus pots. Then they rose, dried themselves, slipped into flowing *yukatas* and left the bath for the use of Toshi and Sumiko — an order of use that was inflexible.

Squatting crossed legged on his usual *zabuton* with his red lacquered tray in front of him, Takeo felt satisfied with his meal of rice topped with sliced raw halibut and seaweed dipped in dough and fried into solid wafers. Similarly seated, his father, brother, and mother were finishing their meals when the young fisherman laid aside his bowl and short wooden *hashi,* deciding to broach a subject that had been troubling him for many, many months.

Addressing his father first, *"Otōsan,"* and then his mother *"Okāsan,"* and then returning to Yoshikazu, he announced evenly, "I feel that it is time for me to serve the emperor."

All eyes turned to Yoshikazue, who remained silent for a moment, staring meditatively at his empty bowl. Takeo knew his father was a good Buddhist, believing a man's fate in this life was fixed. In addition, he had the conviction that service to the mikado strengthened karma, leading to a better rebirth in the next life. And, perhaps, with the good fortune of a glorious battlefield death, a warrior could even attain nirvana; the place of exquisite peace, escaping both life and death. Furthermore, as a fervent follower of Shinto the elder Nakamura was versed in the samurai ethos of Bushido, worshipping Emperor Hirohito as the direct descendent of the Sun Goddess, Amaterasu. Takeo knew his father believed honorable service to the emperor was the most exhalted duty of manhood. In fact, Takeo felt he was looking into his father's mind as Yoshikazue raised his eyes — eyes that glowed like coals in craggy hollows — and said, "All of us have our duty to the son of heaven." The coals burned into his son's eyes. "But we are only poor fishermen — can you serve and perhaps die as a samurai?"

The reference to the storied warrior class brought a hard gleam to the young man's eyes. To serve the emperor in the samurai tradition was the goal of all Japanese boys — even the sons of poor fishermen. "Yes, *Otōsan,*" Takeo said with new eagerness. "I would try to serve as honorably as Hiroshi Fukanaga and Timoro Kawasaki."

Takeo moved his eyes to his mother as the mention of Hiroshi and Timoro brought a sudden tightening to Sumiko's lips, widening of her eyes. Sons of the island, both had been killed the same year; Hiroshi fighting Russians on the Manchuko-Siberian border, Timoro attacking the Chinese Nineteenth Route Army in Shanghai. When the ashes of the two boys had been returned in small white boxes, their parents' incalculable pride could not mask the enormity of their grief. Sumiko cleared her throat before asking a carefully calculated question. "Are you a carp, my son?"

For the first time, Takeo felt a smile touch his lips. The carp was the most admired fish, swimming gallantly upstream, leaping the sheerest falls, fighting the angler's hook, but once caught able to lie quietly on the cutting board accepting serenely what must be. *Sayonara,* (so be it) was the word he had heard for a lifetime. The indomitable carp had been immortalized in his memory by the annual May 5 Boy's Day display of a pennant emblazoned with the image of the fish. Every family with a son had the right to fly the bunting, but the Nakamuras' pennant was the largest and proudest. "Yes, *Okāsan,* I am a carp," the young man answered. The small smile vanished and he suddenly appeared much older as he continued, "I pledge you no dishonor. You know I have studied the *Hagakure.* I know the codes of Bushido." He gestured at a leather-bound volume on a small table in a corner of the room. The sacred book had occupied the same place on the same table for as long as he could remember.

"Then you know when and how to die," Yoshikazue injected bluntly.

Out of the corner of his eye Takeo saw his mother stiffen like a board. "Yes, *Otōsan*. The samurai knows 'There is a time to live and a time to die.' "

The fisherman beamed at his son's quote of one of the samurais' most famous maxims. "You have been studying, Takeo-san," Yoshikazue said, new respect softening his voice. And then quickly, "When would you like to begin your service?"

"Next month — after Toshi completes his school. He can take my place in the boat. I will join the army." Toshi moved his eyes, which glowed with envy, over Takeo's face, but remained silent.

"Of course," his father responded as if no other choice was possible. "The army."

Takeo decided it was time for his bombshell. "I have been accepted for officer training."

"You did this without my knowledge?" his father said incredulously.

"Yes, *Otōsan* — last year at school. My scores were the highest."

Staring at his son with the brown of his eyes heightened by moisture, the fisherman swelled with pride. "Once," he began with a thick voice, "the Nakamuras were a great warrior family. And then came the terrible events of 1871, when all samurai were declared outlaws — became *ronin* overnight — lost their property. And we came to this." He circled a finger over his head. "But you," — he leaned toward his son — "have restored our honor, and you deserve the sword." He turned to Toshi. "Get the sword."

"Yes, *Otōsan*." Takeo's brother rose, moved quickly to the next room and returned, carrying a great sword. More than a meter long, it was curved, its scabbard emblazoned with a pearl-and-diamond-inlaid, sixteen-petalled chrysanthemum, representing the emperor. Its leather-wrapped *tang* (grip) was fitted with elaborately molded silver. Toshi handed the sword to his father, who came to his feet quickly.

Holding the sword before him, Yoshikawa continued with a tale Takeo had heard many times. "This is the Nakamuras' most valued possession. In the twelfth year of Ashikaga, when the Nakamuras ruled in Aomeri, our most eminent ancestor, Mokunosuke, ordered this blade fashioned by the master swordsmith Yasumitsu." He gripped the *tang* and pulled the blade from the scabbard with one easy motion. There was a ringing sound, almost of joy, as the sword leaped free from its lair like a cobra sensing a kill. Yoshikawa held the glistening blade vertically before him and rotated it from side to side, catching the light and reflecting it like polished silver.

Yoshikawa stared at the blade like the subject of a hypnotist's spell, and his voice dropped to reverential tones. "The Nakamura blade is fashioned of layered and tempered metal, folded and drawn nine times, as finely wrought as the Empress's jewelry and as sharp and spare as a Lotus Sutra scroll." He raised his eyes to the tip of the blade and exulted, "Always remember, Takeo, the sword is life! This is the samurai's soul!"

Eyeing Takeo and lowering the sword, Yoshikawa ran his fingers over ideograms inscribed in the silver. Watching his father's fingers trace the inscription, Takeo knew what was on his mind. The expected words poured from Yoshikawa's lips, "Here is the story of your grandfather Shoin's glorious death. He was leading an attack at Port Arthur when a Russian bullet sent him to our ancestors." He raised the sword and stabbed it at the ceiling. "But the blood of at least five filthy Russian dogs stained this sacred blade." He dropped the point of the blade to the floor. "Not even bullets could separate your grandfather from the sword. He was still gripping it firmly even in death."

"I will not dishonor it, *Otōsan*," Takeo said softly, coming to his feet. Yoshikawa slid the blade back into the scabbard and handed it to Takeo, who accepted the sword with the adoration reserved for a temple icon. All eyes were on the young man as he slipped the sword under his *obi*, holding the *tang* with his right hand.

Yoshikawa nodded at a leather-bound copy of the *Hagakure* that rested on a corner table. The book had been there for as long as Takeo could remember. Yoshikawa said to Takeo, "The *Hagakure* teaches, 'If a sword is always sheathed, it will become rusty, the blade will dull, and people will think as much of its owner.' "

Takeo smiled. "And *Otōsan*," he replied. "It also teaches, 'If one's sword is broken, the samurai will strike with his hands. If his hands are cut off, he will bite through ten or fifteen enemy necks with his teeth.' "

Yoshikawa beamed and said thickly, "You are a Nakamura, my son."

Sumiko spoke in a husky, tremulous timbre. "My cousin, Tumio, has promised a belt for you for when you are called. She will stand on a Tokyo corner until it is finished — one stitch at a time from a thousand strangers, and a prayer to go with every stitch, Takeo-san."

Takeo bowed, smiling, knowing the "belt of a thousand stitches" would bring good fortune and enlist the aid of the gods in dying well, if death claimed him on the battlefield. "Thank you, *Okāsan* — thank you." He tightened his grip on the *tang*. It was warm, almost hot. It seemed to pulse like a live thing.

Staring through the gun port, Lieutenant Takeo Nakamura gripped the *tang* of the Nakamura blade tightly. His ears still rang with the blast of the great shell, his nose still dribbled sticky red drops. Bringing his glasses back to his eyes, he focused to the south, where he found Aguijan, which was visible sporadically through the smoke and dust. He smiled a grim little smile.

Three

"It's called Aguijan," the marine captain said, pointing at a chart mounted on the bulkhead. Quartermaster Michael Carpelli, Signalman Dennis Warner, and Pharmacist's Mate Bryan Kohler crowded forward, cursing the cramped mess hall and the smell of the thirty-eight unwashed men packed into it.

Dirt! Filth! Doesn't anyone ever give a clean war? Carpelli wondered. His eyes moved to the marine, Captain Christopher Welly, a short young man whose straggly blond hair escaped his helmet and hung over his ears and over hazel eyes red-rimmed with fatigue. He was thin, like all marines. Michael was convinced they stopped eating the first day of an invasion, ignoring even their K Rations until battle's end.

"We believe they have a radio station here," Welly continued, stabbing the pointer at the center of the island. "And we suspect a radar station, too." He moved the pointer. "And up here, we suspect artillery — number and caliber unknown. Could raise hell with us when we attack Tinian." He turned to Ensign Robert Bennington. "You're in command, correct Mr. Bennington?"

"Correct, Captain," Bennington blustered nervously. "I'm sorry I didn't meet you when you came aboard. But I just returned from the *Relief*."

"I know and I'm sorry about Lieutenant Bennett — terrible luck."

"You know it's food poisoning?"

"Yes." The marine snorted. "What a lousy break. He survived D Day and then got poisoned by his mother. *C'est la guerre.*"

"That's right, Captain," Bennington said. "Food poisoning—he loves herring. His mother sent him some and he's been saving it since Kwajalein. It damn near killed him. They have him on the *Relief.* It was touch and go for a few hours, but he should be back in a couple days."

Carpelli's stomach felt sick and empty. Bennington in command. And a dangerous mission appeared imminent. He bit his lip.

"Your second in command is Ensign John Manning, Mr. Bennington?" the marine asked.

"Correct, Captain. He's on watch. I'll introduce you after this meeting."

Kohler nudged Carpelli. Michael nodded. Manning was a former University of Michigan fullback and a blustering, posturing fool, even more incompetent than Bennington, if possible—two ensigns, two "ninety day wonders" in charge of a warship and sixty-one lives. Again Michael had an empty, sinking feeling as he stared at the chart.

The captain was not finished with Bennington. "You have your orders?"

"Right, Captain. From Commander Task Group Fifty-Seven Point Seven," Bennington said reluctantly, pulling a document from his pocket. He read, spitting the words like a man who had bitten rotten fruit. " 'You will conduct a reconnaissance of Aguijan Island on 19 June, 1944. For this mission you will embark Captain Christopher Welly, commanding officer of Company B, First Battalion of the First Marine Division. You will maneuver your vessel in accordance to the requests of Captain Welly whenever such requests do not imperil your command. You are to reconnoiter the island at close range, marking enemy works. Targets of opportunity may be engaged at your discretion.' " Bennington looked up at Welly, perspiration burnishing his forehead. "Ah . . . please . . . ah . . . continue with the briefing."

The marine studied the ensign curiously for a moment and then moved his tired eyes over the sailors — a blue mass covering benches and tables and jamming the corners of the room. Every face was drawn and grim. Carpelli leaned forward, staring at the chart. The young marine spoke. "Aguijan is small, about three square miles, has sides like slabs of marble, and no beaches to speak of. We know it's farmed, and up here"—the pointer moved—"a few houses and a derrick."

"A derrick?" Bennington said nervously, a trapped look in his eyes.

Again the curious stare. The thin lips compressed. "Yes. The cliffs are so steep, supplies are hoisted up the cliff from lighters." A muttering filled the room. Carpelli heard Bryan Kohler whistle softly.

"You're going to take that place?" Kohler asked incredulously.

Silence while the marine stared at the pharmacist's mate. "Yes. That's our job. My company will make the assault."

Kohler grunted. A great plow horse of a man with gray eyes and hair harvested from a wheat field, his shoulders and arm looked like they were made of boulders and timbers. Before the war Bryan Kohler had been a premed student at the University of Southern California and the number one man on the wrestling team. Then came the war. Despite the hysterical pleadings of his mother he had volunteered on 8 December and by August 1942 had been assigned to Guadalcanal, a corpsman for the marines who had no medical orderlies of their own. He had first met the savage enemy here — an enemy who laughed at the Geneva Conventions and used the corpsmen's white crosses for bull's eyes. Within hours, Kohler learned to carry his kit in one hand and a Thompson submachine gun in the other.

But the slaughter—especially of corpsmen—embittered the former premed student, and he soon became far more devoted to taking life than saving it. To him, the Thompson was a delicious weapon, spewing forty-five caliber slugs like a garden hose. His great strength permitted him to hold the bucking weapon down easily, controlling its natural tendency to climb when on full trigger. He respected the Thompson and used it with artistry.

Late August found Bryan Kohler fighting against the Ichiki Battalion at the Ilu River. Here, standing over a BAR man with his chest ripped and lungs pulsating through shattered bone like red balloons, Kohler—morphine Syrette in hand—was charged by a half-dozen banzai-screaming infantrymen. Without rising or dropping the syringe, he pointed the submachine gun and bowled over the six Japanese like pins on an alley. For this he received the Navy Cross. A month later a Purple Heart was added when his back was shredded by a knee mortar. Months were spent in the San Diego Naval Hospital before he was finally released to the receiving barracks on Terminal Island in Los Angeles Harbor. Here he met Carpelli, who was also awaiting assignment after the sinking of the subchaser 3028. The two survivors became inseparable friends. In fact, when Kohler was assigned to the PCS 2404, Carpelli volunteered. "I might as well get some of that cushy duty with you," he had said, grinning. "Probably never leave stateside. Just USO commandos, that's all we'll be—a pair of pussy mechanics helping keep up home front morale."

Kohler had laughed raucously as he pounded his friend's back. But now Kohler was back in the fight, watching an exhausted marine describe an island so tiny, so obscure, that he had never heard of it until that morning, an island where he would find new

73

horrors and perhaps his grave.

Captain Welly waved his pointer impatiently. "Save your questions for later." He returned to the chart. "There's a low spot in the cliff here — a rocky beach and a path. We call it 'Green Beach.' " The pointer moved upward. "I expect to land my company there at night using rubber boats and move up the path." He turned back to the crew. "Now. Are there any questions?"

Warner spoke. "How do you know so much about Aguijan, Captain?"

"I was on it last night. Seven of us went ashore at Green Beach. We found the path and no sentries. The Japs must believe the place is impregnable."

Carpelli gestured at the chart. Welly nodded. Moving to the bulkhead, the quartermaster stabbed a finger and ran it upward. "If this is the path" — the finger stopped near the top of the cliff — "there is probably a Nambu about here. They could enfilade the path with no dead ground. Their stuff would all be good."

Michael saw Bennington's eyes widen. "I was just getting ready to say that," the ensign said, rankled, glaring at Michael.

Welly ignored Bennington. "You're very perceptive — ah . . ."

"Carpelli, Quartermaster Michael Carpelli, sir."

The young marine nodded. "We figure the military crest is where you indicated, Quartermaster."

"And in caves, Captain," Kohler added suddenly. "For sure."

The marine signaled agreement. "Yes. Their usual disposition. And almost impervious to air attack and high angle shelling." The pointer moved up the cliff. "We think we found another machine gun here — in a cave with a triangular mouth. They've piled a lot of brush in front of it." He turned back to the sailors. "Your three-inch fifty-caliber with its high velocity and flat trajectory is ideal for this mission." He looked at Bennington.

74

"Ah, yes," the ensign said haltingly. "We can use AA rounds set for contact bursts and mix in AP to penetrate timber and whatever else they pile in front of their guns."

"The forty?"

Bennington ran a hand over his forehead. "The same mix."

There was a long silence. Finally, Kohler spoke. "How can we find them? They'll have no trouble finding us, Captain." There was a rumble of voices.

The young captain raised his hand. Silence. "If you get close enough, they'll pull the brush aside to open fire. You'll see the flashes."

"They should have flash-hiders," Kohler said quickly.

"If a gun's pointed right at you, they can't hide the flashes."

"They won't need to," Kohler scoffed. "We'll be dead."

"Not necessarily," the marine answered, his voice rising sharply to the challenge. "You can be within a five-degree cone of a weapon's bore sight and still see the flashes."

"Jesus Christ," a buffalo of a man with long hair, sideburns, and shaggy mustache said as he leaned against the rear bulkhead.

" 'Jesus Christ' what?" the marine retorted hotly, finally piqued.

The man straightened, bared his teeth in a smile that held no humor, continuing in low leisurely tones that spoke unmistakably of a lifetime spent south of the Mason-Dixon line. "Schultz—Chief Gunner's Mate Algernon Schultz, gun captain of the three-inch," the sailor drawled. "I ain't no greenhorn, Cap'n. I got me my Purple Heart already at Salerno, and I ain't hankerin' for another—leastways posthumous."

Another murmur swept the room like a swell before a storm. The marine's eyes widened. "You know this briefing is not mandatory. You have your orders. We could leave it there."

75

The voice was harsh. Welly glanced at Bennington, who returned the probe with a shifty-eyed nod. Carpelli was sure he saw terror in the ensign's eyes. "I was trying to clarify the mission—the problems," the marine said, raising both hands palms up in a gesture of futility.

"Respectfully, Cap'n," the Southerner drawled on. "None of them boys," he circled a finger, "is fixin' to cut an' run." He looked around at the mass of silent faces. "But it don't seem right to find guns by gettin' a passel of swabbies killed."

"They could slaughter my men on that path."

"Ain't no one wantin' that, Cap'n."

"May I say something, sir?" a slight boy with unruly sandy hair said. Standing at Schultz's side, the youth raised his hand much like a schoolboy in a high school classroom.

"Why, of course," the marine said, obviously relieved to disengage the chief.

The boy pursed his lips thoughtfully, giving his visage a cherubic aspect, but his eyes glinted mischievously with a look one might expect to find in the eyes of a leprechaun hiding in ambush. "Lindsay, sir. Gunner's Mate Third Class Don Lindsay, pointer on the three-inch," the young gunner said. And then thoughtfully: "We don't want to see one marine killed, sir—not one." There was a rumble of approval. "But I fire the three-inch and, don't forget, sir, we're on a rolling gun platform. We don't have the stability you have on the beach."

"I know—I know." The marine waved impatiently. "What are you trying to say?"

"They may hit us before we hit them, sir."

"Not if we stay out of range," Bennington injected, hastily.

Welly waved the ensign off. "It's not that, Mister Bennington." And then to the crew, "We will be exposed and I with you." He paused, eyeing the mass of blue

76

through narrow lids. And then in an obvious attempt to placate them, "No one plans on taking casualties and, don't forget, you won't have a crazy marine leading a bayonet charge." He chuckled, but the sound was lonely. He turned to Bennington, "You have your own captain. He'll give the orders."

Smiling weakly, Bennington looked up.

Carpelli choked back a sour taste.

Dawn was coming, drawn across the sky like a sheet of steel rolled from a mill, deep blue and lilac at first, then brightening to faint reds as it spread above the sea. Viewed from the sea, Aguijan rose with majestic abruptness, a green tower soaring from the burnished copper of the flat water reaching for the blue vault of the sky. As the PCS 2404 moved slowly toward the island, Quartermaster Michael Carpelli levelled his binoculars.

"Main battery manned and ready — numbers one, two, three and four twenties manned and ready, Mr. Bennington," Malcolm Murphy said over his head set. "Mr. Manning is aft standing by the forty."

"Very well," Bennington said. "Damage control?"

"Standing by, sir."

Bennington turned to Carpelli. "Quartermaster, get me a bearing on the derrick."

Michael turned to the bearing circle, squinted. "Two-nine-zero, Mr. Bennington."

"Very well." The ensign moved to the voice tube. "Come to two-nine-zero, all ahead standard."

Carpelli glanced over his shoulder, glimpsed the rising sun. It was very red, spilling over the horizon like blood. He turned to Bennington, "I suggest we swing slightly south, sir. Then come to three-zero-zero. We'll have the sun at our back."

Captain Christopher Welly, dressed in dirty green fatigues with a thirty-caliber carbine slung over his shoulder, dropped his binoculars. "Fine idea — good infantry tactics."

"Give me a course, Quartermaster."

"I suggest two-six-zero, sir."

"Very well." Bennington hunched over the voice tube. "Come left to two-six-zero."

"Left to two-six-zero," echoed up from the pilot-house. Michael Carpelli felt the ship heel into her turn. "Steady on two-six-zero, sir."

"Very well." Bennington glanced at the talker. "Tell radar I want a range and bearing to the nearest point of land."

Murphy muttered into his mouthpiece. "Range four-thousand. Bearing zero-three-zero relative."

"Very well." The ensign glanced over his shoulder, found the sun, a glowing yellow disc balancing on the string of the horizon. He turned to Carpelli. "Give me a mark when the derrick bears three-zero-zero."

"Aye, aye sir," Carpelli replied, pleased with the ensign's performance. Maybe Bennington could handle it. Maybe there would be no foul-ups, no casualties.

For over three minutes every man studied the island silently. Only the rumble of the diesels and the boil and surge of water could be heard as the small warship shouldered its way through the calm sea, sluicing the slashed surface aside with her prow and letting the streaming water cream along her flanks and then tumble away astern in a long smooth wake.

Leaning on the gyro-repeater, Carpelli glanced around. It was a magnificent summer's day, a light and fickle breeze scratching dark patches on the calm surface. There was just enough swell running to heave the surface like heavy breathing, changing the hues of the dark blue water. The phosphorescence in their wake had vanished with the morning sun and the stars, too, had been snuffed out by the growing light. Above and behind the island the sky was clear. Swarms of gulls were shrieking, fussing, and gliding on wide-stretched wings, like twinkling flurries of snowflakes swirling in the sunlight.

The empty sky extended to the south. However, in the east, tattered streamers of clouds reflected the sun in bloody carmine and turned the sea below into dull brass. To the north, a thunderhead—so typical of these latitudes—poked its head over the horizon like the finger of a gargantuan hand. The top was nearly flat, in the shape of a fast-growing mushroom, burning with the richer, mellower colors of sunrise—silver and gold touched with fleshy pink tongues and the tinge of wild roses. Its distant thunder growled like an angry lion and it was lit by its own spectacular internal lightning. It was a beautiful day for killing.

Squinting through the repeater's sight, Carpelli waited until the ship moved to the desired bearing. "Mark!" he shouted. "Derrick bears three-zero-zero."

"Very well," Bennington said. Into the voice tube: "Come right to three-zero-zero." To the talker: "Murphy! Radar-range?"

The talker spoke into the mouthpiece, listened for a reply, and said to the ensign, "Range two-thousand-five-hundred, Mr. Bennington."

"Very well. Let me know when the range is one-thousand."

Five minutes passed with the speed of thick oil dripping. The storm swirled closer, outriders of line squalls clearly visible moving ahead of it like skirmishers before an advancing army. Bellies close to the sea, rain slanted beneath the squalls in solid sheets like pearl dust. There was turmoil in those unruly clouds, and Michael knew the surface would soon heave with heavy swells and chop. This would make an unstable gun platform even more unstable.

The sun climbed quickly, haloed by an unearthly fine mist like a medieval painting. Its strengthening rays fumed and glowed orange, green and gold where they sparkled on the ocean, brushing the twisting clouds of the squalls with blood. But no one noticed the magical show. Instead every man stood rigidly in a silence as heavy and lucid as crystal. It seemed they had been struck deaf, shorn of all their other senses and left only with their vision, which was concentrated on the island.

Michael pressed his binoculars to his eyes so tightly it hurt. The island loomed now like a lion crouched for its leap. It was very clear, stagy, almost two-dimensional, like a meticulously painted Hollywood mat. It would be an excellent day for gunnery. He felt ominous stirrings, dread a cold, heavy lump under his ribs. He sighed out some of his tension. Finally, Murphy shouted, "Range, one-thousand, sir."

"Very well. Come right to zero-two-zero. All ahead slow. Port battery stand by." Heeling, the ship began its turn and the pulse of the engines slowed. The ensign spoke to Jay Barton and Glenn Winters: "Lookouts, we want the path—two machine guns—look for cleared trees, a fire path. Could be artillery. You remember the briefing."

"Aye, aye sir," chorused the young lookouts as they stared through their binoculars.

"I have the path, sir," Warner said, excitement edging his voice. "Bearing zero-five-zero, it climbs left to right up the cliff to the derrick and houses."

"Ah—ah, very well," Bennington said. For the first time Carpelli found what he had expected: fear, and—worse—signs of indecisiveness. Bennington continued, "All guns, base of the derrick, look for a machine gun." Murphy repeated the order.

Captain Christopher Welly spoke. "Just below the crest. It should be there. And look for the triangular cave." He stared through his glasses. "We're too far out. What are you afraid of?"

Every man turned, stared at the marine who leaned against the windscreen glaring at the ensign with eyes dimmed and reddened by fatigue. But Carpelli was not surprised. He had seen officers argue before even in the heat of combat, seen ill-advised or reckless decisions kill men. An icy emptiness began to spread with freezing fingers. Anxiously, he watched the two officers.

Bennington dropped his glasses and stiffened like a man jolted by electricity. He mumbled through tight lips, "At one thousand yards we're out of range of small arms and can score with all our armament, Captain."

"I know, but you can't see a fuckin' thing."

"This isn't the infantry, Captain."

"But we're fighting the same fuckin' war. Those guns will knock my boys off the path like clay pigeons. Do the marines always have to do your dying, Ensign?"

Glaring, Bennington fingered the voice tube, turned to the marine. "I'm acting captain of this vessel and I'll . . ."

"Oh, fuck it," the marine spat. "You goddamned USO Commandos don't know how to fight and don't want to fight."

Every man stared with incredulity. Even Michael was shocked by the words. Staring at the emaciated death's-head, the quartermaster knew the young marine had seen too many men die. Every man had his breaking point. Welly had found his. Anxiety turned to fear as Carpelli moved his eyes to Bennington. He knew the ensign was in a no-win situation. He would either tuck his tail and run like a whipped cur or disguise his cowardice by charging like an animal crazed by the sun. The young Latin found the animal.

Bennington turned to Carpelli and shouted in an uneven, throaty voice, "Bearing on the derrick!"

"Two-eight-zero, sir."

"Left to two-eight-zero." The ensign straightened and stared over the bow. Then he returned to the voice tube. "Radar. Give me a range every one hundred yards."

Carpelli moved to the log and scribbled an entry:

19 June 1944: 0623. Closing on the NE coast of

Aguijan on course 280, speed 8. Crew at general quarters . . .

"Fuck the log, Quartermaster. Put your binoculars on that beach. You're the great warrior," Bennington growled.

Michael felt rage clot darkly in his throat. He answered gutturally, "Aye, aye, sir." Then he moved to the windscreen where he took a position between Signalman Dennis Warner and the ensign.

"Eight hundred yards," came from the voice tube.

"Very well."

Slowly, the patrol craft closed on the island, silence broken only by the rumble of her diesels and the shouts of the helmsman relaying ranges.

Malcolm Murphy turned to Bennington with a puzzled look. "I've lost the forty. The circuit's dead."

"Shit!"

Carpelli inclined his glasses. The derrick was at least three hundred feet above the base of the cliff. A gun fired from that position would probably send its first bursts high. And the first bursts would be the most dangerous. They could register before the counterfire of the three-inch could take effect. He eyed the teenage lookouts standing on their platforms like young saplings, and Warner, almost as tall, standing on a light platform. Targets! Easy targets. He turned to Bennington, "May I suggest, sir, that Signalman Warner move his watch aft—next to the forty. I can signal him from here with my hands using code."

Bennington moved his eyes to the signalman. "Move your watch aft, Signalman."

"Aye, aye, sir." Quickly, Dennis Warner plunged down the ladder and moved aft.

Carpelli sighed. At least one less man was stationed on the bull's-eye.

"Five hundred yards."

"That's more like it," the marine said.

"We're within range of small arms and knee mortars, Mr. Bennington," Carpelli said.

"I know — I know. Anyone see the fuckin' guns?"

"No, sir," chorused the lookouts.

Carpelli stared, fascinated by the view through his glasses. Slab-sided, with boulders littering a narrow beach of crumbled basalt, the island reared skyward, covered with trees brilliant green in summer foliage. It was Guadalcanal all over again: he saw great mango trees heavy with red and yellow fruit; stands of tall bamboo, pole-like palms; drooping acacias; and red-splashed flame trees interspersed with wild orchids and hibiscus. Vines were everywhere, tying the mass together in a riot of color. And the surf was spectacular. When it rose and crashed against the rocks it spouted geysers of blue water, haloed by white spray flashing rainbows. And washing against the rocks, the young quartermaster could see the red stain of summer seaweed rising and falling like the heaving chest of a dying man. He saw a blaze of color moving from one tree to another. Then more color moving in irregular patterns. Birds. Moving through the forest. Carpelli expected myna birds, cockatoos, and kingfishers. But he saw something smaller, flashing white wings. "Those are butterflies," he muttered to himself. He continued staring, fascination pushing fear aside. He was in the forest.

"Watch for flashes," the marine said, suddenly coming to life.

Suddenly, a dozen splashes leaped from the sea a few yards off the starboard bow. "Six-point-five millimeter," the marine shouted.

Michael heard a gasp. He turned. Bennington seemed to be strangling. His face was as white as bone china, beading with perspiration, glasses dangling chest-high, eyes wide and glassy. *He's tied up,* Carpelli's mind flashed. *It's happened.*

"Jap small arms," Michael shouted in Bennington's

ear. The ensign nodded stiffly without turning. Michael cursed, bruised his knuckles against the windscreen, and gagged on the bitter taste of disgust welling in his throat.

"Three hundred yards."

"Flashes! Flashes!" Barton and Winters screamed in the high-pitched excitement of cheerleaders at a high school football game. "Base of the derrick!"

"See it! See it!" the marine shouted.

Bennington wheezed, turned to Carpelli, and pointed at the voice tube, whispering, "Fire."

The quartermaster grabbed the tube. "All guns commence firing at the base of the derrick as you bear." The ensign nodded.

The marine — face twisted with contempt — eyed Bennington. "What are you going to do, show everyone how brave you are by sailing this boat up the fuckin' cliff?"

But Bennington, glasses dangling, both hands gripping the windscreen with white knuckles, said nothing. He seemed to be hypnotized by the derrick.

More splashes. But Gunner's Mate Schultz's crew was ready, cranking the muzzle of the three-inch up quickly. There was the usual thunderclap and ribbon of yellow flame followed by a taut string of white smoke that ended in a flash at the base of the derrick. Carpelli heard Schultz bellow, "Rapid fire," and the cannon began to boom like a great automatic shotgun. It was joined by the ripping of numbers one and two twenty-millimeter Orlikons, sixty-round magazines emptying quickly as their gunners held them on full trigger. Now scores of tracers smoked toward the island, and Michael was assailed by the familiar smells and sounds of battle: the strong sharp smell of cordite, the crash of the cannon, the raving of the machine guns, the hollow clatter of ejected brass shell casings striking the deck and clanging together, and the excited shouts of gunners.

"Two hundred yards."

"Jesus," Carpelli said. "They can hit us with sling-shots."

Bennington leaned toward Michael. "Course, course — change course."

The quartermaster put his mouth to the voice tube. "Left full rudder." He glanced at the island and then at the three-inch. Knew he must keep the cannon bearing on the target and unmask the forty-millimeter gun. "Steady up on two-zero-zero. All ahead full!" he shouted into the tube.

A shout from Barton. "Flashes — low — near the beach and just below the path — the triangular cave."

"Good! Good!" the marine shouted, elated. "Kill those motherfuckers!"

"Steady on two-zero-zero, all ahead full."

With relief Carpelli saw Bennignton lean to Murphy and rasp, "Three-inch engage the gun at the crest, twenties strafe the path." He turned to the quartermaster. "Forty engage the gun in the triangular cave."

"Aye, aye, sir." Moving to the back of the bridge and standing at the head of the ladder, Carpelli waved his hands. Instantly, Dennis Warner, who was standing next to the Bofors supporting himself on the gun tub, flashed a "K" with his fingers. Then, in seconds, Carpelli had flashed the message. With the pounding of the Bofors in his ears, he returned to the windscreen. "Sent and receipted for, sir."

"Very well."

Now there were splashes all around the ship, some in rows while others fell in random patterns like handfuls of thrown pebbles.

Even without glasses Carpelli could see yellow lights winking at him from the base of the derrick while others flashed near the beach. The triangular shape of the cave's mouth was clear. He felt the ship steady on the new course, the rhythm of the straining diesels sending their vibrations through every frame and plank, her fourteen-knot speed leaving a boiling white wake. His ears rang with the booming of the cannon, the pounding of the Bofors, and the raving of the machine guns. Tracers like hordes of smoking locusts stormed. But they were too close; they had thrown away the advantage of their heavier calibers.

Michael heard a hissing overhead, as if a bag full of snakes had been suspended from the yardarm. Severed, a pair of halyards flailed in the wind, snapping against the mast like whips in the hands of madmen. The starboard recognition lights exploded, raining green, red, and yellow glass. A great insect fluted and then a hammer struck his helmet, knocking it from his head as if he were in the grip of a crazed wrestler. Legs rubber, he staggered backward, crashed into the repeater, and slid slowly to the deck. The helmet rolled across the deck and thumped against the base of Barton's lookout platform. Horrified faces turned toward him. He heard Barton screaming, "Carpelli! Carpelli!"

He looked at the young lookout and mumbled, "Okay — okay." But his head was a ganglion of bruised, raw, screeching nerves sending messages of pain to muscles that jerked and trembled. He felt something sticky on his temple, creeping down his cheek. He reached up. Blood. Then the hammers struck wood, and splinters rained.

Barton stopped screaming and began to blubber strange animal-like sounds. Michael watched, fascinated, as the boy's life jacket disintegrated — kapok, shards of ribs, and blood swiftly turning his chest to a mire of gore. Then, with blood gouting from his mouth, the lookout pitched backward, clawing at the sky, finally draping over the edge of the windscreen like a bloody mattress being aired.

More screams. Knocked from his platform, Winters crashed into the binnacle, helmet clattering across the deck. The magnetic compass exploded, raining alcohol and shards of glass. Murphy spun from the windscreen, blood gushing from his stomach and sheeting across his legs. Death came so fast the only sound he made was the expulsion of his last breath. But he did not fall. Instead, an arm caught between the voice tube and the windscreen suspending him grotesquely like a broken mannequin.

Then a dirty green figure catapulted over Carpelli and fell on top of Winters, whose legs and arms shook and twitched like an epileptic suffering a seizure.

Gripping the repeater, Carpelli pulled himself erect, ears singing like a million mosquitoes. Supporting himself on the windscreen, he faced Bennington, who stood unhurt, hand to mouth, sweating, breathing hard, eyes wide and unfocused. Incongruously, Carpelli thought he heard cheers. But he was beyond fear, horror, even comprehension. He was wood like the mast, bending to the wind and sea, snapping back, but dead and unfeeling. He peered down on the forecastle. Indeed, led by Chief Schultz, the three-inch gun crew was cheering, pointing. There was smoke and flame at the base of the derrick. Then, suddenly, most of the hissing snakes and fluting insects were gone. But there were still a few splashes, and an occasional bee buzzed.

Michael looked again at Bennington, expecting orders. He appeared unhurt but in shock, frozen and mute like a granite monument. Carpelli knew they had to come about, to move out of range. He shook his head and groaned with pain. However, the trembling had vanished and his mind was clear.

He made a decision that was contrary to pages of regulations; it could lead to a court-martial. Ignoring the horror that had been Murphy, he moved to the voice tube. "Left full rudder," he shouted. "Steady up on one-two-zero. All ahead flank."

The ship swung into its turn and the great diesels roared to full power. "Pass the word for Mr. Manning and Pharmacist's Mate Kohler to report to the bridge on the double."

Bennington remained silent.

Carpelli looked at Murphy. Eyes wide, jaw slack, the cadaver stared back. Michael tasted something sour. He turned and spat a mouthful of bile.

The young quartermaster felt the ship come erect. "Steady on one-two-zero," came from the voice tube. Now the three-inch was silent but the forty and numbers three and four twenties continued firing over the stern. Suddenly, more cheers. Flame and smoke were pouring from the triangular cave. The Japs had been ready for a long siege. Too much ammunition had been stored at both emplacements.

He looked down. A charnel house. Still twitching, the marine lay facedown atop the dead lookout. There was blood everywhere: splattered on the windscreen, on the bearing repeater and smashed binnacle, blood in pools, moving with the roll of the ship. Blood filling the scuppers, streaking the sides of the bridge, dripping on the main deck and coagulating in the hot tropical sun. The young Latin moaned, "No! No!" He rubbed his forehead. Then something clawed his ankle. It was Captain Welly. He was alive. He was wheezing.

There was the sound of frantic footsteps. First Ensign Manning and then Pharmacist's Mate Kohler heaved themselves onto the bridge. Manning, in the lead, recoiled from the slaughterhouse like a man stabbed by a red-hot poker. Kohler pushed him aside and slipped in the blood as he dropped to his knees next to Welly, whom he already sensed as the only man left alive. He rolled him over. Welly's mouth, jaw and throat blended into a single mass of blood, shattered bone, and teeth. Although covered with blood, the marine bled little, the gelatinous wound pulsing and bubbling with his strained breathing.

Suddenly, Bennington came to life. "Manning. Take the con." He glanced at the marine. "Set a course for the *Relief.* I'll send them our ETA on the SCR."

"What about General Quarters?" Manning said

hoarsely as he moved to the voice tube, stepping around the bodies, slipping.

"Cease fire and secure. Set the sea watch."

"Aye, aye, Bob," John Manning said with strength that surprised Carpelli. He leaned over the voice tube and began to shout orders.

Bryan Kohler looked up at Carpelli. "Michael. I'll need your help." There was desperation in the voice.

"Okay! Okay!" the quartermaster said, dropping to his knees.

"He's strangling on his own blood. It's coagulating in his trachea."

The marine captain made a wheezing sound like a Force-10 wind through the rigging, eyes wide open and on Carpelli—pleading, frightened, and not understanding, like a dog crushed by a car's wheel.

Muttering, "Morphine," Kohler jammed a Syrette into Welly's arm. Then, frantically, the pharmacist's mate rummaged through his bag. Curses. He hit his breast pocket. Cursed again. Suddenly, he turned to Carpelli. "A pen. Your Parker."

Michael groped with his life jacket, found his breast pocket, and found the Parker.

"Just the cap. Hack off the end. I need a tube."

Michael nodded. He pulled his knife, an eight-inch, razor-sharp government issue. Placing the cap on the bearing repeater's platform, he hacked the end off neatly.

After opening a small bottle and pouring alcohol over the wounded man's neck, Kohler turned to Michael. "Give me your knife. It's sharper than mine." Then returning to the marine, he shouted over his shoulder, "Hold him. He's conscious."

Welly was blowing bloody bubbles from his throat and from a red hole that had been his mouth. Carpelli squatted across the wounded man's legs, holding each arm in his big hands. Kohler placed the point of the knife against the strangling man's windpipe and began

89

to cut gently but firmly. Carpelli felt Welly stiffen and attempt to thrash. He pushed down, gripping harder. Blood trickled, but Bryan moved the blade down, reversed it, and came up, cutting the windpipe neatly. Then he placed his thumbs on Welly's throat, popping the windpipe open. "Push the cap halfway in," he said calmly. Gently, Carpelli pushed the tube into the wound. Slowly, Kohler removed his thumbs and reached into his bag. In a moment, he had taped the tube in place. Immediately, there was a whistling sound, and Welly relaxed, eyes narrowed and dulled by the morphine, but still fixed on Carpelli.

"You'll be all right, Mate," Carpelli said, leaning close. "You're okay, understand? You're okay, Mate."

Two drops escaped the wounded man's eyes, ran across his cheeks, leaving trails of partially dissolved blood. If Captain Christopher Welly had had a jaw, he would have smiled.

"Jesus, those bullets must've had eyes—went around you, Michael," Kohler said softly without taking his eyes from the wounded man.

"The one with my name on it wasn't there, Bryan," Carpelli said hesitantly, his mind suddenly fogging with pain.

"Like your subchaser."

"Yes—yes, like the subchaser," the quartermaster said, fingering the numbing pain at the base of his skull gingerly. There was a sudden dizziness. Sagging against the windscreen, he closed his eyes, blotting out the horror of the dead boys and Welly's face, but strangely the subchaser came back, spinning through his mind with a kaleidoscope of more dead faces. And his leave—the survivor's leave, Terminal Island and Bryan Kohler. A long time ago. Just after New Year's, 1944.

Within forty-eight hours after the Submarine Chaser

3028 had been sunk off New Britain's Cape Gloucester on 30 December, 1943, Quartermaster Second Class Michael Carpelli's orders had been cut, transferring him to the receiving barracks on Terminal Island in Los Angeles Harbor. Similar to scores of installations scattered worldwide, the base was a nondescript collection of Quonset huts and concrete and wooden barracks interspersed with mess halls, theaters, sick bays, and classrooms. Here Michael encountered naval personnel of all ranks and ratings, some wide-eyes boots wearing round white hats and new dungarees, others old salts in washed-out dungarees and savagely creased blue hats. All awaited assignment, all were apprehensive, all feared the amphibious force.

Two days after arriving and standing at ease in ranks with hundreds of sailors in dress blues, Michael had waited impatiently and uncomfortably in his new uniform for his first medal, the Purple Heart. At the far end of the asphalt grinder, the young quartermaster saw wooden stands, where his tearful mother and Kristie sat in a crowd of civilians, while at the other end of the parade ground a band struck up "Anchors Aweigh."

"What are you up for?" a deep voice rasped in his ear, suddenly.

Turning his head slightly, Michael had caught his first glimpse of Bryan Kohler—a startling visage, hard yet friendly. His sharp, bright eyes glinted in the sunlight reflected from the grinder like a drawn blade, giving the big man the aspect of an artist or a killer or both.

"Purple Heart," Michael answered. "Got blown off a SC and broke my nose. Got a few bumps."

"Shit! Some mortarman used my back for a dart board." The big man moved his eyes toward the band, where an approaching group of officers was visible. "This'll be a MGM supercolossal production."

"What do you mean?"

Kohler inclined his head slightly. "Robert Montgomery — he's a commander — he's going to decorate us."

"No shit? The actor?" Michael moved his eyes down the ranks, found the approaching officers led by the dark-haired actor dressed in a smartly tailored uniform.

"No shit, Quartermaster. His girlfriends are in the stands."

"Girlfriends!"

"Yeah. According to scuttlebutt, he got decked by dengue in the Solomons. He's ship's company now and spends his time banging starlets on crash boats.

"Crash boats? Where?"

"Right here, at the Small Craft Training Center. He takes them for rides. The girls love the boats. They're built by yacht companies and even have chintz curtains."

"Well I'll be damned." Michael was not to be outdone by the stranger. "A girl I know screwed Errol Flynn on his yacht."

"The *Sirocco,* at Santa Monica?"

Michael nodded. "Right. I went to high school with her. She was seventeen."

"A little old for that prick. He likes 'em in pigtails," the pharmacist's mate snorted.

The metallic blare of, "Attention," echoing from the public address system halted the conversation.

"You were in God's arms — God's arms, my son," Maria sobbed, clutching Michael and kissing her son after the ceremony while Kristie hovered nearby, dabbing her cheeks.

"They can't hurt me, Mom."

"You got the Purple Heart," she said, fingering the decoration pinned to the young sailor's breast. "They didn't tell me you were wounded."

"Knocked silly, Mother. Broke my nose."

"Why the Purple Heart?"

"Because I'm an enlisted man and they didn't want to give me the Navy Cross."

"I don't care, *Bambino Mio*. You're all right — all right. That's all that counts." She pushed away and studied Michael at arm's length. "When are you coming home?"

"I'll be home tonight on liberty after chow. I begin my thirty-day survivor's leave tonight at eighteen-hundred — I mean six PM."

"Hey, mate. I want you to meet my mother and sister," a familiar sonorous voice boomed from the milling crowd.

Turning, Michael found the big pharmacist mate approaching. He was followed by a slender, fortyish woman with smartly coiffed auburn hair and widely spaced green eyes, rheumy with recently shed tears. She was clutching the hand of a young girl not more than eleven with waist-length red pigtails, excited blue eyes, and a face showered with freckles. "I'm Bryan Kohler," the big man continued. "This is my mother and my sister, Linda."

After introducing his mother and Kristie, Michael learned that Bryan was on a survivor's leave and had been assigned to his barracks. Staring at the tall man with the big laugh, Michael knew the two would become close friends. And that evening, after chow, the pair poured the first cement of their friendship — a bond that grew and hardened quickly as can only the miter between two lonely, frightened boys at war. In fact, before making liberty, the two survivors agreed to spend as much of their leaves together as possible.

Walking to Kristie's after breaking from his mother's smothering embrace, Michael was troubled. Over and over his mother had spoken of God. "Bad luck for the other boys. God was watching you. God protected you."

"Yes, Mom. Yes, Mom." But Michael was skeptical,

93

and he wondered about God. He had seen little evidence of Him in the South Pacific. Did He turn his back on the rest of the crew? Why? The Japs had many gods; vastly outnumbering the one Christian God. And the Germans had a slogan: *"Gott ist mit uns."* Maybe Napolean was right: "God is on the side with the best artillery." If there was a merciful God, why hadn't He looked after Michael's shipmates? As far as he knew, most of the boys had been believers. Why had they been abandoned? Some of the dead were certainly more worthy than he. The radioman, Don Ringstaff, had been a saint—a true believer, who wore his cross with his dog tags, said his beads, and always spoke grace before chow. Nevertheless, he had been dismembered by the blast, and his entrails were mingled with those of the atheist, Machinist's Mate Leo Van Dyke.

Michael threw his head back, filled his lungs with the cold winter air, and stared at the infinite universe filled with stars that whorled and eddied icily, filling the young man with awe and shrinking him with its immensity and loneliness. Maybe there was a God. He just moved in mysterious ways; very mysterious.

He reached the familiar frame house and turned up the walk.

Short and stocky, Kristie's father, Desmond Wells, was heavy in the stomach, bald with dark bee-bee eyes and large round ears that stood out from his polished scalp like a ship's running lights. *Just like Clark Gable,* Michael thought as he relaxed on the sofa next to a misty-eyed Kristie and sipped his bourbon and soda.

"God was with you on that subchaser," the engineer insisted.

Silently, Michael toyed with his drink, swirling the liquid until the cubes made a bell of the glass. "Ah, yes, Mr. Wells," he said simply. "I was lucky."

"How long will you be here?" Kristie asked, clutching the sailor's hand.

Michael sighed. "I have a thirty-day survivor's leave starting tonight and then I report to the General Detail at Terminal Island for reassignment." And then he explained that he was a small craft sailor and would probably be reassigned to another small vessel.

"And then you'll go back to the war," Kristie said, catching her breath.

Before Michael could answer, Brenda Wells, middle-aged, matronly with graying brown hair, entered the room carrying a tray of cookies and cakes. "Chow down," she said with forced levity. But the somber mood in the room was smothering. Self-consciously, she placed the tray on an oak coffee table in front of Michael and seated herself opposite the young quartermaster.

Reaching for a cookie, Michael said, "Lord, they look good, Mrs. Wells." Savoring his cookie, Michael wondered about these people who he had known for over two years. They were suddenly strangers—people from another galaxy. Discreetly, they had not asked him about the death of the subchaser, and he had volunteered nothing. They only knew what the navy had told his mother. And he felt no desire to discuss the horror, the anger, or the hatred. There was too much to tell and they knew nothing of his world. Only the boys who had been there knew; only they could talk of that world and listen with understanding free of pity. With them he could shoot the breeze and listen to tales of ships and crews and scuttlebutt that brought laughter, hiding sorrow for lost comrades. It was a compulsion and a catharsis. But these people, even his mother, could never understand.

Shifting uneasily, Desmond turned to his wife, "Ah, Brenda, I have a long day tomorrow. Maybe we'd better retire." In a moment, the two older Wellses were gone.

Anxiously, Kristie moved close to Michael and pulled him on top of her as she sank back into the cushions. Pressing down on the girl, Michael felt her firm,

95

swollen breasts stabbing at his chest, pelvis pushing.

The abstinence of over a year at sea, the loneliness and longing, fanned a sudden, consuming heat that sent fire through his veins to his groin, hardening his manhood to steel. Clamping his mouth over hers, he felt her tongue darting, her hands clawing at his neck and his back. She moaned deep in her throat.

Roughly, he unbuttoned her blouse, pulled away her brassiere, and moved a hand over a breast, fingering a nipple until the girl winced. Then, quickly, came a repetition of the same maddening script they both knew so well: his hands ranging her body everywhere—waist, hips, hot flesh of her legs, finally the mound of her womanhood swelling under her panties. But this time he went further than he had ever gone before. For the first time, he pulled the panties down and found her warm depths, penetrating and caressing her deeply until she groaned and muttered guttural, incoherent sounds, until she shuddered spasmodically like a girl who had touched a live wire, sighed, sagged, and then pulled him between her legs.

"Desmond! Are you coming to bed?" resounded from the back of the house.

"In a moment, dear."

The lovers pulled apart, sat up. Hastily, the girl pulled on her panties, straightened her skirt, palmed her hair back.

Trying to control the trip-hammer pounding his ribs, Michael cursed through his laboring breath, "Kristie, this is crazy."

"Let's get married, Michael."

Sighing unevenly, the young man smothered the girl's hand with his. The hammering subsided. "Things are too uncertain and you know it. I couldn't do that to you, just for a—ah . . ."

"A piece of ass?"

"Kristie!" Michael exclaimed, shocked. "You shouldn't."

96

"Well, isn't that what the boys say?"

"The boys say a lot of things."

"Why shouldn't we?"

"You're in your first year at City College. They have a great Drama Department. Why, when I went there, Alexis Smith, Esther Williams, and Donna Mullenger were all enrolled."

"You mean Donna Reed."

"Well, yes, Donna Reed, she changed her name." He rubbed the hard bone behind his ear. "They're all successful—will be great stars, someday you . . ."

She interrupted, startling him again with her encyclopedia knowledge of Hollywood. With her eyes staring over his shoulder at something far away, she said with a voice as monotonous as a metronome, "Donna Reed broke in with *The Getaway* in '41, Esther Williams in *Andy Hardy's Double Life* in '42, Alexis Smith in *The Lady with Red Hair* in '41. Why Donna Reed and Esther Williams had contracts with MGM by the time . . ."

"I know. I know," he said impatiently. "I was trying to tell you, you must stick with your studies—with school. They did. You have talent and you're in the right place."

"But I want you, too. I want you more than anything. Why can't I have both? We could get married and I could go to school while you're away."

"Please, Kristie, I can't—we can't."

Scowling, the girl sank back. "There's something terribly wrong with this world, Michael."

"There's a lot wrong with this world, Kristie."

"We want each other and there are so many barriers—so many things that say 'you can't.' "

Taking her hand, the young man sank back. He breathed slowly and deeply like a recovering marathon runner. "Yes. You're right. 'Thou shalt not.' Our lives are full of 'Thou shalt nots.' But this war will be over someday and then . . ."

"Yes, Michael. I try to remember that. I tell myself

that at night when I can't sleep—when I hold your picture, your letters, when I cry . . ." Choking back a sob, the girl turned away.

"Please, Kristie," he murmured, kissing her neck. "I'd better go."

"I love you, Michael." She turned her tear-streaked face to his. "When this war's over, we'll marry."

"Yes."

"When will it be over?"

"When we kill every last one of them."

"All?" Her eyes widened. "Men, women, children?"

"Yes." The tone was matter-of-fact. "That's the only way."

"How horrible. You can't mean that. What have you become?"

"What my country has made me."

She sighed, a hopeless little sound like an animal defeated by a steel trap. "We know it must be horrible. We know you were sunk, but we promised each other not to ask you."

"Thanks. I couldn't tell you about it, anyway."

"Why? Is it that bad?"

He knuckled his forehead. "I think it's because it's a different universe and you've never been there." He punched a palm. "There's too much to be told so there's nothing to tell." He pulled away. "That doesn't make sense, does it, Kristie?"

"You always make sense, Michael."

"I'd better leave." The quartermaster rose slowly.

The girl came to her feet, circled the boy's neck, and found his lips. "I love you, Michael."

"I love you, Kristie. I love you."

When he pulled away, it was like tearing new flesh from an old wound, and the empty ache wrenched his guts like a hot dagger. But he managed to wheel and step through the door into the cold night air.

Not even an Arctic gale could have cooled the young sailor's ardor. Maddened by the beast unleashed by Kristie and upset by his inability to explain the drives forced on him by the war, the young man turned toward home.

He pounded his head, knowing something had to remain beautiful, pure and inviolate. The beauty of the Solomons, the beaches and lagoons, hid sunken ships, mines, rotting corpses, rusting tanks, and guns. Everywhere, corruption and death. Kristie was life, was beauty — pure, undefilable, and immutable like the cosmos. She must remain that way, a pristine thing in a putrescent world.

Throwing his head back, he stared into space. But ironically, his mariner's eye found the skies of home suddenly strange. Lipping the horizon, the moon was edging toward a fleeing caravan of clouds, its weak light failing to pale the splendor of the stars. Polaris, which marked the axis of the earth and provided latitude by a simple reading of its altitude, was visible. But the Southern Cross was gone. The Big and Little Dippers, Pegasus, and Andromeda blazed across the black heavens; his old friend Sagittarius and Capricorn could not be seen.

He shook his head, knowing he did not belong here. Even the stars seemed to deny him. He stopped, cursing, and turned away from home and toward Firestone Boulevard, where homeward-bound swing-shift traffic streamed at midnight.

His mother was gone, working the graveyard shift at Goodyear and earning enough money to rent a house and buy meat. With the thought of being alone intolerable, the young sailor strode briskly toward the busy street. Surely there must be a bar nearby. He would have a drink. Find other servicemen, shoot the shit. Instant friendships could be made with other men in uniform.

Stopping at the intersection of Firestone Boulevard

99

and Alameda Street, he leaned against a lamppost and extended a thumb — a gesture that would propel him into one of the most violently erotic experiences of his life, a source of flaming memories that would torture him in lonely bunks for years to come.

The shiny black 1938 Pontiac two-door sedan pulled to the curb in a single quick motion. Smiling, the driver, a young woman of perhaps thirty, gestured. Accepting the invitation, Michael opened the door and slid across the seat.

"What's your port?" the driver asked, smiling and obviously pleased with her quip while eyeing the red traffic light.

"Any port in this storm, ma'am."

She laughed, a shrill nervous sound, like a violin bowed by a beginner. "The first bar?"

"Why not?" Michael answered, feeling the car lurch as the light turned green and the clutch was released too quickly.

Turning his head slowly, the young man eyed the driver. She was a stunner. Reminiscent of Veronica Lake, her hair was long and brushed into a fine cascade that valanced her forehead and flowed to her shoulders, shimmering and shaking with the motion of the car. Brown eyes glinted darkly like chips of black glass, and her nose was small and upturned. But the mouth was a little too thin, slashed by a chisel in a hard, sharp chin that told one he was in the presence of a woman who had known life and had been singed by it.

As the woman moved the car through the gears, her dress hiked up to midthigh, revealing Betty Grable legs. Catching his breath, Michael felt an aching hunger beginning to gnaw deep within.

"Why don't you come to my place — have a drink with me? I just got off work."

Michael felt like a man who had discovered oil in his

100

backyard. "Your husband?"

Empty of humor, her laugh was bitter, "Gone."

"Service?"

"Ha! That bum! No, he ran off with his cousin."

"Oh, too bad. Not really normal, ma'am — is it?"

"Ha! I should say so. His cousin's a guy."

Located in southwest Los Angeles and typical of thousands of homes built during the building boom of the early 1920s, the woman's house was similar to Kristie's, a large three bedroom frame building with a natural rock fireplace and rock pillars supporting its wide porch. The expected dark veneers dominated the decor of the spacious, tastefully furnished living room and adjoining dining room, which boasted a mahogany table, chairs and matching buffet. Expensive rugs were scattered casually on a glistening hardwood floor like lazy pets drowsing on a warm summer's evening.

Sinking slowly, the young sailor seated himself in the center of a plump three-cushion sofa faced by a walnut coffee table. Facing her young guest over the table, the woman stood, arms akimbo, each hand resting on a slender hip. "What's your name, sailor?"

"Michael Carpelli."

"Mine's Alma — Alma Sisk." And then with quiet humor that awakened incipient wrinkles sleeping at the corners of her eyes: "The bar's open. What's your poison?"

"Bourbon and soda, please."

"In a jiffy." Walking sinuously through the dining room, she pushed her way through swinging doors into the kitchen. Michael stifled a gasp while eyeing the wonderfully easy flow of the woman's buttocks under her tight skirt, and he groaned inwardly when the spectacle was cruelly obscured by the swinging doors.

With the woman gone, Michael's mind returned to Kristie. Kristie had numbed his senses with desire and now Alma, who reeked with worldly sensuality, aroused him further. The young Latin was confused. He wanted this woman despite his love for Kristie. Was he searching for an outlet, a safety valve? That was it. Deny himself Kristie and, perhaps, find someone else to free the beast that lurked just below the surface.

And it had been so long. Over a year. Endless nights in the forward hold of the subchaser, tossing and turning on the hard mattress, staring in the dim red light of battle lamps at rivulets of seawater seeping through the thin planking, staining the sides in long runs to the bilges. Interminable nights on the bridge, seeing every woman he had ever had or wanted to have smiling and gesturing from the forecastle, a cloud, the horizon, spectral nymphs who flitted from his memories to taunt and torture.

The pinups. He had cursed Betty Grable, Rita Hayworth, Marie Wilson and all of the others who promoted their careers by posing in the near-nude for *Time, Life,* and *Look* — poses that provoked and at the same time denied, frustrating hundreds of thousands of miserable boys with erotica they could never know.

And the dreams — wild, erotic dreams that led to embarrassing consequences and ribald jokes amongst the crew. The cruel sport of looping cloth around the erections of sleeping sailors and tugging gently until the squirming victim finally awoke to face laughing, jeering tormentors. He had been both oppressor and victim.

He had a right to this woman — if she would have him. Certainly, the release of the pent-up storm would serve Kristie. That was it. *He owed it to Kristie,* he managed to convince himself, having no trouble with the strange reasoning.

Suddenly, the doors flew open and Alma entered the room, wiping Kristie, the subchaser and lingering doubts from the sailor's mind. After handing Michael his highball, the woman seated herself next to the quartermaster apparently unaware of a dress that was hitched above her knees and a hand that rested palm to palm with the sailor's. She raised her glass. "Here's to a short war and . . ." Michael felt her fingers entwine his and found her eyes over his glass. She finished her toast, ". . . and to us."

Despite the strength of the drink—it was almost straight bourbon—Michael drank deeply, sighing "Amen." Then he emptied half his glass with a quick toss of his head and tabled his drink next to the woman's.

"You've been to sea, sailor—I mean Michael?"

"No," the young quartermaster lied, deftly avoiding the subchaser, explanations, and the inevitable sympathy that came with being a survivor.

"But you're a quartermaster second class, she said, nodding at the rating badge on his right arm. "Even I know that's a deck rating—earned at sea."

Michael pondered for a moment and spoke hesitantly as he found his story. "Not necessarily. I'm ship's company at Terminal Island. I teach signaling and navigation to ninety-day wonders and quartermaster strikers." Michael took another drink and felt a familiar warmth begin to glow. "Occasional training cruises, that's all."

"Navigation. That must be difficult," she said, pulling her legs up on the sofa and leaning against the sailor.

Catching his breath, Michael drained his glass, and the heat spread on glowing fingers through his viscera. He was suddenly very articulate. "Not necessarily."

"But, a lot of math?"

"I had math through differential equations—even spherical trig before the war."

"Jesus." She stood and walked quickly to the kitchen, returning with full glasses. Dropping to the sofa and pulling up her legs, she crowded the young man, breast against his arm. "Tell me about navigation."

103

"You're kidding."

"No, I'm not."

He took a large gulp. Again, the drink tasted like straight bourbon and the glow began to permeate his whole being. Slowly the war faded in the haze and a sense of lethargic well-being began to course through his veins, bringing an involuntary smile to his lips. "Any idiot can navigate."

"I can't believe that."

"Dummies do it all the time." He took another drink and discovered the table leaning mysteriously when he placed his glass on it. He spilled a little and muttered apologies. She urged him on. He moved on, slurring his words, "All you need is a chronometer, sextant, plotting sheets and charts."

"Yes."

"And the Nautical Almanac, HO Two-Fourteen . . ."

"I'm lost."

"Okay. You've got to get accurate sightings—elevations on the sun, planets or stars."

"How do you know which stars?"

"I know the constellations." He took another drink. "They're my friends." The room began to move.

She nodded in agreement, obviously accepting and believing the ludicrous statement.

"But if you don't know where to find your friends, there are star finders."

"Then?"

"You use your estimated position Greenwich Mean Time and the elevation of the body sighted as arguments and cut in the line."

"Oh, Lord."

Feeling sudden frustration, he began to plead. "It's not hard—all the triangles have been solved—the thinking's been done. That's what HO—I mean Hydrographic Office Method Two-Fourteen is all about." He drained his glass. "You don't have to think." It all made sense to him. Why didn't she understand?

She chuckled. Rising slowly, she grasped both glasses. "Now, if I can navigate my way to the kitchen, I'll refuel us both." Laughing, she walked to the doors with slow, deliberate steps.

Shaking his head, Michael focused his eyes with an effort as he watched the catlike undulations of her perfectly balanced buttocks beneath the tight skirt. He caught his breath, began to sober.

But in a moment, she returned with fresh drinks and the persistent breast resumed its pressure. He felt soft lips against his cheek. "I'm glad you came over," she said, nibbling his ear.

His skin was suddenly hot, and a familiar hammer began to pound his ribs. And the room was turning. He pressed his foot against the floor, but the motion continued.

"What's wrong, Michael?"

"Nothing. Nothing."

Her lips were close. He slipped an arm around her. Covered her mouth with his. She blended into him, her tongue a firebrand, circling his lips, and then she nibbled at the corners of his mouth. Gasping, he covered her mouth with his and the kisses became hot and liquid, leaving them both breathing hard. She pressed her hands to the back of his head, pushed her breast against him, thrust her tongue deep into his mouth until she found his—toying, attacking, running the tip of it over his teeth and gums.

"My God," he managed, stretching her full length on the sofa and pressing down on her, mouth to mouth. There was that terrible heat in his groin and his manhood became steel. He pressed against her. She pushed back, hips moving elliptically.

Slowly, his numb fingers traversed her blouse, leaving a trail of loosened buttons. In a moment, the garment was on the floor, a discarded rag. He fumbled with the hook on her brassiere. Impatiently, she sat up and shrugged out of it, freeing her full, round breasts.

105

Then she pulled the sailor back down on top of her.

His lips found the hard pulse in her neck and his hands moved down over her supple body. He marveled at the exquisite contours of her sleek back, the firmness of her buttocks. Her hands moved over him, too, finding the hard muscles of his arms and back, caressing, exploring.

He moved his lips downward to the slope of her breasts, moved up full unswept mounds with large, hard areolas. He kissed, licked, and then nibbled a swollen nipple. She moaned and squirmed. He moved a hand down, found the zipper of her skirt. She raised her lips. Quickly, the skirt and then silk panties joined the blouse and brassiere on the floor.

Michael was breathing short gasps. A frantic urgency drove his head down to her waist and lower where his tongue left fiery trails on the firm flesh. The woman writhed and moaned like a child being whipped.

His hand clawed downward, seeking the treasure so long denied. But, somehow, despite the heat and desperate desire, he had to know every inch of her, find and caress every nuance of every mystery, because she was not one woman, but all women. Every desire. All frustrations unleashed.

While his hungry mouth ate at the firm flesh of her flat stomach, his hand caressed her knee and then began its upward journey inside her thigh. Michael marveled at the heat of the flesh. Slowly, the fingers crept upward, searching, fondling, until finally they arrived at the bristling hair.

He sank a finger into her hot, liquid depths. She hissed loudly, thrashed and then pushed him away. "Not here, sailor."

"Jesus. We can't stop now."

"My bedroom—my bedroom," she said, rising quickly. "This is too good for a couch." She took his hand and led him to a hallway.

Hurriedly, they entered her bedroom, which was lighted only by the glow of a single bulb that spilled in from the hall, a soft glow that gave the woman's flesh the aspect of ivory. They moved to the bed, embracing, kissing, and running their hands over each other.

"Your clothes, Michael."

With jerky motions, he ripped off his jumper and then his skivvy shirt. He began to claw at the buttons of his trousers, but his fingers were clay and the buttons were tank traps. He cursed.

"Let me." She dropped to her knees and began pulling the buttons loose one by one while chanting in a little girl's voice, "Thirteen buttons, thirteen buttons — thirteen chances to say no."

"Jesus Christ! Hurry! My hard-on's so angry it hurts."

Laughing raucously, she pulled the last obstinate button free and rose slowly, tracing her nipples in tingling trails from the young man's groin to his chest. "Now, Michael. Now!"

Trembling, Michael embraced her, cupping her buttocks, pulling her against him. Her hands were busy, too, a warm palm fondling his erection. The touch was too much for the young sailor. There was the warning of a mighty surge of feeling, then the turgid shaft convulsed, spilling his manhood down the woman's leg and dribbling on the floor.

"Jesus," he said, embarrassed. "I'm sorry."

Sighing, the woman moved to her dresser and then returned with a tissue. "We don't want to waste any." And then awed, "You're still hard."

"Of course. That was only the first quart. I've been storing it for years."

In a moment, the bed received the two thrashing bodies.

Dawn's weak light crept into the heavily draped room

slowly and stealthily like game wary of the hunter. Nose-to-nose, the drowsy lovers lay basking in the euphoric afterglow of their hot, frantic unions, savoring the delicious fulfillment reserved for those who had gorged themselves on passion. Languidly, Alma ran a finger over Michael's arm, through the hair of his chest, down his back to his small waist, then over tight buttocks to his pubis. Then she groped further, finally taking him in her hand. He stirred.

"Lord. What a great reveille," he said, stretching and rolling to his back.

The woman stroked and caressed him. "I can't believe you. You're ready again."

He laughed. Rolled to the woman, pushing her onto her back. "Complaining?"

Her answer was a wet, passionate kiss. Slowly, the sailor covered the woman's body with his own, finally lowering himself between her legs. As she guided him into her hot, dewy center, he braced himself above her with extended arms, looked down on her slitted eyes and half-open mouth, and knew he was locking a vision into his memory forever—a memory that, perhaps, someday would torture him in lonely bunks with a thousand red-hot barbs.

Clawing his back, the woman pulled his head down and he found the pulse in the hollow of her throat with bare teeth. He drove into her with long, leisurely strokes feeling, as if he was swimming inside of her, a daring fish gliding through a warm, dark jellylike sea.

They were spent of their early passions, so the last time endured, driving both lovers to unusual pinnacles and shattering climaxes. Finally she shouted and twisted while the young man convulsed into helplessness, spurting the last of his life into her. They sagged apart, breathing hard.

"I can't believe you—I can't believe you," she managed.

"Why?"

108

"You're inexhaustible."

He laughed. Then in mock seriousness. "You know, it's a good thing women aren't allowed in war zones."

"Why?"

"There wouldn't be any energy left over for killing Japs."

She giggled. Ran a hand over his cheek. "You know something?"

"What?"

"You're what every girl dreams about."

"You mean I'm Clark Gable, Tyrone Power, and Robert Taylor all rolled into one — the answer to every maiden's prayer?" He laughed boisterously.

"Yes, you are. You're inexhaustible — made love all night long. You're the lover every girl fantasizes about — hopes to find but never does."

"I told you I stored it up."

"I thought you didn't have sea duty."

"Ah — I don't, but I told you I go on training cruises."

"This last one must have been a long trip."

"What do you mean?"

"I feel filled up."

"Are you sore?"

"A little, but I love it. And you?"

"Satisfied. Very, very satisfied."

"How long will it last?"

"A couple hours."

She laughed. He dressed quickly and moved to the door followed by the still nude woman. They embraced and kissed — a long lingering kiss.

"You have my number, Michael."

"Yes."

"You'll phone?"

"Yes."

"I'll see you again?"

"Of course."

They kissed again with more intensity. Then he turned and walked out of her life.

Tired and strangely depressed despite the warm afterglow of sexual satiation, Michael turned toward home. But his mother would not return for nearly two hours and his high school friends were gone; every single one was in the service. And Maria would need her sleep after the long graveyard shift.

He had told himself he despised crowded crew's compartments and barracks. Yet, years of enduring rolling, pitching compartments filled with tired, unwashed boys had been his life. Shocked, he realized he felt a void.

Uneasily, he turned toward Alameda Street, which was crowded with the cars of shipyard workers streaming south to Terminal Island. Wearily, the young sailor raised his hand.

The long blue line wound around the mess hall and down the street named after the immolated battleship, *Arizona*. Huddling at the end of the line and shivering in the mist descending from a low, solid marine layer as gray and dark as a smokescreen, Michael cursed Southern California and its myth of perpetual sunshine.

A big hand closed on his shoulder. "You look tired, mate."

Whirling, Michael found Bryan Kohler standing behind him. "Must've been good duty," the pharmacist's mate continued.

"What do you mean?"

"Man, you look as beat as a seagull in a typhoon." A grin spread like a puddle of spilled oil. "Too much poontang?"

"Poontang?"

"In the vernacular, pussy!"

"Yeah, I know. But it's none of your business."

Kohler's eyes glinted maliciously. "Your little actress?"

The voice was hard. "No! And I said it was none of your business." And then curiously, "How did you know about the acting?"

"I heard her talking to your mother. She wanted to meet Robert Montgomery. Said one contact could boost her career. More likely, her little fanny would be boosted right onto a casting couch."

"Shit!" Michael kicked at the asphalt. "She never said anything to me."

"She will." The pharmacist's mate scratched the bristle on his chin. "Why'd you come back?"

"I miss the chow."

Bryan's laugh boomed. "Yeah—right! Tuesday morning. Shit-on-a-shingle day. Of course."

Michael chuckled. "Why'd you come back?"

Bryan's eyes moved up the long blue line to the still distant mess hall. Levity eroded, replaced by grimness. "They're all gone, Michael."

"The guys?"

"Yes. Every last one."

Michael nodded. "I know. I know, Bryan. Like the Pied Piper vacuumed them up."

"He didn't miss one, Michael."

"Yes, Bryan. True. Not one."

Watching the line compress, the boys shuffled forward. "Hey, Michael, I love my mother, but I can't stay home for thirty straight nights." The line lurched a few more steps.

"I know what you mean."

"You, too, Michael."

Michael nodded and nudged Bryan toward the entrance to the mess hall. The slap of steel serving spoons on stainless steel trays could be heard. "Bryan, we agreed to spend our leaves together."

"Roger. But you're in love with Kristie. You'll want to spend your time there."

Michael tapped his chin with a single finger, moved

111

to the entrance where the rumble of hundreds of voices could be heard over the clatter of steel. "No. I don't—I can't."

"Why?"

Michael's face clouded. " I just can't." He turned away.

"I got a plan," Bryan mused.

"What?" Michael looked up.

"Let's tell 'em there's a manpower shortage."

"Shortage?"

"Sure. I've been assigned to the sick bay and you to the signal tower."

"They won't believe that."

"Sure they will. We'll tell them it's port and starboard duty."

"Then we'll be home every other night."

"Right, Michael. You can see your Deanna Durbin and we can cruise, too."

Nodding, Michael stepped into the entrance of the vaulted, barnlike mess hall, where his nostrils were suddenly assailed by the smell of overcooked beef. "You're on." And then, gesturing toward a long stainless steel steam table manned by white-aproned sailors, he said "Our *chef-d'-oeuvre* awaits."

Chuckling, Bryan reached for a tray. *"Oui, oui monsieur.* Gourmet all the way, mate."

They both laughed.

Clouded by an alcoholic fog and dimmed by fatigue induced by the lack of sleep, Michael's memory of the next four weeks was disoriented, flickering fitfully like images flashed by a defective projector. Bars and dance halls and bowling alleys were there: the Elbow Room, Trianon, and Palladium standing out. And a carousel of women, horrified by lengthening casualty lists, spun by eagerly lavishing affection.

To Michael's surprise, Bryan's plan worked surprisingly well. In fact, Maria's schedule demanded a daily sleep schedule, precluding time spent with her son. And although Kristie was bitterly disappointed, Desmond and Brenda seemed relieved—pleased to see less of the young sailor who left their daughter with flushed cheeks and feverish eyes.

New friends were made. The long wooden barracks lined with lockers and double bunks with planks for springs was filled with strangers. Here Michael met Don Lindsay and Algernon Schultz. Lindsay, a young gunner's mate striker from Philadelphia, was assigned to the bunk above Michael's. At that time, the slight young man with the untamed mop of sandy hair and elfin glint in his eyes was fresh out of boot camp and gunnery school. He became attached to the quartermaster and hung close by whenever Michael and Bryan talked of the sea and the great battles in the Solomons. And Don's best friend, Gunner's Mate First Class Algernon Schultz, occupied the bunk next to Michael's.

Sunk off Salerno when his mine sweeper struck a mine cut loose by a sister ship, the burly gunner's mate's youthful face was incongruously etched with hard lines radiating from the corners of his eyes and mouth. Assigned with Lindsay to a new vessel nearing completion at the Sackheim Boat Works, Schultz was a "plank owner" awaiting the completion of "fitting out" and the beginning of sea trials. Schultz was up for chief and it was he who introduced Michael to the new-type patrol craft.

"A PCS," he said, seated on his bunk the first evening in answer to Michael's question. "The PCS Two-Four-Oh-Four."

"What's a PCS?" Kohler asked.

" 'Patrol Chaser Small'—a converted wooden minesweeper."

"Yeah," Don Lindsay piped from his upper bunk. "A new secret weapon. The Japs'll quit as soon as they see it."

113

The boys laughed,

Often, the boys made liberty together, thumbing their way north from the harbor to bars and dance floors scattered over the four-hundred-square-mile sprawl of the city. For Michael and Bryan, the Palladium was a favorite. Here they could listen to Tommy Dorsey, Jimmy Dorsey, Benny Goodman, Charlie Barnett, Frank Sinatra, Jo Stafford, the Pied Pipers, and all of the other musicians and singers they loved. And there were women — partners for dancing and usually much more.

On the first liberty they made together, Schultz and Lindsay introduced Michael and Bryan to South Gate's Elbow Room.

"It's only down the road a piece and there's plenty of shaky puddin'," Schultz offered in his Texas drawl while waving his thumb.

Standing with the gunner's mate, Bryan and Don Lindsay at the corner of Pacific Coast Highway and Alameda Street, Michael nodded skeptically and waved his thumb.

"He means there's plenty of pussy," Lindsay explained. "And there's a drive-in on one side and the Trianon Ballroom on the other."

Schultz nodded. "If you can't find some poontang there, yo' sure 'nuff should be gelded."

Lindsay laughed, turned to the gunner's mate, and began one of the strangest conversations Michael would ever hear. "Hey, cone pone."

"Yeah, Yankee."

"You stick Thelma, yet?"

"No, but I'm fixin' to cut it."

"You should, she's been poked by everyone else in South Gate. In fact, if she had as many of 'em stickin' out of her as she's had stuck in her, she'd look like a porcupine."

Everyone laughed. Eyeing the sparse traffic, Michael leaned back on a telephone pole and stared in amuse-

114

ment.

"You're hot because you can't get in her pants," Schultz retorted hotly.

"Horse shit! I wouldn't bang her with a preacher's dick," the striker said. "By the way, scuttlebutt says she has a pair of boxing gloves branded on her ass. But I hear they're nothing but warts."

"Sure 'nough?" The tone was sarcastic. "Well, they ain't warts and they ain't on her ass."

"Chancres?"

"No, asshole," Schultz spluttered. "They're gloves and they're tattooed on the inside of her thigh."

"Well, you won't see them," Lindsay said matter-of-factly.

"Why not?" Schultz said, obviously walking into a trap.

"Because, even if you get there, they'll be covered with crabs."

Algernon turned to Michael and Bryan. "Don't pay that boy no never mind." He gesticulated at the snickering Lindsay. "He's as full o' shit as a Christmas goose." Chuckling, the quartermaster and pharmacist's mate nodded. "You'll see — you'll see."

A Buick four-door sedan pulled to the curb. Reaching for the door, the gunner's mate shouted, "Yahoo! Elbow Room, here we come!"

"Sho' 'nuff, sho' 'nuff," Don Lindsay mocked.

Laughing, the four sailors entered the car.

"That's Vivian the Virgin," Don Lindsay said, gesturing with his drink and spilling some on the black formica table top. "She's built like a brick shit house."

Michael eyed a tall exotic redhead dressed in a mid-thigh length black taffeta skirt, tight white satin blouse, and black high-heeled shoes as she passed, carrying a tray full of drinks on her shoulder.

The boys had entered the bar, which was jammed

115

with servicemen and women, only minutes before. Don had ushered Michael and Bryan to a corner table, but Algernon, gesturing to the end of the long bar, had shouted, "I've got to find Thelma." Then he vanished into a horde of leaping, twisting dancers, keeping time to the blaring sounds of a four-piece band which played from a raised platform pushed against a far wall.

Seated in a stiff chrome-and-leather chair, Michael eyed Vivian the Virgin's trim rear as she swayed past, vanishing into the crowd. "Nice ass," Schultz appraised expertly, raising his voice over the cacophonous sounds of a trumpet, trombone, piano, and drums mixed with the alcoholic babble of scores of voices.

Nodding in agreement and running his eyes over the long, shiny walnut bar backed by glistening mirrors where glasses were stacked and liquor bottles stood in rows like infantry ready for inspection, Michael was filled with astonishment. Although the room was large and he had spent years in crowded crew's compartments, he wondered how so many people could voluntarily elbow their way into such a limited space.

"The Elbow Room, *Elbow Room*," Schultz said, seemingly reading Michael's mind.

Michael nodded, chuckling and moving his eyes to the postage-stamp-sized dance floor. People were actually jitterbugging. "It looks dangerous," he observed in a loud voice.

"Groovy, man—real hep. And I mean hep," Don said, gesturing at the tall, thin trombonist. "That's Cobra Phillips. Great musician—hip group." He emptied his glass with a quick toss of the head and waved to Vivian.

"Waddaya have?" the sultry redhead said, nudging the table with a shapely hip.

"Another round of doubles and a box to put it in," Don giggled.

"Sorry. This box is gift-wrapped for someone else, sailor."

116

"Don't waste it."

Silently, the girl whirled and walked toward the bar. In a moment, she returned with the drinks, tabled them noisily while eyeing Michael, picked up Don's money, and left.

The quartermaster said to Don Lindsay, "You called her 'Vivian the Virgin'?"

"Yeah. Actually, she's married. Her old man's in the Eighth Air Force."

"In England?"

"Right. And nobody gets in her pants. That's why the handle."

"Shit," Bryan exclaimed sarcastically. "I'll bet her old man's cherry."

Laughing, the boys drank deeply. Don noted, "True as hell—I hear he'll screw anything that'll hold still for thirty seconds. Was the biggest cocksman in South Gate before he got his ass shipped out."

"Figures."

The boys drained their glasses and Michael began to feel a mellow glow spread, and the room was not nearly as crowded and noisy anymore. He was jarred by the striker's shout, "Hey, man—there's Guns and Thelma." Don gestured erratically at the dance floor. "The one built like a Sherman tank."

Squinting hard to focus his eyes, Michael found Schultz whirling across the dance floor, arm around a stocky brunette perhaps ten years older than himself. Broad-shouldered with a bull neck and waist almost as large as her hips, the woman crowded the gunner, mouth clamped to the sailor's neck. Obliviously and with closed eyes, the couple spun around and around, sending other dancers scurrying out of the reach of the woman's flying heels and swirling skirts that revealed plump legs, short hose, and a straining garter belt over bulging flesh.

"I saw her tattoo," Bryan said, quiet humor turning his lip.

117

"Hair!" Michael countered.

"You're both wrong," Don protested. "Flies! Nothing but flies."

The banter was interrupted by the angry shouts of Cobra Phillips. "For Christ's sake, watch where you're going, Thelma."

Without pausing or even opening an eye, Schultz and Thelma continued whirling. But suddenly the woman extended a hand and raised a finger, flashing it under the bandleader's nose in a single flying arc. Quickly, Phillips raised his instrument, extended the slide and spat a stream of saliva through the horn, splattering the side of Thelma's head.

The crowd shouted with glee while Thelma bellowed like a bull goaded by picadors.

"That's why they call Phillips 'Cobra,'" Don laughed. "He can strike anywhere in the room."

But Michael's eyes were on Thelma, who had broken from Schultz and was charging the bandstand, knocking dancers aside. But Algernon recovered quickly and brought the woman down with a flying tackle that sent them both crashing into a group of dancers who were knocked from their feet like pins on a bowling alley.

Michael, followed by Lindsay and Kohler, raced across the floor. In a moment, the struggling woman was pinned to the floor by the quartet of sailors while a crowd spilled around the group.

"Motherfucker! I'll kill that faggot motherfucker," she screamed hoarsely, spraying spittle.

"Woman! Woman! We ain't gonna turn you loose 'til you stop actin' like dry gulch trash," Schultz roared, face flushed.

The woman struggled, frothing. Then, slowly, she began to relax her arms and legs, and her breathing became slow and nearly normal.

"Okay."

"You promise?"

"Yes. Let me up." The men, taking a cue from

Schultz, stepped back. Slowly, the woman rose, all the while glaring at the trombonist, who held the horn at his side defensively like a frightened native holding a spear, prepared for battle or flight.

But the woman turned and walked away into the crowd, which parted like minnows before a cruising shark. Followed by Schultz, Thelma did not stop until she reached the bar. To Michael's relief, the music resumed and couples began turning.

Seating themselves, Michael, Bryan and Don finished their drinks and signaled Vivian, who replenished them quickly.

"I can see why he's crazy about her," Bryan said gravely.

"Dainty and helpless," Michael agreed, affirming the charade.

"Yeah," Bryan said. "Like Anita Louise or Frances Farmer."

"More delicate," Michael chided softly. He traced a figure in the air with a single finger. "Gossamer and wispy—delicate as a breath of fog."

"Ah, cut it out, you guys," Don said. "He's really gone on her."

A tight black skirt and satin blouse materialized. Eyes on Michael, Vivian asked, "You boys lookin' for a little action?"

"I'd like to unwrap a box," Linday said, eyeing the girl's body with unabashed lust.

"Sorry," the girl retorted. "Christmas isn't here." She jerked a thumb toward a table in a far corner where three young women sat. "Some friends of mine. They like to dance, but," she waved a hand airily, "these idiots are all getting too drunk."

Glancing at the boisterous drinkers and unsteady dancers, Michael nodded. And in a dark corner near the rear exit several bodies were stretched full-length. "What the hell?"

"Cordwood Corner," the girl said.

"Yeah," Don Lindsay concurred. "The solicitous, patriotic management does its bit for the war effort by stacking indisposed clientele — saves them from the foul clutches of the SPs and MPs."

"Praise the Lord," Bryan shouted suddenly, throwing his head back and flinging out his arms.

"And pass the ammunition," Michael added. "At last, we've found true patriotism."

"All's right with the world," Bryan said. And then waving a hand: "What about your friends, Vivian?"

"They'd like to dance with you boys."

"We're not exactly rock sober," Don conceded.

"You're better than the rest of 'em."

"We'd be delighted to trip the light fantastic with your charming friends," Bryan said, tossing off the remainder of his highball. And then solemnly, "But remember this, Vivian, let your friends have no illusions, a dance with me does not imply that I will surrender my lily-white body."

"Here! Here!" Don shouted. Everyone laughed.

Quickly, Vivian pushed more chairs to the table and in a moment the three young women were seated. Bryan ordered a round of drinks.

The women were young, all appearing to be in their early twenties. One — a trim brunette — sat next to Michael.

"I'm Vicki," the brunette said, edging close to Michael.

She was a lovely girl with dark brown hair shot through with tones of russet and chestnut, and her skin was clear and fresh as rose petals. But her eyes were what transfixed him. They were wide and bright as polished emeralds, with a latent sadness challenging the gay twist frozen on her full lips. As she smiled, the quartermaster glimpsed white, even teeth.

"This is Marilyn." Vicki gestured daintily to a small, mousy girl with poorly peroxided hair, who had sat next to Bryan. "And Rose," she continued, nodding to a dark-haired, olive-skinned girl with bleary brown eyes who snuggled up to Don.

Don stood and spoke gravely, with an air of gallantry, while swinging an arm in an irregular arc. "My brothers in arms . . ."

"Ah, shit. Knock it off," Bryan said, chuckling.

Everyone laughed while Lindsay collapsed in his chair. Then, after quick introductions, the three couples moved to the dance floor.

Holding Vicki close, they twisted slowly to "Deep Purple." He could feel the soft contours of her back, the points of her breasts against his chest. She was a nice armful, all warmness and sweet-smelling softness.

Pulling her head back, the girl looked up, and Michael found himself drawn to the depths of the remarkable green eyes. "On the beach, Michael?"

Michael decided to answer truthfully. "Temporarily. And you?"

"I'm a singer."

"A singer! You mean with a band."

"I'm trying, Michael. I have an audition with Larry Elgart this week and Stan Kenton next week."

"Why music?"

"Why not, Michael? I love it. I love songs and songwriters."

"Songwriters? They're musicians."

"They're poets, Michael."

"Well, I guess so—they're dreamers."

"Oh yes, that's what a poet is."

"Really? A dreamer?"

"Why yes, a poet dreams when he's awake."

"Of course."

The voice was earnest as if the girl was articulating emotions instead of thoughts. "Songwriters are a special breed, Michael. They can look in our hearts and find things that tear our souls. Put light on secrets we all hide in the dark corners. They tear the truth about us out of us, rhyme it and put it to melody."

121

"They do all that?"

Her laugh was brief—almost forced. "Sometimes—some of them."

The eyes moved over his face, moistened as if searching the visage of someone beloved. He felt strangely uncomfortable, but at the same time drawn strongly to this stunning girl with the sorrowful eyes. He felt pushed by curiosity. "How can you live?"

"I've had a few jobs in nightclubs." The eyes darted to the bar. "And I have a small inheritance."

"Lucky."

The voice was barely audible. "Yes. Lucky."

"You have someone in the service?"

She continued staring away. "No. And Michael, please, let's not talk about the war."

"I'm with you."

She turned back to him, smiled up into his eyes, but the haunted look was still there. Then, sighing, she placed her cheek against his and he felt her body move closer. He had an urge to comfort her, kiss her. He brushed her forehead with his lips.

Suddenly, the band launched into a disorderly version of "Blues in the Night." He felt her lips against his cheek. "Michael."

"Yes."

"Have you ever felt those blues in the night?"

Michael slipped both arms around the girl and placed his lips to her ear. "Oh, yes, Vicki—many, many times." He had known her for years, not minutes, and Kristie and Alma had never existed.

"So have I, Michael."

Michael felt new warmth fanned by the closeness of the girl and the growing effects of the liquor. But, strangely, her dark, dispirited tone stimulated him most, making him search for something to break her mood. He began to croon softly in her ear. " 'My momma done told me . . .' "

"What did she tell you, Michael," she said, her demeanor sharpening, voice lifting.

Michael took the cue, pushed on into the popular lyrics. " 'A woman'll sweet talk . . .' "

"Oh?"

" 'And give you the big eye . . .' "

"Really?"

" 'But when the sweet talkin's done.' "

"What happens, Michael?"

" 'A woman's a two face . . .' "

"Can't believe it." She giggled, a delighted, little girl's sound.

" 'A worrisome thing who'll lead you to sing . . .' "

"Sing what?"

He stopped, stepped back and then chorused with the girl, " 'Those blues in the night.' "

"Yeah, man—groovy," Don Lindsay shouted over Rose's shoulder.

Laughing, Michael pulled Vicki close and the pair whirled around the dance floor until the song ended. Then, ignoring the absence of music, they continued to sway in the middle of the dance floor.

"Hey you guys, it's over," Don shouted. Slowly, the couple returned to the table.

For nearly an hour, the dancing continued. "The joint's going to close soon," Bryan said, glancing at his watch.

"Come over to my place for a nightcap," Vicki said, staring at Michael.

The young quartermaster felt a familiar surge—a sudden racing of the pulses and warmth far down that could bring an ache. Kristie came back, but he pushed her aside.

Bryan said, "We don't have a car."

"Don't need one," Vicki said. "I only live two blocks away."

Built in the nineteenth century, when South Gate

was a distant suburb of Los Angeles, Vicki's house was a small two bedroom with uneven hardwood floors and an earthquake-weakened chimney that listed five degrees toward the street. Lying on a blanket on the floor in front of a restless fire, Michael and Vicki had finished two drinks after Bryan and Don had taken Marilyn and Rose into the bedrooms.

"I love your fire," Michael said, turning his head on his pillow until his nose almost touched the girl's. "My mother and I never had one." He slid a hand to her hip.

"I like it. It brightens up the old house."

There was a sudden, triumphant twang of bedsprings from the back of the house, and Bryan's groans, spiced with Marilyn's cries, seeped into the room. Michael laughed. "Well, they'll be relaxed tomorrow."

"What about you, Michael?"

The quartermaster felt a hand test his bicep, move down his back to his waist. Lips brushed his cheek. "What about me?"

"Are you relaxed?"

"No."

"Neither am I." She gripped the back of his head, pulled him to her. In a moment the girl was on her back, Michael sprawled on top of her.

The kisses were wet, hot, and frantic. For the last time, Michael's mind wandered to Kristie, and he felt the acid stab of guilt deep inside. But it was brief, washed away by the heat of the writhing body beneath him.

She kissed him gently. "You're wonderful, Michael."

"You were great, yourself," Michael said, standing and pulling his jumper on. He moved to the door. "Bryan, Don and the girls left?"

"An hour ago," the nude girl said, rising and moving to him. "I thought you were asleep." And then with a sardonic twist to her lips: "You relaxed?"

Circling her tiny waist with his big arms, he laughed. "Almost to the point of collapse."

She laughed. "Me too."

Then, for the first time, he noticed the picture on the mantel — the likeness of a swarthy young pilot with a flat hat and Eighth Air Force shoulder patch, staring deep into his eyes eerily like a man frozen in time. "Who's the flyboy? He's dark like me."

"Very much like you, Michael."

Michael moved closer to the portrait. Felt shock. "Like a goddamned mirror." He turned to the girl, "Who is he?"

"My husband."

"I didn't know you were married." He felt anger knot in his stomach.

"He was killed over Schweinfurt six months ago."

"Oh Christ. No! No . . ."

"This airdale looked just like me and he sat on the mantel and watched — watched the whole thing." Sitting at a table in a corner of the bar of the A-1 Bowl, Michael stared at Bryan, who moved his drink back and forth on the marble tabletop like a hesitant chess player toying with a pawn. Bored with the base and with a free gangway, the pair had hitchhiked to the nearest bar which was an anteroom of the bowling alley. Still an hour before noon, the small room was deserted except for the two sailors and the lone bartender.

Bryan held up his drink. "I'm waiting for my mother to tell me I'm drinking too much."

Michael looked up sharply. "What does that have to do with the pilot — Vicki?"

"Everything. We *have been* drinking too much. Everyone seems to get drunk every night."

"Why not?"

"Those girls were drunk last night, Michael."

"I know."

125

"Including your Vicki."

"It wasn't just booze."

Bryan shifted his weight uneasily on the upholstered chair and stared at his distraught friend in the dim light. "She's a very young widow. Maybe she's a little out of her mind."

The quartermaster stared at the glow of the indirect light over the bar. Two fixed black eyes stared back. He drained half his glass with one gulp, palmed his forehead, and felt a compulsion to talk, to bare dark thoughts. He had never had a father, and he found confiding in his mother impossible. Anyway, baring one's soul was unmanly. But an ineffable guilt gnawed at him, a guilt that, somehow, was rooted in the dead boys off Guadalcanal, Savo, the Slot. For the first time in his life, he felt as if he had done something obscene. And he had to tell someone or burst. Bryan waited. Bryan understood. Bryan had been there, too. Michael drained his glass, but there was no visceral warmth, no easing of tense muscles.

The pharmacist's mate picked up the empty glasses, walked to the bar and returned with refills.

Michael took a long drink, blurted out, "I'm no puritan, Bryan, but to screw some sailor in front of a guy . . ."

"Jesus, man. It was only a picture, that's all."

"She should've turned it around." He drank again and then slapped the table. "You're going to think I'm corny."

"Try me."

Michael chewed his lip. "You won't laugh?"

"I promise."

Michael's words clotted deep in his throat. "He was part of me."

"The airdale?"

"Yes. Vicki's husband."

Solemnly, Bryan nodded, stared over his glass.

Michael continued, "I can't help it." He took a deep

breath. Exhaling, he spoke rapidly, anxious to articulate the pain. He ran his words together. "It's the SC."

Unblinking, Kohler stared, the gray of his eyes heightened by moisture.

Carpelli plunged on, "It's part of being a sole survivor. I don't belong here—I don't belong anywhere except with them."

"The guys? The subchaser?"

"Yes. I didn't have the right to outlive them. And now it's worse. I die with each guy who gets it."

"We all feel that way."

Carpelli felt as if a burden had been lifted from his shoulders. He sagged in his chair. "Then I'm not the only one."

"Right, Michael. It's kept inside."

"That flyboy dragged it out of me."

There was understanding in Bryan's eyes. "Yes. Yes. Of course he did. But remember this, Michael, you can't die with every guy who catches one."

"You do, don't you, Bryan?"

Kohler's eyes moved to the floor. His jaw took a hard set. "Maybe."

Michael felt an inexplicable surge of anger. "Maybe, shit! You feel guilty because you're alive!"

"Well, don't you? Don't you? If anyone should be dead . . ."

"Stop it! Shut up!" the quartermaster shrieked, losing control. Flaring like burning summer grass on a hillside, he leaped to his feet, fists balled. The bartender put aside a glass he was drying and stared.

"Easy, man. Easy," Kohler said, rising slowly and placing a hand on his friend's shoulder. "She really got to you, didn't she. Sit down, Michael. Sit down." The two sailors sank in their chairs. The bartender resumed toweling his glasses and turned away.

"We don't belong here, Bryan," Michael said in a flat voice.

"Maybe you're right." The pharmacist's mate turned

127

his palms up in a gesture of helplessness. And then he leaned forward, saying, "You going to see Vicki anymore?"

Michael sipped his drink. "I guess so. How about you and Marilyn?"

"Tomorrow night. At the Elbow Room. She said she'd bring Vicki." Bryan's eyes narrowed. "A personal question."

"Shoot."

"Kristie. You're gone on her."

"Yes."

"You don't sleep with her, do you?"

Shocked by Kohler's perceptiveness, Michael could only stare for a moment, chewing his lip. "She's a virgin."

"And you'll keep her that way."

Michael nodded in acceptance. "Yes. She *must* remain that way."

"And that morning we met outside the mess hall—two weeks ago at the beginning of our leaves, you'd sacked-in with someone."

"Her name was Alma."

"Seeing her?"

"Negative."

"Why not?"

Michael shrugged. "I couldn't tell you. I just haven't."

"But you want to see Vicki again?"

"I guess so. . . . Yes."

"And Kristie, Michael. You want to see her, too." Bryan looked into Michael's eyes as if he were scanning a letter and reading every word at a glance.

Michael felt his face warm, cloud with trouble. "Why the third degree?"

"You're not going to tell me it's none of my business?"

"No. Not this time."

"You're torturing yourself, Michael."

Sighing, the quartermaster sank back. "What would

you suggest. What's the solution?"

"You know you don't have to face that."

"What do you mean, Bryan?"

"The navy and our Japanese friends have first priority on your time — on your future."

"Of course."

"Put your bows into the wind, set the sea anchor and ride it out and see them both. You need them both."

"More guilt, Bryan."

"We can live with it." And then with quiet humor stirring at the corners of his eyes, "You ever read *Strange Interlude?*"

"Eugene O'Neil," Michael answered, surprised at the sudden change in topics. "Yeah, at gunpoint in an American Lit class. I don't remember much about it."

"It's about this old broad whose boyfriend gets it in WW-One." Michael's nod encourages Bryan. "Well, she can only replace him with a whole platoon of guys. . . ."

"You mean I need a bunch of broads. One for music, one for art, one for PE . . ."

"Something like that," Kohler acknowledged, chuckling. "Isn't it true?"

"Who knows?"

"See Kristie tonight?"

"Yes."

"Come to the Elbow Room tomorrow night?"

"Yes."

"We'll both become schizo before this is over."

Pursing his lips, Michael nodded. "You know Bryan, if we become crazy enough, we might just understand what we're doing."

"Amen, brother. Amen."

The passage of years would never dampen the burning images of Michael's second visit to the Elbow Room and his last moments with Vicki. It began innocuously enough: the coveted corner booth saved by Vivian,

Bryan and Don dancing with Marilyn and Rose, Schultz and Thelma making their dry run on the dance floor.

And Vicki close at his side on the thick cushions, leaning on an elbow, green eyes riveted to his, her smile broad and warm. Her first words had been, "I was afraid I'd never see you again."

Michael remembered staring back at the emeralds, having no trouble with memories of the previous night, Kristie and pledges of enduring love. Then, with a shock, he realized he was adjusting to this dual existence. Maybe the perceptive Bryan had been right. Maybe he was living his own "strange interlude." "I wanted to see you," he said, taking her hand. He felt her lips brush his cheek, breast pressure his arm.

"Dance with me, Michael."

Hand-in-hand they walked to the dance floor as Cobra Phillips led the band into the opening bars of "Where or When." She came to him without hesitation: the lover, close and warm, filled with desire. Turning slowly to the opening refrain, she held him with fierce possessiveness, lips pressed to his neck. He felt warmth, a quickening of his breath. Slowly they turned, disembodied, aware of nothing except each other, gliding effortlessly, stepping from one wispy cloud to another.

Vicki picked up the lyrics. Although her voice was soft, almost a whisper, the luxuriant strains still came through. He felt the sadness as the song mourned of lovers who had met, dreamed of the past, of a time and place that had slipped by, yet seemed to be repeating. Then, halfway through the song, she stopped abruptly.

Pulling away, Carpelli looked down into her eyes, wide-open, unblinking and shining with such an eerie intensity they appeared back-lighted, looking not only at him, but through him like a sorceress reading the book of the past. He felt haunted and his skin grew cold, the hair on the nape of his neck stiffening. Hastily, he escaped the eyes by putting his lips to her cheek.

"What's wrong, Vicki?"

Ignoring the question, she picked up the lyrics precisely on beat and finished by repeating "where or when," over and over until he silenced her with a finger to her lips. She began to cry.

"What's wrong, Vicki?" he repeated.

"It's so beautiful," she said, watery eyes focused on his.

Don Lindsay's voice interrupted, "Swell! Great! *The Hit Parade* comes to the Elbow Room," he exulted, applauding while a smiling Rose leaned against his shoulder.

Dabbing at her cheeks with a handkerchief and blinking her eyes free of tears, Vicki turned to Lindsay, "More like *Major Bowes' Amateur Hour*," she managed.

Everyone laughed at the forced humor. Then, hand-in-hand, Michael and Vicki followed Don and Rose back to the booth where Algernon and Thelma clutched each other passionately. With a groan, the gunner and his date pulled apart as the dancers settled in their chairs.

Without warning, Cobra Phillips crashed into "My Reverie," with each member of the combo apparently choosing his own key and rhythm.

"Jesus," Lindsay said, holding his ears. And then raising his glass, "Here's to 'My Reverie.' If it survives this, it'll become a standard."

"Enjoy it anyway, mate," Bryan said. 'Cause soon that's all you'll have—reveille and reverie."

Vicki covered Michael's hand with both of hers. "But we're real tonight."

"Jesus, Mary and Joseph, we're beholdin' to you for that," Algernon said, raising his hands supplicantly.

"Here's to the whole damned family," Lindsay said.

"Bottoms up," Rose cried.

"Roger, wilco and out!"

In an instant, the glasses were empty and an alert Vivian scooped them up and returned with refills.

131

"That gal's faster'n a hound with a peach stone up his ass," Algernon said. He waved his glass vaguely to the west. "Can't get this stuff out yonder."

"There's a lot of stuff you can't get 'out yonder,' " Thelma giggled in a high-pitched voice.

Schultz leered. "We'll get ahead—like a coon stores chestnuts."

"You can't screw chestnuts," Thelma snickered. And then lighting a cigarette, she said, "Here's another nail in my coffin." With a sound like the wind whipping a halyard, she exhaled, and a puff of blue smoke joined the permanent cloud that hung in the room.

Wide-eyed, Don shouted, "Lucky Strike greens have gone to war!"

"Thank God for that," Bryan said.

"I feel safe now," Michael added.

Everyone laughed. Thelma exhaled another fog bank. "Why don't you come to my house?" she said, her eyes moving around the table. "We'll have a party."

"No indecent advances," Don said with mock gravity.

Marilyn came to life. "Of course not. What do you think we are?"

Don spoke to Thelma, "You don't want my virginal blood on your sheets?"

The woman laughed raucously. "Honey, if I ever get to you, you'll leave more than blood on my sheets." The corner of the room rocked with laughter.

Fixing her eyes on Michael, Vicki said, " I think we'll take a rain check."

Staring into the wide eyes, Michael shrugged. "Why?"

"Come to my place, Michael."

"Oh," everyone chorused.

"Anyone can come," Vicki added defensively. "There's plenty of room."

"Let's go with Vicki and Michael," Marilyn said, turning to Bryan. And then to Thelma, "No offense?"

"Of course not, dearie. Some other night."

Mischievously, Don eyed Michael over his glass. "Be careful, Michael."

"Don't worry about me," Carpelli said, rising and pulling Vicki with him. "I'm in good hands."

As the foursome left, Michael could feel eyes on his back. Glancing over his shoulder, he caught Vivian's dark eyes boring into his. He felt uncomfortable as he pushed his way through the swinging doors.

Stretched full length in front of the fire, Michael cradled his drink, his eyes riveted on Vicki, who leaned on an elbow and stared down, humming "Where or When."

"Pick another one," he said, sensing the return of her eerie mood and the inexplicable gulf it brought. " 'Where or When' is here and now."

"Here and now—that's all there is, Michael," she cried bitterly. "No past, no future, no . . ."

"That's right, Vicki. How can there be anything else?"

Shoulders shaking, she turned away. He sat up and turned her slender shoulders with his big hands. Tenderly, he kissed the tears from her cheeks. "Oh, Vicki, I didn't mean to hurt you."

She pulled away. "I know, Michael. But there's no escape from this damned war."

"Yes there is."

"Where, Michael? Where?"

"In each other."

She came back fiercely, kissing him with little groaning sounds deep in her throat. He pushed her on her back and began to unbutton her blouse.

"No!" she said, pulling him to his feet. "This time in my bedroom."

As he walked to the hallway, he passed close to the mantel. The picture was gone.

"No lights, no lights."

"But it's so dark in here, Vicki. I can barely see you."

"I know," she said, dropping her panties to the floor. "That's how I want you." She pulled the cover back, stretched full length on her back, raised her arms. "Love me, darling. Love me."

Throwing his clothes on the floor, he stared down. In the dim light the woman's exquisite form was barely discernible. He dropped to his knees, touched her knee with a single finger, and ran it up the inside of her thigh.

Breathlessly, she pulled him down to her breast, hands to the back of his head. As his tongue circled the swollen nipple, she said something strange — strange even in the disorienting heat of the moment. "I love you, darling, always have, always will — since I was a little girl."

But Michael did not wonder. The hot, sinuous body blotted out the world.

The soft light of the morning sun crept through and around the heavy drapes and entered the room gently like a luminescent mist, touching everything with bright fingers. Fighting off wakefulness and basking in the afterglow of a night of frenzied lovemaking, Carpelli stretched and sighed, throwing an arm over the girl's waist.

She sighed, "Joe — Joe."

Jarred, he raised himself on an elbow. "I'm Michael Carpelli . . ."

"Joe, Joe," she insisted, sitting up. "You're wonderful."

Angrily, Michael threw the covers off and came to his feet. There seemed to be mirrors everywhere. But they weren't mirrors. Pictures. Pictures of the pilot. A dozen. Two dozen. Staring back at him from the dresser, night stand, the walls. Frozen, dead eyes.

She was out of the bed, pressing her body against his, eyes like bottomless gems, brimming with love. "You're back, Joe. I knew it. Knew it. All those stories about Schweinfurt were lies."

He grasped her shoulders. "I'm Michael! Michael Carpelli—quartermaster . . ."

She laughed. "It's time to stop kidding, Joe. You've always been a joker. Even when we were little kids." She began to plead. "Stop it; please stop it. You're alive and home." She pinched her arm. "See, I'm awake. I'm not dreaming it this time. You're here, really here. And we made love all night." Running on faster, the words melted into each other. "I'm whole again, Joe. Don't tell me I'm dreaming with my eyes wide open. Not that corny song. No, indeed. You're here—standing in front of me. And last night we had it again; our honeymoon again. I've been dreaming about that. I've lived and died the twenty-five missions with you. But now you're back . . ." She began to sob.

Michael felt his stomach knot with a new horror, a new helplessness he had never felt before. Circling the girl with his arms, he gave in. "Of course I'm back."

"You won't go back?"

"Of course not, Vicki. I've put in my twenty-five. I'm back for good."

"I'm so lucky."

They dressed quickly while Vicki babbled on at express train speed about times together in high school, even junior high school, running her thoughts and words together in a fearful jumble of half-finished sentences and phrases.

Michael felt panic. "Marilyn? Marilyn?"

"At the end of the hall."

In a moment, Michael's pounding had roused the girl who stepped into the hall clad only in a robe. Hastily he explained Vicki's bizarre behavior.

"No. No," Marilyn gasped.

135

Bryan, dressed only in his skivvies, appeared at the door. "What's wrong?"

"Vicki's sick. Get dressed," Michael said. Bryan vanished.

Following Marilyn, the young quartermaster returned to the bedroom. Vicki, dressed in a filmy black negligee, stood before a full-length mirror, twisting and admiring the fit of the garment. She turned to Marilyn. "I can wear it now, Marilyn." Her eyes moved to Michael. "Joe's back."

"I know, Vicki, I know," Marilyn said, taking Vicki into her arms. She turned away, passed Michael as she walked to the door. "I'll call for help," she whispered.

Michael slumped in an easy chair and stared at Byran, who sprawled on the couch. "An ambulance," Michael said with disbelief. "They took her away in an ambulance." The sight of the girl struggling and screaming burned from his mind's eyes, searing his senses.

"Marilyn said they'd gone together since they were kids," Byran offered softly.

"Shit! Shit! Where will they take her?"

"A sanitarium out near a place called Camarillo."

"Then the Krauts killed her, too."

Puzzled, Kohler looked up.

"I mean, over Schweinfurt. It's not just the guys who get it."

The pharmacist's mate nodded agreement. "I guess it never is, Michael. Never . . ."

Looking back on the days following Vicki's breakdown, Michael found blurred images mingling with fragments of crystal clear recollections. Two nights after the breakdown and after breaking a date with Kristie, the quartermaster clearly recalled being seated with Bryan and Marilyn in their usual corner booth at

136

the Elbow Room, sipping drinks served by an unusually taciturn Vivian.

Studying the murky depths of his drink, Michael opened the conversation. "She's gone—out of her mind."

Marilyn brushed strings of blond hair from her eyes—blue-gray eyes that appeared sunken, giving her thin face a cadaverous look. "Yes," she answered. "Gone. Gone from this world."

"What do you mean?" Bryan said, slumped over his drink.

"She's schizophrenic," the girl said.

Michael asked, "You understand these things, Marilyn?"

"Who does?" the girl answered. "But I'm an RN and took some training in a psychiatric hospital."

Bryan nodded. "I put in some time in the psycho ward at the San Diego Naval Hospital when I was in training, too." He studied the girl with narrow eyes, chewed his lip. "They use schizophenic a lot; too much."

The girl took a drink and wiped her mouth with the back of a hand. "Vicki is officially diagnosed as 'paranoid-schizophrenic.' "

"They all are," Bryan spat.

"Of course," the girl agreed. "The county won't pay the psychiatrists until a diagnosis is made."

Michael felt anger flare. "So they're all schizo and paranoid?"

"You have to understand, Michael," Bryan noted scornfully. "Psychiatrists don't know much more and they all love their Cadillacs."

"Shit!" Michael studied the small blonde. "What will they do with her?"

Marilyn took several deep breaths and tapped the table. "Shock treatments and sedation."

"Is that it?"

She bit her lower lip. "No. There are prefontal lobotomies."

"That sounds horrible."

"It is. They sever the front of the brain . . ." Gagging, the nurse halted, pressed her lips to a knuckle like a child seeking security.

Gently, Michael placed a big palm on the girl's back. "Sorry, Marilyn. I didn't think."

The blond caught her breath, shook her head. Pressed on, "It's all right, Michael. You must understand, she's living in a fantasy world. She could snap out of it, or withdraw completely. Become catatonic."

"Catatonic?"

"Mute. Like a vegetable."

Michael punched the table. "I did it to her."

"Don't say that, Michael."

"I look just like her Joe."

"An accident of birth, Michael. She's been on the edge for months," the girl said. "In fact, Rose and I kept hoping she'd meet someone like you." She took another drink, dabbed at her cheeks. "You were the first since Schweinfurt."

"You knew her well?"

"I knew them both. We grew up together in Pomona. His name was Joe Centinero. He was of Spanish descent — he was dark."

"I know. I know." Finishing his drink, Michael beckoned to Vivian, who quickly and silently replaced them.

Michael continued, "He was a singer, wasn't he?"

The blonde sipped her fresh drink, thin lips curling into her first smile. "Oh, yes. All through school and even in church, they sang together. They had uncanny ears for melodies and could memorize lyrics almost instantly. And Joe was more than a singer; he was a real talent — could play the piano, drums and accordion. They were putting an act together when the war broke out." She took several swallows from her glass. Stared off into the smoke and spoke very softly. "They could actually talk to each other with lyrics."

138

"And he was a songwriter?" Michael asked, staring at the far wall.

Mutely, Marilyn nodded her answer to the rhetorical question.

The quartermaster rubbed his forehead. "Jesus. Jesus. She wanted me to be him. Made it come true. Found her own 'Where or When.' "

Michael felt the girl's hand on his. "Don't blame yourself, Michael."

Bryan came to life. "The Krauts did it, Michael."

The Latin squinted at the pharmacist's mate and felt his words rise from deep in his throat. "Bastards! Bastards! Kill them all. Every fuckin' one. That's the only way."

Eyes wide, the nurse came erect. "Michael! Michael!"

But she was cut short by Cobra Phillips, who launched his group into a deafening assault on "Josephine."

Grasping the girl's hand, Bryan pulled her to her feet and led her to the floor. Michael followed them with tired eyes. Then he noticed the civilians. Two swarthy young men in baggy suits standing at the bar. One was engaged in an earnest conversation with Vivian while the other — back to the bar — eyed the dancers with a haughty, disdainful look. Immediately, the quartermaster felt repugnance and antagonism. "Zoot suiters," Michael said to himself. "Fuckin' four-F zoot suiters."

A quick flurry at the bar and shouts brought the sailor out of his chair. Vivian, obviously angered, had slapped one civilian who grabbed her and pushed her against the bar. Before Michael could cross the dance floor, a marine sergeant — employed as bouncer on his duty-free nights — and two corporals had grabbed the baggy suits by the shoulders and pants and propelled them headfirst through the padded doors. One of the young men shouted, "I'll get you, motherfuckin' cunt!" as he was hurled through the door.

139

"Filthy vermin," the waitress fired back.

"You okay?" Michael asked, elbowing his way to the waitress who had returned to her station at the bar.

"Oh, sure, Michael," she said, smiling. "Just some horny insect I knew in high school."

In a moment, Michael returned to his table.

"Zoot suits," Bryan said.

"Bums," Michael answered. "Nothing but bums."

"I have to work tomorrow," Marilyn announced suddenly. "We'd better leave, Bryan." And then to Michael, "Maybe we can visit Vicki. I'll find out."

Quickly, the blonde and the big pharmacist's mate vanished into the crowd.

Michael was suddenly struck with loneliness. Strange, how you can be alone in a crowd. He held his empty glass above his head. But Vivian did not answer. Instead, Nell—a short, plump girl with a pleasant smile and seven-ax-handle ass—swayed her way across the floor.

"What'll you have, big boy," she asked seductively, smile revealing uneven teeth.

"Bourbon and soda."

"Is that all?"

Eyeing the breasts bulging against white satin, spacious pelvis and remarkable buttocks, Michael felt no arousal. In fact, he was strangely repulsed. "No," he answered. "Where's Vivian?"

"She's not feeling well—gone home," the girl snapped. Then she whirled and walked to the bar, tight skirt rolling over her buttocks, which wriggled through the taffeta like two angry animals locked in combat.

But the drink brought no solace, no relief from Vicki and her tragedy. Cursing, Michael rose and pushed his way through the door. The base. He needed the base. He needed the guys.

Lightning pulsed in the black southern skies, sending flickering light to cast shadows of poles and buildings on streets and sidewalks, glistening from a misting rain. Shuddering, Michael pushed his hands into his tight pockets and wished he had worn his peacoat. Taking long, fast strides, the young sailor hurried down the dark deserted street, which was lighted only at a distant intersection by a single street light. Occasionally, a car passed, tires hissing as they peeled water from the pavement in sheets of spray, lights glaring from the wet asphalt.

As he passed a trash-filled alley, the young sailor's peripheral vision detected movement where there should have been none. He heard men curse, a woman groan. Stopping, Michael squinted, finally finding a cluster of forms twisting and struggling on a decaying mattress pushed against an ancient brick building.

Holding his breath, he moved into the alley. Gradually, in the dim light, two men and a woman became visible. The woman, flat on her back with her skirt hiked to her waist, rolled and groaned while one man held her arms and other—pants down to his knees—pushed himself between her legs. The men wore zoot suits. The girl was Vivian. No one noticed the sailor.

As Michael moved closer, he heard the man holding the girl speak shrilly, "Hurry up, man. Get it off. I don't mind a wet deck."

"Here it comes, man. Sloppy seconds," the other grunted, thrusting hard.

The first man giggled. The girl twisted and gasped.

Michael felt a sudden flare of anger knot in his stomach like a burning rope. "My, how romantic," he managed casually.

Releasing the waitress's hands, the first man came to his feet slowly, hard eyes beady and cold as chips of black ice, glinting from sharp features fashioned by a hatchet. The other man remained between the girl's legs, moving his hips frantically, gasping and then shuddering. Then, leaning on his arms he turned his

141

head, revealing a wild-eyed, demonic visage.

The hatchet spoke, "This is none of your business, sailor. Get lost before you get hurt."

"Thanks for your concern, but I think I'll stay for the party." Michael felt a familiar sharpening of the senses, his eyes brightening like a bared blade. Then, as he stared at the whimpering, bruised girl, rage came on with startling ferocity, as though a beast had pounced on his back with bared claws, goading him with sharp fangs. Fists balled, he stepped forward.

The man reacted with the speed of a gutter fighter, leaping unexpectedly toward the sailor and swinging at his head. But he made the mistake of underestimating his opponent's speed and great strength.

Michael had fought many times, and he was ready, stepping to the side and bringing a huge fist up from the hip like a mace. Catching the hatchet squarely on the jaw as he followed the momentum of his own swing and charge, the quartermaster felt bone give way, cracking and popping with the sound of dry gravel under a boot.

Hurled backward by the impact, the man flattened against the bricks, eyes rolling, blood gushing from his mouth and nose. Slowly and with eyes glassed by shocked disbelief, he sank to the ground and pitched face-down in the mud.

Vivian's voice, "Michael!"

Whirling, Michael found the second man on his feet. There was a glint in the man's hand. A knife. Cold steel. The sailor felt a tremor deep in his guts.

Vivian was up, backing fearfully against a wall.

"Prick," the man spat. He waved the knife. "Now we'll see how much of a hero you are." And then, squinting, "Hey, man—you're dark. What's going on, man? You're not a *gringo*, you're one of us."

"I've never been any part of you. Never have been, never will be."

"You'll bleed for the fuckin' Anglos. That right

142

hero?"

"I won't hide from it like a coward."

"Leave, Michael, leave," Vivian shouted suddenly, wiping blood from her cheek. "Antonio will kill you. I've known him since high school. He knows how to use that knife."

"Yeah, man," Antonio said, gesturing with the knife. "I've been hot for a piece of that tight little snatch for ten years."

There was a groan. Antonio gestured at his stricken companion. "You're a hero, man. A real all American boy. Broke Pepe's jaw with one punch. Cool it, man. Run off to your ship like John Wayne and kill more Japs."

Michael stared at the blade. Pointed, it was at least eight inches long and sharp on both sides. No doubt Antonio was an expert. Could stab and slash with equal dexterity. Carpelli feared bombs and guns. But they killed from a distance. The knife held its own terror. It was intimate, bringing killer and killed together as no other weapon ever could. It had to be pushed into the victim, ripping intestines, cutting tissue, pouring a torrent of blood on the user. Only a special kind of lunatic could use it. And now he faced one alone, in a dark, wet alley.

There was a pounding in his temples and his mouth was a desert. He couldn't swallow. Every instinct commanded him to flee, but he planted his feet and balled his fists. Flight had been impossible in the Solomons and it was impossible now.

The woman watched.

"Have it your way," the man said, advancing, holding the knife lightly at his waist.

Michael stepped back, feeling the side of the building for a brick, board, anything. There was a glint of faint light and the man lunged, extending his arm for Michael's groin. Feeling a breath of wind, the quartermaster leaped back, clutching his waist. The cloth was

143

ripped, but no blood.

The man laughed. "Next time a little lower. I'll cut off your balls. Then"—he waved at the cowering woman—"she won't like you no more."

Michael continued the retreat, but kept square to his enemy. An animal pounded at his ribs, trying to get out. His breath was hard. But his jaw tightened and the cords in his neck bulged.

"Michael, leave. Please, Michael, leave."

Ignoring the woman and staring at the advancing blade, Michael took another step back. Stepped on something round and hard. A bottle. He scooped it up, smashed the end against a building, and waved the jagged edges at his enemy.

"Come on, Valentino. Let's see your balls, if you have any," he hissed, a sneer on his face, mockery in his voice.

The man stopped and circled the knife. Michael expected a head-on lunge, but instead, the man leaped to the side, dropped to his knee, and stabbed upward.

Staggering backward, the quartermaster felt a red hot flash of pain. He gripped his chest. His hand came away warm and sticky.

"Ha! I'm going to cut off your dick and stuff it in that *puta*'s mouth." He gesticulated with the knife.

The woman's face was a look of horror. She keened softly.

Pain brought rage to the surface, pushing fear aside. Michael felt a sudden calmness, a new resolve. Somehow, he would destroy his enemy. Punch that gloating smile from his face. Kick him. Choke him. Hear him scream. Hear him beg. He had one advantage—reach. He would lure the overconfident zoot suit into a moment's carelessness.

The sailor stepped back and felt a pile of wet garbage. He took another step, faked a misstep, and lunged for the building.

With a shout, Antonio leaped forward, landing in

the garbage, sliding. Michael jumped, swinging the bottle down. There was the butcher-shop sound of cleaving meat as the bottle thudded into the man's upper arm.

An animal caught in a steel trap howled and the knife dropped into the mud.

Shouting triumphantly, the sailor stepped in close and pulled the bottle down with all his strength. Pulling himself free, the man staggered against the building, gripping his shoulder.

A monstrous, primal emotion swept through Carpelli like lava. The pain in his chest and pressure in his head, behind his eyes blurred his senses and blotted out everything except the twisted face of his tormentor.

Destroy the face. He dropped the bottle and stepped in close. Attacked instinctively. A massive fist cracked the cartilage of the man's nose with the popping sound of teeth biting an apple. Antonio sagged. Michael straightened him with a hand to the neck and punched straight-on with the other. First the knuckles, then the back of his fist. Over and over. Spittle sprayed. Teeth flew.

A blow to the eye, then another. A scream. Pleas for mercy. A short, brutal punch cracked Antonio's jaw. The pleas became cries and the man's head hung loose like a punching bag. More blows flopped it from side to side. Michael felt a spray of mucus, saliva, and blood. He heard an animal growl. It was himself.

Then a hand was on his shoulder. "Michael! Michael! You'll kill him," Vivian screamed.

"Of course. That's what I'm paid for," he spat.

"Please, Michael. Enough! Enough!"

Stepping back, the quartermaster released his enemy. The man collapsed like a sack of potatoes dropped from a truck.

"This way, Michael. This way," the woman said, leading the sailor out of the alley.

Numbly, the quartermaster allowed himself to be

145

led. But he was smiling — a small, hidden smile of satisfaction.

Her apartment was tiny, a studio of one room with a small bath and cooking alcove.

Standing at the foot of the neatly made Murphy bed, Vivian gently fingered Michael's ripped jumper. "You're hurt," she said in a voice husky with concern and exertion.

"Only a scratch," he said, gazing at the girl's ripped blouse and skirt torn to the waist. "And you?"

"I'm all right, Michael. Really. Sit down, Michael." She gestured at a couch. "I'll get you a drink."

"Thanks. I need one."

In a moment, the girl returned from the alcove and her small icebox and handed the sailor a bourbon and soda. She sat next to him. The torn taffeta fell away from her long, slender legs. They were bruised and blood had trickled from a scratch and coagulated on one thigh, staining ruined nylons.

Not even the blood, bruises and torn nylons could impair the classic lines; exquisite turn of her perfect calves and firm thighs. In fact, the abuse had exposed her vulnerability — enhanced her femininity, making her even more attractive. Her waist was tiny and her brassiere white and full and heaving through the torn blouse.

For the first time, Michael felt the full impact of her beauty: high, smooth forehead, vaulted cheek bones, flawless ivory skin like a Dresden doll, wide-spaced hazel eyes and full lips sculpted into a fragile chin. He felt fingers on his cheek.

"Thanks, Michael."

"It was a pleasure."

"It really was?"

"Yes, Vivian. It really was." He saw a milky substance on the inside of her thigh. "He really did it to you."

She shrugged. "He's been trying for ten years."

"He left something on your leg."

"The pig."

"Did he hurt you?"

She laughed. "He didn't get into me, if that's what you mean."

"But he . . ."

"He came, sure. But he didn't get inside me." She sank back on the couch, fingering her leg. "Filth!" And then with her eyes averted and voice thick, "After all that, he couldn't even get it up enough to put it in. He just rubbed it against me until . . ."

"Okay, Vivian. I understand."

She stood suddenly. "Michael, take off your jumper."

"What?"

"You're hurt. I can see the blood."

Raising his arms slowly, Michael felt a sharp pain in his chest as the girl pulled the jumper over his head. "Two small rips," she said, holding the jumper up by the shoulders. "I can mend them on my electric Singer before you can say Jack Robinson." She pointed to a sewing machine in a corner. "Now your skivvy shirt."

Michael raised his arms again as the girl peeled the torn, bloody garment from his body. "Jesus," she said, examining the young man's broad chest, thick neck, and muscular arms. "You are a bull. No wonder your punch was so hard." Michael laughed.

Examining the cut on his chest and the coagulated blood in the mat of hair, she rued softly, "He got a piece of you, too, didn't he? You bled a lot."

"It's nothing."

"Nothing, my eye." She stood quickly, moved to the bathroom. In a moment, she returned with a basin, gauze, tape, and iodine. Quickly, she dabbed at the cut with a washcloth, applied stinging iodine, and then taped gauze over the wound. "There," she said with detectable pride. "I feel better about you now."

"I'll live. It isn't bleeding."

"I know, but you lost a lot of blood, and it could pop open."

Michael's head was light, but he spoke calmly, "I'll let Bryan look at it. For sure, I won't go to the sick bay."

"Why not?"

"They'd confine me. Maybe even hold me for injuring two fine citizens."

She snickered. "I'd better bathe." And then, gesturing at her thigh, "Get Antonio off of me. Then, I'll sew up your jumper and skivvy shirt."

"Good. I don't want the SPs to spot me when I return to Terminal Island. All my clothes are there." And then thoughtfully: "Vivian, why don't you call the police? You were raped."

The girl straightened, face crossed by sudden gusts of anger, her hazel eyes narrowing, her lips slashed down into hard lines. "Rape? Are you serious?" she asked, incredulously.

The young sailor was startled by the transformation. "You were attacked," he countered defensively.

Her laugh was bitter, voice vapor off dry ice, "Do you have any idea what the cops would do to me if I reported a rape?"

"And an assault," he added, gesturing at her torn clothes.

"Yes, and an assault." He looked at her expectantly. She sighed, and the hard look eased into one of resignation, but there was still vitriol in the timbre of her voice. "First, the cops think all waitresses are whores."

"But, Vivian . . ."

She waved him to silence and pointed to her short skirt, ran a hand over the remnants of her low-cut satin blouse where her big silky-white breasts bulged above her brassiere like half-moons. "They'd point to my clothes and say 'You asked for it. Showed your tits, wiggled your ass in front of 'em until they could sniff your pussy.' "

148

Michael was shocked by the girl's rancor, her choice of words that could usually be found only in the mouths of sailors.

She raced on, voice cutting with the razor-edge of sarcasm, "And then they'd make cracks about how it was. 'Did you like it? How was he hung? A sweet-pea or a cucumber? How many times did you come?' Then they'd laugh, suggest they could do better." She punched a cushion with a tiny fist. "Fat-assed, horny, stupid sons-of-bitches."

"I can't believe it."

"Better believe it. It's happened to two of my girlfriends."

"The cops did nothing?"

"To the cops, both of my friends were the perpetrators, not the victims. They almost got raped again in the police stations."

"Christ, great world we're fighting for."

She took his hand and her voice softened. "And Michael, you're worried about the SPs finding out about this. You've got to remember, we *can't* let the police know about any of this, either."

"What do you mean?"

"You really hurt Pepe and Antonio. It's true—you might be arrested for beating up those two fine citizens. The law always protects the bums."

The sailor ran a finger over the end of his chin. The stubble was like the short bristles of a brush. "I guess you're right," he agreed.

"A woman's got to be murdered before those bastards do anything." She smirked. "And then it's a trifle too late."

Silently, he drummed his nearly empty glass with restless fingers, swirled the contents and studied the sloshing, peaking liquor while his mind sifted back to something he had heard in the alley. "You've known Antonio for ten years. I heard him say so."

"Since high school. Antonio Lopez is his name. We

149

graduated in the same class." She tossed off the rest of her drink. "I think you hurt both of them badly."

"They won't be shooting off those big mouths for a while."

She stared at the wall, troubled. "You were going to kill him," she mused.

"Yes," he said matter-of-factly.

"Training? the war?"

"No! No! Not at all." He drained his glass with one gulp. "It's not that at all. It's just that he had it coming — came at me with a knife, earned it." He shrugged. "That's all."

"I can't disagree." She rose and recharged Michael's glass but did not seat herself. "I've got to bathe." She waved a hand the length of her body. "I feel foul." Michael nodded and sipped his drink.

Within twenty minutes, the girl had bathed and dressed in a tight white chenille robe. Then at her insistence, he crammed his large frame into the tiny bathtub. He could hear her working at the sewing machine while he gingerly washed around his bandages, removing the blood that had run down his stomach and abdomen. Then, dressed only in his shorts and trousers, the quartermaster sat on the couch with his third highball. Vivian sat next to him, nursing a recharged glass.

Vivian's bitterness seemed to have been drained away with the bathwater. Slowly and haltingly she told him of Vicki and Joe Centinero. How Joe and her own husband, Craig, a gunner, had been in the same squadron in England. The fascination with music. Michael's amazing resemblance to Joe. How she had suspected Vicki was slipping.

He had heard enough of Vicki and Joe. The tragedy left him depressed, his stomach churning queasily to the point of nausea. He began to push himself to his feet.

"No! Please!" She grabbed his arm. Pulled him down. "Stay. Stay, please stay." There was near-panic in her voice.

"Stay?"

"Yes. I can't bear the thought of being alone—not tonight."

Michael sighed. Then, for the first time noticed two small pictures of a soldier on the mantel of the artificial fireplace. Young, with wispy blond hair and a scattering of freckles, he grinned down at the couple. "Your husband?"

"Yes. That's Craig."

"The Eighth takes heavy losses."

Fear crossed the girl's face like the shadow of a squall. "Please, Michael—don't."

The quartermaster felt an amalgam of anger and self-loathing at his cruel gaffe. "I'm sorry. I didn't think," he pleaded. He studied the boyish face on the mantel. "You'd have me stay the night?"

"I can't bear the thought of being alone." Her voice was tremulous.

"What about Craig?" he asked, stabbing a finger at the photographs. "They're shooting at him."

"I've been true. Lord, I've been true. They even call me 'Vivian the Virgin.' But after what Antonio did—I can't bear the thought . . ." Her voice trailed off into sobs.

Placing a hand on Vivian's trembling shoulders, Michael felt the full force of the girl's sexuality—a force that contracted his chest and lungs, taking his breath, causing a prickling of hair on the nape of his neck and sending a stinging warmth to his skin and cheeks that spread like burning oil on water.

But Craig stared down relentlessly like Joe Centinero did at Vicki's. Maybe Craig was dead, too. Tapping his forehead, Michael cursed his luck. Twice he had been subjected to this cruel punishment. Joe Centinero was dead and Vicki was mad. And here he was with another Air Corps wife who could be an Air Corps widow at any moment. The bed waited and Craig stared.

Slowly and with the girl's hand on his arm, he came to his feet. "My jumper?"

The girl stood very close. "I'll sleep on the couch," he said.

"Something might happen. I can't do that to him and I don't care how corny I sound."

"Joe Centinero?"

"And all of the others, Vivian. All of the others. There's something rotten . . ." Suddenly, the room moved and Michael sat heavily. "Jesus, I didn't think I'd lost that much blood," he said, bewildered and palming his forehead. "I don't understand."

"That settles it, Michael. You've got to rest for a while." Carefully, the girl led the quartermaster to the bed.

With a sigh, he sank back on the firm mattress. Slowly, like a cat settling for a nap, the girl followed, wrapping an arm around the young man's waist and snuggling her head against the curve of his neck.

"Now, relax, Michael. Relax."

Sighing unevenly, Michael put his lips to the girl's forehead. "Yes, Vivian — relax."

He moved his eyes. Craig was still there.

The next morning Michael hitchhiked to the base early. After chow, he returned to his barracks with Bryan. There, seated on his bunk, he told the pharmacist's mate about the previous evening: his fight with the zoot suiters, the night with Vivian and Craig.

"Craig Johnson," Bryan said, nodding. "Jesus, Michael, just like Joe Centinero. How do you find such luck? I can't believe it." And then carefully, "You stayed all night?"

The Latin felt a pulse of contentment. "She's still Vivian the Virgin. She's not looking for a strange piece of tail. I slept — that's all Bryan."

Bryan released his breath audibly. "I never thought

I'd be happy to hear my buddy passed up a piece of ass." And then his voice deepened with concern. "According to scuttlebutt, one of those zoot suiters died and the other has a broken jaw, cheek and nose."

Michael spluttered, "Dead?"

"Yeah. Bled to death. His arm was almost chopped off." He hunched forward. "No clues, though."

"Insanity!"

"What do you mean?"

"Over a year in the Solomons and I never saw a single, live Jap. All that fighting and killing and I didn't hurt a soul."

"I don't understand, Michael."

"I mean, I never killed anyone. I had to come back here and do it in an alley." He tapped his temple with a closed fist. "Does that make sense?"

"No. And don't look for it or you'll go nuts."

"I've committed murder, Bryan."

"According to the law, yes."

"But in the Solomons I could've been decorated for doing the same thing."

"I got the Navy Cross for killing six men with one burst."

"But if you'd killed them here, you'd be a criminal."

"There you go trying to be logical. Don't you understand? Murder is a function of geography. So, don't kill anyone this side of the one-hundred-eightieth meridian."

Feeling a sudden weakness, Michael lurched.

Bryan put a hand on his friend's shoulder. "Hey, mate, you're hurt. Let me see that wound."

"I'm okay."

"Bullshit! Let me see it."

Assuring himself that the barracks was deserted, Michael removed his jumper and skivvy shirt. Bryan whistled as he examined the wound. "Clean, but it should be sutured."

"Not here," Michael said.

153

"Of course not. There's a doctor named Woolsey near the A-One Bowl. I've seen his shingle."

"Know anything about him?"

"No. But the job is simple. I could do it if I had the sutures and equipment."

"Let's go."

Doctor Hubert Woolsey was a short, round, middle-aged man with shining pate and sagging jowls. He marveled at the wound's cleanliness and antiseptic dressing, and in less than fifteen minutes it was stitched and the patient dismissed. However, the boys were enraged when the receptionist—a young blonde with large, flirty eyes—presented Woolsey's bill for seventy dollars.

"That's nearly a month's wages," Bryan roared, shocking the receptionist and an office crowded with patients.

"What do you expect?" Woolsey asked, hearing the uproar and entering hastily from his examining room, stethoscope dangling over his white smock. "Suturing is highly skilled work."

"It took you ten minutes," Michael shouted. "That's seven dollars a minute."

"That's right," Bryan agreed. "Killing Japs is highly skilled work, too, and we do it for pennies."

Every eye was on Woolsey as he flushed and sputtered. "You can't expect something for nothing."

"We didn't come back to be robbed," Michael said.

Woolsey turned to his receptionist. "Take whatever they'll pay." And then to the sailors, "Don't ever come back!" He returned to the examining room.

Michael stared at Bryan. "I'll give him a day's pay."

"Four bucks?"

"Three-eighty."

Carpelli turned to the receptionist and handed her four one-dollar bills. "Three-eighty for his surgical

154

skills and a twenty-cent tip."

"Tip?"

"Yeah. For the thread."

The sailors laughed as they left.

"Pricks," Michael said, sipping his drink in the bar of the A-1 Bowl. "The whole medical profession."

Studying his glass, Kohler said contemptuously, "You won't find philanthropy there."

"Greed."

"That's the name of their game, Michael. They'll steal anything they can get their hands on. Phony diagnoses, fake tests, useless x-rays. Anything to run up bills."

"What are we fighting for?" Carpelli asked rhetorically. "Thieving doctors, profiteering contractors, bums who rape and try to kill us in alleys?"

"I've been screwed by barbers, tailors, and bartenders," Bryan said angrily. And then, thoughtfully: "Maybe we just fight for each other, Michael."

"And that's it? Not for country? Not for democracy, God, and all that other shit?"

"Well," Kohler added, his gravity eroded by a sly smile, "there's always pussy."

"For sure! For sure!"

They both laughed.

Bryan walked to the bar, returned with fresh drinks. He studied his friend and spoke softly. "Marilyn told me we can't see Vicki for a while."

"Damn!"

Bouncing an ice cube with a single finger, the pharmacist's mate hastily changed the subject. "Have you heard the latest about the *Arizona?*"

"Why do you bring her up? She's still on the bottom of Pearl."

"Because the navy's still promoting the story about the wonder bomb that dropped down her stack."

155

"And set off her forward magazines. That never did make sense. No one believes it."

"Civilians do," Bryan countered. "But I got the real poop from Schultz." He hunched over his drink. "Eleven hundred guys are dead because some lazy gunnery officer stored two tons of black powder on the second deck. The Nips were dropping finned fourteen-inch shells. One penetrated and . . ."

"That figures," Michael said, bitterly. "But the navy adapts—it's inventive."

"What do you mean?"

"Next, they'll invent the super bomb that penetrated six decks and set her off."

"Probably. When this story wears off. The civilians would believe it, Michael." Sighing, the pharmacist's mate sank back. "Would you believe I've been assigned to the Two-Four-O-Four?"

"No. Not before your leave's up."

Bryan drained his glass and then slammed it to the table. "I volunteered."

"Oh, shit. Why?"

"You ask me why, Michael?" The tone was incredulous.

Carpelli bit his lip as Kohler continued. "We don't belong here, Michael. We're foreigners." Eyes gleaming, the pharmacist's mate hunched forward. "The oh-four needs a QM deuce, Michael."

Michael laughed. "I'll get in line. Take a number."

Bryan rocked with laughter. "Come see my mother tonight. She'd like to see you."

"Tomorrow night, Bryan. I've got to see Kristie and my mother. Mom doesn't work tonight. I promised to stay with her."

Bryan nodded. "Okay, tomorrow night. And remember the Two-Four-O-Four. Picked crew, you know."

"Picked my ass."

They both laughed.

"Check with the assignments officer, Michael."

156

"Maybe. Maybe."

"And Michael. They did find a dead zoot-suiter."
Michael nodded silently.

Kristie's Majestic superheterodyne radio festooned with flashing lights and cyclopean dial reminded Michael of a pinball machine gone mad. Squatting in a corner, it dominated the Wells's living room arrogantly like a temple carving of a Hindu devil.

Monday night was sacred. This was the evening for the *Lux Radio Theater.*

Seated on the couch with Kristie while Desmond Wells and Brenda slouched in easy chairs, the quartermaster sank back, unable to ignore the booming voice of Cecil B. DeMille as the producer introduced the night's production, "Men in White," starring Spencer Tracy and Virginia Bruce.

Although Michael had been brought up on radio, he resented the intruder who commandeered an entire household. Yet, he too, was a creature of the electronic monster. "The Lone Ranger," "Phantom Pilot," "The Shadow," "Fibber McGee and Molly," "Duffy's Tavern," "Evelyn and Her Magic Violin," "Jack Armstrong, the All-American Boy," Eddie Cantor, Jimmy Fidler, Fred Allen, Jack Benny, Burns and Allen, and scores of others had shared his meanest rooms, bringing distraction from the horrors of the depression.

But he chafed watching Kristie, the aspiring actress, ignore him, spellbound, as Hollywood's fantasy enveloped her. He knew she had dreams of the silver screen, of acting like Bette Davis and Josephine Hutchinson. Even of someday appearing on the *Lux Radio Theater.* He felt rankled but remained silent as the drama unfolded.

An hour later, a bored Michael and misty-eyed Kristie rose, hand-in-hand. "Spencer Tracy is so romantic," she sighed.

"They'll do 'The Thin Man' with William Powell and Myrna Loy next week," Brenda said. "Why don't you come over, Michael?"

Michael said, "I'm not sure I can. My leave will be up and I've been assigned to a ship."

"Oh, no," Kristie gasped, hand to mouth. "So soon?"

"I've no control," Michael lied. Then firmly: "They need me."

Before Michael could be dragged into a conversation with her parents, the young girl pulled the sailor through the door, muttering, "Let's go for a walk."

"Be home early," Brenda protested. "You have school tomorrow."

As the couple walked hand-in-hand, Kristie spoke. "They'd send you out there again, Michael?"

"It's the job Kristie. It's not finished."

"You love it," she said rancorously.

"Love it?" Carpelli asked, shocked. "You sound like my mother."

"The sea, I mean. Not the war."

Michael thought for a moment, wondering about the girl's words. There had been afternoons on the sub-chaser when he had sat on the hatch of the lazaret staring over the stern eagerly, watching row after row of humped-back swells overtake the ship like brooding, forbidding mountains, raising her like a kite on a thermal and spinning her screws furiously on the front slope while slowing them on the back as the tiny ship tried to slide backward. Then there were days when the wind whined through the rigging and whipped the halyards, ripping the top from the chop in lacy sheets like torn bridal lace, and a man's tongue found salt on his lips.

And there were the quartering seas that lifted the ship's stern while the bow crashed down, sending the shock of thunder through the hull, snapping the mast like a green stick and throwing up spray in long tattered banners as high as the bridge. The drowned exhausts gurgled on one beam and barked on the other while firing spray that rainbowed in the tropical sun.

He had found that the sea had its own sky. This was the big country. Nothing crowded a man's eyes here. In fact, a quick turn of the head even revealed the earth's curvature.

And steaming after the sunset, one found clouds and sun giving a show Cecil B. DeMille could never produce. Stately, immobile thunderheads and fleeing cirrus clouds conspired with a sky of translucent blue to awe a sailor with paintings and sculpture not found anywhere in any museum on earth. Love it? Yes. He probably did. But he would never admit it.

"I prefer being with you, Kristie," he managed, simply.

"Michael." Her tone was querulous. "What's happened to us? You've broken dates—been cool. Is there someone else?"

He felt his stomach tighten as a car's headlights turned into the street. As the car passed, he saw the girl's lovely face clearly—innocent, cheeks pale, blue eyes huge and moist with distress. And Alma, Vicki, and Vivian were there, looming, watching. He had betrayed Kristie as he had betrayed the boys on the subchaser. He didn't deserve them and he didn't deserve her. Steeling himself, he spoke hoarsely, "I've been a son-of-a-bitch, Kristie. I don't deserve you."

The girl stopped in her tracks, "You love someone else! I knew it!"

Hands on her shoulders, he looked down. "No," he answered honestly. "That isn't true. I love you."

The girl had the look of a drowning swimmer grabbing a life preserver. "Then it's all right—all right."

"No, it isn't all right. I—you should be free of me . . ."

"No. I don't want that, Michael. I don't care if there were others. Men need—I mean, I'm a virgin. You want me to stay . . ." He turned away. She tugged at his

159

arm. "Michael, please. This is crazy. You're leaving. Why break up now?"

"Kristie," he cried, whirling to her. "But you know what I've done — what I've been?"

"Yes. I told you. I felt it weeks ago." She kissed his cheek. "My love, you're going back out . . ." She choked.

"Please, Kristie."

"You're going back out there. The worry will begin again. Not knowing if my letters will come back marked 'deceased.' " She bit her knuckle.

"All right," he breathed. "But you owe me nothing."

"If it makes you happy." She pulled him into the darkness of a large ash and raised her face. Her lips were warm, wet, and very hungry.

Ignoring his injured chest, he kissed her fiercely, then pulled away. "These are terrible times, but I'll return."

"Promise." The voice was a tiny whisper.

"With all my heart."

Sighing, she placed her head against his cheek, "Promise me one thing more, Michael."

"Name it."

"Don't volunteer. Don't volunteer for anything."

He smiled — a slow, ingenuous smile. "Of course." And then quickly: "I've got to leave, Kristie. It's my mother's night off and I promised to be home early."

He kissed once more — long, hard, and passionately.

Throughout his life, Michael Carpelli tried to forget the look on his mother's face that night when he told her he was returning to sea.

"Why? Why? Michael. They almost killed you the last time. You've done enough."

Despite a burning in his chest, Michael managed to conceal his injury, and tried to hide the truth from his mother. He spoke quickly, "I have no control, Mother. I

160

do what I'm told to do. And the Two-Four-Oh-Four is a small patrol craft. A PCS. We'll probably only see coastal duty."

"Which coasts?" Maria responded, bitterly. "The subchaser was small, too. Don't give me that bullshit again." She narrowed her eyes, probed with uncanny perception. "Did you volunteer?"

Shocked, Michael sputtered, "Why no—of course not." The lie flushed his face.

"You hate the war?"

"Of course . . ."

"But you'll go back."

"There's no choice, Mother."

Her jaw tightened. "That isn't it and you know it, Michael."

"No, I don't," Michael retorted warily.

"Yes, you do." She struck home. "Killing makes you a man, doesn't it. And you don't even have to pull the trigger yourself. Just being there is enough, isn't it?"

Michael felt as if his soul had been bared. "No, Mother. No!"

She raced on. "You've found a place where you belong—a home your no-good father and I could never give you. And you've escaped from the depression." She waved a hand vaguely at the nondescript furniture. "It's your friends. First it was Wally, Ernie, Dale, and Max. And now it's Bryan, Lindsay, Schultz, and the rest. You can't turn your back on them if it kills you. Isn't that right Michael?" A tear streaked her cheek.

Galled by his mother's insights and worn by her intransigence, the quartermaster pounded his temple with a balled fist. "Please, Mother. I don't know. I just don't know."

She dabbed at her cheeks with a handkerchief. "Promise me one thing, Michael."

"Anything, Mother."

"Don't volunteer anymore."

"Volunteer?" He chuckled. "I just heard that from

161

Kristie."

"I don't care who you heard it from. Give me that one thing—one thing, to know my son won't volunteer." She looked deep in his eyes, her eyes huge and liquid, black as the bottom of a grave. "I don't want that insurance—that ten-thousand dollars when you're . . ." She trailed off, choking back tears with her hand.

Slipping his arms around his mother, Michael whispered in her ear, "Of course, Mother. I promise. I won't volunteer for anything."

Four

"By bushido is meant perceiving when to die. If there is a choice, it is always preferable to die quickly. There is nothing else worth recording."
Hagakure ("Under the Leaves"), the classic manual of samurai conduct.

> This is a journey
> With no return
> Wholly drenched
> Is the island of tears
> > Lieutenant Takeo Nakamura, June, 1944

> Keiko, a camelia
> In full bloom
> I long for her
> Far away
> Lost in the mist of time
> > Lieutenant Takeo Nakamura, June, 1944

"Sir, I volunteer myself and my company as reinforcements for Aguijan Island," Lieutenant Takeo Nakamura said, bringing his six-foot frame to bent attention in the low-ceilinged, crowded bunker.

Admiral Nagumo's leathery, lined face was broken by a sad smile. "You are a fine son of the Mikado with strong karma," he said, lowering his binoculars and turning from a gun port. He continued, "My last patrol craft was sunk this morning."

Nakamura bruised his knuckles on the rough concrete. "But Lieutenant Isobe is dead," the young lieutenant persisted.

"Yes, true, Nakamura-san. He and twenty of his men died gloriously for the Emperor, honoring their *hachimachi* headbands." The old admiral nodded toward a group of communications men manning phones and radios. "According to the reports, a small vessel took them by surprise, almost rammed the island. They used the sun cleverly — fired high velocity shells right down the throat of the cave."

"The Americans will take it, sir."

" 'When in doubt, choose death,' " the old man said, quoting an ancient maxim from the *Hagakure*. "I am confident the garrison will make a judicious choice." He gestured to the east. "We only have a dozen barges in Tanapag Harbor and we need them."

Moving to a port, Takeo raised his glasses. Focusing to seaward, he saw enemy fire-support ships which fired leisurely salvos, puffing flame and smoke like old, gray dragons. It had been a hard campaign. Ignoring losses, American marines had attacked with abandon, pushing the defenders off of Mount Tapotchau, north up the spine of Saipan toward Marpi Point and a series of ridges above Tanapag Town and the harbor. Japanese commanders had reacted with the usual reckless counterattacks, squandering the lives of their men like drunken gamblers throwing away chips.

Despite the sacrifices, the Japanese were forced back slowly, always maintaining an unbroken army front. They still had most of their artillery, but the majority of their armor — 25 Chi-Ha Type 97, medium tanks — had been lost in a single charge against Charon Kanoa. American anti-tank guns and a new weapon they called "bazooka" had opened the Chi Has like fish tins. The crews had been massacred. Only two tanks escaped.

Takeo liked the new bunker better than the old wrecked observation post on Tapotchau. Just below the crest of a ridge and on the northern slope of the mountain, the new,

164

large bunker was a true command post. The walls of the bunker, itself, were made of concrete four-meters thick, reinforced with thirty-millimeter steel rods. It interconnected with a storage area for rice and dried vegetables — which were almost exhausted — a small medical aid station, sleeping chambers, and even a small kitchen. The entire complex was perfectly camouflaged with small trees, shrubs, and rocks scattered about on the surface in natural patterns. The 180-degree view was to the west, where Garapan, Tanapag Harbor, and the American anchorage were clearly visible.

Shifting his glasses to Tanapag, Takeo Nakamura saw a shallow harbor choked with the superstructures of dozens of sunken ships. Some still burned. An ideal anchorage, on the south the harbor was sheltered by a long narrow neck of land called Mucho Point, while to the north protection from the sea was given by a thin, sparkling white reef which ran in nearly a straight line east and south for several kilometers, terminating in a small island called Manigassa. Here a "sleeper" battery of 120-millimeter guns was emplaced. The young lieutenant knew the Yankees could never use the harbor while the battery commanded the entrance.

He returned his glasses to the jungle of wrecks and found a large freighter with a fieldpiece mounted on its stern on a circular platform. Turning quickly, he spoke to General Saito, who hunched over a map table with two aides. "Sir, may I suggest manning some of those wrecks close to the channel with snipers?" Nakamura stabbed a finger in the direction of the harbor. "They could interdict any vessels slipping past our battery on Manigassa and enfilade the marines on Mucho Point."

The old soldier looked up thoughtfully and then moved to an embrasure, raising his binoculars. After studying the harbor for a moment, he turned to Nakamura. *'Ronins'* work, but an excellent idea."

The old general shouted at a young lieutenant — one of a half-dozen communications men manning four radios and a bank of field telephones. "Lieutenant Yamaoka.

165

Call Forty-Third Division. I want Commander Sachiko Matsushima."

Bent, with sunken cadaverous cheeks and chest and stomach hollowed to ribs and hipbones by dysentery, the young officer turned to one of his men and rattled an order.

Admiral Nagumo whirled, snarling. "Matsushima is one of mine!"

Nakamura feared another clash between the two old warriors. But General Saito put the young officers' fears to rest with flawless logic. "Matsushima has a full company of naval personnel. This mission calls for men with shipboard experience."

Sullenly, Nagumo nodded his approval and turned to a gun port.

Takeo knew there was more to the assignment than experience. Matsushima, tall like Nakamura and as thin as a bamboo stalk, had been born in Corvallis, Oregon, but had earned his degree at Tokyo University, putting him in the ranks of thousands of other *kibei* — Japanese born in America and educated in the homeland. Held in contempt by the armed forces, these men were invariably given the least desirable assignments. Matsushima was about to receive his.

There was a commotion. "General!" one of the communications men shouted. "Intelligence reports the Americans have taken Hill Two-Three-Zero — Hagi Ridge."

"In what strength?" the old man asked, voice edged with alarm as he moved to the map table.

"Company strength, sir."

Drumming his fingers, the old man leaned over the map. Takeo moved to the table and stood between Admiral Nagumo and General Saito.

"My barges! We must counterattack immediately," Nagumo said, staring at Saito.

"Yes, Admiral. If they hold that ridge, they can cut us off from the harbor."

A short, squat major with the physique of a Buddha, incongruously wearing polished brown cavalry boots, stabbed a finger at the map. "My battalion could push them off, sir. We are in ideal position now, on the next ridge, Hill Two-One-Zero."

Takeo eyed the cavalry officer, Major Masomichi Noyori. The squat, powerfully built man's tanned face matched the leather in his boots. His was as unreadable as that of the Buddha he resembled. And there was steel in him; his command of himself and those around him told Takeo he was in the presence of a soldier.

Still, Takeo disliked the man. It was well known that in 1937 as a troop commander in the Fourteenth Cavalry Division, Noyori had not only allowed his troopers to run wild in the Chinese capital of Nanking, but had actually raped a woman in full view of hundreds of soldiers and then rammed a bayonet up his victim's vagina, pulling up and gutting her from groin to chest. Takeo felt revulsion at the killing of the woman, but that was not the point. Although her death, the massacre of tens of thousands of other 'Pake,' the burning, the looting were unimportant to the Imperial Army, criticism in the world press was. The army had lost face. That was unforgivable.

The major spoke in a crater deep voice. "Tonight, sir. Just after sunset. Americans hate to fight at night."

"No," Saito disagreed. "They will dig in, reinforce. We must attack now. Let them feel the full fury of the Thirty-First Army."

Nagumo's solitary voice rang through the bunker. "Banzai! Banzai!"

Animosity forgotten, the two old commanders bowed to each other while the other men remained silent.

Takeo looked away, baffled by the fantasy world in which the old men sought refuge. The Thirty-First Army was a myth. At best it was a corps with two basic units—the Forty-Third Division and the Forty-Seventh Independent Mixed Brigade. Both units had been bolstered by odd companies and battalions composed almost entirely of survivors of submarine attacks. In fact, on 6 June the last convoy had arrived—two ships out of an original seven. Thousands had died hideously in the attempt to run the

167

submarine blockade. Only 2,600 men landed, with most of their equipment and ammunition on the bottom. The two transports were promptly sunk by dive bombers.

Casualties had been heavy. Two weeks of fighting had reduced the original force of 32,000 men to about 20,000. Nevertheless, Saito still spoke of his Thirty-First Army. Nakamura ground his teeth in frustration.

Major Noyori's voice penetrated Takeo's torment. "I am short a company commander, General."

Nakamura had found a straw. A chance for action on the field. He could shed the chains of liaison between the two senile old men. The lieutenant whirled. "Please, General," Takeo said so loudly all heads turned. "My company is in reserve. You denied my request to reinforce Aguijan. For two years, I have been assigned to a company, yet I have done nothing but staff work. Please General — please Admiral, grant this one request. Allow me the privilege of serving the Emperor as I have been destined. Let me die as a samurai, not hiding in a hole like a mole."

Nagumo bit his lip.

Saito's face darkened. "Very well," he said. "I speak to you as an old friend, Takeo-san, an old friend who has known you since Rabaul." He sighed. "You have earned it."

"Thank you. Thank you," Takeo said joyfully.

Nagumo spoke to Takeo, concern adding new wrinkles to the serrated face. "Do not seek your battlefield death on Hagi Ridge, Lieutenant. Of course, if the gods claim you, you are theirs." Shrugging, he turned his palms up in a gesture of finality. "But, I order you, do not use this attack to seek *seppuku*. At this moment, I need you more than the gods."

The reference to ritualistic suicide brought a glint to Nakamura's eyes. "You have my word on my ancestors, Admiral."

Saito stared at his watch, then turned to Noyori and said, "We attack as soon as I can establish an order of battle."

Noyori nodded. "Armor, sir? Artillery?"

Innervated by the scent of battle, the old man's eyes

burned, and he shed the traces of senility like a butterfly breaking free from its chrysalis. Even his voice showed new energy and he spoke like a businessman filling orders for a factory manager. "I can give you our last two Chi-Has."

"Artillery?"

The old general turned to his artillery officer, Captain Tamon Yoshikawa. Yoshikawa sat before a grid map next to his spotter, Sergeant Hajime Tomonaga, who squinted through his huge, range-finding binoculars. The captain wore a sling on his shattered right arm, the sergeant had head and ribs bound with dirty white bandages. Both had been wounded the first day when a fourteen-inch shell had demolished the command bunker on Mount Tapotchau. As was true of most artillerymen, both were hard of hearing. In fact, Captain Yoshikawa's last vestige of hearing seemed to vanish after the shell hit. Neither had missed a day of duty.

Studying his grid map and stabbing with a pencil, the artillery officer said loudly, "I can range Hagi Ridge with most of Forty-Seven Division artillery. Four batteries of seventy-millimeter howitzers, six batteries of seventy-five millimeter field guns, two batteries of one-hundred-twenty-millimeter dual purpose and four two-hundred-millimeter mortars."

Saito's voice filled the chamber, "Our Whitworth-Armstrongs at Magicienne Bay?"

"Both destroyed this morning."

"Sacred Buddha!"

Major Noyori interrupted. "American artillery?" he shouted at the hard-of-hearing artilleryman.

All eyes were on Captain Yoshikawa as he thumped the southern tip of his grid map. "One-hundred-fifty, one-zero-five and one-five-five millimeter pieces still here in their artillery park."

Everyone nodded silently.

Noyori spoke, "Their counterbattery fire will stop us in our tracks."

"Not if they are turned the other way, Major," Lieutenant Nakamura said, stabbing a finger at Tinian.

"Of course," General Saito concurred. "I will order an artillery mission from our largest pieces on Tinian. Easy range for our heavies." He glanced at Yoshikawa, who stared blankly.

"Tinian!" the general shouted.

The artilleryman nodded. "Four one-hundred-fifty-millimeter, forty-caliber naval guns and," he smiled slyly, "two six-inch Whitworth-Armstrongs contributed by our British friends at Singapore."

The men chuckled, remembering the early salad days of the Greater East Asia War and the easy conquest of Malaya.

Saito spoke to Yoshikawa, "How long would you estimate it would take the Americans to pull up their trails and respot those one-zero-fives and one-fifty-fives?"

The artillery officer pondered. "The Yankees build cities when they go into battery. Very permanent. Officers' clubs, ice-cream stands. Intelligence claims they even have a radio station there and plan on a theater by the end of the month."

"Kabuki?" Saito jested.

Everyone laughed heartily at the general's quip.

"No, Sir," Yoshikawa continued. "But the Americans have dug their pieces in behind high earthworks. They will be forced to pull their guns out of their revetments to respot."

"How much time, Captain?" There was impatience in the voice.

"Twelve to fifteen minutes for the one-zero-fives, twenty minutes for the heavies."

"Good. You will order a ten minute bombardment of the American artillery park from Tinian. Then our mobile pieces are to be moved. The Whitworths will take their chances in their caves." Then as an afterthought, "Their chances are good. The enemy's fire will be unregistered."

"Yes, sir. I understand, General."

Major Noyori spoke in a troubled voice, "Their fire-support ships, sir. They react very quickly."

The old general scratched the sparse white stubble on

170

his chin. Then, leaning over the grid map, he placed a finger on the harbor. "Our four one-hundred-twenty-millimeter sleepers on Manigassa. They will open fire when Tinian does. They will engage the ships in the anchorage."

Yoshikawa spoke, "They will be doomed, sir. There will be no escape."

" 'There is a time to live and a time to die.' " General Saito said, quoting the *Hagakure*. "That decision will be made for all of us." His eyes moved to Yoshikawa. "You still have a battery of seventy-fives on Marpi Point?"

"Yes, sir."

His face a book of thoughts, the old general's finger returned to the white stubble. "Have it open fire on the American destroyer off the point. This should pull some of their heavy ships north."

"The destroyer has been replaced by a patrol craft."

"Sink it! The *California* and *Tennessee* will react like the forty-seven *ronin*."

The officers smiled wryly at the reference to the classic tale of samurai vengeance.

The old soldier glanced at his watch. Again, the rheumy eyes found Major Noyori. "How soon did you say your battalion could attack?"

"We are dug in behind the Third Battalion. We can pass through at any time, sir."

"Good. The tanks are in reserve behind your front. They are not to warm up their engines. They may attract fire. They are too noisy, anyway. Have them attack as soon as they start their engines." He moved his eyes to the skeletal Lieutenant Yamaoka and the soldiers manning the bank of field telephones. "We will begin our bombardment from Tinian and Manigassa in fifteen minutes, ten hundred hours. Thirty minutes from now, ten hundred fifteen, our guns will begin a bombardment of Hagi Ridge. This bombardment will continue for one half hour.

"Yes, sir," the communications officer said. He spoke rapidly to his men, who began talking into their mouthpieces and microphones.

Saito addressed Major Noyori. "Jump off with your infantry and tanks ten minutes before the bombardment is scheduled to end." He traced a line on the map. "On this axis."

"We may take casualties from our own fire, sir."

"True, Major. But it should be to our profit. We must keep those barbarians in their holes and close with their infantry. Drive in so close — so fast their artillery will not dare counterfire."

"Excellent, sir. We will do it, sir," Noyori enthused. But Nakamura detected a hollow ring — skepticism.

Noyori turned to Takeo. "My company is code named 'Cherry Blossom.' You will lead 'Lotus' Company. They are fine men, all veterans of Manchuko. They have been blooded by our Russian friends. You cannot die in better company."

"I am honored, sir," Takeo said, gripping the *tang* of his sword. Following the major, he moved toward the entrance.

He was halted by the general's shout. "Major! Lieutenant!"

Turning with Noyori, Takeo saw Saito and Nagumo facing a paulownia-wood shrine hanging from the wall. Built much like a tiny flat log cabin with one wall missing, it was crowded with both Buddhist and Shinto icons and talismans. In the forefront was an exquisitely carved golden Buddha that had been given personally to the general by a priest at the shrine at Ise-Shima. Seated in repose, was a finely carved figure of the six-armed Nyōirin Kwannon. Four of his six hands held symbols, including a rosary, the "Jewel that Grants All Desires," a lotus bud and the "Wheel of the Law." The fiercest and largest figure was that of the god of war, Hochiman San. Standing in full armor, he clutched his great sword before him and glared at his enemies with eyes of ruby.

Every man stood and faced the shrine. All bowed and then clapped twice to attract the attention of the gods — odd numbers were considered bad luck.

"Jimmu Tenno," General Saito said reverently, calling on the god who had founded the Imperial dynasty, "I invoke your blessings. Bring success to our arms this day. Let us attack as the tiger, devouring the enemies of the Son-of-Heaven." The voice rose and Takeo recognized the *Hagakure* creeping inevitably into the prayer, "Let us bloom as the flowers of death, always remembering duty is as heavy as Fujisan, death as light as the down of a swan." Grimly, the old soldier turned to Noyori and Nakamura. "Teach the Yankee filth-eaters a samurai does not sleep on logs, eat stones, drink gall," he said, eyes flashing, back straightening. He waved a tiny fist. "Drive the barbarians into the sea!"

A dozen fists were raised and shouts of "Banzai!" and *"Tenno heika banzai!"* filled the bunker.

As the shouts faded, Admiral Nagumo said softly to the young lieutenant, "If you die, Nakamura-san, die facing the enemy."

After bowing and saluting, Nakamura and Major Noyori left the bunker.

The assembly area was perhaps a hundred meters north of the crest of Hill 210. Free of the tangled growth found on most of the island's lowlands, Takeo crouched in a scraggly undergrowth that reminded him of Shikoku's south shore. Looking to his right and then to his left, the young officer felt confidence as his eyes found scores of gray-green-clad infantrymen crouching in their holes, checking rifles, bayonets and grenades. And on the crest he saw Major Masomichi Noyori, standing erect and staring at Hagi Ridge. An Arisaka Type 38 cavalry carbine was slung casually over his shoulder, and he gripped his sword in the precise parade ground angle. Grenades hung from his belt.

Takeo pulled his eight-millimeter Otsu from its holster, checked the eight-round detachable box magazine, palmed the magazine back into the grip until he heard the spring-loaded locking mechanism snap into place, cocked it, set it on safe, and reholstered it. Then he fingered the rings of four Type 97 grenades hanging from his belt.

He disliked the Type 97 grenade. With an explosive charge of only sixty grams of TNT, he deemed it little better than a Chinese firecracker. And the igniter system was complex and slow. First, a two-pronged safety pin had to be pulled, then the head of the striker had to be struck against a solid object — boot, heel, rock, helmet — which drove a firing pin into the cap and lit the fuse. Then you, supposedly, had four and one half seconds before detonation. However, too often, the contraption exploded immediately or not at all.

Shaking his head, Takeo moved his hand to the hilt of the Nakamura sword. He never questioned the efficiency of this weapon. Lovingly, he ran his eyes over the sixteen-petalled chrysanthemum inlaid on the scabbard with pearl and the sixteen diamonds glistening back from the stamens like the eyes of deities. The beautiful design always reminded him of his obligations and duties to the emperor. Softly he swore to himself the traditional oath, *"Schichisei Hokoku"* ("Let me die seven times for my Emperor").

Like a bolt, Keiko Yokoi came back, lovely as a cherry blossom, amorphous as a wind-driven cloud. With a curse, he put her out of his mind. A woman did not belong here. Never! Never on a battlefield.

He heard a shout. Major Noyori had descended from the crest. Standing on the battalion's front and waving his sword back toward the enemy, he began chanting an oath that Takeo recognized as a samurai's ancient prebattle liturgy. "I am Masomichi of the Noyori clan. Son of Shojiro who personally slaughtered seven Russian dogs at Mukden before an enemy bullet sent him to the Yasakuni Shrine. My father, Kuribayashi, was an aide to General Nogi and served as his *kaishaku* when the immortal general committed *seppuku* as Emperor Meiji's funeral cortege passed. My life has been useless, only a half-dozen 'Pake' and two Yankees have wet my blade." He stabbed the great curved blade toward the sky. "I, myself, have little personal merit, wishing only to find vengeance as the forty-seven *ronin,* destroying the enemies of the Son of Heaven and sell my life as dearly as possible, leaving my body to rot on . . ."

The harangue was interrupted by a cataclysmic clap of

174

thunder as a battery of howitzers concealed behind the next ridge to the north opened fire. Then, over the spine of the island, the deep rumble of heavies. Still more blasts and rumbles from Manigassa Island. Then a score of sixty-millimeter and eighty-one-millimeter mortars — the artillery of the infantry — began firing from a draw near the bottom of the ravine. Now the air was filled with hissing, warbles, rustles, and ripping canvas as shells of all calibers tunneled through the air overhead.

There was the blast of a whistle, and the major stabbed his sword toward the crest. It was time to move up to Third Battalion's positions — the last stop before the assault.

As a man, five hundred infantrymen rose. Unsheathing his sword, Takeo gestured to his company and shouted into the din. Scrambling over loose rocks and burdened with combat packs, ammunition belts, grenades, canteens, and rifles, Lotus Company followed its new leader.

Takeo's breath came hard and fast — too fast for the amount of exertion. Excitement, that was it. His nose caught the pungent cut of cordite. The sharp smell struck like a liter of saké. An animal pounded at his chest, clawed at his dry throat, burst from his lips as a hoarse, "Banzai!"

Now they were at the crest, crouching in Third Battalion's holes. He and a sergeant tumbled in a hole with the two-man crew of a Type 96 light Nambu. Ignoring the newcomers, the pair tended their weapon like lovers caressing a concubine, the gunner sending a steady stream of bullets up the gentle slope, perhaps three hundred meters, to the crest of Hagi Ridge, while the loader jammed 30-round magazines into the top-loading breech.

Hagi Ridge had become the great volcano Oshima, one hundred meters of explosions, dust, smoke, flames, and smoking rocks and debris flung in every direction by invisible giants.

Takeo felt a surge of spirit. Nothing could live in that flaming maelstrom. And, indeed, they needed all the artillery they could get. Marine firepower was awesome, the Garand rifle was the finest infantry weapon in the world. Semiautomatic, it completely outperformed the Arisaka,

175

while the Browning automatic rifle—it seemed every squad had one—was actually a machine gun that sprayed 600 rounds a minute. Hopelessly outclassed in firepower, the Japanese compensated with *Yamato damashii* (Japanese spirit) and a joyful willingness to die.

"Sir!" the sergeant shouted in his ear.

Turning, Takeo saw the hard, grizzled face of Top Sergeant Koiso Hamaguchi—the second in command to himself. The face was flat, almost featureless, with a stubby nose abused by numberless fists and pounded down to a lump that blended into pockmarked cheeks. His eyes were slits, his pupils cold black beads, and his mouth was a slash chipped into granite.

Hamaguchi spoke quickly, spitting out his words like the Nambu. The voice soothed the animal in the lieutenant's chest. "Your runner, Private Saigo Takamori, is in the next hole, sir." He jerked a thumb.

"Thank you, Sergeant." Takeo raised his head and caught a glimpse of Takamori, a smooth-faced schoolboy who appeared to have rushed into uniform before he was fully weaned. He was very small and very frightened, huddling in his hole like a cormorant caught in the cave of the winds. Takeo would never forget those eyes—brown saucers dipped in clear water.

The pounding of the Nambu was making jelly of his eardrums. He tapped the sergeant's shoulder, gestured, and rolled to the next hole, tumbling in next to the terrified boy. Hamaguchi followed. Takeo tried to shake the bells out of his ears.

Hamaguchi pointed a finger and shouted over the uproar, "We only have one field radio left, Lieutenant. The major has it."

"Thank you, Sergeant. I was briefed." Nakamura glanced at his watch. Ten more minutes. He dropped a hand to his waist and felt his "belt of a thousand stitches." He smiled as he found the talismans his mother had sewn in, believing they would protect him—"Eight Myriads of Deities" and the tiny "Buddha from Three Thousand Worlds." Every man was loaded with tokens, amulets, belts, mementos, and charms. Notwithstanding, many would die.

He wished he had had time to clip nails and hair for his parents. Then, in the event his ashes could not be returned to be buried with his ancestors, his parents could cremate his nails and hair, consecrating them in the family's plot, or better yet, the Yasakuni or Minatogawa Shrines, where he would dwell for eternity with the spirits of countless heroes.

Sighing, he turned his eyes to the tortured hill. The rocky ridge seemed close. Just a short walk in the morning sun. Suddenly he was distracted by a commotion in the rear.

Hundreds of civilians, led by a young girl brandishing a sharpened bamboo pole, poured into the ravine like spilled oil and began racing up the slope. Takeo was stunned. Some carried pitchforks, others scythes, and a few had rifles, but most carried only sharpened bamboo. All were dressed in filthy rags. All wore *hachimachi* headbands and all carried bottles of saké.

Standing, Takeo waved his hands. "Go back! This is no place for you!"

A rough hand whirled him. "Quiet, Lieutenant!" Major Noyori shouted in his face. "Let them come!" He pulled the lieutenant down into the hole.

"They will be slaughtered."

"Fine. They know the barbarians will murder the men and rape the women. Better to improve their *karmas* here and now."

"They are not samurai, Major."

"They are Japanese, Lieutenant, with *Yamato damashii*."

Takeo felt anger well. "I will follow my orders, sir. But under protest."

"Protest all you like, Lieutenant. But we will take that hill with any weapon we have." He waved at the civilians. "They can stop bullets — save our men."

There was a new presence. The girl had dropped into the crowded hole. She lay beside Takeo, breast against his arm. Placing her bamboo spear on the rim, she handed the major her saké. "I am Kimishiko Toyoda." She waved a hand. "These people want to die with you."

She was lovely, delicate as a Kyoto doll with porcelain skin flushed by excitement, wide black eyes like a young deer, and long black hair that tumbled to her shoulders. Her body — clothed in a sleeveless, cotton-padded jacket, work pants gathered at the ankles and the usual wooden clogs — was slender, athletic, yet womanly, the soft curve of her hips and the thrusts of her breast attesting to her newly found womanhood.

After taking a drink, Noyori spoke. "Loyal sons and daughters of Nippon are always welcome." He looked at his watch. "We attack in five minutes. You have the honor of leading, Kimishiko."

"No!" Takeo shouted. "This is madness!"

"Quiet!" Noyori roared. "When this is over, we will settle this at a court-martial, Lieutenant."

"At my request, Major."

Staring at the lieutenant, the girl spoke far too harshly for one who appeared to be so young and innocent. "Madness? What is madness, Lieutenant? We have been driven from our towns, our farms. My father was the mayor of Tanapag Town — they murdered him. And what awaits us? Sanity?" She waved at the sea. "The filth-eating barbarians will kill the men and rape the women. Many hundreds have already hurled themselves from Marpi Point. Is it not better to fling ourselves upon the enemy instead of uselessly dying in the sea?"

"Like samurai," Noyori bellowed, preempting Takeo's objections.

Feeling a deep anger, the young officer turned away. But a new sound penetrated the cacophony of explosions — singing. All up and down the line civilians were mingling with soldiers, drinking and singing, throwing bottles down the slopes to gleam in the sun, becoming mementos that would be found decades later, burned and discolored, to be taken home reverently by grieving relatives.

Gradually, organized singing penetrated the bedlam and Takeo felt a new emotion as hundreds of throats chorused the national anthem, the "Kamigayo," at the marines on the boulder-strewn ridge. "Corpses drifting swollen in the sea depths, corpses rotting in the mountain grass. We shall die, we shall die for the emperor. We shall never look back."

Cheers. "Banzai!"

There was a blast. Takeo felt concussion punch his head with an invisible fist. He turned in time to see a farmer arc through the air. More explosions. Screams.

Noyori shouted in his ear, "American counterfire."

"But the general said they would turn . . ."

"Ha! Senile old fools—both of them." Then he said harshly, "The Americans are professionals. Of course they kept ready—guns spotted and registered." He glanced at his watch. "It is time."

Together, the officers leaped to the rim of the hole, both waving swords. "Banzai!"

"Banzai!" roared back from over a thousand throats.

But the major hesitated, pointing the curved blade, staring at Kimishiko. "Banzai!"

Joyously, the girl leaped from the hole to her feet and raced toward Hagi Ridge, waving her bamboo spear. Shouting, screaming, cheering, waving their weapons the horde of civilians swarmed after her. And Noyori waited.

Howling like devils, the American shells came in, flinging rocks, bodies and parts of bodies in every direction. Undaunted, over a thousand civilians raced into the gentle ravine facing the ridge, covering the first hundred meters in minutes, and began pouring up the slope toward the enemy positions where Japanese artillery still burst. For the first time, through the din, Takeo heard the unmistakable rapid fire of American Garands and Browning machine guns. And a new sound—a gun that fired so fast its bursts sounded like tearing sheets. The first ranks of attackers seemed to be struck by invisible scythes that stopped dozens in their tracks, tumbling them backward in heaps. Some screamed. Others writhed. Most lay still.

"The last are the hardest to kill," Noyori said, quoting an old infantry maxim. He turned to the rear and waved.

There was a roar of engines, a squeak of bogies and a clatter of steel tread and two Chi Has broke through their camouflage netting and wallowed up the slope. Although they were very close, Nakamura had never seen the armor. He almost chuckled at their clumsy, lurching gait. In a moment, the two medium tanks staggered over the crest and moved toward Hagi Ridge like a pair of ungainly steel beetles.

Waving his sword and blowing his whistle sharply, Noyori signaled the battalion and five hundred infantrymen charged down the slope adding their own cries of "Banzai!" "Americans die!" and "Japanese drink American blood! Eat American flesh!" to the bedlam.

With his sword in one hand and his Otsu in the other, Takeo ran at the head of Lotus Company, Sergeant Hamaguchi on his left and a suddenly grim Private Takamori on his right. Following the tanks, it seemed to take an eternity before Takeo reached the bottom of the ravine and began his upward climb.

Dead civilians littered the slope. He felt horror. Death in civilian clothes always seemed more grotesque. More final.

Suddenly, most of the artillery ceased. Now, only the shriek and blast of American shells. Heavy, but not a curtain barrage. One battery. Maybe two of 105-millimeter guns. But it slackened, too. The guns on Tinian. They must be scoring.

The animal in his chest was pounding. But, strangely, not as violently as before. As he scampered and stumbled through loose blasted rubble, his breath was labored, but he felt strong, and his senses had never been more alert.

Now he was halfway up the ridge but could not see the girl and the leading horde of civilians that had vanished into the smoke and dust that shrouded the ridge. And Noyori was far to his left.

He began to thread his way through a thick carpet of the dead. Those who had died instantaneously were strewn casually, arms outflung like broken marionettes. Those who had a few moments of awareness between the wound-

180

ing and the dying had drawn up their legs and arms in the fetal position, hands clenched in tight fists. Somehow, they looked small. Strange, how cadavers always seemed smaller than life.

He entered an area where shrapnel had shredded a large group of people. He felt hot gorge sour in his throat as he waded through gore, splintered bones, ripped and mangled flesh. And the tanks crunched through the carpet, adding to the horror as the steel treads tore through the legs of a wounded woman who howled like an animal. The other crushed an old man's head like a melon. Takeo tasted vomit. Concentrated on the crest.

A sudden breeze cleared the ridge. The girl and a handful of survivors among the boulders were locked in hand-to-hand combat with men in green, camouflage fatigues.

"Banzai!"

The tanks were firing their fifty-seven-millimeter cannons and machine guns. Suddenly, one exploded and flamed like a defective *o-bon* lantern. Bazooka! Then the other lost a tread but kept firing. Then it exploded. The hatch flew open and a burning crewman tumbled out and raced through the brush, a screaming torch.

Takeo heard screams and the staccato barks of Garands and Brownings. His men began to pitch and tumble. There was the unmistakable slap of a ball round striking flesh and bone. Turning, Takeo saw Private Takamori, eyes filled with disbelief, face contorting like a sheet of hot metal struck by a hammer, sink slowly to the ground, a red stain spreading across his chest. Moaning and blowing red bubbles, the youngster rolled to the ground.

The young lieutenant waved his sword, shouted, and was sickened as he stepped on a woman's head. He was almost to the top, but half the company was down. He cursed and prayed. Then he heard Sergeant Hamaguchi's heavy footsteps and felt new confidence. Now he could see an American machine gun. Wedged between two boulders and protected by sandbags, it spit flame toward him, bowling over an entire squad with a single burst.

"Hamaguchi!" the lieutenant screamed, stabbing his

sword.

"Yes, sir. Flank it, sir. Grenades!"

Takeo turned his head and blew two short blasts on his whistle. Instantly, the company went to ground, vanishing as a man behind brush and rocks. Then, with the sergeant behind him, the young officer slithered up the slope on his stomach, working his way close to the crest and to one side of the gun. A few marines' guns actually fired over him. There were only a few, but they were the hardest to kill. No live civilians were visible.

Suddenly, the corpse of a civilian tumbled past him, arms and legs flailing ludicrously in that rubbery, disjointed manner of the newly killed. Then another and another tumbled past, like rag dolls thrown by a petulant child. The marines were pushing bodies out of their way, clearing fields of fire. Professionals. Real professionals.

Now the Browning was in range. Followed by the sergeant, Takeo tumbled headfirst into a shell hole. A big crater blasted by a large-caliber shell, it stank of high explosives. Its pulverized soil was powdery and still warm. An outcropping of rocks near the edge of the crater gave added protection from enemy fire.

The Browning was at least thirty meters to their left. Both men sat a moment to catch their breath and gather strength. Then the lieutenant holstered his pistol, returned his sword to its scabbard, and unhooked a grenade from his belt. Sergeant Hamaguchi was already bouncing a grenade in his hand like a young boy weighing a rock before throwing it at someone he disliked. Both men came to their knees and faced the ridge.

A Garand cracked, dirt spurted, and fragments of rocks flew, raining on the pair. Ricocheting slugs whined and hissed. A marine marksman had them spotted. They would be exposed for a moment when they hurled the grenades. They had no choice.

"Now!" Nakamura muttered. As one, the two soldiers pulled the pins, struck the grenades against their helmets, rose, and lobbed the bombs at the enemy emplacement. The Garand barked off three quick rounds before the pair

182

could drop back into their shelter. Slugs hummed like angry insects. Then two explosions, screams, and the machine gun fell silent.

"Banzai!" Exulting and grinning, Takeo turned to the sergeant. But Hamaguchi did not reply. Instead, seated with his back to a rock, he stared at his stomach and clutched at his abdomen pushing, gray intestines back into a huge hold ripped from hip to hip. It looked as if he had been disemboweled by a sword. Already, a thick pool of blood was spreading.

"Orderly! Orderly!" Nakamura shouted.

"No, Lieutenant," Hamaguchi gasped, lips pulled by pain into a rictus of agony. "Soon I will join my ancestors. The ridge. For the Emperor, sir."

He knew the sergeant was right. Hamaguchi was a dead man. His face was already a ghastly gray, and he was slipping into unconsciousness. The momentum of the attack must be pressed. The Yankees must not be allowed to regroup, to bring up reinforcements. The ridge was within reach, it must be taken now or not at all.

Takeo knew he must rise, lead the charge. Above him, the air teemed with the snapping, cracking sounds of bullets like bullwhips. Shells whistled and warbled. He could hear the shrieks of the wounded, wild with anguish, filled with terror. It was the agony of the world, of gutted creation. Hamaguchi toppled over on his side like a fallen log. Takeo felt frightened and restless, unbearably so, like some form of illness. A deadly tension scraped along his spine like a gapped knife. Hesitation. An instinct as old as mankind froze him. He could not bring himself to leave the sheltering earth.

To no man does the earth mean so much as to the soldier. The young lieutenant felt an atavistic compulsion to press down upon her, dig into her with his fingernails, bury his face and limbs deep in her, safe from the howling death above. The earth was his mother, his sister, his mistress. She sheltered him, held him in her embrace, safe from the annihilation in the bellowing death of battle.

But he had his duty as a samurai and a servant of the

Emperor. Never did the samurai turn his back on battle. Old Admiral Nagumo's admonition came back, *"If you die, die facing the enemy,"* he had said. Bolstered by the ancient maxim and the knowledge that when in doubt the samurai always chose death, he gripped his pistol and sword with new resolve, rose to a crouch, took several deep breaths, and blew a long blast on his whistle. Then, rising quickly, he leaped from the shelter and raced the last few meters to the crest.

Screaming "Banzai!" he jumped over a few rocks the marines had stacked and dropped into the American's position. The first Japanese soldier in, he expected to find bayonets waiting, but, instead, he saw nothing but bodies. Because of the zigzagging alignment of the works, he could only see a few meters in both directions.

The civilians had done their job magnificently. Corpses were everywhere. Bodies in heaps, sprinkled with blasted and chalky loam, covered every square centimeter of the interlocking trenches and holes as far as he could see. Here and there he detected movement and a wounded soldier or civilian groaned or screamed. And Americans were there, their bodies mixed with the civilians. No wonder the hideous slaughter; many of the enemy clutched a new submachine gun. Despite numbness, Nakamura felt anger, knowing the old Arisaka was no match for this kind of firepower.

Thankfully, the artillery had stopped. Takeo nursed the infantryman's hatred for the guns and the men who struck at him with impunity from so far away. But they were forced to cease fire, now unsure of who owned the ridge.

He heard shouts of "Banzai!" and the remnants of his company began to pour into the works. Immediately, his men started to bayonet the Americans, seeking those who might still harbor a spark of life. An occasional scream signaled the dispatching of a wounded man. Eagerly, his troops began pulling rings and watches from the dead.

Takeo stared at the Browning machine gun that he and Hamaguchi had destroyed. He was pleased with the work of the grenades. They had performed much better than he

184

had expected. With one leg of its tripod blown askew, the gun was tilted on its side. The gunner had been hurled back by the blasts, face blown off and one arm gone up to the elbow. The loader was draped over the tilted weapon, head pulled down by the weight of his helmet. The helmet moved and the Japanese officer heard a bubbling moan.

Takeo holstered his pistol, gripped the *tang* of his sword with two hands, and raised the curved blade over his shoulder. The back of the marine's neck was very white, and he could see the vertebrae quite clearly. The sword was his soul, now, his compulsion. It seemed almost as if it were in command, demanding its destiny be fulfilled. Heart pounding, he felt an amalgam of excitement that approached sexual intensity.

He moved to the loader's side and brought the sword up, paused, and then down with all his power. The blade slashed through the air with a soughing, joyful sound, razor-sharp edge impacting the neck precisely between two vertebrae. The finely tempered steel slashed through skin, bone and tissue so easily, it felt as if it had met nothing more than the tissue paper sides of a *hi-matsuri* (fire festival) lantern. The head dropped to the ground and rolled from side to side in the helmet like a potted red cabbage. The body twisted and rolled from the gun. Blood squirted onto Takeo's boots. The deep-down warmth swelled. It was almost like being with a beautiful woman.

"Banzai!" a private shouted, rushing past, hands gripping watches, rings and wallets. One ring was still on a finger.

Turning, Takeo glanced over the American fortifications. They had been very thorough, digging in under rocks and boulders, reinforcing with sandbags and logs. He moved a few meters down the ridge to an area where shell fire had done heavy damage. As usual, plunging fire from howitzers and mortars had been far more effective than the flat trajectories of high-velocity weapons which tended to rip right over the ridge or explode on the front slope. Sides of the works had been caved in by the blasts, splattering dismembered Americans against parapets and rocks. Bits and pieces of flesh, bone, and torn camouflage uniforms were scattered everywhere.

He tripped over a leg blown off just above the knee and caught himself on the side of the trench. His hand sank into soft spongy soil, the pink color of freshly sliced carp. He pulled back in revulsion. An American had been blown to bits and some of his soft tissue driven into the soil.

A sudden movement, a stifled groan jarred him. An American sergeant was sprawled against a boulder, chin resting on his chest. His right shoulder was a scarlet mass of torn tendons, muscles and bone splinters. The right side of his chest had been ripped open. Blood from a ripped scalp streaked his big beefy face and ran down his neck. He was a husky man, bearded and built as square and strong as the boulder he rested against. A Garand was at his right hand. Two dead civilians lay across his feet.

Takeo kicked the weapon aside and stepped close. A corporal, bayonet leveled, raced up, but Takeo waved him aside. The soldier stepped back and watched. Gripping the bloody sword before him, the lieutenant moved to the wounded American's side. Unafraid, the man stared up at the Japanese officer.

Round and gray-green, his eyes were hard and smoked with hate, glinting like the tips of bayonets. His lips skinned back, "We're evicting you, you big yellow-assed Nip bastard," the man spat in a surprisingly strong voice. He raised a hand as hairy as that of a bull gorilla and extended a single finger.

Nakamura felt grudging admiration for the man. Obviously, the extended finger was a sign of respect for his conqueror. The American represented a nation of fighters. While an isolated Japan had enjoyed nearly three hundred years of peace during the Tokugawa Shogunate, the Americans had been fighting incessantly from the moment their state was born and before. So fond were they of killing, they slaughtered each other in one of the world's bloodiest civil wars when their neighbors tired of fighting them and wars were hard to find. And this sergeant was one of the tradition, a warrior to the end. Certainly, he deserved to be treated as a samurai.

Smiling, Takeo replied in the precise English he had learned in middle school, "Welcome to Saipan, Yankee."

The American's eyes moved to the bloody sword. For the first time, fear darkened the big eyes. "No!" he said. He raised the hairy hand defensively and then pointed at the holstered Otsu. "For Christ's sake, if you've got to do it, use that."

"You have fought well—like a samurai. I am going to honor you. You have earned the blade." Raising the sword, there was a contraction of his chest and lungs that left him breathless and he felt the familiar warm tingling begin again.

"No!"

"Banzai!" Takeo brought the sword down in a flashing semicircle. But the marine rolled to his right. Instead of impacting the American's neck, the blade bit into his left shoulder, cutting through flesh and muscle. The tremendous force of the swing chopped through the clavicle, severing the top of the scapula, shattering two ribs and jamming into the sternum. The marine howled. Arterial blood spurted and pink flesh and muscle was laid bare like a slaughtered calf.

Takeo tugged on the blade, but it was firmly wedged in bone. Cursing, he placed a foot on the marine's chest and pulled the blade free. More screams as he raised the blade over his shoulder. The marine twisted his torso and kicked out at the bodies lying across his feet. "Hold still!" Takeo scolded.

He was answered by more screams and the fearful, glassed-over gray-green eyes rolled wildly.

Again the flash of the blade, the happy hum of steel parting air, the impact. This time the cutting edge slashed precisely into the neck, severing the head and sending it rolling across the floor of the trench. Two infantrymen who had been watching shouted, "Banzai!"

Standing erect and watching the spurting blood and the spasmodic jerking of the marine's limbs, Takeo felt very little joy. It had been a sloppy job, indeed. "Why did he not hold still? he asked himself in a soft voice. "He ruined what

187

could have been a magnificent death." He felt disappointment and disgust for the dead sergeant. He had died very poorly. Behind him he heard the infantrymen mumble agreement.

Turning from the corpse, the Japanese officer continued down the ridge, sword ready, stepping carefully over bodies, unexploded grenades and dud mortar shells. He passed two live civilians; a groaning old man rolling on the ground holding a gory hole where his left eye had been and a young boy of perhaps thirteen who leaned against a parapet holding a bloody bamboo spear. The boy appeared unhurt, but he stood as motionless as a temple icon, staring blankly.

Takeo was looking for the girl. The lovely Kimishiko Toyoda. The mayor's daughter. But he could not find her. Nothing moved except his men who were now pulling clothing from the dead marines.

It was shocking. There were very few marines. Thirty. Perhaps forty. Not even a platoon. He looked down the slope with disbelief. It was a garden of hell. Hundreds of dead cut down in windrows with medical orderlies moving amongst them. And the smell. Already, in the hot tropical sun, the pungent odor of death, coating his mouth, his throat. And big blue flies had begun to swarm and feast. Soon the rats would be gorging themselves.

Then he found her. The lovely girl curled into a fetal position with her own spear rammed through her throat. She must have died slowly, horribly. A scarlet pool of blood had spread around her head like the penumbra of the dying sun at sunset. The face was no longer beautiful. Contorted by pain, it had been twisted into a terrible mask of agony.

He tore his eyes from the cadaver and shouted at a sergeant who was pulling leggings from a dead gunnery sergeant, "Major Noyori! Major Noyori? Have you seen him?"

Dropping the American's legs, the man pointed to the rim of the trench. "There, sir."

At first Takeo thought the man was insubordinate — jesting. Then he saw it. A leg encased in a shiny cavalry boot, ripped wiwth a ganglia of stringy red tendrons and flesh draped over the edge of the trench. Flies buzzed.

"Is that all, Sergeant?"

"Yes, sir. Probably an eighty-one-millimeter mortar. Direct hit. On the helmet, sir."

Mutely, Nakamura stared. Then, under his breath " '. . . leaving my body to rot . . .' "

The sergeant turned back to the dead marine.

Lieutenant Takeo Nakamura leaned numbly against the concrete, staring unseeing through a gun port. The torpor and lethargy that strike all men after combat had seeped through his veins, turning his brain to battered jelly, sapping his strength. The blood lust was gone and with it the fierce samurai warrior. Beyond horror, he was just another man who had been pushed to a plateau of such heights his emotions had flaked away like leaves in an autumn gale, leaving him light-headed and unresponsive like a man suffering from the lack of oxygen.

It had come on immediately after he had made his report, avoiding mention of his clash with Major Noyori. The men in the bunker had cheered as he described the advance, the annihilation of the defenders. General Saito had called for saké while Admiral Nagumo led toasts to the emperor with shouts of, *"Tenno heika banzai!"*

Then Takeo had emptied like a punctured balloon, his emotions as dead as the concrete around him. He leaned against the wall, staring blankly through the gun port at the far horizon where a single thunderhead ranged upward in layers of dark colors from blue to purple to black. And lightning flickered like muzzle blasts while thunder rumbled in a supernal cannonade. Even the gods were at war.

The touch of a bony hand turned the lieutenant's head. "Great victory!" Saito enthused, waving his tin canteen cup filled with saké.

Takeo mumbled, "Great, sir."

"Yamato damashii defeated the enemy."

"Yes, sir." Slowly a troubled thought forced its way into Takeo's mind. "I submit myself for court-martial, General." Every man in the bunker turned.

The old man's eyes became slits. "What are the

189

charges?"

"Insubordination."

"Who brings these charges?"

"Major Masomichi Noyori."

"He is dead. Witnesses?"

"Sergeant Koiso Hamaguchi."

"He is dead, too."

"Any other witnesses, Lieutenant?"

"Myself."

The old soldier tossed off the remainder of his saké. "Specifics?"

"I disputed the Major's decision to allow civilian participation in the assault. I carried out my orders under protest. The major pledged to take me before a court."

Saito gestured to an orderly, held up two fingers. In a moment, Takeo held a full cup while the general sipped his recharged drink.

Saito spoke, "To Major Noyori. He had the full, free balls of a hero, not the shriveled walnuts of a coward. May he dwell with the gods." And then raising his cup to Nakamura: "Drink."

Tilting his cup up, the lieutenant felt the heat of the liquor course downward, start a small glow. He drank again.

Saito continued, "It was a costly victory, Lieutenant."

"Very costly." The lieutenant emptied his cup. The orderly refilled it.

"Many samurai entered the Yasakuni Shrine, Lieutenant."

Takeo drank again, felt the warmth spread, his tense abdominal muscles relaxing. "Yes, sir. And civilians, sir." He shuddered.

"Your charges against yourself are serious."

"Yes, sir."

The old man tapped his cup thoughtfully. "I will convene a court at the end of this campaign—entertain the charges at that time." Straightening, the little old man became very military. "Until that time, Lieutenant, you are to carry on with your duties."

Fatigue, shock and the effects of the saké combined to

render logical the ludicrous statement. Every man knew defeat was inevitable and with defeat, death was just as inevitable. But the general had said a court would convene. That was enough. The decision had been made and a small part of a future that did not exist was locked in place.

There was a quick movement of khaki, the flash of a bottle, and Takeo's cup was full again. There was the sudden need for saké. He drank heavily. The others turned away. The floor moved. A concussion. But there was no shell fire. It made no difference. He steadied himself.

His young runner came back. What was his name? He shook his head in frustration and drank. Oh, yes: Takamori, Private Saigo Takamori. The dead all looked alike. Death was democratic. But he had an identity. Thank the gods. He had been so young, he had hardly had time to get used to life. No doubt a virgin. And the mayor's daughter — so lovely, so young, so dead. In a heap with Americans, too. And like the cherry blossom, she had been most beautiful in her moment of death.

Drinking again, he noticed the liquor had no flavor, just a warmth that seeped into his veins and spread pleasantly. The orderly appeared with the bottle.

Leaning to the embrasure, he stared into the failing light of late afternoon. The thunderhead had faded and a solid blanket of cirrus clouds had mackereled the sky, graying it like the corpses that covered Hagi Ridge. And the enemy ships were toys on the flat pewter sea while the ridges below dropped off to Tanapag Harbor, pointing their green fingers at Manigassa Island, where a few palms stretched skyward defiantly. Gulls, free of the hate below, wheeled in a single great flock like litter caught by the southwest monsoon, dropping and pouncing greedily on the refuse of battle. Many corpses were losing their eyes. Takeo's lips found the cup.

Were the gods sated with blood? There had been no firing for almost an hour. Even the enemy's fire-support ships had stopped their bombardment, and the ochre-colored clouds of smoke had long since dissipated in the fresh breeze. It was one of those anomalous lulls in battle which occurred unpredictably and without reason. Silence, a beautiful, hypnotic absence of sound, filled the bunker like a cool viscous fluid, flooding every niche and corner, coating everyone and everything.

On the far horizon he saw a glow, then a glint of light from low cruising clouds. Had he drunk too much saké? Shaking his head, he gripped the port. The declining sun was playing tricks, reflecting light from a low cloud. It was a warm glow — lovely as only nature's magic could conjure in the tropics. Abruptly, the glow became eyes, warm soft pools brimming with love, with desire. He felt a sudden desperate yearning. Keiko Yokoi flooded back from the distant past, filling the pool of his mind. Exquisite with features as delicate as bridal lace, her hair shone with the blackness and sheen of fine lacquer. Vividly, the full lips glowed from his mind's eye, her visage surreal and nebulous as wind driven mist. And he could hear her voice, the soft and gentle sounds of a robin greeting spring. Closing his eyes, he shook his head, but her memory sparkled like a golden butterfly caught in the web of his soul, unable to escape and not really trying.

He had met Keiko Yokoi in August of 1942. A trainee at Shikoku's officer training center at Matsuyama, Takeo had just graduated with Keiko's brother, Seiji, a slender young man with the build of a long-distance runner, the warm eyes of a libertine, and the jaw of a fighter. Seiji was hard to understand and somewhat aloof. Nevertheless, under this veneer, Takeo felt warmth, perhaps need. Slowly, Nakamura learned to like young Yokoi and the pair soon became fast friends. In fact, Seiji invited Takeo to his home to meet his family.

Euphoric with graduation and proudly wearing their lieutenant's rank badges on their lapels and the two blue rings of the commissioned officer on their khaki caps, the pair boarded an old dilapidated bus at the Matsuyama bus depot destined for Uwajima — a crossroads where Seiji's father Makoto was to meet them.

192

Because gasoline for civilian use was almost nonexistent, the old bus had been converted to an exotic fuel consisting of compacted household garbage, coal dust, and oil residue that had been baked into solid bricks. Frequent stops were made as the old driver, limping and cursing, walked to the rear of the bus and hurled more bricks into the bunker. And the road was terrible: worn asphalt filled with potholes and cracked, flaking concrete.

Nevertheless, spirits were high and the passengers, most of whom were farmers, sang patriotic songs and shouted slogans at the two officers and a pair of sailors seated themselves near the front.

Since his childhood, looking north from his home on Tama Shima across the turbulent mist-shrouded Bungo Suido, Takeo had caught glimpses of the gray, mysterious south coast of Shikoku. When the west wind freshened and tore away the mists like ripped curtains of fine silk, the dark mass of the island was visible rearing up like the keel of a capsized ship, dark and two dimensional, like sepia on a *shoji*.

But now he was driving across it wide-eyed as a first-time tourist. He passed through a place typical of every part of Japan he had ever seen, with steep forested mountains, narrow valleys, and tiny plains where every inch of cultivatable land was planted. Inevitably, the crop was rice—the single crop upon which the survival of Japan depended.

As the antiquated bus chugged over the road, which had deteriorated to a mule path, Takeo saw tiny villages with wooden houses crowned with big thatch roofs which he knew kept the inhabitants cool in the summer and warm in the winter. Tall, soaring *sugi* trees clustered around the houses. Scattered randomly were the ubiquitous Shinto shrines and Buddhist temples, each with the upturning roof that reminded the young officer of cresting waves.

Finally, the ancient vehicle exited a narrow pass and entered a long valley bounded by forest-cloaked mountains to the north, east and west, but open to the sea to the south, a vast blue plain flickering and glistening in the sunlight like an endless tray of diamond chips. Houses were scattered among the rice fields, each with its manicured gar-

193

den defined by carefully trimmed hedges.

With a squeal of worn brakes, the old bus lurched to a stop at a roadside shelter marked Uwajima.

"Father! Father!" Seiji shouted, gesturing to a small, round, graying man seated on the high seat of a one-horse cart.

Laughing and with the passengers chorusing the *Komigayo* behind them, the young officers scrambled from the bus.

Despite his dazzling first glimpse of Keiko Yokoi in the main room of the Yokoi home, Takeo managed a stoic exterior when he first met her, her mother, Fumiko, and an unexpected guest, General Shojiro Kobyashi. Although restricted to short steps by her pale blue, richly embroidered kimono, Keiko walked as if moving to music, showing the inherent grace of a fawn as she bowed to the men with downcast eyes. She tried to keep her face an unexpressive mask, but her cheeks were flushed and she brought Takeo visions of a midsummer rose in full bloom. Beauty! He had seen nothing but beauty since Makoto had met them at the crossroads. Riding in the cart, he had felt as if he had known Makoto for a lifetime. Laughing and joking as he prodded the old mare along with a long bamboo switch, the short, husky middle-aged man with streaked ebony hair had seemed youthful as he gestured and talked incessantly to his son and at the same time told Takeo of his family and the valley.

And what a valley. Broad and flat with the typical yellow-red soil of Shikoku, it was a mass of intense green — an emerald mosaic of rice paddies where women in brown pants, printed smocks, and wide-brimmed straw hats hunched over the priceless crops, transplanting seedlings from tightly packed beds to the more spacious rows of the paddies. And water was everywhere; standing between rows, flowing beneath the road through rock and concrete culverts and tumbling down the distant mountains in spectacular, mist shrouded waterfalls.

Staring at the mountains, Takeo caught his breath.

These proud fortresses were many times higher than Tama Shima's Toriyama, soaring so high they seemed to be reaching for the heavens in search of their creators, Izanami and Izanagi. And the northeasterly trade winds added to the spectacle, pushing high-cruising clouds across an aching blue sky, some pausing to cling to the highest peaks like filmy nightcaps. Stands of pine, beech, ash, poplar, and oak cloaked the steep sides in a solid blue-green mass.

They had passed many houses. All were superior to the average farmer's dwelling. Of sturdy wood construction, they boasted auxiliary buildings and meticulously tended gardens. But when Takeo first glimpsed the Yokoi home, he knew he had found the most spectacular. A rambling dwelling, it boasted a gray tile roof and spacious gardens. When he leaped from the wagon and followed Seiji and his father to the front entrance of the large home, he entered a fairy land that surprised with carefully tended terrain of both the traditional "hill" and "flat" gardens. Enclosed by an *ikegaki* — a high green hedge which had been carefully squared off — rocks of varying size were grouped on flat ground raked to symbolize ocean waves. Artfully tiered trees, stone lanterns, a well, and a single stone bridge enhanced the symbolic ocean. And in the tradition of bonsai, lovely dwarf pine and cedar, growing in flat trays and glazed flower pots, were grouped around the building.

When Takeo entered the house, he had been shocked by its spaciousness, the main room at least twelve mats in size. In the Japanese tradition, the construction was of unpainted wood, modular with *shojis* separating living spaces. But the furnishings were expensive and the floors richly finished.

But now, as he stared at Keiko, the beauty of the valley, the mountains, and the gardens faded to insignificance.

With an effort, the young lieutenant tore his eyes from the girl as Makoto introduced him to General Shojiro Kobyashi, who was a cousin to Makoto. The general was thin to the point of appearing emaciated, and his expensive uniform hung from his gaunt frame, unable to conceal the starkness of his physique. His gray-streaked hair was thin, crowning a death's-head face with large brown eyes under thick brows that gave the aspect of holes burned in old parchment.

The general answered Nakamura's deep bow with the expected *mokurei*, a quick movement of the eyes that politely acknowledged the young officer, yet maintained the dignity of superior rank. Stiffly, the general seated himself in the place of honor — a *zabuton* opposite Makoto and in front of the *tokonoma*; a raised paltform with a hand-painted landscape and a vase holding the mandatory three stocks of flowers. Following Makoto's gestures, Takeo sat in the second honored position to his host's left while Seiji sank to the *zabuton* opposite Takeo.

Instantly, there was a flash of expensive kimonos, the feather like padding of *tabi* on wood and Fumiko and Keiko entered, carrying a lacquered box and steaming kettle which they placed on a small serving table next to the men. Slowly and reverently, Fumiko slid the top from the box, uncovering powdered green tea, and with a small bamboo scoop measured out portions into porcelain cups. With studied precision, Keiko poured hot water and then stirred the mixture with a bamboo whisk. Bowing, the women served the men.

" 'Froth of liquid jade,' " Fumiko said, quoting an ancient adage as she handed Takeo his cup.

Completing the ceremony, the young officer bowed, turned the cup's intricate design of cherry blossoms toward his host and tabled it, waiting for Makoto's toast.

Raising his cup, the elder Yokoi quoted an old aphorism, " 'A man without tea in him is not in tune with the universe.' "

The men drank.

The women returned and Takeo was handed a porcelain *sakazuki*, brimming with hot, spiced saké. Looking up, Takeo saw Seiji's mother as if for the first time. He knew Fumiko had to be at least forty, yet her skin was clear, her eyes bright, her lustrous black hair upswept into an elaborate hairdo held in place with jeweled combs. Slender and girlish, her body was sheathed in a wrapper kimono with huge pendant sleeves all done in eggshell blue and brocaded in Meiji period designs. A tight white silk *obi* emphasized her tiny waist.

Beautiful people Takeo thought. *So beautiful*.

Makoto held up his *sakazuki* for the obligatory toast. "The emperor," he said.

Quickly, the cups were drained and Seiji recharged them from a silver server.

"In my youth, I served in Korea with the army, Takeo," Makoto said proudly, staring at Nakamura.

"Where, sir?"

"Near Seoul, Lieutenant. Chasing garlic-eating bandits into the hills and at the same time trying not to freeze to death." He nodded to General Kobayashi. "My cousin has a division in south China."

"The Twenty-Third Infantry," the general said with obvious pride.

"The Twenty-Third, the Minokomo," Takeo mused. "One of your battalions was involved at Chingtao?"

The old officer nodded, looked around for the women who were busy in the kitchen, leaned over the table, and spoke softly but with obvious relish. "We avenged our pilot."

Seiji stirred to life. "Vengeance, sir. I do not recall."

The general held up a hand. "Vengeance that would have honored the forty-seven *ronin*." His eyes narrowed. "One of our fighter pilots parachuted near Chingtao. The next day one of my patrols found him tied to a tree, skinned with his privates stuffed in his mouth." There was a murmur of horror. Kobyashi continued, "I sent a battalion under one of my ablest commanders, Colonel Tohaku Hideyoshi." He drained his *sakazuki*. The silver server flashed around the table.

"Your revenge?" Makoto asked, eyes burning with excitement.

The tone was conspiratorial. "Hideoyoshi nailed the men and boys to the huts with their privates jammed down their throats, let his troops have their way with the women and then nailed them all to the huts."

"Then he burned it to the ground," Makoto said eagerly.

"The next day," the general said, nodding.

"Of course, let them feel the pain," Seiji acknowledged.

"Exquisite," Makoto said, raising his cup. The men drank. "But still, not a very good trade — a village of 'Pake' for a samurai."

"True, cousin. But Hideyoshi solved our problem."

Takeo stirred uneasily. Since his earliest days, he had been taught the necessity for defense of honor and revenge. Always the forty-seven *ronin* were held up as the classic example of vengeance. Still, he felt troubled. "The women, too?" he said tensely.

All eyes turned to Nakamura. "Why of course, Lieutenant," Kobyashi retorted sharply. "They were all guilty and they were only 'Pake.' "

Abruptly, Makoto changed the subject. "Seiji has been assigned to Colonel Kiyono Ichiki's battalion."

"You will be seeing the Solomon Islands, soon," the general observed, turning away from Takeo.

"Yes, sir. A place called Guadalcanal," Seiji said.

The general nodded. "Yes. The Americans have occupied it. Ichiki has the honor of annihilating them." He raised his cup, "As our Yankee friends would say, 'good hunting.' "

Chuckling, the men drained their cups and again the silver server made its circuit.

Makoto turned to Takeo. "You have your assignment, Lieutenant?"

"Yes, sir. I have been assigned to Seventeenth Army headquarters."

The general raised an eyebrow. "Rabaul?"

"Yes, sir."

"Your duties?" Makoto asked.

"Liaison between the army and units of the navy stationed at Simpson Harbor and Blanche Bay." He nodded to Seiji. "I would prefer to serve in the field — meet the enemy face-to-face."

"Banzai! Banzai," Makoto cried, slurring the words.

"Fine *Yamato damashii*." Waving his cup, he spilled a few drops on the highly polished table. "But the navy will soon sweep the barbarians away like a great *tsunami*." He held up his cup. "To Admiral Nagumo and his great victory at Midway. The Yankees cannot last much longer now."

Takeo thought he detected a tightening of the general's jaw while Seiji seemed to find new interest in his cup. The rumors. That was it. Civilians were not aware of the rumors about Midway: four carriers sunk, 4,000 dead, the best air groups massacred, hundreds of horribly burned survivors unloaded at Sasebo, Yokosuka and Hiroshima, closed wards, top secrecy, the press and even survivors giving false stories of a great victory when, according to the rumors, the navy had been dealt a crippling defeat.

Smiling, Kobyashi raised his cup. "To Admiral Nagumo. He destroyed the Yankees at Pearl Harbor and again at Midway, sank the Dutch fleet in the East Indies, and swept the British from the Indian Ocean. Truly, the greatest carrier commander on earth."

The men drank.

Pushing himself to his feet slowly and somewhat unsteadily, Makoto gestured and the officers followed to a room at the back of the house that was actually an attached structure. Kobyashi and Nakamura murmured with delight when they caught sight of a two-meter cauldron filled with hot water. Quickly, they removed their clothes, scrubbed themselves thoroughly with hot water taken from buckets, and then sank sighing into the tub's warm caress.

Oblivious to the men's nudity, Keiko served more saké. But Takeo smiled as the girl seemed to lurk above him and sneak looks when serving the other men, who seemed unaware of the girl's interest.

Because the young officers must depart early in order to catch the returning bus, the bath was reluctantly cut short and the men returned to their *zabutons* in the main room. There Fumiko and Keiko served an elaborate dinner of raw fish, sliced eel on rice, pickled turnips, peppered string beans, fish soup, and a superb *cha-wan-mushi* — steamed custard filled with vegetables and fish. To Nakamura, the supreme dish was a serving of *ume-bo-shi* — blood red pickled plum seed. He nodded to his hostess, pointing to the dish, smiling his appreciation.

Fumiko seemed not to notice. Instead, she punctuated the serving of each dish with deprecatories which were extreme even for the Japanese tradition: "Just common left overs," "Poorly cooked scraps," "Not fit for a Korean," "Scraps of Chinese garbage."

The guests protested, praising the food: "Superb," "Magnificent," "A feast for Amaterasu," and the ultimate, "Fit for the Imperial palace."

But the controversy died as the diners first savored and then began devouring the gourmet feast, filling the room with the clatter of *hashi,* grunts and Makoto's sighs as he consumed *sakazuki* after *sakazuki,* constantly replenished by Keiko.

"Never let the cup be full," Seiji said, nodding to Takeo, quoting the first half of an ancient maxim. "But never let it be empty," he continued, turning toward his father.

"It's never full," Makoto said, raising his *sakazuki* and hiccupping.

The general chuckled. Then everyone's attention turned to the meal and silence filled the room except for a brief, halting, self-conscious exchange between Takeo and Keiko, who sat with her mother at the small serving table.

Scanning the girl's hairdo, a short *okappa* which was worn by most female students, the young lieutenant inquired, "You are a student?"

"At the Matsuyama Women's College," the young woman replied, busying herself with her *hashi*.

"Why that is near my station," he said, concealing his elation. "Where do you stay?"

"I have a room in my Aunt Kyoko's house. It is in Akama."

"Oh, yes. A suburb." The young officer studied his *ume-bo-shi* while Seiji, his parents and Kobyashi appeared not to hear the conversation. Setting his jaw and sneaking a sidelong glance at the lovely girl, the lieutenant pressed on,

"Perhaps, with your parents' permission, I could escort you to the Akakusa-za Kabuki. The two masters Tananama and Ito are doing *The Forty-Seven*."

The two young people stared expectantly at the girl's father. But Makoto, lost in his eighth or tenth *sakazuki*, studied the table numbly.

"Makoto-san!" Fumiko called sharply. "You have been asked for your permission."

"Huh!" Makoto responded, bleary eyed. "Ah, yes—of course. You have my permission, Keiko. You young people should enjoy yourselves—yes, indeed. Enjoy yourselves." He raised his *sakazuki*.

Seated cross-legged on *zabutons* in a box under the balcony of the Akakusa-za, Takeo and Keiko fell silent with the rest of the audience as hardwood *hyoshigi* clacked and a stagehand cloaked in black hauled back the curtain to reveal paper cherry trees in full bloom along a river made of tin. A castle was on one side of the metal waterway while a vast paper and paste rice field occupied the other. Eagerly, the young couple hunched forward as a row of musicians kneeling at one side of the stage began to pluck their *samisens* and a narrator entered his chant, describing the story of *The Forty-Seven*—a romantic tale of vengeance taught to every Japanese before he reached puberty.

Enchanted, Takeo and Keiko watched as the actors appeared and the action unfolded, spilling over onto the *hanamichi*—an auxiliary stage like a runway that extended into the audience.

Kabuki actors had always fascinated Takeo. The deathly white skin makeup highlighted by eerie black lines of mascara and the garish vermillion mouths mesmerized and amused him. Certainly, the dramatic costumes—some weighing as much as fifty kilograms—with wings, horns and even spider legs radiating from the neck—were spectacular. And the *onnagata*—men playing the parts of women—duped even the knowing. Extraordinary performers, they spoke in squeaking falsetto voices, mimicking female mannerisms. In fact, the leading "woman," Haruchiko, was quite lovely.

But soon the action consumed the young officer as he became involved in the familiar tale of Lord Asano of the western domain of Akō who in 1701 as a guest of the imperial court at Edo, was tricked by a scoundrel, Lord Kira, into unsheathing his sword. A mortal breech of etiquette, Asano was compelled to commit *seppuku,* his estates confiscated and his forty-seven samurai relegated to *ronin* — dishonored vagabonds. Cleverly, the *ronin* feigned debauchery and drunkenness until a year had passed, and on the anniversary of their lord's death they fell on Kira and hacked him to pieces. Then, in the finest tradition of *bushido,* the forty-seven committed *seppuku.*

But a romantic fantasy was woven into the tragic fabric. Haruchiko, Kira's daughter, had fallen in love with one of the forty-seven — a young samurai, Onoe Kamezo. Shattered by Kamezo's *seppuku* and kneeling before a heap of bodies, the young woman disemboweled herself.

Takeo brushed tears from his cheeks. Keiko wept openly.

After the play, sitting in the small dark confines of a swaying rickshaw — the gasoline shortage had caused a resurgence in popularity of the ancient means of transportation — Takeo slipped his hand under the blanket covering his and Keiko's knees. He found her hand waiting. Turning to her, he stared at the radiant face that because of the jerky motions of the rickshaw appeared blurred like a camelia held in trembling fingers.

Takeo's heart thumped and his collar was suddenly tight and hot despite the cold outside. Face lifted, she leaned to him. Gently, his lips found hers — soft, warm rose petals in the spring. But the moment was brief; tragically brief.

She turned away, pulled her hand from his and spoke in a tremulous voice. "I enjoyed the play, Takeo-san."

Choking back his frantic heartbeat, he managed, "I — I always enjoy it."

"The ending was beautiful," she said in a thick voice.

"Yes. A perfect way to die."

She returned her eyes to his. "Do you believe a girl should follow her lover in death?"

"Thousands have done it. Certainly, it improves *karma.*"

She nodded. "Yes. Many have hurled themselves into Oshima's lava." Biting her lip, she hastened to a new subject, "When do you leave, Takeo-san?"

"Three weeks."

"Is Rabaul safe?"

There was bitterness in his voice. "Yes, unfortunately."

"You will be there permanently?"

"Who knows? I could be transferred to the Marshalls, Gilberts, Carolines, even Saipan. I understand a new army group will be headquartered there."

"You do not like staff work."

"Of course not, Keiko-san. I am an infantry officer. I belong on the field like your brother."

"Seiji will meet the Yankees in that strange place. I — I forget the name."

"Guadalcanal."

"Yes, Takeo-san: Guadalcanal." Her hand returned to his. "You would like to go there?"

"It is my duty — my destiny."

"To die on the battlefield."

"Of course. We all know that."

Turning away, her voice was very soft. "Of course, we all know that — true, true."

Uneasily, Takeo changed the subject. "Would you like to visit the museum at Okoshiri Castle tomorrow? I hear the grounds are beautiful and we can take a bus."

She continued to stare out the yellow, celluloid window. "I would like that very much, Takeo-san."

He felt her hand tighten.

Okoshiri Castle was built on a wooded promontory just north of Matsuyama in 1601. In 1922 an earthquake completely destroyed it — a feat never accomplished by its enemies. Completely restored, the great castle with its manicured gardens served as a famous museum of art and as a gathering place for families and couples cultivating blossoming love affairs.

Walking with a thin crowd through the gardens leading to the entrance of the great stone structure crowned with battlements like shark's teeth, Takeo nodded and chuckled as Keiko pointed and exclaimed over the magnificent sights upon which generations of landscape artists had labored so that passersby could feast. Actually, the grounds were a park. A large pond surrounded an island flaming with roses, lilies, camelias, and many other blooms, like a multicolored bull's-eye in the middle of a blue target. Hundreds of stone lanterns were on the banks and on the island, where Takeo detected a cluster of cranes. Pointing, he laughed aloud. "Cast iron."

"They look so real, Takeo-san."

Passing a tall pergola covered with blossoming grape and lilac, the couple found a waterfall leaping from the top of a small hill covered with sculpted dwarf pine. The water bubbled and tumbled gaily over red and green rocks to a riverbed of volcanic stones, where it swirled like a great blue-white serpent beneath a graceful bridge to the pond.

"Lovely," the girl murmured.

"Yes, Kaiko-san. But I hear the art collection is one of Japan's finest."

"Sepia ink drawings, classic calligraphy, haniwa sculpture, paintings even from the Heian period . . ." she stopped, breathless with excitement.

Laughing, he gestured at the massive entry doors decorated with two large pounded brass sixteen-petaled chrysanthemums, guarded by a pair of stone lions. "Let us discover for ourselves."

"Yes," she answered, eyes bright. "A feast."

"Tomorrow night the feast, Keiko-san," he said. Then he looked around, saw no one, took her arm, and moved up the steps.

"Tomorrow night?"

"Yes. Shimagawa. Finest restaurant on Shikoku."

"Oh, I would love it, Takeo-san." Her lips were close to

his ear.

Laughing, the couple entered the castle.

Takeo knew they had found the restaurant when he saw the paper-and-bamboo lantern high above its entrance displaying the restaurant's name in elaborate calligraphy. Answering the officer's knock, a bent, wizened little man opened the door — actually a portal in a high wall that surrounded a landscaped compound containing a dozen small wooden huts.

"Jochu! Jochu!" the old man called as he closed the door.

A polished jewel of a woman dressed in a fine kimono appeared, smiling and bowing. "This way — this way, please," she murmured, leading the couple through a garden shrewdly contrived to be a miniature of the garden at Okoshiri Castle, with a small pond, tiny island, miniature cranes, trickling waterfall, and dwarf trees and shrubs. Beckoning, the young woman led the couple to a hut and pulled the *shoji* aside.

After removing their shoes, Takeo and Keiko entered a small room austerely furnished with a low table from which a small lantern glowed, two silk cushions, a *tokonoma* and several *shoji* masked alcoves.

Seating themselves, the young officer stared at Keiko as the soft lamplight fell on her. He had never seen her so attractive. Her kimono was a deep purple of fine silk brocaded with camelias and wrapped around the waist with a laced, gold-colored *obi*. And her coif was elaborate with willow sprigs and gold pins scattered in the lustrous folds. But most exciting was her face, radiant as if she were restraining latent emotion.

Feeling a familiar pounding in his chest, Takeo turned to the waitress. *"Jochu-san,* sak 5e *please."*

In a moment, the couple held sakazukis, made the usual salutes to the Emperor, their ancestors, parents, and the war effort, while riveting each other's eyes over the table. Within minutes, they were drinking their third cup of the hot, spiced wine.

"The specialty of Shimagawa is roast eel," Nakamura said.

"I know. I hear it is exquisite."

Almost as if overhearing the exchange, the young waitress entered and placed two black lacquered boxes containing sliced eels layered on white rice in front of the diners. With a sigh, Takeo reached for his *hashi*.

Leaning over his hot tea, Takeo watched the waitress as she slid the *shoji* closed. The meal had been finished and the table cleared, and the diners were sipping their tea. She would not enter the hut again unless summoned.

Keiko's eyes were on her cup. She spoke hesitantly, "You have strong *karma*, Takeo-san."

"Thank you. I am certain you do, too."

She pressed on, "You wish to seek *nirvana* on the battlefield."

"Why of course. I have told you before. You studied the *Hagakure* in school. We all did." He chuckled. "But I will be attacking our enemies with a pad, pencil and typewriter."

Peering over her cup, she smiled. "They can be devastating weapons, Takeo-san."

Pleased by her concern, he reached across the table, capturing her hand. Her flesh released magnetic waves, tugging at every fiber of his being. He wished he could smash the wooden barrier between them.

She read his mind. "Come closer to me, Takeo-san." There was a burning in her eyes.

Slowly he rose, pulling her up with him. Then a quick step to the side and he felt the smooth silk of her kimono under his hands as she came to him. He found the warm lips, open and demanding. He felt an ineffable joy — an ecstasy that seemed to suspend him in space and time. But undeniable urges claimed his hands, sent them downward to her tight buttocks, and back to her waist where he found the bow of her *obi*. He tugged on the silk.

Straining for air like the victim of an executioner's garrote, she pushed him away. "I love you, Takeo-san."

He stiffened. Those words. Those precious words. He choked his heart back down his throat. "I — I love you, Keiko-san." And then holding her close and talking to her ear: "Your family has never met mine."

"You never talk of them."

"We are fishermen."

She kissed his cheek. "You told me that much."

"I did not tell you we are poor."

"I do not care, Takeo-san."

"Your father would."

"You are of good samurai stock, Takeo-san. General Kobyashi said so."

"But poor."

She kissed his neck. "Father likes you. And if ever you . . ."

"If ever I approached him, he would listen—might approve if we . . ."

"Yes, my love. But at this moment, Takeo, I do not care."

Her mouth found his with a hard hunger. He kissed her cheeks, eyelids, forehead, neck while she twisted against him, her breath hot and short, fanned by a sexuality that grew, surging with an existence all its own, filling the room with its steamy presence.

Pulling the *obi* free and tearing at her undergarments, Takeo found her flesh burning his fingertips. His hands slid upward to the hard cones of her breasts, cupping, squeezing, tantalizing the swollen nipples.

She pulled back, her black eyes velvet and swimming with passion, lips parted thinly, her kimono off one shoulder. She began to push the garment from the other.

"No," he commanded. "Let me." He raised his trembling hand.

Her skin was hot to his touch like candle wax under the flame. Warmth spread from his groin rising like waves of heat from Oshima-yama's lava, tingling his flesh with a thousand crawling insects and sending a hammer in his chest to frantic pounding.

She shuddered and gasped as her kimono dropped to the floor with the finality of a dead leaf in autumn.

Takeo stared at the sculpted body of a goddess, wondering if this was a dream, a drunken fantasy. Her breasts were firm mounds topped by the rosettes of her nipples, her stomach flat and flaring to slender hips and the mound of black hair covering her sex. Her legs were slender, colored, and textured like fine amber jade.

He took her shoulders in his hands and pulled her toward him.

"No," she cried, turning away. Hastily, she moved to an alcove, pulled back a *shoji* and removed a quilted *futon* and two pillows.

"Let me," he said.

"No. I will spread it." She waved a hand. "Your clothes."

Frantically, the young man tore at his clothes with nerveless fingers that no longer had joints. Cursing, he threw his shirt then his trousers on the floor while the girl spread the *futon* and then lay back on a pillow.

Nakamura stared down at the girl who smiled up at him. Strange. He wanted her so much he ached. Yet, he waited; perhaps, to savor the moment. Yes. That was it. The longer this moment, the stronger the memory. Someday, that would be all that he would have of her. He feasted his eyes.

She reached up. He took the hand and he felt her pulling. Releasing his breath with the sighing sound of wind through a pine, he sank to the pad and covered her body with his.

"I will follow you anywhere, Takeo-san."

"Anywhere?"

"Yes."

"Into death?"

"Especially into that kingdom."

"I do not wish that."

"But we would be together, loved by our ancestors."

"In time that comes to all of us, anyway, Keiko-san."

"Without you I would have nothing here."

"You can find another samurai."

"There are no others — could never be."

"You are beautiful — could find many more."

"That is not my choice. There can only be you." She ran a hand over the hard muscles of his arm, then to his back.

He felt the heat again. Pulled her body against his. With a sigh, she rolled to her back. He lowered himself between her legs gently, and again they commenced the frenzied movements, climaxed by an explosion of feeling so intense he felt as if his life had been drained from him and he sprawled on top of her helplessly like a dead man.

There was a strong thrust of her hips and Takeo felt her legs lock him in. Slowly, her fingertips traced random patterns through the rivulets of sweat streaking his back as she whispered, "Come back to me, my love."

He could only breath, "I love you. I love you."

Had it been two years or two centuries since that night? Because of a week spent on Tama Shima, they had only two weeks together — a time of such heat that each exquisite night was torched into his memory, indelible reflections of a writhing body, lustrous black hair framing the bloom of her visage, eyes narrowed by ecstasy. And her sighs had been a soft breeze in a garden, parted lips like rosebuds.

But the gods of war were stirring, pushing the girl back into the dim recesses. Manigassa Island was writhing and heaving like a dying man. Only a few kilometers off the coast, the *California* had opened fire, her fourteen-inch shells sending boulders, concrete, men, and palm trees twisting into the sky. And a small patrol craft was heading for the reef.

"Keikō. Keikō," the young lieutenant whispered. "Come back." He pounded the concrete. "Please come back."

But the roar of battle filled the bunker, driving phantoms into the mists.

Five

Someday, what you're doing will be the stuff of
movies and actors will be heroic and boys will
watch and feel the itch to kill.

Maria Carpelli, 1944

The day of the attack on Hagi Ridge was the day
Quartermaster First Class Michael Carpelli almost
killed Ensign Robert Bennington. It happened during
a patrol—a two mile ping line five hundred yards
north of Marpi Point.

Michael Carpelli despised ping lines. Without a
doubt, a ping line was the most tedious duty conceiv-
able. Two miles at 10 knots on a 270 heading, then reverse course and run the reciprocal while the sonar
gear made its monotonous search, cranked from beam
to beam by a thoroughly bored soundman. Although
there were rumors that over twenty Jap I-Boats had
been sunk in the Marianas in less than two weeks, the
2404 had not made a single submarine contact.

However, other elements promised to enliven the
patrol. There were reports that small groups of Japanese troops had been trying to flank the marines by
pushing off from the northern shores of Saipan and
rowing south in small boats and rafts. Armed with
small arms and grenades, they would rush ashore behind American lines, killing and destroying until shot

down. Others tried to make Tinian. Destroyers had been posted on close inshore patrols, but the reported presence of a Japanese carrier task force in the Philippine Sea had lured off most of the men-of-war.

Dawn of 28 June crept across the sky with spectacular malevolence, the sun a satanic red ball sifting through a high milky scum of cirrus. The entire northeast horizon was walled off by a slippery, smooth, and dark gray cloud, like the slimy body of a gigantic slug. The sea was as substantial as metal, brooding with a deep swell that changed the hues from one monotonous gray shade to another, like bending and twisting lead. Here and there the surface was whipped to a froth by the fickle wind.

Steadying himself with a hand on the windscreen, Michael could feel the throb of the diesels as they drove the stem through the sea like Saracen steel cutting lace, sluicing crests of white-flecked ridges to both port and starboard while astern the frothing wake still flashed with swirling phosphorescence in the weak light.

Dawn always brought with it the danger of air and submarine attacks. Standing at general quarters, the entire bridge force swayed mutely with the ship like silent drunks, eyes glued to glasses. Michael felt a little comfort because Don Lindsay—now an experienced, alert veteran of seven months at sea and rated as a Gunner's Mate Third Class—stood on the port lookout's platform, glassing his quadrant in short jerky sweeps.

However, the other two new members of the bridge force brought no confidence. Bill Whitlow, a slender, acne-faced boy with hair like a poppy field in full bloom, manned the starboard lookout platform while another youngster, Isadore Nash, who was as dark as Whitlow was fair, manned the phones. The pair had been brought aboard from the repair ship *Agenor* when the PCS's bullet-riddled bridge had been patched.

211

Both were less than a month out of boot camp; both were perpetually frightened.

Rotating to the south, the quartermaster studied Marpi Point. Much like Aguijan, with sheer cliffs towering hundreds of feet straight up, it was the most forbidding part of Saipan's coastline. They were so close he could see the deep bays and crevasses that rent and split the cliffs into shadowy depths of darkest gray and black. The sea piled in, surging and cresting in rock-strewn shallows before it crashed against the battlements, creaming up in explosive bursts of purest white spray. A few casuarina and hardwood trees crowned the cliffs, but unlike the southern reaches of Saipan, growth was sparse. Occasional columns of smoke were to be seen, but the wind leaped on the columns like lions on prey, ripping them to tatters before the columns could form their towers. Not one human was visible.

"Keep your eyes peeled," Lieutenant Andrew Bennett said. "There's supposed to be a battery of seventy-fives up there."

"Sir," Ensign Robert Bennington said, "request permission to bring small arms to the bridge."

"Good idea. Both Thompsons and both M-One carbines." He turned to Seaman Nash. "Kohler to the bridge."

"Aye, aye, sir."

Carpelli yawned. This was the third day of the patrol. They had sighted nothing but the corpses of civilians. Floating in schools in the weird way the dead clustered and attracted debris almost as if seeking company in their final journey, the PCS had not sighted a single live Jap. But the dead had been disturbing; most had been women, some with children tied to their breasts. Always, the black triangles of dorsal fins crisscrossed as great whites lashed themselves into a frenzy of greed, slashing and tearing with razor-sharp teeth, sending the carrion into whirling,

212

bobbing motions—a final macabre ballet.

He heard Whitlow's high-pitched voice, "Jesus! My God!"

"My God what?" Bennett shouted angrily. "Bearing and range, goddamn it."

The boy's voice trembled, "Bodies, sir. Bearing zero-zero-zero, range . . ."

"I've got 'em, I've got 'em . . ." The captain waved the youngster to silence.

Refocusing, Michael swung his glasses. Dead ahead, five women and three children floated. All were bloated with huge gas-filled stomachs and bulging, splotched cheeks and enlarged round limbs thrust straight out.

Dennis Warner spoke. "We'll ram them, sir."

"We won't hurt them, Signalman."

"Ensign Bennington requests permission for target practice, Captain," Isadore Nash reported.

Bennett studied the bodies and flotsam. "Very well."
Nash mumbled into his headpiece.

Dropping his glasses, Michael moved to the starboard wing of the bridge. He was looking almost straight down as the bodies were suddenly caught in the sluice from the stem, whirling outboard crazily. Then Michael saw the ropes that bound them together and the great white shapes fathoms deep.

There was the unmistakable popping sound of an M-1 carbine being fired as fast as its 15-round magazine could be emptied. Leaning over the windscreen, Michael could see Bennington bracing himself on a stanchion next to the Number One twenty-millimeter directly below, firing down into the dead, a few broken boxes, cartons and other offal. The quartermaster expected to see the trash shatter and leap. But, instead, two women jerked. A baby's head exploded.

"Why do that? Why Captain? Why?" Michael shouted, incensed.

"Easy Quartermaster. He can't hurt them."

213

"I'm letting gas out of them," Bennington shouted up through the wind. Laughing, he added, "They're a menace to navigation."

Leaning over the windscreen, Bennett brought cupped hands to his mouth, "Secure from target practice, Mr. Bennington," he shouted. "Ammunition is valuable. Save it for live Japs."

Whitlow and Nash laughed nervously. Don Lindsay and Dennis Warner remained silent.

Michael's voice came from deep in his chest. "Not live Jap women and children, Captain?"

"A Jap, is a Jap, is a Jap," Bennett said, chuckling over his clever paraphrase of Gertrude Stein. Then seriously, "We haven't killed any civilians, have we Quartermaster?"

"No sir. But Ensign Bennington . . ."

"He didn't hurt anyone." The captain waved a hand. "Resume your search."

"Aye, aye, sir."

"But sir," Whitlow piped, suddenly. "Why? Why do they kill themselves?"

"Because they believe they'll be raped and their children murdered and it's the Jap way, anyhow," Bennett answered.

"And they really believe that, Captain?" Dennis Warner said, lowering his binoculars.

"You saw them."

Feeling a deep, acid, burning in his stomach, Michael swept the sea directly ahead. But now the sea was empty, and Michael knew they would experience another interminable day. When he saw Bennington fire on the women and children, he had felt a hot cord twist in his stomach, releasing the acid. He hated the man. He was a coward and a murderer. He had tried. Oh, Lord, he had tried. Since the massacre off Aguijan, every night when he closed his eyes, he could see clearly in his mind's eye the ripped bodies of Malcolm Murphy, Glenn Winters, Jay Barton, and the marine

214

captain, Christopher Welly. Also, glaring like the cliffs of Marpi Point, was his memory of the captain's face the day he told him of Bennington's incompetence and cowardice.

With trouble crossing his face like a ten-tenths cloud cover darkening the sea, Michael had met with Andrew Bennett in the wardroom the morning of the captain's return to duty. After requesting and receiving permission for an "off the record" report, Michael began, "Ensign Bennington's a coward. He choked — couldn't even give commands — murdered three men," he said, standing in front of the captain's desk.

Looking up from his chair, Bennett's voice cracked like breaking ice, "Watch your mouth, Quartermaster. You're talking about my executive officer. Why don't you tell him?"

"I did."

Shock seamed and wrinkled Bennett's pudgy face. "You told him?"

"Yes. Alone. In the chart house the day after the action. We were alongside the *Agenor* being patched up."

"You — you called him a coward?"

"An incompetent, murdering coward, sir."

"Jesus. You could spend the rest of your life in the brig."

"I don't give a damn, Captain. I told him if we survived this war, I'd track him down and kill him."

"He's never told me."

"Of course not Captain." Carpelli placed a hand on the desk, leaned on it. "Court-martial me. But that man's a killer."

Sinking back into his chair, Bennett looked up at the tall quartermaster, who returned to attention. The captain spoke but the cold edge was gone. "This is off the record, so give me your charges," he said, resign-

215

edly.

Quickly with perspiration beading his forehead, Carpelli described the horror of the attack — Bennington's cowardly paralysis and inability to cope with Welly's mad tactics. Bennett nodded silently.

"You know, of course, you are an enlisted man charging an officer with the gravest offense in the book. Technically, an offense that can lead to execution."

"I know."

"And how much chance do you think you'd have before a review board?"

"I know, Captain. Kohler, Schultz and the guys have told me, too. But I can't stay silent."

"And your witnesses are dead."

"Not the marine."

"He has no face, can't talk, is in a naval hospital back in the states. He's dead as far as your case is concerned."

"Then he'll kill again."

The captain's fingers drummed polished oak. "Michael, I know you dislike the ensign."

"Please, Captain. That has nothing . . ."

"No! Listen to me. We lost men but Bennington did a good job."

"Good job?"

"Yes. On paper, he was bold, decisive, completed his mission and punished the enemy."

"Our casualties?"

"Within acceptable limits, Carpelli. *C'est la guerre.*"

"Why don't you decorate him, Captain?"

"Comseronten probably will."

"Transfer me."

"Now? Where?"

"Anywhere. If not afloat, to the beach. I can signal. A beachmaster can use me. If I stay on board with Bennington, I'll kill him."

The fingers stopped their drumming abruptly. "Mi-

216

chael, we're all under stress. We've all seen too many boys die. But life isn't that cheap. I can't transfer you. You do my navigating and you can signal. You're a leader. This ship needs you — the crew needs you. Control yourself. We all react violently — we're paid and trained for it. We're pros but it's not a way of life. Think about it, Michael. It's controlled and directed at our enemies, not our shipmates."

Michael felt a cold hand clutch his throat. His voice came out like a hiss. "May I be dismissed, sir?"

"No. Not before you realize every word said has been off the record and that not one word of this conversation can be repeated by either of us."

"Of course, sir. It was at my request. I understand."

Hunching forward, Bennett's eyes narrowed. "I respect you, Michael. I'll keep this conversation in mind. I can promise you that much."

"Yes, sir." A phrase the captain had used disturbed the quartermaster. "You said 'on paper,' sir. What paper? A battle report, sir?"

"You're very perceptive."

"May I see it?"

"Classified."

"I won't tell the Japs, Captain."

Bennett chewed his lip before nodding in acceptance. "You won't tell anyone?"

"You know me better than that, Mr. Bennett."

"I guess I do." Then, sighing, Bennett reached into a drawer and removed a folder. "All right. I trust you. I have your word?"

"My word of honor."

Seating himself, Michael's eyes eagerly scanned the document. Slowly, the lids widened and anger flared.

PCS-2404/A12-1/(WHB)
    U.S.S. PCS-2404
    c/o FLEET POST OFFICE
    SAN FRANCISCO, CALIFORNIA

SECRET
From: The Executive Officer. (Acting
              Commanding Officer as per
              above date.)
To: The   Commander-in-Chief,
              United States Fleet
Via: The Commander Task Group
              57.7. The Commander Task
              Group 57
Subject: Action Against Aguijan Island,
              Marianas, 24 June 1944
Reference: (a) Pacflt Conf. ltr. 2CL-44 Se-
              rial 03 of 1 Jan. 1944

1. Pursuant to the requirements set forth in reference (a) and particularly Enclosure (c) of reference (a) the following report is submitted herewith:

Part I.

1. All times in this report are Zone Description minus ten.

Early in the morning of 24 June 1944, this vessel opened fire with 3"/50, 40 MM, and 20 MM weapons upon Japanese installations, machine gun emplacements, and geographic points and areas in the immediate vicinity of GREEN Beach, Aguijan Island, Marianas. GREEN Beach is that beach on the southwest coast of the island consisting of a small landing step and paths leading to the plateau upon which is situated four corrugated metal and wood buildings and to an inclined structural steel boom and cables which lead to anchors on the sea floor.

The enemy returned fire with light machine guns which were being fired from a triangular cave a short distance to the northwest of the landing step and from other more obscure positions in the green vegetation adjacent to the paths leading up the cliff to the plateau.

After obtaining several positive hits with 3"/50 caliber shells in the interior of the cave, enemy fire ceased from that position, but continued from other nearby positions. These points were promptly swept with 40 MM and 20 MM guns. Upon completion of the bombardment and the destruction of the enemy positions, the ship retired.

2. (a) At 1000, 23 June 1944, Captain Christopher Welly USMC, Commanding Officer of the Aguijan Special Landing Force, boarded this vessel at anchor off Charan Kanoa (BLUE Beach 2.)

Captain Welly briefed the crew concerning a surface reconnaissance of Aguijan Island, particularly GREEN Beach and areas adjacent to the beach containing machine gun positions.

(b) While at anchor a conference was held between the ship's officers and Captain Welly, charts, maps, and photographs were consulted and the mission was discussed and planned in detail. This vessel weighed anchor at 0330, 24 June 1944, departed the Charan Kanoa anchorage and proceeded to a point off Aguijan Island bearing 260, range one mile with the sun astern. Because illumination and visibility were not adequate in the twilight, I ordered a close approach to the beach on a course of 330. I took advantage of the rising sun on the approach. At 0535 this vessel began to receive small arms fire. Disregarding this fire, I continued closing the range and a close reconnaissance was made and enemy works were brought under fire from a range of 150 yards.

219

Part II

1. During the run, I directed fire on the buildings on the cliff top, ravines adjacent to the buildings with the 3"/50 caliber gun at ranges varying from 500 yards to 150 yards. 75 rounds of 3"/50 ammunition were expended. At the same time, the 40 MM machine gun and the numbers 1, 2, and 3 20 MM machine guns kept up continuous fire on two caves, a single path, adjacent brush and targets of opportunity. The average range was 200 yards with a close of 150. At 1545, I ordered a change of course to 230 . . .

Michael realized the last course had been taken from his last entry in the ship's log. Squinting, he raced on, knowing Bennington had to construct the rest.

. . . 3 inch shells were seen to land inside the triangular cave and burst, much smoke and recurring flashes were observed emitting from the cave as a result of these hits. Enemy machine gun fire began coming from other adjacent areas, bullets were heard coming over the ship, and splashes were observed on the opposite side of the ship, as well as close aboard the side toward the beach. At this point, Boatswain's Mate Third Class Malcolm Murphy, seaman First Class Jay Barton and Seaman Second Class Glenn Winters were killed, apparently by 6.5 MM machine gun fire. Captain Christopher Welly USMC received serious wounds to the neck and face. Disregarding casualties, I brought this vessel to a course parallel to GREEN Beach and continued punishing the enemy until all his guns fell silent. At this point, I ordered a change of course to 120, the range was opened and all guns secured.

2. Gun ranges used varied from 500 yards to 150 yards depending upon (1) the range of the beach from the ship and (2) the range of the various targets designated. The 40 MM and 20 MM machine guns were on a separate telephone circuit with a talker on the conning bridge. However, because of a breakdown, the signalman was posted next to the 40 MM and commands were relayed from the bridge by the quartermaster using hand signals.

Radar was used (SO-1-4 mile scale) in connection with fire control to give help in making a more accurate estimate of the proper range to set on the 3"/50 gun.

Michael skipped over descriptions of preparations, expenditures of ammunition, damage control, communications, and fire control. Scanning quickly, he moved to the last paragraph.

Part IV

1. (a) The enemy's fire was very effective. In general, it was well directed and very accurate. Performance of personnel was exemplary throughout the action. Especially gallant were our dead: Boatswain's Mate Third Class Malcolm Murphy, Seaman First Class Jay Barton and Seaman Second Class Glenn Winters who manned their posts until struck down by enemy fire. Captain Christopher Welly also displayed great courage. Quartermaster First Class Michael Carpelli and Pharmacist's Mate First Class Bryan Kohler displayed great resourcefulness in saving Captain Welly's life. Respectfully, I feel all of the above should be considered for decorations.

2. Transmission by Registered Guard Mail or

U.S. registered mail is authoritzed in accordance with Article 76 (15) (e) and (f), U.S. Navy Regulations.

Robert H. Bennington acting for
Andrew B. Bennett, Jr.

cc/Cominch (advance)
Cincpac & POA (2)
Comseron 10
File

Michael shook his head in rejection. Numbly, staring at the captain, he allowed the report to slip through his fingers and drop on the desk. "You can't believe that, Captain. It's 'Alice in Wonderland.' He froze — couldn't give commands, killed those guys . . ."

"Carpelli," the officer said sharply. "You must understand my position. I trust you and believe you're sincere. But I can't destroy an officer's career because of the accusations of one man."

"But Captain . . ."

"No!" Bennett waved a hand indicating he was not finished. "No, perhaps the truth is somewhere in the middle. It usually is."

Raising his arms, he spread his hands. Then, dropping them he hunched forward, "I'll do this much, Michael. I'll watch him very carefully."

"Not enough!"

"It's got to be enough. And remember this, you must live with this man — even stand watches with him. Now straighten out and fly right." He knuckled his forehead. Then continued with the timbre of his voice softened, "He recommended you for a decoration."

"For what, Captain? A scratch on my chin when a slug knocked my helmet off?" He leaned over the desk. "I already have a Purple Heart — got it when I was blown off the SC."

"You saved Captain Welly's life."

"Bryan did that and he has his medals already."

The officer sighed in exasperation. "You want the man's scalp and there just isn't a case." He tapped the desk top with a single finger. "There is one thing you must keep in mind, Michael."

Silently, Michael stared.

"Always remember this, Michael. It is not easy to command."

There was a long silence before Bennett pressed on. "Now return to your duties, Quartermaster. We have a date with some Japs on Marpi Point."

Burdened by two Thompson submachine guns and a pair of M-1 carbines and followed by Bryan Kohler, Robert Bennington returned to the bridge. Choking back the acerbic gorge of his resentment, Michael ignored the ensign and continued studying the cliffs.

"How's World War Two going?" Kohler asked, looking slyly at Carpelli and Lindsay while accepting a submachine gun from Bennington.

"Send us more Japs," Don Lindsay mocked theatrically without taking his eyes from his glasses. A chuckle swept the bridge.

"How's about manning the USO, buying bonds, and chasing pussy?" Kohler responded.

"If you can get that duty, include your captain," Andrew Bennett said, staring at the horizon.

Laughter swept tension from the bridge. Nevertheless, Michael seethed as he checked the empty chamber of his weapon, slung it over his shoulder, and returned to his watch.

"The funny war's over, gentlemen," Bennett said. "Concentrate on your sectors and maintain bridge silence." He nodded to the pharmacist's mate. "Maintain a watch ahead, Bryan."

Kohler moved to the windscreen.

For several minutes, only the ship's sounds could be

223

heard; the slap of the hull cleaving swells, tatters of spray raining back into the sea like gravel thrown against asphalt, the hissing and snapping of wind-whipped halyards and the staccato bark of exhausts.

The patrol craft had just completed its turn at the western end of its run when Lindsay shouted, "Object bearing two-seven-zero, range five-thousand."

As if choreographed, the bridge force swung to port in unison.

"Blue sail, Captain," Michael said, glassing the sighting. Then, moving to the gyro-repeater: "Bearing one-three-five, true, sir."

"Come right to one-three-five. All ahead flank," Bennett shouted into the voice tube. Then turning, "Kohler and Carpelli stand by with the Thompsons, Mr. Bennington and Lindsay the M-Ones. Mr. Bennington report the sighting to Old Hickory and tell him 'am closing.' "

Bennington repeated the order and spoke into the microphone.

As Carpelli made a notation in the log, cocked his weapon, and set it on "safe," he heard the hard sound of steel on steel as three bolts were worked.

"Be sure you're on 'safe,' " Bennett shouted. "We're here to kill Japs, not each other." He leaned to the talker, "All gun stations wake up. You may earn your pay today."

As the ship heeled and the diesels roared with new life, Michael studied the sighting.

"Radar reports one or two objects bearing zero-zero-zero, range five thousand," Isadore Nash said.

"Great," Andrew Bennett said, sarcastically. "Those mothers are really on the ball." He turned to Isadore Nash, "All guns, target bearing zero, zero, zero, range five thousand. Three-inch use contact fuses, forty a one-to-one mix of AP and contact. Stand by to engage."

Nash repeated the commands into his headpiece.

As the ship steadied on its new course, it smashed into the swell at sixteen knots, sending a blue-white shroud of water and spray flying while astern a white wake swirled and boiled angrily.

Michael cursed through the salt crusting on his lips and wiped spray from his lenses. Focusing, he found a crowded boat perhaps twenty feet long, with very little freeboard, wallowing — first rising sharply on a swell and then plummeting into a trough. A dozen oars worked frantically and a small blue tattered sail bulged in the wind. A small raft was astern, lashed to the boat with a single line. He saw steel helmets.

"Long boat towing a raft, sir. Steel helmets, sir," Michael said.

"Very well. I've got them, Quartermaster."

Lindsay spoke, "Twenty soldiers in the boat — four on the raft and . . ."

"And what?"

"And a couple women in the boat, sir."

"Women?" Ensign Bennington challenged. "How can you tell from here?"

"Long hair, female features . . ."

"Bullshit, Gunner," Bennington said. "Jap broads are flat-chested, bowlegged and built like their men. If you can't see a pussy . . ."

"Belay that crap," Bennett roared. "They're Japs! That's all that counts." To the talker, "Radar, give a range and continuous ranges every five hundred."

"Radar reports range twenty-five hundred."

"Very well."

Michael studied the boat as the PCS quickly reduced the distance.

"Range two thousand."

He saw rifles, bayonets and on the stern a long barrel coiled with air-cooling fins. "Nambu on the stern, sir. A heavy, Captian. Probably a seven point seven."

Bennett turned to Kohler, "Best range of that Nambu?"

"We were taught five hundred yards. But I've seen effective fire from six and seven hundred, sir."

"That's what I thought."

"Range fifteen hundred."

"All ahead slow."

Michael saw a pair of bare heads with long hair flying in the wind. Then a tiny form held close. "Two women and a baby, sir."

Robert Bennington spat, "How the fuck do you know, Quartermaster?"

"Carpelli, Lindsay, Mr. Bennington. We're not concerned with sex and age. Only nationality and range," the captain bellowed.

"Range one thousand."

"Come left to one-zero-zero."

Despite the breeze and fine spray, Michael's face felt warm. But he concentrated on the enemy, swinging his glasses as the ship turned to her new course.

"Steady on one-zero-zero."

"Very well. All stop."

"All stop."

"Helmsman, let me know the instant you lose steerageway," Bennett barked down the voice tube. He spoke to Isadore Nash, "Three-inch! One round across her bow. All weapons that bear, stand by to open fire." And then as an afterthought, "Arm the depth charges for a fifty-foot pattern."

He was interrupted by the blast of the three-inch that vibrated every frame right down to the keel. A column of water shot from the sea ahead of the boat and at least five hundred yards beyond it, held its life for a fleeting instant and then vanished in the wind.

"Jesus Christ! We're not shelling the fuckin' island," Bennett shouted. Then to Nash, "Tell Chief Gunner's Mate Schultz to fire his popgun on the down roll. He's liable to airmail one all the way back to Pearl."

Isadore Nash repeated the order, paused, turned to Bennett, "Chief Schultz wants to know if you want the hedgehogs armed, Captain."

"Negative. Just the depth charges."

"They may have a mortar with them, Captain," Kohler said. "They're damned good with them."

"I know." The captain stared at the enemy boat where the oarsmen still pulled and the tiny sail continued to bulge. "Shit," he said with disgust. He shouted to the talker, "My stewart's mate to the bridge on the double."

Stewart's Mate José Garcia was born in the Philippines but educated in the United States, graduating from the University of California as a language major. He spoke Spanish, Italian, English, French, and Japanese fluently. A short, swarthy, powerfully built man with a flat nose and thick lips, he was captain of the depth charge racks and the two K-guns. It was joked that if the K-guns misfired, Garcia could throw the 300-pound charges. Breathing hard, he pulled himself onto the bridge. "Yes, sir," he said, standing at attention despite the roll.

Bennett handed him the loud hailer. "It's on full volume." He gesticulated at the enemy. "Tell them to heave to and surrender. Tell them I'll give them the Geneva Convention and tell them I'll open fire in two minutes if they don't surrender."

Michael felt the ship wallow and begin to rock on her beams. "Losing steerageway, sir," came from the voice tube.

"All ahead slow and hold her on one-zero-zero."

Michael felt the tempo of the diesels pick up. He concentrated on the boat and raft. All oars had been shipped and at least twenty rifles and the Nambu were trained on the PCS.

Garcia's metallic voice boomed across the thousand yards. Michael wondered how many words made the transit and how many were ripped away by the wind. Deep in his heart, he knew it would make no difference. As in a Greek tragedy, the ending was preor-

227

dained.

There was movement on the raft. Then he saw the short tube. "Mortar, sir. Small. Probably two-three feet long."

Bryan spoke: "If it's their eighty-one-millimeter, Captain, they can range us now with seven pounds of HE."

"Very well." The captain turned to the talker. "On my command, starboard battery will engage the raft."

Garcia's voice continued to crack with a hollow, metallic ring.

Four heads on the raft suddenly turned away from the tube. Then blue smoke torn to atoms before a cloud could form.

"The mortar's taken us under fire," Kohler shouted.

There was the hum of a huge insect passing close through the rigging, followed by a blast off the port beam, the flash masked instantly by a towering white waterspout as high as the bridge, steel fragments pockmarking the sea.

"Super-quick fuse, Captain!" Kohler shouted. "Daisy cutter!"

Bennett never acknowledged. Instead he shouted at Nash, "Commence firing—commence firing—commence firing!" Out of the side of his mouth to the stewart's mate: "Secure! Return to your battle station."

Michael had never seen a mortar crew in action. He was stunned by the speed. As the gunner cranked range adjustments, two men passed the projectiles while the loader dropped the charges down the tube, all turning away from the muzzle blast as the weapon fired. Despite the heaving seas, there was grace and coordination there, like a quartet choreographed by Fred Astaire. But the swell heaved the raft and the mortar sprayed its charges wildly. Only one shell hit close, near the stern just off the port depth charge racks, splashing the deck and spraying the hull and bridge with spent shrapnel.

"Casualties?" Bennett boomed.

"Two, sir. At the depth charge racks," the talker responded. "One knocked out by shrapnel to the helmet, the other with a leg wound."

"Kohler aft!" the lieutenant shouted.

Slinging his tommy gun over his shoulder, the pharmacist's mate vanished down the ladder.

Michael opened his mouth wide, rocked as the three-inch lashed out with its yellow tongue, assaulting his ears with its thunder. Above the din, he could hear the pointer and trainer shouting like madmen, the rasp of steel, the clang of the breech block. Again and again the cannon fired, but the heavy seas and slow speed rocked the ship like a cradle in a gale and the shots flew wide.

Garlands of tracers glowed and left faint trails as the starboard twenty-millimeters and the forty-millimeter ripped and pounded, spraying wide of the target, the gunners fighting the heaving deck. But the sheer volume of machine gun fire brought death to the raft. Michael was staring through his binoculars when a twenty-millimeter shell hit a soldier squarely in the diaphragm. Flinging his arms out like a martyr on a cross, he was flung from the raft backward. Other shells exploded in small flashes, ripping splinters and debris from the raft while dozens more scored the sea, sending angry exclamation marks leaping in twenty-foot columns. Within a minute, the raft was empty of men, reflecting the sun's red glow with its own crimson smear.

Flashes came from the boat and splashes leaped from the sea between the longboat and the patrol craft. "They're firing, sir," Michael said.

Bennett cleared his throat. "We're out of range." Then to Isadore Nash: "All guns engage the boat."

Staring at the women, Michael swallowed with an effort, his throat a dry well seared by cordite. The captain had no options and every man on the bridge knew it. The Japs had dictated the action.

Coughing gunsmoke from his lungs, Michael caught a glimpse of the island which had grown. "We're being set in, Captain," he shouted.

"Radar, range to the nearest point of land."

"Five thousand yards, sir."

"Fathometer?"

"One hundred thirty fathoms."

"Very well. Let me know when we cross the one hundred fathom line. This stuff shoals fast."

The action had forced the patrol craft to steam perhaps three miles south of Marpi Point to a point off a wooded promontory called Lagua Lichan. Michael knew that if an enemy battery was emplaced, it would not be on the northern cliff tops or on top of the bluffs at Lagua Lichan, but would in all likelihood be inland, spotted on some reverse slope, possibly only six thousand yards away.

"If there's a battery up there, Captain, we're cold meat," Carpelli shouted.

"I know," the lieutenant answered. He waved a fist at the long boat. "Goddamn it! Kill the motherfuckers."

The guns responded, the three-inch making its first hit on the mast — a shell that exploded in a bright flash and puff of white smoke, sending the blue sail flapping into the sea and raining shrapnel on the occupants, who hunched low like people in a storm. The machine guns were scoring, the twenties bursting with small flashes, sending puffs of splinters into the wind while the two-pound forty-millimeter shells sent planking, soldiers, and parts of bodies flying. All around the boat, the surface was whipped to a froth, spray leaping and blowing in misty clouds. There were hoarse shouts and cheers from the gunners.

A three-inch shell struck the boat squarely amidships at the waterline. The explosion broke the boat into two pieces that rose slowly on a column of water like an inverted "V." Bodies twisted and catapulted into the sea. Michael heard screams. Then, except for scattered planking and debris, the swell wiped the horror from its own face.

More cheers and shouts.

"Cease fire! Cease fire!"

Michael groaned with relief as the assault on his eardrums came to an end. "Debris, sir. Debris—maybe survivors," he said, studying scattered wreckage.

"Give me a course through the center of the area, Quartermaster."

Sighting through the bearing ring, Michael said, "I suggest one-nine-five, Captain."

"Three survivors, sir," Ensign Bennington said, shifting his M-1.

"Very well. Come right to one-nine-five."

"Depth charge run, sir?" the ensign asked. "Saltwater enemas?" He chuckled.

"Negative." The lieutenant turned to Nash, "All charges on 'safe.' Secure the K-guns."

Michael heard Bennington's soft groan of disappointment.

Michael made out three forms floating on a large chunk of hull probably kept afloat by a flotation tank. He saw long hair, a tiny head, and a steel helmet. "Woman, baby, and a soldier, floating on wreckage, sir." He saw no long barrels. "No rifles."

"Grenades?"

"Can't tell, Captain." Then staring anxiously at the island, "If there's a battery . . ."

"I'm aware! I'm aware," Bennett said sharply. "Old Hickory wants prisoners. We'll try to take these." Then to Isadore Nash: "José Garcia to the bridge."

Within minutes, the stewart's mate was pleading through the loud hailer, explaining the virtues of the Geneva Convention while the patrol craft, with all engines stopped, drifted down on the wreckage.

The soldier came through Carpelli's lenses with the

youth of a high school freshman. Helmet askew, he sat on the wreckage, bracing himself with arms extended rigidly behind himself. The woman took the young quartermaster's breath. Leaning on one elbow, she held the child and stared directly into Michael's binoculars. She was young, with the doll-like face of all young Japanese women. Long black hair was flattened by saltwater and hung down her back to her waist, her slender body clearly defined under a soaked blouse and pants — nubile breasts peaking, the soft round line of female buttocks clear. Now only a half-cable's length away, her eyes came through his glasses like bright, polished black pearls reflecting the ascending sun. She looked like a wounded fawn staring down a hunter's gun barrel — helpless, innocent, in pain, and not understanding.

The baby was tiny, perhaps two years old, clinging fearfully to the woman's breast, staring at the ship and whimpering. The woman talked into the baby's ear and stroked its head.

Michael licked salt from his lips and cursed to himself. "Surrender, damn you. Surrender."

Isadore Nash spoke, "Depth charge reports port rack jammed, number four charge ticking, sir."

'Ticking! Depth charges don't tick."

"Stewart's Mate Garcia reports shrapnel damage from the Jap mortar, sir. The tracks are bent and the charges won't roll. The detonator on number two is damaged. He believes the diaphragm is leaking."

"It's safe — can't go off."

"He's worried, sir. Wants to jettison. Needs crowbars, torches. Says he needs you aft and Pharmacist's Mate Kohler reports the two wounded are only slightly injured."

"Very well. Chief Schultz and damage control to the stern." Then to Robert Bennington, "Try to take them prisoner. I'd better go aft. There's four tons of TNT back there." He strode to the ladder, turned with an afterthought, "Watch the soldier, if he has a grenade he can set us off like a cherry bomb. And remember, when you come within heaving range, none of our weapons will depress low enough to score." He disappeared down the ladder.

Slowly the ship drifted down on the survivors. Bennington turned to Isadore Nash. "Rescue party man the starboard rail amidships." Quickly, four seamen carrying life rings and boat hooks took station.

Nash spoke. "We're too close. None of the ship's armament bears, sir — can't depress enough."

"Very well. Carpelli stand by with your tommy gun — Lindsay, the M-one."

Michael rested his submachine gun on top of the windscreen, locking the drum between the wind deflector and the plywood slab of the screen. Raising his carbine, Lindsay braced himself on the lookout platform's rail.

Ensign Bennington shouted at Nash, "Get a line over."

Looking down at the ship's waist, Michael saw a seaman whirl a "monkey's fist" over his head like a cowboy preparing to throw a lasso. Then, with a hum, a line pulled by the lead-weighted monkey's fist arced over the short span of suddenly calm water, landing on the far side of the wreckage and draping over the Japanese. It was a perfect heave.

Slowly, the young soldier came to his knees, grasped the line, and hurled it back onto the ship.

Now they were drifting down on the wreckage in an eerie, windless calm — an absence of motion and sound as if the sea and wind had conspired to stop heaving and blowing and turned to watch the inevitable.

"Son-of-a-bitch," Bennington shouted, leaning over the windscreen and pointing his M-1. "Surrender!"

Blankly, the soldier stared back while the woman held the baby close, brushing its forehead with her lips. Hesitantly, she pointed at the sky and kissed the child on the mouth.

"Let me swim over, sir," Carpelli pleaded. "I can take that runt dripping wet and with one hand."

"Negative, Quartermaster. They could have knives, pistols."

"I'll take that chance."

"No you won't!"

Warner's shout ended the argument. "He's on his knees."

"Shit," the ensign exclaimed. "He's got something in his hand!"

"No he hasn't," Carpelli shouted.

"Fire! Fire!"

Carpelli hesitated. Lindsay brought up his carbine but the weapon remained silent.

"You fuckin' fags," Bennington spat, squinting down his barrel.

The carbine fired almost like a machine gun, the ensign's finger working like a high-speed piston.

"No!" Michael shouted.

The baby's scalp peeled back above its eyes and a red mist flew into the screaming woman's face, shrieks that were cut short by a half-dozen slugs that ripped her breast and flung the child into the water while the soldier added his hoarse screams, dropping like a felled tree and slipping head first into the ocean leaving a crimson stain. But even in death the woman refused to surrender the wreckage, draping full length on her back over the shattered hull, arms flung out, mouth open and running with blood, dead eyes staring at Michael.

"The captain, sir," Nash said.

Grinning and ignoring Carpelli, Bennington moved close to Nash and the voice tube. The ensign spoke to Isadore Nash, "Tell the captain the soldier had a grenade. I opened fire. The woman was in the line of fire."

There was the sound of hasty feet on the ladder, and a breathless Kohler pulled himself onto the bridge.

Staring at the woman, Michael's vision was clouded with a red mist, his stomach bound up into a hot ball, and his throat constricted. Words were there, but they could not form, and he could only grunt and react instinctively. Bringing up the Thompson, he pointed it at the ensign's back as the officer hunched over the tube.

Something big was in the way, and an arm was suddenly around his neck. Kohler came from the front and Lindsay from the rear. In a moment, Kohler had wrested the weapon from Michael's unfeeling hands. Michael could hear Lindsay whisper close to his ear, "Easy, easy, easy." The arm relaxed and then dropped away.

"What the fuck's going on?" Bennington said suspiciously, turning and staring at Michael.

Carpelli saw nothing but the woman and Kristie — the woman bleeding, Kristie crying.

There was a howl overhead. Every face turned skyward as the howl became a shriek like banshees screaming down from the clouds in anger. Four huge columns of water geysered from the sea five hundred yards beyond the port bow. Shrapnel whined and skipped, kicking water from the sea like rain from a squall.

Ensign Bennington stared numbly.

Carpelli shook his head, mists and ghosts vanishing with the shell fire. He knew an observer high on a bluff at Lagua Lichan had them in his range finder. Somewhere on a reverse slope an artillery officer hunched over his grid map, making corrections while his guns prepared a second salvo.

"Captain's on the bridge," Andrew Bennett shouted, leaping from the last rung. "All ahead flank! All ahead flank," he screamed into the voice tube. "Steady up on the salvo."

Michael felt the ship surge and heel and his mind was suddenly a crystal. "Respectfully, sir. They're registered and those are ranging shots."

"So?"

"They'll expect you to chase the salvo. The next one will be in exactly the same spot and right on top of us."

The Captain bit his lip, winced. "Left to three-two-zero. Three-inch and forty fire on the bluff."

"Target, sir?" came back from the talker.

"Japan, goddamn it."

The cannon and machine gun roared to life. Michael saw bursts on a cliff top but knew the captain had no target and at best their counterfire could only distract.

The banshees returned, and feeling the lash of shells overhead, every man hunched down instinctively as all men do when under shell fire. In exactly the same piece of tortured ocean, four columns leaped and shrapnel flew.

"Score one for Carpelli," Bennett grunted. To the voice tube, "Right to zero-seven-zero. Then to Kohler, "Seventy-fives?"

"Looks like it, sir."

"Best range?"

"Up to sixteen thousand yards, sir."

"That's what I thought." He glanced over his shoulder. "They'll probably stop their salvos and come to rapid fire."

As the captain predicted, the enemy battery began firing a steady stream of shells but, twisting and turning, the PCS gradually steamed out of range.

"All ahead standard," Bennett finally ordered. "Come left to three-one-five. Secure from general quarters. Set the sea watch."

The SCR squawked. After hunching over it, Ensign Bennington turned to the captain. "Old Hickory, sir. He wants us to patrol the reef to Manigassa Island."

"No relief?" Where's the PCS two-four-nine-six?"

"No word, sir. Just proceed to the reef."

Michael heard thunder, far in the distance, quaking and booming.

"Ah, shit," Bennett muttered. "Aren't there any other ships to fight this fuckin' war?" Then to the ensign, "Report the battery, our action against the boat and the raft and tell him we have two slightly wounded." Then to the bridge force, "Well, gentlemen. Manigassa, here we come."

The run from the PCS 2404's position off Lagua Lichan to the Manigassa Island reef was about sixteen miles. Steaming at full speed, the little warship had a full hour's run ahead. After jettisoning the damaged depth charges, the vessel cleared Marpi Point, and Michael was able to "shoot" tangents on both Mucho and Marpi points. Then he descended to the charthouse, which was directly beneath the flying bridge where he "cut in" the sightings with parallel rules and a drafting machine, locating the ship's position precisely on a large chart tacked to the waist-high chart table.

Although the captain was officially the ship's navigator and his sea cabin—a narrow padded bunk more like a bench than a cot—occupied one side of the tiny room, this was the quartermaster's country. Here were kept all of the portfolios of charts, sextant, stadimeter, star finder and publications. The bulkheads were lined with volumes: rows of *Hydrographic Office Publication 214*, *The Nautical Almanac, The Air Almanac, Bowditch, Dutton's, Sailing Directions, Tide and Current Tables, Notice to Mariners* and *Light Lists,* which was useless in wartime.

The chronometer, which was set on gimbals and stored in a padded, fitted locker, was handled as carefully as a newborn baby. Daily, at exactly 1600 hundred hours, Michael walked to the radio shack, clamped earphones to his head and listened for a time tick broadcast from the naval observatory. After starting a stopwatch, he returned to the chart house, carefully removed the timepiece from its little fortress, checked and logged the instrument's error, wound it with exactly eight turns, and returned it. Size of error was not important: only consistency.

After marking his fix—a small "X" with the time, 1100, penciled next to it—Michael lay his parallel rules on the chart and marked a line from the ship's position just northwest of Marpi Point to a point west and north of Manigassa Island and just seaward of the one hundred fathom line. Then working the rules across the chart, he read the course from a compass rose which was the printed face of a gyroscope placed in a corner of the chart.

Reaching up, he opened a voice tube. "Bridge."

"Bridge aye," Bennett's voice echoed back.

"Suggest course two-two-zero."

"Hundred fathom line?"

"Outside of it Captain. We'll steam parallel to the reef, one to two miles seaward of it."

"Very well. ETA Manigassa?"

"Eleven hundred forty, sir."

"Very well. Forty minutes. I'll have Warner relay bearings to you every fifteen minutes."

"Thank you, Captain. Try to get a tangent on Tinian. San Hilo Point should be visible in twenty minutes."

"Very well."

Michael welcomed the challenge of piloting—a problem that focused his mind—but it could not remove the vision of the butchered woman, whose face glowed inside him with the pain of a new wound. Deep down he knew Ensign Bennington had been justified. The ship could not be risked. The cold, diabolical scales of war had a way of balancing blood against humanity and humanity was always outweighed. But the ensign had displayed his cowardice again. Bold and decisive against the helpless, fumbling and frozen when confronted by an armed, resolute foe.

He struck the chart with a clenched fist, rechecked the course. Reaching for the voice tube, "Bridge."

"Bridge, aye."

"There's a three to four knot northeast current off Sabaneta, Captain."

"Could set us in, Quartermaster. I remember. Thank you Michael."

Carpelli returned to the chart. Although he enjoyed the challenge of piloting, celestial navigation was by far the true test of seamanship. With over two years of sea duty behind him, he still thrilled when, with only a chronometer and sextant, he was able to locate the position of a ship smaller than an atom in a 25,000-mile universe. And the methods were crude: Warner steadying him by wrapping an arm around Michael's waist while gripping a stanchion, freeing both of Michael's hands (one to hold the sextant the other to adjust the vernier), dipping the sun, star or planet in an arc until it touched the horizon. The shout of "Mark!" and the quick read of the stopwatch by Andrew Bennett. Bennett would nod and grin as Michael read the altitudes from the counter.

After pouring over the plotting sheets with Andrew Bennett and cutting in a half-dozen sights, Michael never failed to feel a surge of accomplishment. Only infrequently the lines would meet in a "wagon wheel," usually converging on a point and often — when in convoy — morning position hoists would actually locate the ships in formation. Then the skipper and Carpelli would laugh and slap each other on the back.

Without turning, Michael sensed a presence in the cabin.

"Found the New World, yet, Columbus?" Bryan Kohler asked.

Turning, Michael chuckled, "Still looking, but I

239

predict we'll fall off the edge of the world first."

Bryan sat on the bench called "The Captain's Night Cabin" and spoke softly, "Were you about to fall off up there?" He pointed a finger straight up.

Leaning with his back to the table, Michael spoke, "What do you mean?"

"The way you held that tommy gun — pointed it at Bennington."

Michael sighed. "I went a little crazy when he killed that woman."

"I saw it from the stern. His decision was militarily correct."

Michael struck his open palm with a fist. "I know!"

"He had to do it."

"I know! I know!"

"But the woman, why'd you lose your head?"

"She had a baby. Did you want to see them dead?"

"You know me better than that, Michael. She was the first Jap woman I'd ever seen."

"And those were the first live Japs I'd ever seen." Michael stared at the bulkhead. "Did you hear the gunners yelling? Like a football game. They enjoyed themselves."

"Yeah."

"It's true, isn't it Bryan?" Silence. "Did you enjoy yourself when you killed those six?"

"I've killed more than six."

"Whatever."

"Yes."

"Because they were Japs?"

"No. Because they were men and I was there."

"But you hate Japs, Bryan."

"I've never said that. I'll hate whoever my country happens to hate at the time. That'll do. It always has." The voice was matter-of-fact.

"And you happened to be there with a tommy gun."

"That's always how it is, has been, and will be."

"I don't get it."

"Nations always have the weapons and war is an excuse to use those weapons."

"You're a butcher, Bryan."

"What were you in the alley?" He waved off Michael's objections. "We're all butchers, given the opportunity."

"But we can't kill women—kill women and babies." Michael almost gagged on the words.

"Why not?"

"It's inhuman."

"Come on, Michael," Bryan chided. "We left humanity east of the one hundred eightieth meridian."

"No way, Bryan. You couldn't kill that woman."

There was silence for a long minute. "Michael, didn't Bennington fire with unusual speed?"

Michael nodded.

"It seemed that way to you because I got in a burst." The words rocked Michael. "No!"

"Yes."

"Why? Why?"

"The captain ordered me."

"You should've refused."

"We don't refuse."

"I can, Bryan."

For the first time, Bryan's voice rose. "No! No! No! You must obey orders. We all obey orders."

"Even to kill women and babies."

"Of course. There are no options. If we don't, there's no meaning to our lives."

"Bullshit! You sound like Admiral Nimitz."

"Bullshit, my ass. Nimitz, my ass. We have always obeyed our orders—always have." He waved a hand. "That's why all of this works—has meaning." Grimacing, Kohler's white teeth bared. "The Germans are killing Jews."

"That's the rumor."

"It's also rumored they're gassing them."

"I can't believe that. Starvation, gunfire. But mech-

241

anization . . ."

"If it's true, they're still dead, regardless." The pharmacist's mate shrugged.

"What's the point?"

"Someone's giving the order."

Michael thought for a moment. "You mean up the chain to the last link. 'Schicklgruber?'"

"Sure. Why not? That's the system. It works for all of us."

Michael sagged. "Oh, Christ, Bryan. I hope you're wrong."

Bryan pushed himself erect. "You hate Bennington."

"He's a murdering coward."

Carpelli looked up. The pharmacist's mate stared back silently, eyes unusually bright like polished stones.

"You should be transferred, Michael."

"You think I'm crazy."

Kohler smiled back sadly. "Unfortunately, you're the sanest man I've ever met. Sane people don't belong here." Gripping the edge of the bunk, Kohler leaned forward. "But it's the ensign and you know it. You can't serve with him."

"I asked for a transfer."

"What happened?"

"The captain turned me down."

Kohler drummef the bench. "Then you've got to control yourself. You must . . ."

He was interrupted by the captain's voice, pouring from a bulkhead-mounted speaker. "Now hear this. This is the captain speaking. We are underway for Manigassa Island. I just got the word over the SCR and things must be hot because it was in plain language. The *California* will engage a Jap battery on Manigassa as soon as we arrive off the reef. This battery has been firing on our transports as part of a Jap offensive. They're attacking on Saipan and even their artillery on Tinian is firing. But our problem is the battery on Manigassa. They have Tanapag Harbor blocked. In fact, a duck couldn't squeeze his dick into Tanapag without losing his foreskin. Most of our cans are off chasing a Jap task force in the Philippine Sea. So it's up to us. We're to patrol the reef—there's blue water right up to it—and kill any Jap motherfuckers who try to make it to the beach. We'll use all of the ship's armament. The three-inch and forty will use contact fuses.

"We'll go to general quarters in a few minutes. The deck force will give weather decks a clean scrub-down fore and aft—especially around the guns. And keep your sleeves rolled down.

"One thing about the gunnery problem. Our targets will be running on top of a coral reef. Anything high is no good. So aim low—cut off their legs and if you aim low our shot will hit the reef. Exploding coral makes excellent shrapnel. A Jap can't run for shit with a chunk of coral up his ass.

"Don't let one of the bowlegged, yellow sons-of-bitches escape. Remember Aguijan!"

From the sea the mile-long reef stretching to Manigassa Island gleamed in the noon sun iridescently like bleached bones, a long white exclamation mark terminating in the green dot of the island. Pushing his helmet back, Michael swept the panorama of battle with his lenses, finding great clouds of smoke puffing skyward from a ridge just back of Tanapag Town while in the transport area an LST burned and more smoke hung over the southern tip of Saipan and the northern parts of Tinian. At sea, two destroyers and a pair of cruisers were firing on both Saipan and Tinian while the battleship *Tennessee* moved slowly to the south like a great gray tortoise, her fourteen-inch guns punishing Tinian. The *California*, under forced draft, plowed north from Tinian toward Manigassa, her great cannons trained fore and aft.

Sheets of flame leaped from Manigassa Island and shells sent water towering next to a transport.

"Goddamn it! Get the lead out of your ass, *California*," Bennett shouted.

"Why doesn't she fire, sir? She's in range," Dennis Warner asked anxiously.

"Mucho Point is too close to the target. She doesn't have a clear field of fire, yet. But she will when she clears Mucho."

"That won't be long, sir," Warner noted.

"Not long, Signalman."

Whitlow's voice squeaked like the taut string of a violin, "She's training her main battery."

"Those fuckin' Nips are going to get a lesson in gunnery," Bennett said. And then to Ensign Bennington: "Mr. Bennington, move your watch to the forecastle and make sure Chief Schultz keeps his fire low. Longs will hit Mucho Point. This would not make our marines happy—since they occupy it."

"Aye, aye, sir." The ensign vanished down the ladder.

The captain turned to Isadore Nash. "Kohler to the bridge with the tommy guns."

Michael dropped his binoculars. "We can't get that close, sir—fifty yards."

"The charts show blue water right up to the reef."

"Respectfully, the data are old and . . ."

"I know, Quartermaster. We'll have the weapons here, anyway. Now give me a course parallel to the reef and a hundred yards from it. I want to clear Manigassa by at least a mile as soon as the *California* engages the battery."

Michael sighted through the repeater and checked a small chart tacked down on a table. "Zero-five-zero, Captain."

"Very well."

There was thunder at sea and lightning leaped from great clouds of brown smoke as the battleship opened fire. Everyone stared expectantly at Manigassa Island. No one was disappointed. A great pyrotechnic display of exploding shells, flying trees, guns, men, and boulders filled Michael's glasses. There were cheers.

More salvos, and the battery on the convulsing, dust-choked hell fell silent.

"Still zero-five-zero, Quartermaster?"

Michael sighted. "I suggest zero-four-five, Captain."

"Very well. Come left to zero-four-five. All ahead slow." Then to the bridge force, "Keep your eyes peeled. If any of those mothers are alive, they'll make a break for it across the reef." To Nash: "Fathometer, I want continuous readings. Let me know if we shallow less than ten fathoms."

"Captain!" Don Lindsay shouted. "Men on the reef."

"Very well. Radar, range?"

"Six hundred yards."

A crowd of men were fleeing the island. Some staggered, others fell on the jagged coral; all appeared to be in panic. They were helpless.

"Commence firing—commence firing!"

The guns blasted, the ship trembled.

Slowly, the PCS closed on the reef, her fire sweeping men from the sparkling reef like a great broom.

"One hundred yards, Captain," Nash said.

"Left to zero-three-zero."

The twenty-millimeter fire was devastating. Traversing their weapons slowly, the gunners sent hundreds of tracers streaming into the enemy, knocking some from the reef and killing others in heaps. Soon blood was streaming over the coral and into the sea where it spread in red stains.

And the crew cheered hoarse and wild like animals howling in the heat of killing lust. And it was infectious. Carpelli, gripping his weapon and leaning over the windscreen next to Kohler, felt a sudden compulsion to pull the trigger despite the range. There was no fear, no doubt, no conscious thought. Just a primal impulse to destroy other men.

Inspecting the reef piled high with corpses, Bennett laughed. "Cease fire! Cease fire!" Then to Kohler and Carpelli, "Stow it, Jimmy Cagney and Edward G. Robinson. You'll get your chance to use your Chicago pianos, yet. There's plenty of war left." Then waving seaward, he shouted in the voice tube, "Left to zero-zero-zero."

As the ship steadied on the new course, the captain moved to the PA system. "Now hear this, to all hands, well done, well done."

Cheers, wild and uncontrolled.

The lieutenant continued, "We've had a busy war. Now Old Hickory is sending us back to the anchorage. Not exactly R and R, but you've earned a break."

More cheers.

Handing his weapon to Bryan, Michael averted his eyes. The beast was there and they had both felt its claws. He was no better than a jackal. He had wanted to kill those helpless men, not because they were Japs, not because his country had been attacked, not in anger, not in hate and not in vengeance, but only because a weapon was in his hands and they were there to be killed. The alley and Antonio Lopez's face flashed back.

"Secure from general quarters. Set the sea watch."

"You felt it, didn't you, Michael," Bryan said casually.

Without answering, Carpelli turned toward the ladder feeling sick and confused. In one day he had gone from a revulsion to slaughter to a compulsion to kill. And Bryan knew—had read him like a book. How was it possible?

Replacing a destroyer, the 2404 dropped anchor at the north end of the transport area—an anchorage just south of Mucho Point. With the Japanese pushed north to a place called Hagi Ridge, the beaches and anchorage appeared peaceful. For days, the 2404 rode at anchor. With the main engines secured, the ship was very still, with just the gentle hum of blowers and the faint throb of generators deep in her bowels to show a sign of life.

The entire crew welcomed the respite, broken only occasionally at night when bombers sent them to battle stations. Smoke generators as large as water heaters were ignited on the stern, sending billowing black clouds like California smudge pots to hide the scores of transports. But the raiders were few and their bombs did little damage, dropping blindly through the smoke. To every man, the new duty was a welcome change.

Michael, troubled by Bryan's insights and his own mixed emotions, lost himself in his charts. Unable to make his corrections when underway, he spread his charts and made the numerous corrections listed in *Notices to Mariners* with pen and ink. Although he had two quartermaster strikers, Seaman First Class Steve Fleishman and Seaman Second Class Bernie Foat, who could stand bridge watches and man the helm, neither could signal and neither could be trusted with the charts. In fact, many of the charts were inaccurate, some surveyed in the nineteenth century, lacking reefs, rocks, and sometimes even small islands.

Hunched over his table early one afternoon, Michael heard the door close behind him. Turning, the quartermaster found Ensign Robert Bennington standing in the middle of the room. Slowly Michael came to his feet. There was no attempt to conceal the contempt in his voice. "What do you want?"

"A word with you, Quartermaster."

247

"Go ahead. I'm your subordinate. Lavish your words on me."

"You think I'm a dirty, stupid son-of-a-bitch."

"What are you trying to do, Ensign, hustle me into a court-martial?"

"Off the record, Quartermaster."

Michael smiled. "Who said you're dirty?"

Ignoring the rejoinder, the ensign pressed on, "You think I fucked up off Aguijan."

"I *know* you fucked up off Aguijan. We buried your mistakes—Winters, Barton and Murphy—at sea. Remember? You invited us to the funeral. I've already told you."

"And the woman?"

"It wasn't necessary, Ensign."

"It was militarily correct."

"I keep hearing that. And the Germans are telling themselves that very thing every time they kill another batch of Jews."

"She was in the line of fire, Carpelli."

"And Winters? Barton? Murphy? Welly? Whose line of fire? And who tied up?"

"We executed our mission—punished the enemy."

"You executed my shipmates."

Forehead seamed and glistening and brows pinched down to an arrowhead, the ensign leaned forward. "It's easy for you. Oh, yes, the hero. Just stand and watch while your officers make their decisions. Criticize, make your remarks and hide behind the old man . . ."

Michael's face became an oven. Eyes bulging, he interrupted, "I don't take that shit from you. I don't hide behind anyone. If you'd like to find out. . ."

"The hell you won't take shit off me."

"This is off the record. There's no rank in this chart house, Ensign." He eyed the officer from head to toe and back.

Bennington's feet were spread, fists clenched at his

side. There was no fear in his eyes.

"Go ahead and swing, Ensign."

"Not here."

"Where? At home? When we're civilians? A decade from now? A century from now?" The enlisted man's voice was mocking.

"No! The first time we make the beach. Anywhere. Any time. We can find privacy. I'll take these off." He fingered a gold bar pinned to the open collar of his tan shirt. "We'll settle it then."

"It'll be a pleasure, sir."

Turning, Bennington reached for the doorknob. Then, as an afterthought, he spat over his shoulder, "I hope someday you command. You make the decisions. You put men's lives on the line." He closed the door.

Michael returned to his charts. There was a smile on his face.

"You and Bennington still going steady?" Don Lindsay asked, seated on the lazaret hatch, sharpening his knife. Schultz and Kohler laughed as they looked at Michael and ran files over their own blades.

Because of watch schedules, the four friends had found it difficult to meet together. Finally, by some quirk of scheduling, they were all free at the same time. Seated together on the lazaret, they all busied themselves with their knives.

"He turned down my senior ring," Michael quipped back.

"Look at that," Kohler said, waving at the port depth charge rack. "That mortar bomb really tore it up."

"Shoot, man. I done that with my little ol' crowbar," Schultz said. Then while taking long strokes with his file, "Hear about the PCS Two Four Nine Six?"

"She got clobbered. Sprayed by a five hundred

249

pounder. Eight dead, twelve wounded. That's why she didn't relieve us off Marpi Point," Michael answered.

"Wooden ship in a steel war," Kohler said, bitterly.

"Keerect. Don't make no sense. An' her exec got it."

"So? I didn't know."

Schultz pursed his lips. Made a popping sound. "Left some writin'."

Michael, Don and Bryan all turned expectantly.

"He got a chunk of Jap iron in the throat — made it back to his cabin and done wrote on a shoe box with his finger dipped in his own blood . . ." He stopped.

"Well?"

" 'Break the news gently to Helen and give 'em hell.' Then he cashed in."

"No shit?" Bryan said.

Lindsay spoke. "He actually wrote that?"

"Got it straight from the horse's ass — namely, their chief gunner's mate. Met him on the *Agenor.*"

"Can't believe it," Michael said.

"Seen too many movies, I reckon," Schultz noted. Then, quickly changing the subject, he added, "Got a letter from Thelma."

Michael winced. The mailboat, a battle-scarred subchaser, had been alongside that morning. He had received two letters from his mother, one from his cousin Joan in New York City, one from Dale, and another from Ernie. But none from Kristie.

"Still mad about you?" Lindsay asked, raising an eyebrow.

"Sure 'nuff. She's still hankerin' "

"Like a polecat in heat."

" 'Nuff of that, boy," Schultz retorted, waving his blade in a mock threat.

"Sorry," Lindsay said, grinning. "Got a couple letters from Rose," he added.

Bryan nodded. "Yeah. I heard from Marilyn."

Michael turned quickly, "Did she say anything about Vicki?"

Bryan stared at the deck. "Yes, she did."

"Well?"

The voice was funereal. "Marilyn said she was completely withdrawn. Catatonic."

"Oh, no. No!"

For a long minute, there was only the sound of files on steel. Finally, Schultz startled everyone. "Do you boys reckon there's a God . . ."

Lindsay snickered.

"I ain't funnin', Don."

"Sorry."

"If there is," Michael answered thoughtfully, "he's not out here."

"Where is he?"

Kohler spoke, "Back home helping out the war effort and staring benignly down on the four-Fs while they screw our women. He's definitely not interested in PCSs."

"Do you figure he was watchin' off Marpi? Do you reckon he was countin' bodies on the Manigassa reef? How's about that exec who wrote on his shoe box? Is he the skipper of some patrol craft up there?" The chief stabbed a finger skyward.

Lindsay's voice was earnest. "When I was in boot camp, the chaplains always told us it was okay to kill Japs. It was in the Bible."

"Every fuckin' thing you want is in the Bible. Murder, mayhem," Bryan said. "I'll bet the Germans can even justify what they're doing to the Jews by book and verse."

"I'm sure of that," Michael said. He turned to Schultz. "The Japs have gods, Algernon."

"I know. And Hirohito is top dog."

"Right."

"An' they can make it big," he waved a hand, "by spillin' their guts like them dudes on the reef. But they're a bunch of murderin' critters who slaughtered our boys at Pearl for no reason."

251

"Right, Chief," Bryan allowed. "But, in their own minds, they had their reasons."

Everyone stared.

He continued, "I hate the bastards, but like I said, in their own way they had their reasons. People always do for starting wars. Christ, according to the Krauts, the Poles attacked them."

"It don't figger."

Bryan turned his palms up in a gesture of futility. "True, but, you know, every nation in every war has needed a Pearl Harbor."

"I reckon. You mean an Alamo," Schultz said.

"Right, Chief."

"What was the Japs' Pearl?"

Bryan hunched forward. "Oil, scrap iron, their war with China, pride. We cut off their oil and iron and told them to get out of China. Even sent the Flying Tigers to fight them. You don't do that to the Nips."

Everyone nodded.

Bryan pressed on, "And they're a suicidal bunch, dying for a chance to die. You saw that at Marpi and Manigassa."

"Sure 'nuff. An' they're wrong," Schultz said. "That's why we're here. That's why we kick ass."

Bryan and Michael exchanged a look. "True," Bryan said. "But there's something else." He studied his razor's edge.

"What?"

"We watch each other."

The chief was astonished. "You been swillin' white lightnin'?"

Bryan laughed. "No, Chief. I mean there are a lot of reasons why we do this. Don't discount the fact that we can't let each other down."

The chief took a long swipe with a stone. Tested an edge that would have brought envy to Saladin's face. "I guess you're right, Bryan," he said thoughtfully. "Never put it in that mind. True, in a way, we've been knockin' chips off each other's shoulders."

"Of course."

"But you ain't saying we started this ruckus?"

"Not really, Algernon. But it takes two to tango."

"They invited us to this hoedown," Schultz muttered.

Everyone laughed.

Michael spoke to the chief, "You know Chief, if we live through this, someday, we may get a chance to look back."

"I don't get you."

"Looking back, Chief. That's the only way to understand something like this. Separate yourself from it by forty, fifty years minimum. Then look back. Then you can see more and maybe why."

The chief waved at the island. "I saw them critters in the boat. I saw them on the reef. I saw them dead. That's enough."

"It's a way to solve the problem," Lindsay agreed.

Michael and Bryan discarded their files and began running stones over their blades.

"Sharp?" Schultz asked.

"As a possum's tooth," Michael answered, mimicking the chief.

Everyone laughed.

Michael was hunched over the chart table when the captain's acerbic voice ripped through the PA system. He had just moved a small island in the Caroline Islands one full mile west when the cynical, derisive timbre — a combination of Edward R. Murrow and Walter Winchell — poured from the speaker, stopping his pen in midstroke.

"Gentlemen!" the voice cooed, free of military idiom, "This is your tour guide speaking. Splendid news!"

Michael was on guard.

"Now that the battery on Manigassa Island is permanently out of business, harbor tours of Tanapag Harbor are underway."

Michael heard a groan sweep the ship.

"Because of the Two Four O Four's distinguished record these past fun-filled weeks, we have been specially selected to enjoy the first tour of this lovely, historic facility. You may not know this, but this harbor is famous for placid waters, breathtaking views and friendly natives. Prominent amongst its attractions are several vessels which are filled with innumerable delights and surprises for the guileless tourist. At thirteen hundred hours, the first tour will begin. Planning for this happy event will start immediately in my cabin."

The cynical tones vanished, replaced by the military voice, "Ensign Manning, Chief Schultz, Pharmacist's Mate Kohler, Quartermaster Carpelli and Gunner's Mate Lindsay report to my cabin on the double. The deck force will give all weather decks a clean scrub-down fore and aft—especially around the guns."

"Old Hickory believes there are snipers here in this five-thousand-tonner, the *Tomatsu Maru*," Bennett said from his chair, stabbing a pencil at a chart of Tanapag Harbor. "They've been picking off marines on Mucho Point and the marines can't reach them. They can only be had from seaward."

The tiny cabin was jammed, with Ensign Manning, Schultz, Lindsay, Kohler, and Michael crowding around the captain's desk.

"We're to take the first tour?" Michael asked.

"Yes. You four volunteered because you handle the small arms better than any of the other men."

"Oh," Kohler said. "I was wondering why I volunteered."

Everyone chuckled.

"Mines?" Schultz asked.

"Frogmen from the UDT cleared two this morning. The channel's clear to this point." His finger indicated a point just north of Mucho Point. "There's a can sunk here in the main channel."

Michael ran a finger over Tanapag Town, the fueling dock and nearby foothills. "They could have artillery anywhere, sir — five, six thousand yards."

"And they probably do," Bennett agreed. "But we'll have a Piper Cub spotter and the *California*, and two cans will be standing by here." His finger struck the chart seaward of Manigassa Island.

"Reckon they ain't gonna pull down with the big 'C' out there," Schultz acknowledged.

"We'll stand in here" — the captain ran a finger up the main channel — "to the wrecked can here, lay to off the freighter here, and send you over in the wherry."

"You mean," Lindsay said with a wry smile, "we'll board her like Errol Flynn boarded that *greaser* in *Captain Blood*."

"Cutlasses and all."

"May I wear a red bandana?"

Bennett chuckled. "Linsday, I don't care if you wear a red jockstrap."

Schultz's voice cut through the laughter. "If they cut an' shoot, Capt'n, we'll be the turkey's ass at a Thanksgivin' shoot."

"We'll cover you."

Kohler asked, "We'll search the entire ship?"

For the first time, Manning spoke. His voice was surprisingly firm. "Most of the superstructure is above water. Pilot house, wheel house, radio shack. If there are snipers aboard, there will be dozens of places for them to hide."

"We'll need grenades," Kohler said.

"I'll bring a sack of grenades," the ensign answered.

"Nine second fuses?"

Manning was obviously surprised. "Why yes, Kohler."

"Old-fashioned. No good," the pharmacist's mate noted. "On the canal, they threw them back."

Bennett spoke. "Pull the pin and hold them for six seconds."

Manning gulped, "Yes, sir."

"Now get your weapons and take plenty of ammunition. We'll get underway as soon as we can get the hook up."

The men shuffled through the door.

Standing in the ship's waist with the rest of the boarding party and burdened with his tommy gun and two 20-pound box magazines in pouches on his duty belt, Michael watched Manigassa Island slip slowly past the port side, the once lush green cay now a blasted moonscape with every scrap of vegetation obliterated. Rocks, twisted guns, chunks of coral and fragments of concrete had been scattered in casual heaps by the rain of 1,800-pound shells. Nothing moved. Not even a gull. A soft breeze blowing down from the reef brought the faint odor of rotting meat from heaps of khaki-clad cadavers. Feeling a familiar emptiness, Michael turned his head.

On the starboard side only a few feet from the hull he could see the delicate bushlike growth of a jagged, razor-sharp coral reef. In fact, now that he was in the channel, he could see that the ship was actually in a passageway that had been blasted through barrier after barrier of coral. To both port and starboard the jagged edges raised menacing fingers, eager for the unwary ship's bottom. But ahead and astern, Michael saw blue water.

The harbor was a shambles, jammed with the corpses of at least a dozen ships. Blocking the channel a hundred yards in, lying on her starboard side with her stack dipping water, was the destroyer. Her bow had been blown off all the way back to the number two mount. The rest of the dead ships were merchant-men—two oilers and perhaps ten cargo and transport vessels. All had been ripped savagely. Masts, super-structures, and shattered hulls projected above the surface everywhere. At the far end, below the sham-bles of the town, the harbor's lone fuel tank—a jumble of burned-out scrap metal—still smouldered. Just be-low the tank and jutting out into the bay, a long pier had been smashed to matchwood.

High above the hills a lone Piper Cub buzzed and circled like a greedy fly over carrion.

The 2404's target was a classic wreck. She was the vessel closest to Mucho Point. Despite her great dis-placement, she appeared to have been blown up and hurled into the shallows fronting the peninsula. A bomb—it must have been a 1,000-pounder—had struck the stern, tearing the entire stern frame free, twisting it from the keel so that the rudder projected above the water like the dorsal fin of a great dead sea monster. Amidships, other bombs had blasted plating from the hull, exposing rows of bent frames like the ribs of a long-dead whale. Long steel stringers were bent out from the hull like arthritic fingers while the decks were littered with smashed derricks, a downed boom, winches, tackle, and collapsed rigging. Her su-perstructure had been raked by the sharp claws of shrapnel, every port and window broken, long smears of rust etching crazy patterns in burned, filthy white paint. A lifeboat, smashed to splinters, hung from its davits.

"Must have been some party," Lindsay said with un-characteristic solemnity.

"What was left of a convoy. Escaped our subs but not our SBDs," Manning said.

"Lots of places to play hide-an'-seek," Lindsay mut-tered.

But the ship's bow was still intact, *Tomatsu Maru* still visible, a dirty white against the black hull. And high above her forecastle, tilting crazily with stays ripped away, her foremast still supported a crow's nest.

"Shit, look at the armed guard," Bryan said, waving a hand at the bow, where a single seventy-five-millimeter field piece sat neatly trimmed fore and aft on a circular platform built above the foredeck.

Nothing moved. They were in a morgue. Then Michael detected something amiss. The gun *was* moving, turning toward the PCS.

He could hear Bennett's screams from the bridge, "Commence firing! Commence firing!"

Six figures suddenly materialized on the platform and began tugging on the gun's huge ironshod wagon wheels. Incongruously, one was an officer in dress blues, wearing a white headband and carrying a long swagger stick which he stabbed at the patrol craft.

Number three twenty-millimeter was only a few feet from Michael when a bright bar of flickering flame sprang from the muzzle and the hammering clatter dinned on his eardrums. Pressing against the shoulder rests, the gunner eyed his tracer stream as he held the weapon on full trigger, the loader standing by gripping a sixty-round magazine with both hands. Slowly, the gunner traversed the Orlikon like a meticulous housewife sweeping a dirty floor. Smoke blew into Carpelli's face and the reek of cordite stung his throat and made his eyes run.

Firing as fast as the loader could ram shells into the breech, the three-inch hurled three shells over the wreck and into Mucho Point while Bennett screamed in anger and horror. But the tracers from the machine guns were a blizzard as they had been at the reef, brooming every Japanese from the platform before a single round could be fired. Then the cannon made two successive hits, sending the fieldpiece flying, its wheels spinning free

258

of the carriage like giant pinwheels.

"Cease fire! Cease fire!" Then came: "Boarders away."

Gripping the lifeline and standing on the bumper, Michael lowered himself slowly and carefully into the wherry. With five men and their weapons, the small boat was heavily laden, showing only a few inches of freeboard. Then, with a sputter, Manning brought the small outboard motor to life and the party headed for the wreck.

"Amidships, sir. A net," Michael said.

"I see it. They must have used it when they abandoned ship." Manning moved the tiller.

Carefully, Michael studied the vessel. But nothing moved. Not even the wind stirred and the only sound in the harbor was the buzz of the outboard motor. Looking back, Michael saw the 2404 drifting close aboard, every weapon trained on the *Tomatsu Maru*.

The quartermaster felt naked, and he worried about Manning. He was in command. Would the ensign freeze like Bennington had off Aguijan? Would more men be killed? And the ensign carried a sack full of old-fashioned grenades with nine-second fuses. He could kill them all. Or a sniper's bullet could set off the bombs.

Carpelli actually felt relieved when the wherry came alongside the wreck where Schultz secured the bow painter to the net.

Slinging their weapons over their shoulders and with the other boarders close behind, Carpelli and Kohler scrambled over the wreck's bulwark together and tumbled to the rusty, pitted deck. Gripping their weapons, they scampered across the deck like big crabs to a steel locker that gave protection from the bridge. Lindsay, Schultz, and Manning followed.

Then it happened. There was the crack of a rifle and the sound of a hammer striking a pot. Don Lindsay went straight down as though his bones had

259

melted. His mouth worked a few times and he rolled onto his back.

Screaming, "Don! Don!" Schultz grabbed Lindsay by the shoulders and began dragging him. Manning leaped across the deck and hid behind a ventilator. Cursing, Kohler came to his feet and sprayed the bridge. Thudding into steel, bullets whined and ricocheted. Another crack followed by a clang and rusty metal particles were kicked up at Schultz's feet.

"Where are they? Where are they?"

The chief gunner's mate dragged Lindsay to the locker, leaving a trail of thick, black blood. There was a hole in his helmet. Frantically, the chief pulled the stricken man's helmet from his head. Blood, shattered bone and brains oozed from a huge exit wound in the back of the dead man's head.

"Don! Don!" Schultz moaned, dipping his hands in the gore and trying to push it back into the dead man's head. "A dum-dum. Them sons of bitches—a dum-dum."

"He's dead! He's dead," the pharmacist's mate shrieked. "For Christ's sake, Algernon, you can't put him back together. Get down!"

The chief crouched.

Two more clangs on top of the locker, the whine of ricochets and particles stung Michael's cheeks like needles of blown ice. The quartermaster looked up, saw movement high overhead. He screamed, "The crow's nest! The crow's nest! Those sons of bitches."

Howling like a wounded animal, the chief leaped out into the open and rolled over on his back, firing.

"No! For Christ's sake, Schultz," Carpelli shouted. But the gunner's mate ignored him.

Cursing, Carpelli and Kohler slid on their backs from their shelter and began firing upward into the bottom of the crow's nest, shredding the rotten wood flooring of the basketlike platform. A cloud of splinters showered and there were screams. A rifle sailed end over end, bouncing from the roof of the radio shack onto the main deck. Blood began to rain.

Wood cracked and broke with ripping, popping sounds and the bottom of the crow's nest gave way. A body dressed in bloody rags crashed down on the roof of the radio shack and then bounced to the main deck, arm and legs flailing loosely, leaving bloody smears on the side of the radio room like paint thrown by a mad artist. Feet tangled in the flooring, a second sniper hung head down from the nest, convulsing like an epileptic, arms jittering, blood pouring from his mouth, nose and chest. His shrill, undulating shrieks rent Michael's ears like the screech of venting steam from a high-pressure boiler.

Manning's voice, trembling but under control: "Lindsay. How is he?"

"Dead," the pharmacist's mate answered.

"Shut that son of a bitch up," Manning shouted, waving overhead at the howling Japanese.

The chief raised his weapon and fired two rounds. There was a scream, then silence, and the man hung quietly, swinging gently in the breeze like a butchered steer, head lolling from the impact of metal, blood draining from his body in a steady stream that splattered Michael's helmet and coagulated on his face and clothes.

There was a pause while every man caught his breath. Manning spoke, "We'll split the Thompsons. Kohler with me. We'll check out the crew's quarters aft. Carpelli, you stay with Schultz. Check out the bridge."

After seeing Manning and Kohler scamper aft safely, Carpelli turned to Schultz. "You okay?"

No answer.

"Chief. You stay here. I'll check out the bridge."

"No way, Michael. I ain't chicken-shit."

"I know that. You okay?"

"I'm ready. Let's git a-goin', Mate. Time's a wastin'."

261

Clutching their weapons, the pair moved forward, dodging into the shelter of ventilators and doorways. Glancing fearfully over their shoulders, they scurried up a ladder to the wheelhouse, their shoes clanging on the bent and warped treads. Standing on the port wing of the bridge, they found the door to the wheelhouse closed. All was quiet.

Schultz kicked the door open.

A Japanese naval officer with a white band around his head and a sword hanging from the belt of his dress blues was seated behind the ship's wheel, staring at a shattered binnacle. His bloody left arm dangled straight down and a giant swagger stick was on the deck behind him, next to the smashed engine room telegraph. He turned slowly to the Americans.

His youthful face was lined with fatigue; his eyes appeared to hold some secret, cynical amusement. He spoke in perfect English. "Commander Sachiko Matsushima. Born in Corvallis, Oregon, 2 March 1917." A smile cracked a network of lines and the youthfulness vanished. "Welcome to Saipan, Yankees."

Michael stared in disbelief. After two years, a live enemy a few feet away, smiling and boasting that he was an American. He had heard about the nisei, thousands of them serving Japan. And he could hate — hate easily when he thought about his dead comrades. But this slender, wounded officer with the friendly smile was suddenly just another injured, helpless man. But not to Schultz, who could only see blood.

"Welcome your ancestors, Nip prick," he spat. There was the click of a firing pin striking a cartridge. Cursing, the chief worked his bolt. Nothing ejected.

"Shoot him, damn you. Shoot!" he screamed.

The smile vanished from the officer's face and he began to turn. Lindsay's face came back with the red halo of gore splattered around his head.

Michael pulled the trigger. The Thompson leaped like a live thing and he held it down hard, the roar of the forty-five-caliber weapon in the small compartment deafening him, booming and echoing like great drums. Struck by a hail of slugs, the officer spun in a full turn that sent him crashing backward against the opposite bulkhead, blood oozing from huge punctures in his chest. After twitching spasmodically, he sagged back and relaxed in the embrace of death.

Michael could hear Algernon sigh, "Good! Good! A good Jap."

Staring at the corpse, Michael felt no remorse. Instead, he was swept by a strange elation, like a mountain climber who had finally scaled the ultimate peak. *So this is what it's all about,* ran through his mind.

He felt the chief's hand on his arm. "Let's haul ass, boy."

Two blasts jarred them. Quickly, the pair stepped out on the iron grating of the port wing. There, they could hear Ensign Manning's excited shouts. "We got two! They're nothing but fertilizer now!"

Then, for the first time, Michael heard the strange words. He would never forget them. *"Han kook sa ram, han kook sa ram."* The voices came from amidships.

Slowly three sailors crawled out from under the ruins of the funnel and formed a shabby line behind Lindsay's body. They continued to shout the strange words, *"Han kook sa ram."*

After the chief cleared his jam, Schultz and Carpelli descended the ladder and moved aft, stopping side by side in front of the prisoners, weapons leveled.

All were young, all were thin with ribs protruding through yellow parchment and all were dressed only in torn dungaree pants. One had a gold crucifix dangling around his neck on a long gold chain.

"Christian! Christian!" he begged, holding the cross and thrusting it toward the Americans. then, he shouted again, *"Han kook sa ram."*

Michael could hear hard footsteps on steel as Manning and Kohler ran toward them. Manning shouted,

263

"We want prisoners. Don't shoot. They're hard to get."

"Christian! Christian!" the prisoner shouted. His companions bowed and grunted.

"Fuck you, Manning," Schultz bellowed. "Tell it to Don! I don't cotton to that shit!"

Whirling, Michael brought a hand upward under the gunner's carbine and it fired two rounds straight up and then clicked, jamming again. Pushing hard, Michael pinned the chief against a bulkhead.

The prisoners hurled themselves to the deck, crying and screaming. There was the strong smell of ammonia as two of them lost control of their bladders, filling their dungarees with sulphur-yellow urine.

Breathlessly, Kohler and Manning rushed up and helped restrain the chief. Manning took his carbine.

"Okay! Okay!" Schultz managed. "I'm okay."

It took two trips to ferry the prisoners and Lindsay's body back to the patrol craft. Busy conning as he backed the ship down and out of the channel, the captain sent word for Ensign Manning to report to the bridge and to assemble the prisoners amidships with their pants dropped to their ankles.

Suddenly fatigued, Michael leaned against number three twenty-millimeter ready box between the chief and Bryan and stared at the prisoners. They had all dropped their pants and they all wore those strange, diaperlike skivvies. Staring around wide-eyed, they appeared more than thin: they were starved with hollow cheeks, marble pale skin, lips gray, eyes sunken into blue hollows, ribs and bones protruding. None could have weighed more than one hundred pounds. These were the enemy? The cold, diabolical foe who killed so ruthlessly? He shook his head.

And he had killed a man coldly and with very little emotion. It had been over two years. Strange. But in a war very few ever saw the enemy and only a tiny minority ever pulled a trigger. In the alley with Antonio Lopez, he had fought for his life. But here, the fates had singled him out. He knew he hated the enemy. Japs had obliterated the subchaser and killed many of his friends. Notwithstanding, he hadn't felt hate in the wheelhouse of the *Tomatsu Maru*. In fact, the tall thin Jap with the toothy smile exuded friendliness and spoke of home. But he had been there with a weapon when killing was to be done. He had been trapped by converging circumstances. Maybe Bryan was right. He was beginning to make sense.

The gun crews of number three twenty-millimeter and the forty stood silently, staring at the dead man and at the prisoners. Michael's eyes moved to Lindsay. The once happy face was gray, mouth open, eyes staring straight up, a small purple hole at the top of his forehead just below the hairline. And he had his red bandana, a circle of gore that had oozed on the deck from the huge exit wound at the back of his head.

It was hard to believe the wit and humor would never come again, that he would never flirt with another pretty girl, make love and laugh with the sheer joy of life. Michael knew another bit of himself had died with Don Lindsay the same way he had died with every boy on Saipan, North Africa, Normandy, or over Schweinfurt. *If old men know when an old man dies, what do young men know?* he asked himself.

The ship continued backing and the men stared silently. The prisoners whimpered.

Michael heard Schultz breathing hard. Turning, he saw the chief staring at his dead friend, eyes wide and cold as a tomb, jaw tight, neck cords bulging.

"Easy, man," Michael said, taking the chief's arm.

Suddenly, the prisoner wearing the crucifix screamed the strange words again. *"Han kook sa ram."* He held the crucifix in front of his chest.

Snarling like a rabid dog, Schultz pulled free from Michael. In a single motion he grabbed a boat hook from a boatswain's mate, who had used it to steady the wherry, and with all his strength rammed it into the prisoner's chest, knocking him flat on his back and driving the cross into the man's heart. The man screamed once, gasped bloody bubbles and died almost immediately.

The two surviving prisoners hurled themselves to the deck, screaming and crying.

Leaping, Michael caught the chief in a headlock and wrestled him to the deck with the aid of Kohler and a gunner. But the chief was powerful, struggled wildly. Carpelli slapped the man across the face, shouting, "Chief! Chief! For Christ's sake, Algernon, come out of it!"

Suddenly relaxing, the gunner began to mutter, "Okay, Carpelli — okay." Then, slowly, the men came to their feet.

Shouting obscenities, Bennett rushed from the bridge. "Goddamn it! We need prisoners. I'll court-martial your ass, Chief!" He glanced at Lindsay and turned to a deckhand. "Cover him with a tarp — on the double," he said thickly. Then he moved close to the two surviving prisoners who still crouched on the deck. "Queer-looking Japs," he said to himself. And to a seaman: "Moore, get my stewart's mate."

"Aye, aye, sir." Moore vanished into the wardroom.

The gunners began to growl in unison, "Kill the Japs! Kill! Kill!"

"At ease! At ease! Belay that crap." Bennett shouted.

As the men fell silent, Stewart's Mate José Garcia walked up and stared down at the prisoners.

The prisoners stared back at the Filipino as if they had found an old shipmate. *"Han kook sa ram. Han kook sa ram,"* they chorused.

Garcia turned his flat, dead face to Chief Schultz. "Congratulations, Chief. You just killed a Korean."

"Ain't nothin'," Schultz spat. "He's just another fuckin' gook to me." Then he turned quickly and climbed a ladder, vanishing forward.

266

That afternoon the 2404 headed for the Mariana's Deep where Gunner's Mate Third Class Donald Lindsay was buried in 32,000 feet of water. As the burial detail gathered amidships, the dying sun flickered low on the horizon, sinking into a bloodred pool of glowing mist and haze, coloring the western skies with infinite hues of russet and gray, reflecting from the sea with the pallor of a cadaver's flesh.

To the north and west rain was in the air, great ranges of brooding cumulus clouds with dark heads the color of ashes. And rain was to the east, too, where line squalls cluttered the horizon and gray curtains of rain slanted from drooping clouds.

The wind was restless, whipping the halyards and grabbing the sailors' blue hats angrily while the gray sea parted and spumed white before the knife of the stem and then closed in quickly to froth and bubble in the ship's wake.

There was a palpable aura of death in the air. Standing next to the canvass-shrouded body, Michael shivered in its grasp. Two dozen sailors, dressed in foul weather gear, were gathered amidships, holding ranks on both sides of the body loosely as they rolled with the ship. There was a flag over the body and Bennett stood at its head, holding a Bible. With his mind racing with thoughts of Lindsay, death and more death, the nightmare from which he could awake but not escape because the dream was reality and reality a nightmare, Michael only heard snatches of the ancient service when the captain's voice broke through the racing kaleidoscope of images.

"They that go down to the sea in ships, that do business in great water . . ."

Chief Schultz sobbed with unabashed grief. Michael took his arm.

"We commend into thy hands of mercy, most merciful father, the soul of our brother, Gunner's Mate Third Class Don Lindsay."

Closing the Bible, he nodded. Two seamen raised and folded the flag while a pair of boatswain's mates raised the head of the body and it slid quickly over the side. Weighted by two three-inch shells sewn into the legs, it splashed into the sea and plunged quickly out of sight in the black depths.

With suddenness found only in the tropics, a squall was on them, wind howling like a ravening beast, rain hissing down like gray arrow shafts, splashing their faces, stinging their eyes, and pounding on their parkas. Thunder jarred the ship and lightning flashed blue.

"Chief! Chief!" Michael said softly. "Come on—to the chart house."

But the chief was a statue, staring back at the wake.

"Come on, Chief," Bryan Kohler pleaded, taking Schultz's other arm. "Let's get under cover."

The chief muttered to the ship's wake, "I've had my Pearl—my Alamo. I know. I know."

Slowly his two friends led him forward.

Head back, Chief Schultz sagged onto the captain's cot while Bryan sat beside him. Michael, back to the chart table, leaned back, supporting himself on his elbows.

Before anyone could speak, the captain's voice filled the chart house. "Now hear this. This is the captain speaking. We will relieve a DEL'—Destroyer Escort Leader—"in the anchorage and drop the hook just south of Mucho Point. As you know, this is good duty and we have earned it. This ship has fought enough of World War Two for a long while. Now we will give some other units an opportunity for glory."

Michael heard a weak cheer.

"It should last this time because two SCs and two

268

PCs"—steel patrol craft—"will arrive tomorrow from Eniwetok. Also, two divisions of cans have been released for radar picket duty from Task Force Fifty-Eight, which kicked the shit out of the Jap fleet in the Philippine Sea, sank four carriers and the word is the F-Six-Fs had a real turkey shoot—maybe four hundred kills. The cans should arrive tomorrow. The *Agenor* put the Two Four Nine Six back together and she's rejoined the screen off Marpi Point."

Bennett cleared his throat.

"You've had a rough campaign—done enough fighting for all of Seronten. You deserve a rest, and now you'll have it. The campaign is nearly over, the enemy is close to complete defeat. As you know, thousands of Japs are throwing themselves from Marpi Point. Most are civilians. It's unfortunate, but there is nothing anyone can do. I understand that the marines try to persuade them through loudspeakers, but they won't listen. Just like that bunch we caught off Lagua Lichan.

"I wish you could swim at the anchorage, but you know with the bodies and the sharks that is impossible. But we'll relax, use four sections with the forty as the ready gun, lookouts, radio, and radar. You'll have four on and twelve off."

Cheers.

"One other thing, a Jap sub was depth charged by one of our DEs"—Destroyer Escort—"off Magicienne Bay. She could still be around. We'll man the sonar gear on a listening watch, only.

"Once again, you have conducted yourselves as professionals. I'm proud to serve with you. Well done." The PA system hummed and then clicked off.

"Well done? A rat's ass," Schultz said to the deck.

Michael sighed. "You boys wait here. Old dad has a surprise."

"Surprise?" Bryan said, looking up.

"Stay put," Michael said, rising. Quickly, the quar-

269

termaster opened the door to the radio shack, passed two bored radiomen seated at typewriters and with earphones to their ears, and exited onto the boat deck where cold rain lashed his face. A few long strides up a short ladder brought him to the canvass flag bag which was located on a separate platform just aft of the flying bridge. With cold fingers the quartermaster unsnapped the corner of the heavy tarpaulin cover, groped deep, and then grunted with satisfaction when his hand encountered a firm bundle of newspapers. Clutching the bundle, he returned to the chart house.

Watching Michael place the papers on the table, Bryan said, "Going to read us 'Maggie and Jiggs'?"

Michael chuckled as he unwrapped the papers, exposing a fifth of Seagram's V.O.

For the first time Chief Schultz appeared animated. "Doggon' boy, what you done got there?"

"White lightning," Michael answered, handing the bottle to the chief.

"Shoot," Algernon said, admiring the label, "this is sippin' whiskey." He took a long pull, handed the bottle to Bryan who drank and passed it to Michael. Silently and quickly the bottle made two more rounds.

"A miracle," Bryan mumbled.

Michael laughed.

Relaxing, the chief spoke, "Poor Don, never know'd what poleaxed him."

"It was fast," Bryan acknowledged.

Schultz took another drink, smacked his lips. "I know you boys don't put much truck in God, but I'm a hopin' there's one."

"So do I," Michael said.

"Amen," Bryan added.

" 'Cause Don sure 'nuff is with him now," Algernon said. He drank deeply. Bryan and Michael took short sips, returned the bottle to the chief who looked at it wistfully. "Got the next watch on the forty." He offered the liquor to Bryan.

Bryan pushed it back. "I'll take your watch, Chief. Have another pull."

"I can stand my own. I ain't hankerin' to get out of nothin'."

"I know," Bryan interrupted. "It's a trade. Okay?"

The chief nodded, drank again. "He was a good ol' boy—a mite rambunctious, but a good ol' boy."

"He was that."

"I'll write his kin."

"The captain will."

"I'm obliged." Silence while the chief drank again. "He didn't feel nothin'."

"True."

"Ain't no better way to check out." The chief held the bottle up in a salute. Drank. "I don't have no trouble now."

"With what," Michael said. "What do you mean?"

"Knowin' why I'm here."

Nodding silently, Bryan and Michael exchanged a glance.

"What about you boys?"

"Kill the sons of bitches," Bryan said. He took a short drink, handed the bottle to Michael.

After drinking, Michael wiped his mouth with his sleeve. "As Don said once, that would solve the problem."

"Bust every last one," the chief said, taking the bottle. The words were slurred. "Stake out their fuckin' hides."

"Sew salt," Bryan said.

"Salt?"

"Yeah. That's what the Romans did to Carthage."

"Killin's enough," Algernon said. "Don't need no seasonin'."

Bryan and Michael chuckled.

"Whew!" Schultz said, shaking his head and staring at the bottle, "this stuff's shuckin' the hair right off my balls."

271

"Builds muscles," Bryan said, rising.

"Where you goin'?"

"Get some 'joe,' Chief," Bryan said, looking down.

Schultz shook the bottle. "Almost half left."

"For you, Chief," Michael said.

"Shoot man. This much would carry me plum back to Mulberry Creek." He gulped down another big drink.

"Good place?" Michael asked.

"Good? Shoot, when this shindig's over, you boys gonna come back to Texas with me. "I'll fix you up with poontang like nothin' you ever seen."

"Best offer I've had all day," Bryan laughed.

"Man, them Texas girls know how to shake that puddin'. Take you back of the corncrib an' . . ."

"It's a deal, Chief," Bryan said.

"I'm convinced," Michael added.

"Whew!" The chief rocked from side to side, staring at the bottle. "Reckon I'll catch me some shut-eye."

Michael gestured. "On the bunk, Chief. It's comfortable."

"Sure 'nuff." Algernon handed the bottle to Michael and rolled on his side away from the light. Quickly, Michael capped the bottle and placed it in a drawer filled with publications.

Silently, Bryan left and Michael turned to his chart table. As he hunched over the chart with a pair of dividers, he heard Schultz mumble behind him, "Almost over — almost over."

An hour after anchoring, the captain called Michael, Bryan, Chief Schultz, and Ensign Robert Manning into his cabin. Seated at his desk and toying with a pencil, Bennett began, "I'm having trouble with my battle report."

The men looked back silently.

He stared at the chief. "We're not at war with Korea."

Despite a hangover, Schultz spoke up quickly, "How do you rightly figure what's a Jap an' what's a Korean, sir. They'se all gooks."

The captain stabbed a pad with his pencil. "Chief, that isn't the point. I have to write a report and explain how an unarmed civilian was killed on the deck of my ship."

"Civilian?"

"Yes, Chief."

"Sir," Manning interrupted. "They were employed by the enemy."

"I know," Bennett answered. "We've found them in the Gilberts, Marshalls, Solomons, working as laborers. The Japs treat them like slaves and the Koreans hate them. After all, Japan has occupied Korea for over thirty years." He turned to Schultz. "We can't make allies of them if we murder them."

"Murder?" Schultz gasped. "What did I do to them dudes in the crow's nest?" He gestured to Michael. "An' Michael busted one in the pilot house, an' the ensign gutted a couple with grenades."

"Those were Japs."

"But they'se as dead as doornails."

Bennett thumped the pencil on oak. "Goddamn it, Chief! It's who you kill that counts."

"You mean I can get a medal for the Nips but a court-martial for the gook?"

"Of course. The Korean was a civilian—helpless." He scribbled on the pad. "Did he menace you?"

Silence.

For the first time, Michael spoke, "He waved a cross at the chief."

"A cross?"

Bryan joined in, "That's right, Captain. You have to be careful when Christians start waving the cross."

Michael felt encouraged, "They become very dangerous, sir."

273

"I'm a Christian."

"We all are, sir," Michael said. "But it's still true."

"You both agree to that?" Bennett asked incredulously.

"I was worried, sir," Bryan said.

"Me too," Michael concurred. "He was next to the ready box."

Sighing, the captain dropped his pencil. "Goddamndest thing I ever heard." Then to the chief, "Okay, Algernon. According to your buddies and my report, the prisoner made a menacing gesture. You felt compelled to act in defense of this vessel and your shipmates."

"Keerect, Captain," Algernon said, nodding and smiling. "Thank you kindly. I ain't no murderer, sir. I just hanker to kill Japs."

Bennett waved the pencil. "Okay. All of you are dismissed."

The men turned toward the door, but were stopped by the captain's voice. "Remember, it's almost over and we've got some cushy duty."

"You mean the screen's been changed?" Michael said.

"Yes. The cans are on picket duty where they belong. Finally, the screen's been changed."

Six

Forever, I am the sword
of my emperor
Only the hand of death
Can sheath me
       Lieutenant Takeo Nakamura
                              June 1944

If I go to sea I shall return a corpse awash.
Thus for the sake of the emperor I shall not die
peacefully at home.

                      The Naval Lament

"The screen has been changed, Admiral," Lieutenant Takeo Nakamura said, focusing his lenses while leaning against a waist-high parapet of boulders and rocks laced together by the fishnet weave of camouflage netting.

Pushed from their bunker overlooking Tanapag Town and the harbor, General Saito and Admiral Nagumo had moved their command post north to the cave just a few kilometers south of Marpi Point. Here, high on a scrub covered hill, they still had a view of the harbor, anchorage, and Hagi Ridge, where Third Battalion still maintained a tenuous hold.

Leaning against a boulder, the old naval officer raised his glasses slowly to a face scored and riven by crags and deep lines of terrible suffering, a face that

275

spoke not only of age and fatigue, but of dysentery and the yellowing effects of lingering malaria. "That patrol craft is back and the destroyer is gone," he said.

"Sir," the dysentery-wasted communications officer, Lieutenant Mitsumasa Yamaoka, croaked, looking up from a field radio, "Third Battalion reports heavy attacks on Hagi Ridge. The Yankees have pushed them off the eastern end."

"Sacred Buddha," General Saito said.

Admiral Nagumo spoke to the general, "This is our last chance to use my barges. If we do not use them now, we never will."

All was lost and every man knew it. Hammered by relentless infantry attacks and incessant sea and air bombardment, the Thirty-First Army had been pushed north toward Marpi Point, compressing surviving units into masses of starving civilians. Rations were low and ammunition short, but *Yamato damashii* remained.

Raising his glasses, General Saito said, "It is time for a last attack—a glorious rush for the Yasakuni Shrine."

"The barges . . ."

Ignoring Takeo, the general spoke to Admiral Nagumo. "You and I, Admiral; we can lead this last attack."

The old mariner turned slowly, fixing Saito with rheumy eyes, lids drooping away so that the inner flesh showed like wet yellow jade and his voice was wispy, the rustle of wind through dry reeds. "I—I would be honored, but I am weak, General. I will end it here." He drew himself up in bent mockery of military posture and with new strength quoted one of Japan's greatest warriors: "The great samurai Shida Kichinosuke said, 'If there is a choice of either living or dying, when all is lost, choose death.'"

276

Every man turned to the admiral: Lieutenant Yamaoka and his two enlisted men from their brace of radios, the nearly deaf artillery men, Captain Tamon Yoshikawa and Sergeant Hajime Tomonaga from their grid maps, a half-dozen aides and runners who suddenly showed new alertness.

"*Seppuku*, Admiral?"

"Yes." The old sailor turned to Takeo Nakamura. "Lieutenant, you are the best swordsman on this island and you carry the fabled Nakamura blade. I knew your grandfather, Colonel Shoin Nakamura, who gave his life so gloriously for Emperor Meiji at Port Arthur. He was a great samurai." He stabbed a finger at the jeweled scabbard. "Now I would leave my blood on that steel that has tasted the blood of so many of the Mikado's enemies."

All eyes moved to the young lieutenant. "Your blood, sir?" Takeo asked in a near whisper.

The old sailor nodded. "Yes. I want you as my *kaishaku*, Takeo-san."

Takeo drew himself up rigidly. He was awed by the honor. Upon successful disembowelment, the *kaishaku* must behead the condemned with a single clean stroke. Yet, even more important, if the supplicant hesitated — and Admiral Nagumo was very weak — he was responsible for instant beheading. "I and my entire family would be deeply honored, Admiral," Takeo said, bowing.

A slow smile broke through the seams and wrinkles of the old man's face. "Very well, Lieutenant. I know you will honor your duty and send me to my ancestors with one clean stroke." He turned to General Saito and showed his fine mind was still clear, thinking tactics. "Before my ceremony, General, let us plan our final attack."

The admiral's quick shift to the impending attack brought a thought to Takeo's mind that had been gnawing at him since the Americans first landed. "The barges . . ."

"Yes! Yes, Lieutenant Nakamura," General Saito said impatiently. "You can have the barges. To-night—midnight or later. The white devils hate to fight in the dark and you will have your best chance to get around the patrol craft."

"Hagi Ridge, sir?" Takeo asked.

The old soldier rubbed the stubble on his chin. "I will personally lead Thirty-First Army in an assault to relieve Third Battalion."

Nagumo said, "The civilians?"

"Let them come. They have a right to die on the field. And we could not stop them, anyway."

Nagumo jerked a thumb over his shoulder. "Thou-sands of them are down there."

Saito nodded. Anxious to remain near the front and mingle with the troops, hordes, of men, women, and children were huddled just back of the lines, most camped in the shallow amphitheater-shaped Managaha Valley. Here they huddled under blan-kets, cooked their meager portions of rice and tended to wounded soldiers. Some had firearms, but most were armed with picks, hoes, shovels, and bamboo spears. They waited for death quietly and patiently.

Saito glanced at his watch. "I will lead the attack just before sunset—sixteen thirty hours." He turned to Nakamura. Takeo-san, your company has been wiped out."

"I know, sir."

Saito waved the lieutenant to a table and pointed to a map. "The remnants of Second Battalion is in reserve in the Managaha Valley, here. You led them well in our last attack. I will order them to assemble at the top of the path when our attack begins. Lead them to the barges at Tanapag Harbor." He stabbed the map with a finger. "The barges are hidden here under this bluff. At zero one hundred, exit the channel here, circle through the transports and land at Charan Kanoa." He looked up. "Kill the devils — kill them for me, your Emperor, our gods."

"Banzai!" rang through the cave.

"Excellent," Nagumo said, rubbing his bony hands. "Excellent." Then he turned to Takeo, and the old sea warrior was back, "That patrol craft . . ." he waved a hand. "She looks small but she has great firepower, Takeo-san."

"I know, sir. I saw her in action against Manigassa reef." He waved a hand at the long white finger of coral and the heaps of dead still cluttering it. "We will hope she mistakes us for Americans, perhaps a returning reconnaissance."

"And if she is not fooled?"

"We will attack her, Admiral."

"She has a three-inch, a Bofors and four Orlikons."

"But no five-inch, thirty-eight calibers."

Everyone nodded in respect to the awesome American rapid-fire cannon that was the finest piece of naval artillery in the world.

"True, Takeo-san. They have sent a boy to do a samurai's work. You are a fine officer with great *karma*. You have earned your right to a glorious battlefield death — fulfill the promise of your *hachimachi* headband and honor those who contributed to your belt of a thousand stitches." Reaching up, Nagumo clasped Takeo's shoulder with the claw of an old bird. Then, staring into the young man's eyes: " 'If your sword be broken, attack with your hands, and if they be severed . . .' "

" 'And if they be severed,' " the general interrupted, completing the ancient maxim, " 'attack with your shoulders, your teeth . . .' "

"Banzai!" Nagumo shouted. Others picked up the cheer, filling the cave.

The admiral gestured to an enlisted man. "Corporal Minami. Chestnuts and sakte!"

The noncommissioned officer disappeared into the depths of the cave and returned, carrying a large bottle and box. Every man came to his feet, and in a short minute each clutched a single dry chestnut in one hand and a few ounces of sakte in his tin canteen cup in the other.

Saito spoke to Nakamura. "You will lead one hundred seventy men who are filled with *Yamato damashii*, Lieutenant."

Takeo nodded. "With our swords, our hands, our teeth . . ."

Raising his cup, Nagumo croaked, "Duty and an honorable death for the Son of Heaven."

Crying, *"Tenno heiko banzai,"*—"Long live the emperor"—every man mirrored the admiral's gesture. Then the cups were drained and the chestnuts eaten.

"We have eaten stones and tasted gall, sir," Nakamura said harshly.

Both men nodded understanding. "Yes, Nakamura-san," Saito said with surprising gentleness. "And the samurai knows when it is right to live and right to die."

"There is nothing else worth recording," Nagumo added. The old sailor turned to Takeo. "And now it is right for me to die, Takeo-san."

"I am ready, sir," Nakamura said, fingering the tang of his sword.

"Minami," Nagumo said. "A blanket."

Quickly, the corporal spread a worn blanket. The old man dropped, squatting on his crossed legs, and fumbled weakly with the buttons on his tunic. He turned to Takeo. *"Kaishaku!"*

Leaning, the lieutenant unbuttoned the old man's

tunic and trousers. In a moment, the admiral was bare to the hips, ribs protruding, abdomen hollow.

"Wakizashi!"

Takeo turned to Corporal Minami, who handed the lieutenant a nine-inch knife honed razor-sharp on both sides and with the point a needle. Nakamura passed it to the admiral, who grasped it eagerly and looked at it wistfully, almost affectionately, seemingly collecting his thoughts for the last time.

Turning his eyes up, the old sailor spoke to the ceiling, the rancor of years spilling out like acid, "Once I commanded *Koku Kantai*. My eagles darkened the sky, destroyed Pearl Harbor, swept the Pacific, Indian Ocean and the Java Sea clear of the Americans, British, Dutch. And then I led . . ." The voice wavered. Breathing deeply, the old man squared his frail shoulders. "And then I led my eagles to Midway—Midway where I and I alone gave the orders. I and I alone lost *Kaga, Akagi, Soryu* and *Hiryu* and all my gallant eagles. For this crime I disembowel myself and implore you who are present to be my witnesses. May the Emperor find forgiveness in his heart."

The supplicant reached into his pocket, removing a slip of paper. Obviously, Nagumo had been anticipating *seppuku* for some time, because he held a death poem. He read slowly. "The blue sky and sea are one universe blending into the infinite now as life and death form an unending river." He dropped the paper, grasped the knife with both hands, and turned the point toward his stomach. Every man held his breath.

Takeo unsheathed his sword, the fine steel ringing like a chime struck by a monk in a Buddhist temple. Quickly, the lieutenant stepped to the admiral's side and raised the blade over his shoulder. Leaning forward, he stared intently at the old man's face. If the

281

old man faltered, weakness could be read in his eyes, the set of his jaw, first.

As the young officer watched the admiral press the sharp point to the right side of his abdomen in preparation for the first horizontal cut that released the "seat of the mind," the distant cannonading seemed to stop, the wind died, and only the sounds of breathing could be heard in the cave. The old sailor pulled his head far back and locked his jaw tightly, grinding his teeth. He pushed. Blood spurted. He sucked in his breath. Pushed again until most of the blade vanished. Pulled the blade horizontally. Gasped audibly. Stopped. Pulled again. Stopped again. Blood poured down over his trousers and onto the blanket. The watery eyes rolled to Takeo, imploring, filled with pain and despair. He groaned. Turned his head down.

There was no hesitation. Eyeing the back of the scrawny neck, the young officer saw the knobs of vertebrae protruding like old roots. He took a firm grip with both hands and then brought the great killing blade hissing in an arc, striking the old man's neck in a blur of speed and power. There was the dull chopping sound of steel cleaving meat and bone followed by a thud as the severed head fell to the blanket and rolled to one side of the cave, eyes wide open. The headless body remained erect for a moment as if a mind was still present, blood pouring from the abdomen and spurting from severed jugulars in torrents. Then, slowly, it topped on its side.

"Banzai" rang through the cave and hands slapped Takeo on the back.

"Magnificent," Saito murmured.

"Thank you, sir," the lieutenant said modestly, wiping the blade on a corner of the blanket and then sheathing it. Takeo knew it was time to make his own preparations. He turned to Minami. "Corporal,

282

scissors and two envelopes."

"Yes, sir."

Hastily, Takeo cut his fingernails and snipped locks from his long black hair. After stuffing the cuttings into the envelopes, the young officer sealed them, addressed one to his parents and the other to Keiko Yokoi, and handed them to Minami.

Instructions were not necessary. Every man was aware of the ancient custom of preparing clippings for cremation in the homeland when a samurai felt death was imminent and prospects for recovering his corpse for proper cremation and burial poor.

"The I-Eighty-Seven is still in Magicenne Bay, sir," Minami said, staring at the envelopes.

Takeo nodded. The submarine was the last link with the home islands. It had slipped into a remote cove when most of the American destroyers had been taken off picket duty. Badly mauled by patrol craft, the I-boat had been forced to hide under an overhanging bluff, submerging in the daytime while making repairs to a damaged main engine.

Minami placed the envelope in a mailbag with hundreds of others. "I'll try to slip through the American lines tonight, sir."

"May Amaterasu look down on you, Corporal."

"General," Captain Yoshikawa bellowed in his usual loud voice, "Sergeant Tomonaga and I would like to follow the admiral." He gestured at the body that lay in a widening pool of blood.

"I need you."

"Sir. The *Tennessee* just destroyed our last battery — the seventy-fives at Lagua Lichan." He shrugged. "We have no artillery."

"Very well," the old soldier sighed. "How?"

"Grenades, General." The captain pointed to a small clearing in front of the cave, surrounded with boulders.

"You have my permission."

"Thank you."

Rising slowly, both men put on their helmets, took one grenade each from a half-dozen crates of bombs, and walked into the clearing.

Leisurely, they sank to their knees, facing each other. For several minutes they spoke to each other quietly. Then they took off their helmets, struck their grenades on rocks, dropped them into their helmets and then jammed the helmets on their heads, holding them down firmly with both hands.

The two blasts were simultaneous, sounding like the pops of firecrackers inside drain pipes. Rising on red towers of blood, the two helmets flew high into the sky while the decapitated corpses were hurled onto their sides. The bodies twitched and then lay still.

"Banzai! Banzai! Banzai!"

Light was failing when Takeo watched General Saito lead the last attack on Hagi Ridge and the foothills above Tanapag Town. Waving his sword, the old soldier led a motley assortment of troops, walking wounded and masses of civilians against the marines who were now entrenched on most of the ridge. Garands and Brownings flickered flaming snakes' tongues, piling the attackers in screaming heaps. And the Americans had emplaced one of their fifty-caliber machine guns which fired huge dismembering bullets.

Takeo had his glasses on the old warrior as he struggled up the slope pushing aside brush and tripping over rocks. His quest for glory was not long. He had just paused on top of a heap of blasted boulders, pointing his sword with one hand and waving his pistol with the other, when the fifty-caliber bullet hit him full in the face. Hurled backward by the impact, the top of Saito's head was blown completely off, exploding in a red spray, helmet soaring high in the air as if he, too, had died by grenade. The old man tumbled to the ground, sword and pistol flying, limbs flailing loosely.

The charge did not even pause, swirling and surging like a river flowing uphill into the dancing flames of muzzle blasts. And artillery began to come in, adding more flame, smoke, dust, and piling bodies. But some of the frantic attackers reached the summit and even pushed beyond.

Takeo knew it was time. He left the cave and began making his way down to the harbor.

Seven

Death is near
Waiting on the wave tops
I long for you
Far away at home
Keiko, the essence of all
    Lieutenant Takeo Nakamura
        June 1944

Jammed with eighteen sweaty, unwashed men, the amidship's crews compartment was hot and humid. Michael dreaded the compartment. The knowledge that he was below the waterline held its own particular terror as it did for all sailors at war. He remembered the horror stories. They all remembered the tales of men trapped below in the *Yorktown*, *Oklahoma*, *Astoria*, *Quincy*, and many others—stories of the gut-wrenching screams and pleading heard through voice tubes and PA systems as water rose and men died slowly like the rats swarming over them.

Dressed only in his skivvy shorts, Michael twisted and turned, the red glow of the single battle-lamp penetrating his closed eyelids, bringing back Don Lindsay and the corona of coagulating blood spreading from the huge head wound. Rolling to his stomach, the quartermaster punched the mattress. He was warm. Too warm. He rolled to his back.

Feeling nauseous, he ran a finger over his stomach, chest and cheek, finding a slippery patina and occasional rivulets. And his hair was strangely stiff and brittle, eyes set in sand, aching dully in iron sockets. Lindsay was joined by images of Kristie, his mother, Alma, Vicki, Vivian, the Jap woman and her baby, Barton, Winters, Welly, and too many more, racing past like race horses at a finish line. But the race had no end. It was a carousel and his head spun with it.

He sat up quickly, feeling faint, and grabbed the steel-pipe frame of the bunk above. Dully, he pulled himself erect, shook his head free of apparitions and dressed slowly. His back ached and so did his arms and legs. He needed air, fresh sea air. He had to get out of the trap. He turned toward the ladder.

It was very dark on the flying bridge, the moon only a scimitar partially shielded by skittering clouds that blackened the sky, coloring the sea with an ebony brush. But the air was fresh and Michael filled his lungs with huge drafts like a man dehydrated by the desert heat, face down in the cool pool of an oasis. He felt strength returning and the heat faded.

"Jesus, Michael," Dennis Warner said from the starboard lookout platform, "we can win the war without you." The only other man on the bridge, Seaman Bill Whitlow, who stood on the port platform, chuckled.

"Thought you boys might let Tojo sneak aboard — cut our throats."

The seaman and the signalman laughed. Then Michael heard the engines.

"LCVPs," said Warner, raising his glasses.

"Must be marine scouts," Whitlow added, staring north.

Grabbing a pair of binoculars from a box mounted on the wind screen, Michael focused to the north, but saw nothing. The noise of the engines increased—the high whine of at least a dozen marine engines at full power.

"Gray Marine engines," Warner said.

"Bullshit!" Michael spat. "Too high."

"Too high?"

"They're Japs," Michael said.

"Can you see them?"

"No, Dennis. But those are Jap engines."

"Bullshit, Quartermaster. You're not on watch."

"You want to take the responsibility, Signalman?"

Warner cursed. Whitlow stared silently through his glasses.

Michael gripped the voice tube, "Pilothouse."

"Pilothouse aye," a sleepy voice answered.

"Sound the general alarm."

"What?"

"The general alarm!"

"Are you out of your fuckin' mind Carpelli? I need some sleep."

"Sound the fuckin' alarm!"

"It's not your right. Only . . ."

"It's not only my right, it's my duty! Sound the goddamned alarm or you're on report."

"Okay. What a shitty way to make a living."

The honk of claxons brought the crew to battle stations. Andrew Bennett stormed onto the bridge followed by Ensign Robert Bennington and Seaman Isadore Nash. Shrugging into his Mae West and adjusting the chin strap of his helmet, the captain accosted Michael. "What kind of wild hair do you have up your ass now, Quartermaster?"

Silently Michael jerked a thumb to the north where the whine of engines could be heard clearly.

"LCVPs," Bennett said, raising his glasses.

"That's right," Ensign Bennington concurred.

"Those are Japs," Michael said matter-of-factly. "They're making a sortie from Tanapag."

The captain turned to Bennington, "Anything on the SCR?"

"Negative, Captain. It's been quiet."

Bennett spoke to Isadore Nash. "Tell Schultz to give me three star shells to port. Over the north part of the anchorage—sixty-degree elevation."

Cranked high, the three-inch ripped the darkness with a long yellow tongue that lighted up patches of mist, etching the mast, rigging, and statue like bridge crew in millisecond cameos. Then two more snaps of the cruel whip were followed by the popping sound of champagne corks high in the sky.

Three parachute flares blossomed high in the sky like chandeliers in a vast ballroom. Eyes to glasses, Carpelli picked up at least a dozen twin-bowed wooden barges. "Japs, Captain," Michael said softly. "Off the port beam. They've cleared Mucho Point. Range two thousand."

"Bennington!" Bennett shouted. "Call Old Hickory. Under attack by a dozen barges. Request fire support and illumination." He turned to Nash. "Three-inch and forty commence firing. Twenties, when in range. Anchor detail, slip the anchor."

The talker muttered into his headset, turned to the captain, "Anchor chain fouled, sir."

"Shit! To all hands, we'll fight where we are." The lieutenant turned to Warner. "Signalman, break out the Thompsons, M-ones and my forty-five." Then back to Nash: "Kohler to the bridge."

Michael brought up his glasses. The barges were

in a line abreast, charging the PCS like infantry. In fact, bayonets were visible.

The captain screamed, "For God's sake, Schultz! Fire! Fire!"

Michael heard Schultz shout, then the three-inch tore into the darkness, painting the forecastle and bridge scarlet and yellow again and again in short violent images. Carpelli grabbed his ears. The forty began its pounding and the port twenties blazed and ripped, triggers held down by frightened gunners, sixty-round magazines emptying in seconds. The quartermaster groaned with pain as burning rods stabbed at his eardrums.

There was a new shadow, and Kohler was on the bridge. Warner returned with the submachine guns and carbines, handing a Thompson to the pharmacist's mate and the other to the quartermaster. Hastily, Michael wound the drum key until he heard nine clicks. Then, slinging his weapon, he brought up his glasses.

South of the PCS, the anchorage exploded to life like an angry volcano, anchored transports firing five-inch and three-inch shells over and around the patrol craft. There was warbling and ripping overhead, and dozens of star shells blossomed high above the barges.

Although waterspouts leaped all around the Japanese and tracers exploded and ricocheted, flames danced from the strange double bows.

"Nambus, Captain," Michael shouted over the din.

"I see them. They're out of range."

"But not for long," Kohler said.

A shell made a direct hit on a barge, flinging it high in a burst of fragments and tumbling bodies. Another staggered like an injured animal, falling behind and burning in its own fuel, infantry in full marching kit jumping into the hell surrounding it.

Two more barges exploded, and it seemed as if acres of ocean were suddenly burning. Michael felt as if he were in a shooting gallery at Ocean Park. But the charge continued, not one barge deviating or pausing to save roasting comrades.

Illuminated by flares and backlighted by burning comrades, the Japanese were easy targets, half of them destroyed within minutes. Nevertheless, five or six survivors converged on the PCS, moving so close the transports were forced to cease fire. The patrol craft was on its own.

"Anchor!" Bennett screamed, his voice sharpened by the hard edge of anxiety.

"Still fouled, sir."

"Shit! Kill the bastards! Kill them!"

A barge exploded in an intense luminescent ball, then another sank so suddenly it appeared to be a submarine making a crash dive. Still another dropped back, belching flames. But two were left, one swinging toward the little warship's stern, the other closing on the port side.

A giant bee buzzed close to Michael's ear. Then came the unmistakable thumping and ripping sound of bullets striking and shattering wood. There was a cry and Bill Whitlow pitched from the lookout platform, sprawling on the deck, carbine clattering.

Kohler hunched over the boy and then turned to the captain, "Through the head, sir."

"Very well." Bennett gestured to a corner. Dennis and Bryan dragged the corpse aside.

"Small arms to the port side and stand by," the lieutenant screamed through the detonations. Then to Bennington: "Lay aft, Ensign. Stand by the forty. Their accuracy is terrible—they've got to engage the barge astern."

Bennington vanished down the ladder.

Resting their weapons on the wind screen, Michael, Bryan, and Dennis Warner leaned on the plywood, eyeing the barge off the port beam. Its companion had vanished in the darkness astern.

Only one to two hundred yards away, Michael could see every detail clearly: double bows, Nambu firing, infantry crowding the bow with fixed bayonets and firing around and over each other.

The three-inch fired, sending a spout high in the air.

"Shit! Shit, Schultz. Better than that."

As if hearing the captain's blandishments, the port twenty-millimeters both scored, pouring a storm of one-half pound high explosive shells into the crowded boat like a hail of firebrands, knocking the Nambu over the side and killing most of the troops in the bow. Apparently out of control, the barge swung, giving the full length of its starboard side to the patrol craft. A few soldiers fired over her gunwale.

Hunching forward, Warner began to squeeze his trigger. "Out of range!" Michael shouted.

Nodding, the signalman stepped back.

The machine gunners traversed their weapons slowly, decimating infantrymen and ripping chunks of planking from the barge. Belching bubbles from punctured flotation tanks, it sank, leaving a few soldiers afloat, clinging to wreckage.

"Kill them!"

Within seconds, the great bullets shattered the heads of the few survivors. Cheers.

The cheering was halted by frantic shouts. "Japs! Japs!"

The talker turned to Bennett, voice filled with

292

disbelief, "Japs on the stern."

"Impossible! Not in the twentieth century." Grabbing Carpelli's arm, the captain gestured to the boat deck, "Carpelli! Kohler! The cargo lights!"

Scrambling down the short ladder to the boat deck, the pair switched on the two floodlights, illuminating the stern. Carpelli saw a madhouse. The last barge that had swung around the stern had sneaked a line aboard. Not a single gun could bear on it and already three Japanese were aboard, standing on the depth charge racks. One, an officer, was the tallest Jap Carpelli had ever seen. He gripped a two-handed sword, waving it over his shoulder as he advanced on the forty. The gun crew was throwing shells at him.

"Fire, Carpelli! Fire, Kohler! None of our armament bears."

More helmets appeared and more soldiers clambered aboard. Slowly, the barge swung to the port side and Michael could see five or six soldiers gripping the lifeline and pulling themselves aboard. He aimed the Thompson.

The quartermaster and the pharmacist's mate fired together. Holding his weapon down to counteract its tendency to climb, the quartermaster sent a stream of forty-five-caliber slugs to knock soldiers from the ship's side like a man swatting flies. Then the barge drifted out, exposing its interior from bow to stern. There were dead and wounded heaped on the bottom and a few men aimed their rifles. Two streams of slugs swept the boat, piling the few live infantrymen on top of their dead comrades. Manned by dead men, the barge swung away.

Warner handed Kohler and Carpelli fresh drums.

Snapping his new drum in place, Michael raised the hot submachine gun. At least six infantrymen were on board. And gunners were in his sights. One, a tall gangly youngster named Rick Ursich, faced the officer with a boat hook. The Japanese leaped to the deck, and with a single swing of the great curved blade, decapitated the American. Then, one of the infantrymen shot another gunner through the head. Within seconds, three more Americans were hit.

"Fire! Fire!" Bennett screamed.

"Our guys? The ashcans?"

"Fuck the ashcans! Fuck everything! The only live men back there are Japs. Fire! Fire! We'll lose the ship . . ."

Kohler, Carpelli and Warner fired together. The scythes of flying metal harvested corpses the way reapers cut wheat, making a charnel house of the stern. Within seconds, every man was down.

"Carpelli to the stern — Kohler and Warner cover him!"

In a moment, Michael was on the main deck, running to the stern, passing bodies and cowering, frightened gunners, waving their only effective weapon — the eight-inch knife issued to all men in the amphibious force.

Someone was alive on the stern. There was a commotion just to the right of the forty-millimeter gun tub. Back to Michael and armed with a boat hook, Bennington faced the tall Japanese officer whose tunic was red with blood. Crowding the space between the tub and a K gun, they squared off like brawlers in an alley.

"Out of the way, Mr. Bennington."

"Fuck you, hero. This is my personal Nip!"

Gripping his sword with two hands, the Japanese crabbed forward and swung. Bennington leaped backward, tripped over the K gun and sprawled on

294

the deck.

Ignoring the captain's shouts from the boat deck of, "Out of the way — stand clear," Michael faced the Japanese. Blood ran down the man's cheek and welled from a chest wound. But there was defiance and resolve in the flinty, black eyes. And death was there, too.

Michael tightened his finger. There was a click. The Thompson remained silent. Steel glinted. The cold hand of terror gripped his stomach; his heart became a mallet against his ribs. Working his bolt frantically, he leaped back. He caught a blur in his peripheral vision.

The great sword flashed down. Struck on the helmet and from behind simultaneously, Michael was knocked against the gun tub. Ears ringing and head whirling, he leaned against the tub, stunned.

"See what it's like, hero!" Bennington shouted, charging past Michael and driving his boat hook into the officer's chest. But the sword hissed down again, catching the ensign just above the left clavicle. There was a scream — the butcher shop sound of steel cleaving meat and bone — and Bennington was hurled down, draping over the K gun, head nearly severed, a deluge of blood gushing onto the teakwood planking.

The sword was raised. Michael shook his head and regained his balance. Pulled the trigger. The submachine gun bucked. Caught in the chest by a half-dozen slugs, the officer fell, momentum carrying him forward, draping him over the ensign's corpse.

There was a groan, and Michael leaned over the bodies. "Keiko. Keiko," the Japanese rasped, wretching and vomiting blood. After a last shuddering convulsion, he slumped back in the softness of death.

Straightening, Michael turned slowly and surveyed the carnage. American and Japanese bodies were piled everywhere. Blood ran in streams over the tapered decks to the scuppers. There were groans and screams.

Bennington and the Japanese officer were draped over the K gun in a macabre frieze, the American's nearly severed head turned to the Japanese, whose arms were outstretched, seemingly embracing the ensign. Blood from both mingled in a widening pool.

Numbly, the quartermaster stared, realizing the cowardly ensign had saved his life and had thrown away his own recklessly. A coward and a hero. It made no sense. But nothing made sense. Bennington's dead eyes were on him.

"No! No!" Michael shouted. then he waved a fist at the moon and the mute stars. "You don't make sense either! You're part of it! None of it makes sense! There is no reason. No reason . . ."

A cloud obscured the moon and the cargo lights faded. Strength ebbed from his legs, and he sank to the deck, the strange chills racking his bones with spasms again. Face down in the gore, the quartermaster slid his hand through the thickening blood until he touched the tip of the sword. The steel was cold and the air a breeze sweeping an iceberg, freezing his lungs. Slowly, the cloud blotted out everything.

Something was pushing the air from his lungs and screams tore at his heart. He opened his eyes. Framed by the penumbra of a mess hall light, Kohler's face was above him, and the big pharmacist's mate was pushing on his chest.

"Enlarged spleen, one-oh-five temp, jaundiced skin. You have blackwater fever — malaria, boy," Kohler said. He waved. Instantly Warner was there, pulling Michael up. "Here," Bryan said, "take these. Quinine, six hundred fifty milligrams."

Michael swallowed, and the water was cool and fresh in the desert of his mouth.

"The Japs couldn't do it," Bryan said, easing the quartermaster back down. "It's a miracle. I thought that Nip had you for sure. You should live forever. You're going back to the states." He bared a syringe. Michael felt a sharp stab in his arm. "Pleasant dreams, Mate." He turned to Warner, "If he pisses black, call me no matter what I'm doing." He jerked a bloody thumb. "I've got to take care of them, Michael."

As the pharmacist's mate moved to the next table, Michael looked around. The tables were covered with wounded boys, their blue dungarees caked with blood. Some were screaming and thrashing; others lay still, either dead or in the embrace of morphine-induced sleep. The white bulkheads and even the overhead were splattered with blood. The captain, Kohler, Schultz, Warner, and two seamen worked frantically, bandaging and rigging IVs while the pharmacist's mate shouted instructions.

Shaking like a man with palsy, Michael turned his head slowly. "It isn't real," he muttered. Mercifully, the cloud returned.

Eight

Michael had only fragmentary memories of the following days, swept by burning fever mists, where time was disjointed and reality as elusive as blown swamp gas. Days and nights blurred together as life became a succession of compartments: the mess hall, the LCVP, a truck, and then the claustrophobic interior of an aircraft.

There was a slender young woman in khaki who moved slowly through the wounded and leaned over him, taking his temperature, giving him pills and sometimes sticking a needle in his arm. And there was always the IV.

The woman was an angel. When she leaned over him, the bulb behind her sent highlights to play in her blond hair like restless fireflies, giving her a halo. And her eyes were blue — as blue as the Marianas Deep. Lindsay came back. Michael cried out. And then Bennington was there. Her cool hand was on his forehead. Michael twisted.

"Easy, sailor. Easy," she said, her voice soothing like Glenn Miller's music.

Michael sagged back. Lost himself in the swirling dark clouds.

After endless twisting against the straps, an orderly's voice broke through. "He's sleeping, Lieutenant, but his urine's dark."

The soft lines of the lovely face hardened and

her voice came through the murk, "His kidneys are going—must be *estivo autumnal*. He's jaundiced and toxemia is setting in." Fingers pushed against his chest. "Spleen's still enlarged." She sighed. "We'll lose him. Increase quinine to one thousand milligrams and start him on atabrine—five hundred milligrams every six hours."

"Yes, Lieutenant."

"His IV?"

"One hundred ccs an hour, two percent dextrose."

"Let's raise it to one hundred fifty at five percent."

"Yes, ma'am."

Michael opened his eyes slowly. "Don't worry, Lieutenant. "I won't die—I promise."

She smiled, "Of course you won't."

"But do something for Bennington."

"Bennington?" She looked at the orderly.

"No Bennington aboard, Lieutenant."

Michael spoke. "That Jap almost chopped his head off. Please do something for him." He felt a cool hand on his. "He needs help."

"Of course, sailor. We'll do everything we can." The smile could not mask the sadness in the tired eyes.

There was a moan, and another orderly called, "Lieutenant Lee!"

"Coming."

She was gone and fitful sleep returned. But the bulb was always there, sometimes glowing yellow like the sun and sometimes burning dully like the ashes of a dying camp fire. And cruel people roused him to force pills down his throat and to stab needles in his arms. And his urine was so important.

299

"Look, I'm pissing rainbows," he grunted at an orderly, holding up a cloudy beaker.

A marine across the aisle with no legs actually stopped groaning and chuckled.

He could feel the plane bounce and rock as it bored through tropical turbulence. And he could feel it land with jars that sent waves of groans through the compartment. He heard familiar names: Kwajalein, Johnston, Pearl, and finally the magic name, Los Angeles. Impossible. It was all part of the dream, the coma brought on by that hungry mosquito.

The plane had changed—or was it a truck that changed? But now the compartment was long, wide and very white with a high vaulted ceiling. The IV was still there and people were still fascinated by his urine. And he could swear he saw his mother, leaning over him and crying. But an orderly took her arm, and she became another part of the shadow show and faded away like all the others.

Then one day a fresh breeze blew away the gloom and mists and the sun streamed into the bright, white room—a long ward crammed with beds filled with young men.

An orderly leaned over him, "Lieutenant Clark," the young man shouted. "This one's coming out of it."

A youthful physician bent over him. He felt fingers pull his eyes wide open. "Jaundice almost gone. Temperature Peterson?"

"Ninety-nine, sir."

"Blood pressure?"

"One ten over eighty, sir."

300

"Good. Good." Fingers pushed on his chest, then on his abdomen. "Swelling's down." The doctor looked at the orderly. "I don't understand how they let a case of malaria get this bad."

Michael spoke in a bare whisper, "We were busy, Lieutenant."

"You're back," the doctor said smiling. And then grimly: "Obviously, they kept you very busy." He waved at the crowded ward. And then smiling a sad smile, "Welcome back, Quartermaster Carpelli."

"Where am I, Lieutenant?"

Clark chuckled. "Naval Hospital Annex, Torrance California—Communicable Diseases Ward."

"I'm communicable?"

"Not anymore."

"I saw my mother?"

"Yes," Peterson answered. "In fact, she's here waiting." He waved toward the far end of the ward.

"Can she come in?"

"No."

"But I did see her, didn't I?"

"Yes. She sneaked in and I had to put her out."

"Christ!"

Lieutenant Clark spoke. "We'll wheel you out to the visitors' area. You aren't contagious unless you have a pocketful of mosquitos."

Michael was beaming when they disconnected his IV and helped him into the wheelchair.

"Michael, Michael," Maria sobbed as she embraced her son, raining kisses on his forehead, cheeks, and eyelids as she leaned over the wheelchair in the waiting room, which was actually one

301

end of the large Quonset hut called the Communicable Diseases Ward.

"Not on the lips, Mom. I'm a male Typhoid Mary."

Laughing, she pulled up a chair and sat close, holding his hand.

"I thought I'd lost you."

"How long have I been here?"

"Four days. You got sick a week ago."

"I don't understand."

"What Michael?"

"Where I got it—one mosquito, somewhere, someplace."

"I understand the incubation period can be as long as a year." She leaned forward. "But I don't care, you're home—home to stay. They can't send you back out now." A sudden horrifying doubt struck the smile from her face. She questioned herself rhetorically. "They won't—can't send you out again, can they?"

"No, Mom."

She kissed him. Then gently: "Was it horrible, Michael?"

Michael smiled, realizing his mother knew absolutely nothing except that her son had malaria. "Nothing could be as bad as the Solomons, Mother."

"I heard that Saipan was ghastly." He felt her grip tighten. "You were there, Michael?"

"Yes, Mom."

"The fighting was heavy and that small ship of yours can move in so close."

Again Michael was struck by his mother's perceptiveness. She knew more than he had anticipated. She had met Don Lindsay, and sooner or later she would learn the truth. "We took casual-

302

ties, Mother. One was Don Lindsay."

Hand to mouth, she came erect, whispering, "No. No. How horrible."

"He didn't suffer."

"Kohler and Schultz are all right, Mom." There was no need to tell her of Winters, Barton, Whitlow, and the rest. She had never met them.

"Kristie?" he asked suddenly. "I haven't had a letter in months."

Maria looked away. "You know I'm not close to them."

Sensing evasiveness, he pressed on, "You must know something."

Maria bit her lip. "I hear she got a job in Culver City."

"In the movies? She got a break?"

"I don't know. There's a lot of filming going on out there. Not just features, but training films, too."

"You must see her?"

"No. She left home."

"Left home! She's so young. Her folks wouldn't . . ."

"I know. She moved in with some designer—clothes designer."

"Oh, Lord, no," Michael said, stomach nauseous again. "I can't believe it."

Misery streaked Maria's face with new lines. "I didn't want to tell you," she cried.

"Please, Mom."

"I want my boy to be healthy again—back in school—earn his teaching credentials . . ." She choked and buried her head on his shoulder, sobbing.

"I love you, Mom. Please don't cry. I'll be out of this ward soon and then I'll come home."

303

"Don't let Kristie set you back."

"I won't Mom. I promise." He stroked her hair, kissed her. But his jaw was set, eyes grim.

The day after Michael was transferred to the general ward, the destroyed woman loomed over his bed. At first he thought he had lapsed back into a fever and was suffering another apparition. But she was real, a hunched middle-aged wreck of a woman whose riven flesh hung in folds and bags as if she had just pressed her face to a wire fence. One eyelid drooped and the other was narrow, giving a crafty yet sorrowful look to blue pinpoints that burned in a dim watery way as if she had just turned her face to a fierce rainstorm. Her thin lips were gray and cracked, her hair straggly ocher shot through with silver, appearing not to have felt a brush in days. Once she had been tall and stood proud, but now some terrible burden had crushed her down, compressing her spine and bending her like a sapling in a gale.

"You're the quartermaster — Michael Carpelli," she said in a thin monotone, eyes as cold and dark as a crypt, yet familiar.

"Yes, ma'am."

"I'm Evelyn Bennington, Ensign Robert Bennington's mother."

Michael felt a hand of ice clutch his heart. He was looking into the dead ensign's eyes and the ruined face hinted of him, too. "I'm sorry about your son, Mrs. Bennington."

"I'm not here for that."

He felt an emptiness, groped for words, "How did you know?"

"The captain wrote me."

304

"Of course. He had a lot of letters to write."

She stiffened.

"I didn't mean to pain you."

Ignoring the apology, she pressed on, "Bobbie wrote about you."

"About me?" Michael said, unable to conceal his surprise.

"About everyone. He was a journalism major—wanted to be a writer. He practiced by writing long descriptions of his shipmates, the sea, the ship—everything." The network of lines that covered her face contracted into a new pattern that hinted at amusement. "I may know things about your crew that you don't know." Then grimly: "Bobbie was my only child—bright with an unlimited future." She caught her breath and pushed a tiny fist to her lips.

"I didn't know him that well."

"I've come from Vermont to see you. My son is only a memory now, but he can't be totally dead as long as we remember him." She stared at the wall at another place and another time, speaking to no one and everyone. "When he's forgotten, he'll be dead beyond recall."

He began to speak. She waved him to silence. "He's buried at sea?"

"Yes," he answered slowly. "That is customary."

"But where? Your captain didn't tell me where."

"I would assume the Mariana Deep."

"Sounds horrible."

Michael seized the opportunity. "It's beautiful, Mrs. Bennington. The sea is over thirty thousand feet deep and as blue as a gemstone."

"I wanted him in our family plot."

"He's with his shipmates. He couldn't find better company, ma'am." And then firmly: "He belongs there."

Sighing, she pulled a chair close and sank into it. "The clouds? The sky? How is it there?"

Closing his eyes, Michael moved back and searched his memories. He spoke dreamily. "The clouds are whimsical in the tropics. But usually you can find battlements and towers soaring high like flying buttresses. A cathedral of his own."

A sad smile broke through. "You're a poet, Quartermaster."

"Thank you, but there is beauty there like you'll find nowhere else."

"You like it there?"

"Sometimes," Michael acknowledged, surprised by the woman's cognition and his own nostalgia.

"My son didn't like you."

"That's true."

"You didn't like him."

"That's true, too. But he saved my life."

"I know." The keen edge of bitterness sharpened the timbre of her voice. "He took a sword for you."

"Yes."

"The man who—who used that sword?"

"I killed him."

"I find no saitsfaction in that."

"I do."

She shook her head. "Just another dead boy and another grieving mother to match me."

"That's all?"

"Nothing more."

A terrible feeling of distress choked Michael. "But there must be more to it than that." His head came off the pillow as he pleaded, "There's more to it than that—must be. It can't be useless."

Her hand found his cheek and he sank back.

306

She conceded nothing. "There are all kinds of reasons for the killing until you lose your son. Then you suffer a loss that cannot be justified, reasoned — for which there is no rationale . . ."

Slipping from his cheek, her hand found her forehead with bony knuckles.

Michael felt a compulsion to console — to try to ease the anguish. But the woman was beyond all that and had already shrugged off his efforts. He saw his mother. No. He saw all mothers of all dead boys. They had given beyond their ability to give. It was too much. Only empty shells were left and one was beside him. There were no words.

The sad eyes moved over him. "You love your mother?"

"Of course."

"Then don't be killed."

Slowly, with her eyes tied to his, she leaned close. The thin lips found his forehead, his cheek. He put a hand to the back of her head. She kissed him full on the lips. Her mouth was cold and hard. He felt as if he was holding a dead thing — statuary that imitated life poorly.

Stiffly and with great effort she rose. The cold old eyes had softened. "Good-bye, Quartermaster."

"Good-bye, Mrs. Bennington."

She turned toward the exit, stopped, and turned back. "Bobbie was a good officer, Michael Carpelli," she said matter-of-factly. "I know he was — no one has to tell me. He could only excel because that was the kind of boy he was."

Michael stared back. "He did his best, Mrs. Bennington."

She turned and pushed her way through the swinging doors and out of the ward and Michael's life forever.

Michael's recovery moved quickly. Daily Maria visited and Michael began walking not only in the ward, but outside on the spacious lawns. The deep cool grass tickled and caressed his feet, while overhead the sun glared in the usual cloudless California sky. Like all returning veterans, sight of familiar things jarred him with pleasure: automobiles with gas-ration stickers on their windshields, the busy drive-in across the street and rumbling red electric cars racing on the Pacific Electric right-of-way just east of the hospital — all told Carpelli he was home and home was unchanged.

"I never thought I'd enjoy seeing a streetcar," he said to his mother one day as they watched a two car train race by, leaving a swirl of dust and cycloning papers in its wake. They both laughed.

Exactly three weeks after returning, Michael was dozing in the middle of the afternoon when Bryan Kohler stormed into the ward, carrying a long bundle.

"Hey, mosquito bait! Time for reveille. Doctor Kildare's here so stop goldbricking." He placed the bundle under the bed.

"Hey, man, the chancre mechanic himself," Michael said, sitting up, grinning. And then while shaking Bryan's hand vigorously, "I thought you were out there making the world safe for democracy."

"Wrong war."

"Sorry. We're supposed to remember Pearl Harbor."

"Four-oh! You're on the beam. We tied up last night and nobody has liberty yet. In fact, I'm here officially to pick up supplies," the pharmacist's mate said, pulling up a chair.

"What happened?" Michael asked eagerly. "How come you're back? What . . ."

Bryan interrupted him with a wave. "Slow down, mate." He hunched forward, "After you waltzed with that Nip and got decked by malaria, I knocked you out with a shot of happy juice."

"I'm still groggy."

"We off-loaded all the wounded by dawn and the old man went nuts. He ordered a high-speed depth charge run right through the Jap survivors. Gave 'em the works — racks, K-guns and all. Maybe twenty, thirty guys."

"Rough way to go."

"They had it coming."

"Of course, but saltwater up your ass, bustin' your guts . . ."

Bryan's lips thinned, "Couldn't happen to a nicer bunch of guys."

Michael moved his head in agreement. "You came back?"

"We hit a piece of submerged wreckage and lost our port screw, damaged six frames and we shipped water in the auxiliary engine room."

"Why not Pearl?"

"Pearl's jammed and they don't like to work on wooden ships."

"So you're back at Terminal Island?"

"Back to the womb, Michael. The Sackheim Boat Works."

The pharmacist's mate's jawline hardened, and he looked at the wall. "And we need replacements."

Michael felt his throat tighten and his eyes burn. He forced the question, "How many?"

"Fourteen dead, seven wounded."

"No! No, that's a third of the crew." There was agony in the voice. "Who? Who?"

Haltingly and in funereal tones Bryan spoke, "Bennington, Whitlow, Ursich, Fleishman, Carolla, Ringstaff . . ." He reeled off the names, describing for each the way of death or injury.

"How many had forty-fives in them?"

Kohler looked at the floor. "Impossible to tell, Michael, and you know it. But you know when we opened up there were only Japs standing."

Michael hit the mattress with a clenched fist.

"We buried them at sea the next day," Kohler added.

"Lindsay has a lot of company," Michael said in a reverential whisper, like a man at a memorial. And then looking up, "Bennington saved my life and I hated him — even threatened him."

Bryan stared at the floor silently.

Carpelli continued, "I don't understand. How can a man change like that? What happened?"

"Maybe he didn't change. Remember, only his life was at stake on the fantail."

"You mean it's hard to command."

"Of course, Michael. The guy was fresh out of college. He was in way over his head when he commanded a ship, but back there with you and the Jap, he could make his decision for himself only, not the ship."

"And I'm alive," Michael said. He came up on his elbows, propped his head on a doubled pillow. "I met his mother."

Looking up, Bryan's eyes widened with surprise. "She came to see me."

"He was from the East Coast."

"Yes, Vermont." Speaking slowly, Michael told his friend of the shattered woman, her knowledge of him, her son's sacrifice, and even of the hostility between them. "And she kissed me," Michael concluded softly. "On the lips, Bryan."

Shaking his head, Bryan looked away. Hastily, he changed the subject. "How's Kristie?"

"I don't know. I haven't seen her or heard from her. She's gone." Michael told Bryan all he knew about the aspiring actress.

"Shit!" Bryan said. "Maybe she's out there with those 'Culver City Commandos.' "

"What are they?"

"A bunch of actors who got commissions and spend all their time chasing pussy and making training films — in that order."

"Oh, man," Michael breathed. "She couldn't do anything like that."

"Bullshit! She didn't even send you a 'Dear John?' "

"Nothing," Michael conceded.

"When you get out of here, we'll look her up."

"I don't know," Michael said, shaking his head. There was despair in the voice. "I get out in a few days, have a thirty-day R and R leave coming." He palmed his long hair back. "I report to General Detail, Receiving Barracks at Terminal Island. I'm not ship's company anymore."

"I know. Bennett told me he had to cut the orders. Foat's our only QM." Bryan moved to a new topic. "Schultz told me to tell you he'll be here to see you tomorrow. In fact, a bunch of the guys will try to be here."

"Why not today?"

Bryan shook his head. "We're mounting four fifties and the three-inch is being taken ashore for overhaul. They're really rushing us. There's something big brewing out there." He waved vaguely.

311

"And Schultz is up to his ass in gun barrels."

"Four fifties?"

"There are rumors of Jap suicide planes. They call them *kamikazes*. We need all the guns they can bolt to the deck."

"Jesus. They're that crazy."

The pharmacist's mate pressed on, "I phoned Marilyn. She's fine and we have a date in a couple of nights."

"How's Vicki?"

"Better. Much better. She may be out in a few months."

"Thank God," Michael said, spirits reviving. "And Vivian Johnson? Any word?"

"She's still working in the Elbow Room and Cobra Phillips still blows his horn." Bryan squared his shoulders. "Remember how loyal Vivian was to her old man?"

Michael nodded. "Craig. He was a gunner on a Seventeen."

"Right. Well, the asshole finished his twenty-five missions and then went AWOL with some British broad."

"Well I'll be damned. Must be a lot of guys sniffing after Vivian."

Bryan laughed. "She's really pissed off—won't have anything to do with anyone. She's wearing cast iron panties now."

Michael shook his head in disgust.

Suddenly, incipient humor wrinkled the corners of the pharmacist's mate's eyes. "Hey, mate, I've got some great news."

Michael stared expectantly.

"My mother bought me a car."

"A car," Michael gasped.

"Yeah, a 1929 Ford convertible coupe."

"Jesus! You must be rich," Michael managed, stunned by the unprecedented luxury.

Bryan roared with laughter. "Not really."

" 'A' Sticker?"

"Yeah. But I'm saving my gas for your first night out."

"You're on."

Bryan glanced down and pulled up the long bundle. Cradling it in both hands, he offered it to Michael. "This is for you. The captain sent it — said you earned it."

Carpelli unwrapped the heavy paper, exposing a magnificent curved sword sheathed in a jeweled scabbard. Some of the wounded turned and stared curiously. "The Jap officer?"

"Right-on, Michael. Look at these pearls and diamonds. Must be valuable."

Michael searched the scabbard. "The chrysanthemum. It represents Hirohito."

"It's on all their weapons — even their rifles. I noticed that at the 'Canal.' " Bryan ran a finger over the silver fittings of the handle. "There's some Jap scribblings here."

Both young men stared at the ideograms surrounding the grip. Bryan continued, "José Garcia was able to translate most of it. A lot of bullshit about a great Jap warrior named Nakamura who got himself clobbered killing Russians way back in 1905."

Michael felt puzzled. "So?"

"So, the Japs like to have family swords. This one's hundreds of years old."

"So I killed some guy named Nakamura. Right?"

"Probably."

"The dead don't have names, Bryan."

313

"What do you mean?"

"They're nothing anymore, just statistics, the end product of the fuckin' assembly line out there." He waved a hand.

The pharmacist's mate tried to combat his friend's depressed mood. He chuckled. "You're some philosopher, Michael." He held up the sword. "That son-of-a-bitch had guts. You've got to admit that."

"He wanted to die. They all want to die."

"You didn't disappoint him."

The quartermaster's lips tightened down to a thin line. "What did you do with him?"

"We deep-sixed him with his buddies."

"Just garbage now."

"That's right. Shark bait."

Michael stared at the sword for a silent moment. His voice was almost wistful, "Do you think we settled anything out there? Ever will?"

Bryan's face broke with a slow grin. "Still hunting for that white fish, Quartermaster?"

It was the sick man's turn to smile. "Don't we all? And it was a whale, Bryan, not a fish. I took American Lit, too."

Kohler grinned broadly. "Well, remember this, old Ahab wound up with a harpoon up his ass."

Michael found no humor in his friend's jest.

Kohler continued, the timbre of his voice altered by a new earnestness. "Well, we showed them they can't just slaughter us at Pearl and get away with it."

"No. That's not what I meant. Like WW-One didn't do a damn thing—didn't make the world safe for a fuckin' thing."

Turning his lips under, Kohler's voice rumbled up out of his throat. "Of course not. What war

314

ever has?"

Cursing through a sudden shortness of breath, Michael lifted the sword over his head and threw it clattering across the polished floor. A dozen heads turned, stared, but remained silent.

Recovering rapidly and feeling strength flow back into his muscles, the next few days found Michael's spirits rising. In fact, a happy smile wiped the gloom from the sick man's face one evening when Chief Gunner's Mate Algernon Schultz and Signalman Second Class Dennis Warner stormed in. Carrying a box of chocolates, Schultz offered them, saying, "Pogey bait, boy. I was gonna bring you some moon, but them polecats—" he jerked a thumb, "won't let me."

"I'll be out in a couple days," Michael said, coming erect and accepting the candy. "Then we'll make liberty together." He gestured to a pair of chairs.

The visitors seated themselves.

"Get well quick, Michael," Dennis said. "We only have one QM—Bernie Foat."

"Sorry to disappoint you, boys," Michael said, biting down on a cream, "but I've retired from those festivities."

"There's a real hoedown brewin' out there, Michael," Algernon said, stuffing a caramel in his mouth.

Michael patted his buttock. "Yeah. The thought of missing it hits me right here."

The visitors laughed.

Michael's demeanor became serious. "I hear we took a lot of damage."

"Keerect," the chief said. Quickly, the gunner

described the damage while carefully avoiding mention of dead shipmates. "An'" he concluded, "we's back at Sackheim in dry dock."

"Seven days of availability," Dennis Warner added, waving to the west. "They're in a big hurry."

"Obviously," Michael said, "the war can't continue without you."

The visitors laughed again.

"We sure miss you, boy," Algernon said.

"Please, Chief, you'll have me in tears."

Schultz faked a punch. "Don' want that, boy."

"Tell you what I'll do," Michael said with a sly look.

"What?"

"While you lads are out there striking terror into the heart of the Japanese Empire, I'll do my best to bolster civilian morale on the home front — maybe take up free-lance gynecology."

Warner roared with laughter while Schultz sputtered in confusion, "Lance? Lance what?"

"Pussy!" the signalman explained through chuckles.

"Sure 'nuff. I cotton to that," Schultz said slapping his knees. "I'll put in my chit for that duty, too."

"Don't need any help, Chief. Thank you," Michael said.

"Hey, man, got a date with Thelma, Saturday night at the Elbow Room," Algernon said. "Gonna really whoop it up."

"I'll be out by Thursday."

"Make it with us."

"I'll try."

"Try, buffalo chips! Be there!"

"Okay, Chief. But I've something else to take

care of—something very important."

"Must be a piece of ass," Dennis said.

"Not quite," Michael said.

When Michael was discharged, his first call was on Desmond and Brenda Wells. All reserve was gone when they met him at the door. Brenda hugged him while Desmond slapped the young sailor on the back and pumped his hand.

"You're safe—safe," Brenda said, voice breaking.

"Saipan, you were at Saipan," Desmond said. "Your mother told us." And then to his wife, "Brenda, let go of him. Let him sit down."

Michael found a chair, and a bourbon and soda was pressed into his hand. Brenda and Desmond sat in an overstuffed sofa facing him, holding martinis.

"You look fine. Fine," Brenda said.

Michael waved her off, "Kristie? Where's Kristie? I haven't had a letter . . ."

The couple exchanged a hard look. Desmond spoke, "She moved out. She lives with a costume designer in Culver City—Ernestine Carr."

Michael shook his head, indicating a lapse.

"She's big," Brenda explained. "Kristie claims it's a great opportunity."

"Has she had parts?"

"No. But she's taking voice and acting lessons in Hollywood from Roland Deras, and she claims she'll get a screen test next month."

"She's not even twenty," Michael said.

Brenda put her teeth to white knuckles. "I know," she said.

Desmond stared at his glass.

Looking at the distressed couple, Michael shifted uneasily. What they had told him was upsetting, but what remained unsaid was even more disturbing. Everyone knew Hollywood was filled with middle-aged men claiming to be producers, agents, and writers, who preyed on young girls by promising bright futures while persuading the girls to try their casting couches. And Roland Deras was one of the most notorious. Thousands of young women from all parts of the country filled cheap rooms and bungalow courts, walking the streets, working in restaurants and drive-ins while haunting the studios and the offices of agents, forlornly hunting for that elusive part, fame, and big money. They were easy marks.

Michael said to Desmond, "She won't come home?"

Desmond shook his head. "She's over eighteen. She threatens to run away to New York if we bother her."

"How? She has no money."

"She said she'd hitchhike," Brenda said.

"She's out of her mind," Desmond added. "She thinks she'll be a star."

Draining his glass, Michael felt the warm liquid course downward. But there was no effect. "I'd like to see her."

Brenda released her breath audibly. "Oh, Michael. It would be wonderful if you could talk some sense into her."

Desmond's eyes were cold and hard. "She's changed, Michael. She's not our little girl anymore. She's not the girl you knew, the girl you left behind." Shifting his suddenly moist eyes to the far wall, he stood and walked to a desk. Returning, he handed a slip of paper to the quartermaster, saying thickly, "Here, Michael. Here's her address."

Seated in the 1929 Ford convertible coupe parked in front of his house, Michael watched fascinated as Bryan moved through Henry Ford's complicated starting ritual: insert the key, retard the spark, advance the throttle, pull the choke, and pound the starter button with the left foot while the right hovered over the accelerator.

To Michael's surprise, the four cylinder engine coughed and clattered to life, vibrating the old car right down to the last nut and bolt. With a hum of relaxed spring tension, Bryan released the emergency brake and then laboriously turned the steering wheel as he pulled away from the curb.

"Culver City here we come," the pharmacist's mate enthused triumphantly, jamming the car into second gear.

"Sixteen twenty Euclid," Michael said loudly over the typical second gear whine of the Model A Ford. "She's staying with some designer named Ernestine Carr."

"I know, you told me," Brian said, pulling the gearshift down to third gear. "I'm navigating this run, Quartermaster. So secure your sextant and plotting sheets."

Despite his grim mood, Michael managed a smile. "Okay, Bryan. You have the DR track, but do me a favor."

"What?"

"Turn on your running lights. It's almost midnight."

"Shit," Bryan exclaimed, snapping on the headlights.

For the first time, Michael laughed.

Driving west on Washington Boulevard, Michael was glad the top was down. It was torn anyway, and the old car charged through an autumn evening designed by the chamber of commerce with a cloudless sky and stars pulsing like white diamonds. Kristie's face was there and a terrible emptiness gnawed as Michael thought of the only girl he had ever loved and the inexplicable turn of events that had deprived him of her. It had been only seven months since he had left, yet the months had seemed like years. She had been there always: on lonely watches glowing from the darkness of the forecastle, above his bunk in the red glow of battlelamps, disturbing his sleep, sending him thrashing fitfully as the heat in his groin rose. And when struck by malaria, she had permeated the mists—a phantasm who stared down smiling, beckoning, promising eternal love.

Now she was gone—probably lost forever. There had been no letters for months. And she had not even inquired about him—not a word to her parents or his mother. He shook his head and punched the door with the back of a fist.

"Easy, man. This is a valuable machine," Bryan scolded. "I can understand your jealousy."

Michael managed a light. "I didn't know it was obvious."

"Oops," Bryan exclaimed. "Here's Euclid."

With a squeal of tires, the pharmacist's mate wheeled the old car into a quick right turn and after a short search pulled to the curb.

There was a party underway at 1620 Euclid. Not a wild noisy party, but a party, nevertheless, with the soft babble of voices and the sounds of a victrola playing Artie Shaw audible even at the

320

curb. The two sailors closed the doors of the Ford gently and then walked up the long sidewalk to the house.

It was a big house, a two story frame with a wide pillar-supported porch and huge heavily draped windows facing the street. The two big sailors padded quietly across the porch and entered without knocking.

They stepped into a large, dimly lighted living room with deep carpets and a half-dozen couches and love seats scattered casually. Every seat was occupied with couples—drinking, talking, and embracing. Some stood in dark corners, kissing and running hands over each other. In an adjoining unlighted room the phonograph played "Begin the Beguine" and Michael could hear couples dancing and the giggles of young girls.

As Michael's eyes adapted to the dim light, he realized the men wore officers' uniforms of all the services. Some were decorated with American Theater ribbons and Good Conduct citations. Michael snorted. As with most veterans of Pacific battles, he and Bryan disdained advertising and wore none.

As the two sailors moved to the center of the room, conversation faded as if a wet blanket had fallen on the revelers, and someone removed the needle from the record. Silently, the crowd stared at the intruders.

"What do you sailors want?" a short, fat, balding captain finally asked, looking up from a couch where he sat close to a lovely blond girl at least twenty years his junior.

"Ernestine Carr," Bryan said.

"Not here."

"Kristie Wells," Michael said harshly.

"Ever hear of her, Colonel Mackey?" the captain asked an officer who was slouched in an easy chair, cigarette in one hand, drink in the other.

"Never heard of her."

Michael pressed on, "Roland Deras?"

The captain's date squirmed, looked at another girl and then down a long, dark hall. "They're . . ."

"Shut up, Diane."

Quickly, the sailors moved to the hall. The oldest ensign Michael had ever seen barred the way.

"Out of the way," Bryan hissed.

"You're not invited, have no right here and you're cruising for a court-martial and the brig, sailors," the old ensign said.

"After Saipan, that sounds like cushy duty," Bryan answered.

The officer eyed the sailors from head to toe: tailored blues, creased caps, jumpers bare of ribbons, and the square shoulders and poise of young men accustomed to settling disputes with their fists. And there was steely resolve there and self-command that told all they were in the presence of men who knew violence and death.

"Get out of his goddamned way, Jim," the captain shouted from the couch. "If Deras wants to screw around with that kid, let him handle it himself."

Michael and Bryan pushed past the ensign and walked down a long hall. They opened the first door. The room was dark and unoccupied. They opened the second door and Bryan Kohler stopped, wide-eyed in his tracks. Two nude people were on the bed; a very young girl straddling an overweight, balding man who squirmed on his back, groaning. The girl turned. Bryan shouted

"Claudia! For Christ's sake, not Claudia!"

"Shut the fuckin' door!" the man screamed.

"Come on, Bryan!" Michael spat, too impatient to even inquire about Claudia. Claudia could wait. He pulled his muttering friend to the next door. The quartermaster flung it open. It took a few moments, but he had found Kristie.

At first he was not sure he had found her or not because the room was illuminated only by the shaft of light from the hall that fell on the far wall and reflected on the bed. She was sprawled on the bed unclothed with a middle-aged man, thrusting and writhing on top of her, locked in by her legs. So absorbed was the couple, they appeared not to notice the intruders, or did not care, butting, thrashing and moaning. Finally, the girl shouted— a deep-throated animal-like sound—convulsed, and sagged back into the mattress, arms sliding from her lover until they were flung out like a cross. Grunting like a rutting steer, the man shuddered, bit the girl's neck, and sagged as if every drop of life had spurted from him. Breathing hard, he slid from the girl. Both their bodies were beaded and slick with perspiration. Then, for the first time, the man acknowledged the intruders. He reached for his trousers.

Roland Deras was a big man, fortyish and flaccid with tiny piglike eyes set in a face like an unmade bed. His paunch bulged and his pate shone. Kristie could only sit up and stare at Michael in shock.

"What in hell do you swabbies want?" Deras piped in a high, squeaky voice. "Can't a guy have some privacy?" Pulling his pants on and securing the fly, he came to his feet.

Then Michael saw Kristie's face clearly. A red

mist clouded his eyes and he felt the hot lust to kill pour into his veins. Every nerve in his body screwed up to the breaking point. The muscles of his shoulders and arms bunched and knotted, the sinews of his neck bulged out starkly, corded into the heavy bone of his jaw. He was on the fantail again, facing the Jap officer. Growling a primal sound like a beast ready to leap, he came after Kristie's seducer recklessly, bringing up his right fist, catching him squarely on the mouth.

Spittle flew and Michael felt tissue and teeth give and break. The force of the punch sent Deras tumbling over the corner of the bed and crashing into the far corner. Moaning, the officer rolled to his back, face tight with shock, clutching his jaw gingerly. The jagged stumps of his broken front teeth were bright red with the juice. Kristie screamed.

There was no conscious thought, no hesitation, only an atavistic animal urge to destroy and obliterate. Michael went after him again. Bryan, shouting "No!" grabbed his shoulders and pulled him back. "Jesus, man," Bryan pleaded. "This garbage isn't worth it."

"Let me go!" Carpelli tried to pull away, but the pharmacist's mate pushed him against the wall.

"Michael! Michael!" Kristie finally managed, pulling a sheet over herself. "You've hurt Roland!"

"I'm okay, Bryan. Let me go," Michael said, ignoring Kristie. Roland staggered to his feet, but remained cowering in the corner, bleeding from the mouth. Michael rubbed his knuckles. One was slightly gashed and there was a trickle of blood on his hand.

There was a commotion at the door. "You assholes'll spend the rest of your lives in the brig for

324

this," the old ensign said, staring at Michael. Several more officers crowded close behind him. "You just punched Captain Roland Deras."

"That's right," Deras agreed, slurring his words and spraying blood. Cautiously with a single finger he began to feel his already swollen jaw. "Call the SPs, Paul," he said to the man in the doorway. He spit out a piece of enamel.

Bryan spoke. "At the same time, call the cops, because the girl in the next room is only seventeen."

"Seventeen?" the two chorused. "That's Rosselyne Slater and she's twenty," the officer called Paul stated.

"Bullshit. She's Claudia Freeman. I've known her since she was a kid. She lives on the same block with my mother. She baby-sat my sister, Linda, for years. She's only a senior in high school, for Christ's sake."

"That fuckin' Ron. Always fuckin' around with San Quentin quail," the man in the doorway spat bitterly, waving to the next room. The other men muttered angrily.

Bryan chuckled at their discomfort. His voice cut with scorn. "You gallant officers are guilty of statutory rape, to say nothing of running a floating whorehouse and giving alcoholic drinks to minors." He stared silently at the faces that now crowded the doorway. "I'll make the phone call — to the *Times, Examiner, Herald*. Your wives, studios, Hedda Hopper, Louella Parsons, Jimmy Fidler, and even Walter Winchell are going to love this. Man, what great publicity! Remember what happened to Errol Flynn? They hauled his ass into court for screwin' around with a minor. He made the front pages for weeks."

Michael caught Bryan's sardonic mood. "Yeah. You could even get shipped out when the brass finds out. Make a few landings. Get star billing from the Japs. They have a great script out there, filled with action. Better than *The Charge of the Light Brigade*, *Sahara* and *Captain Blood* all put together. You should see the flashy shows they put on—the realism. And it's all in Technicolor." He chuckled. "More fun than a casting couch. Why, hell, an air raid is more spectacular than a premier at Graumann's Chinese."

"Yeah," Bryan agreed, "you should see a thousand-pound bomb go off, greatest special effects you ever saw, and the noise . . ." He gripped his forehead and threw his head back in mock awe, "Better than Vitaphone."

"You could even get a few Purple Hearts to go with those Good Conduct medals," Michael said. "A few could be posthumous, of course," he added slyly.

"I've had enough of this shit," Roland Deras muttered almost incoherently through lips that had swollen to the size of sausages. He grabbed his clothes and pushed through the crowd in the doorway. In a moment, the other men followed him and the hall was silent.

Kristie sat motionless, staring at Michael. "You hurt him," she said.

"Nothing an archeologist can't fix. He'll live." He heard Bryan snicker from a position near the doorway.

"Why did you do it?"

"Why are you here?"

"I wanted a career."

"A career? This is a career?"

Kristie continued, "No, not yet. But some

326

things are expected. Can't you understand?"

"Understand? My God, what about your virginity? Your pledge to your mother, your priest? And you were going to wait for me."

Her voice was hard, and it stung like dry ice, "You forget, Michael. I'm human. While you were out sleeping with your whores, you left me to burn in my bed alone. I'm human, too. You never considered that."

"I did consider that and you forgave — said you'd wait — said you loved me." He waved. "Gave me something to live for out there."

"You changed, Michael."

"So have you."

"Of course. I told you I'm human, too."

His face was hot as if the fever had returned. He spat his words, "So you fucked that fat bum — a goddamned USO Commando."

"Leave, Michael."

"My pleasure."

Heading east on Washington Boulevard, Michael slouched, resting the back of his head on the Ford's hard springs bulging under the sparse, worn upholstery, and stared skyward. His Kristie was gone. He had destroyed her. Or had the war done it.

"She's gone," he said to the sky.

"Maybe she never was," came Bryan's quick reply — an answer so sudden and crisp Michael felt he had been stealing his thoughts.

"Never was?" He rubbed his sore hand. The bleeding had stopped, but there was a dull ache.

"Yeah, Michael. She was your ideal because you wanted her to be your ideal."

"Bullshit! Don't practice Philosophy One AB on me."

"You created her," Kohler said, ignoring the affront. "You wanted something pure, untouched."

"Of course. Don't you?" Michael said caught up in his friend's insights.

"No. This world doesn't tolerate clean, pristine things."

"It corrupts."

"Of course. She was just another pussy, Michael."

"Don't say that."

"Why not?"

"I'll bust your jaw."

Bryan grunted as he wheeled the Ford around a corner. "You saw her on the bed with that pig. What did you see? A virgin?" There was no humor in his laugh.

"This is a fucked-up world," Michael said, waving a fist at the heavens.

"Said like a professor of graduate studies, ol' buddy," Bryan said, pulling the Model A to the curb in front of the A-1 Bowl. "Let's have a drink. You need one or two or a half-dozen."

Bryan was wrong. Michael needed eight drinks before his malaria-weakened constitution gave out and he dropped his head to the table.

The next day, nursing a hangover, Michael received his leave papers and orders. Scanning the single sheet, he could not believe his good fortune. After his leave, he was to report to ship's company at the Small Craft Training Center on Terminal Island, where he was to teach navigation and signaling to ninety-day wonders commissioned directly from universities.

It was late afternoon when he arrived home carrying his toothbrush, razor, and other toilet articles in his ditty bag. Maria was ecstatic. After kissing her son, she pulled him down on the old couch. "The war's over for you, *bambino mio.*"

"Could be, Mom," he agreed, placing the ditty bag on a battered end table.

Her face clouded. "You mean you can still . . ."

"Orders can always be changed, Mom, but it looks like I'll be stateside for a long time."

Sighing, she captured his hand. Saw the bruised knuckles. "You're hurt."

"It's nothing, Mom."

"Another fight?"

"I squashed a cockroach."

She waved a finger in his face, scolded, "You've got to stop that fighting. You'll get hurt." She sank back into the battered cushions. "But you don't have to fight the Japs. You're safe. My boy's home and safe."

"Yes, Mom." A strange uneasiness dried his craw, and he twisted restlessly.

"What's wrong?"

"Nothing."

"Kristie?"

He squirmed like a man too close to a flame. "No. No, that's over."

"Over? I thought . . ."

"No, Mother. She's changed or I've changed or maybe the world . . ."

"I'm sorry, Son."

Leaving out the details of the scene in the bedroom, Michael told his mother about the events of the previous night, telling her only of Kristie's determination to be an actress and her infatuation with Roland Deras.

"Do you think she's sleeping with that man?" she asked innocently.

"I'd hate to think so," Michael answered stonily, choking back the gorge of his lie.

Maria changed the subject suddenly and with trepidation in her voice, "The Two Four O Four is in drydock?"

"Yes."

"Have you visited it?"

"No. I intend to go aboard tomorrow."

"Just to visit?"

"Of course. What else? The only friends I have . . ."

He watched her as she rose, grabbed the ditty bag off the table, returned to the couch, and held the small canvass bag in both hands. "Well, leave this here," she said defiantly.

Michael laughed. "You're holding my toothbrush and razor hostage, Mom?"

She smiled. "Yes. Don't volunteer for anything."

"I promise, Mom."

"Yes, you promise," she mimicked skeptically. "You've done that before." She placed a hand on his while still clutching the bag in her other hand. "I've got to work tonight. I'm still on graveyard shift."

"I know."

"You'll be alone. Go to a movie. *Sahara, Action in the North Atlantic, A Yank in the RAF* are all playing around."

"Good war movies," he said harshly.

"Sorry, Son. I didn't . . ."

"All the guys are gone or dead."

She bit her lip. "I know. I know."

"I'm tired. I think I'll just listen to the radio

330

and go to bed."

"No bars?"

He smiled. "No bars."

"Good, *bambino mio*." She kissed his cheek and held him tight. He thought she would never let go.

Ships in dry dock are awesome—even a PCS. Crossing the gangway from the lip of the graving dock to the 2404's main deck, Michael was struck by the small vessel's sudden appearance of size. Sharing the dock with two PCs and a mine-sweeper and festooned with a latticework of scaffolding, she was free of the sea for the first time since launch, her patched wooden hull gleaming with new paint. Crewmen and yard workmen swarmed over her, scraping, painting, and filling the air with their shouts and the sounds of metal impacting metal, the shrieks of high speed drills, and the Orlikon bursts of pneumatic tools. And the K-guns were gone, replaced by four Browning fifty-caliber machine guns mounted in two pairs.

Schultz waved from the forecastle, where he signaled a crane operator, who slowly lowered the three-inch back down on its mount. "Elbow Room, tonight," the chief shouted, cupping his mouth.

"Four-oh," Michael shouted back.

As Michael reached the end of the gangway, he saluted Ensign John Manning, making the traditional request, "Permission to come aboard, sir."

The officer's smile was big and warm. "Permission granted, Quartermaster Carpelli."

"Is the captain aboard, sir?"

"In the wardroom." The ensign gestured to a pennant whipping at the yardarm.

"Thank you, sir."

Walking to the wardroom, Michael was greeted by Dennis Warner, Bernie Foat, Isadore Nash, and a half-dozen others who grabbed his hand and pounded his back with shouts of "Welcome aboard," and "Welcome home." But there were new faces—many new faces and curious stares. Michael knocked on the door of the wardroom.

"Welcome aboard," Lieutenant Andrew Bennett said, opening the door and grasping Michael's hand while ushering him in. In a moment, the quartermaster was seated, facing the officer across his desk.

"Good to see an alumnus," Bennett said.

"Couldn't resist homecoming, Captain."

"We have an empty bunk if you're overwhelmed by nostalgia, Michael."

"I'll try to bear up, sir."

Both men laughed.

Bennett became serious. "You look well."

"I feel well, Captain."

"You know of our casualties—our damage?"

"Yes. The guys told me."

"We'll be ready for sea in about two weeks."

"No leaves?"

"A week only for one-third of the crew." The captain stabbed a finger, "Something big is brewing."

"Yap or the Philippines, Captain?"

"You're very perceptive, Quartermaster."

"So are the Japs, Captain. We're running out of objectives. It becomes easier and easier to pick the next one. They'll be waiting."

"Of course." Bennett tapped his desk with a single finger. "You don't belong on the beach, Michael."

"I beg to differ, Captain."

"No. It's true. You're no longer part of state-side — won't fit, can't belong to it." He circled a finger over his head. "This is my world and it's yours, too. You belong here, found your place here . . ."

"And I can get killed here."

The captain sighed. "I admit I need you. I admit I'd like to see you ship over. But keep in mind, Michael" — he struck the desk with his knuckles — "we'll be here maybe two weeks and we can use you. No, as I said, we need you."

"Thank you, Lieutenant," Michael said sincerely. "I'll remember and think about it, sir."

Smiling, the captain rose as Michael came to his feet. After a firm handshake, the quartermaster left.

Nothing had changed: the long, shiny walnut bar and paneled room crowded with uniforms and women, the perennial blue thunderhead of tobacco smoke, the lanky Cobra Phillips twisting on the bandstand blowing his trombone like Gabriel calling his flock. The corner table was still tucked in the far end, where Michael sat toying with a highball as he eyed Schultz, Kohler, and their women. Thelma, heavier and going to flab, crowded Schultz while whispering in the gunner's ear and occasionally nibbling on his earlobe. Marilyn, whose stringy hair still showed the effects of a shortage of peroxide, snuggled up to Bryan Kohler, never taking her eyes from the big pharmacist's mate's face — not even when she drank.

And Vivian was there, alluring with her long amber hair tumbling to the shoulders of her tight satin blouse. Michael had forgotten how sensuous she had been until he watched her walk across the room with a trayful of drinks on her shoulder, her short, tight taffeta skirt undulating sinuously over firm buttocks, long world-class legs spectacular in black hose.

"In case you had any doubts, that's what we're fighting for," Bryan muttered under his breath while watching Michael's eyes.

Michael laughed, remembering the expression on Vivian's face the moment he had entered. Women had looked at him often with desire and longing in their eyes. But Vivian, carrying a tray, had stopped in midstride, green eyes wide and fixed unblinking as if a dream had materialized, a phantom had risen to flesh and blood or a beloved had been released after an eleventh hour reprieve. Not even his mother's eyes had ever moved him like Vivian's, because there was passion and aching, painful hunger smouldering there.

Michael had felt a visceral jolt, an urge to reach out and touch her—feel his hand on her flesh, fingers in her hair. Instead, he managed a casual, "I hear you have great highballs."

"The best, Michael," she had answered, eyes riveted to his. And then with a smile and wave to the corner, "The maitre d' has reserved your usual table, Mr. Carpelli." Slyly, she added, "You've been neglecting us."

"I had some prior engagements," he said simply.

"I heard," she said.

Now she was serving another round, leaning over Michael, eyes searching the new wrinkles awakening at the corners of his eyes. "I've got to talk to you," she said, close to his ear.

"Ooh! Watch her, big boy. She may have designs on your body," Thelma bellowed.

Everyone laughed.

"When do you get off?"

"Midnight."

"I'll be here."

The waitress vanished into the crowd. At that moment, Michael met Soul Saver Sal.

"Have you accepted Jesus Christ as your one and only saviour?" echoed in Michael's ear hoarsely.

Turning, Michael stared up at an old man with feral brown eyes and unkempt white hair that hung over his ears. His yellow skin was loose and corrugated like weathered cardboard, thin neck dried and wrinkled like an old turkey's. Slight, he was dressed in a threadbare black suit and plain dirty white collar. Two of his front teeth were missing and he hissed his *s* with a spray of saliva.

At first Michael assumed the man was drunk, but he soon discovered he was mistaken. "I've never met the man," the quartermaster said evenly while Bryan, Marilyn and Algernon stared curiously.

"You have," the old man said sharply. "But sin has clouded your eyes and you cannot see."

Michael wiped spittle from his forehead.

"Can you see the door?" Kohler asked casually.

The women giggled.

"Let him say his piece," Algernon said, obviously fascinated.

Drawing himself erect, the old man extended an arm over the table. "Repent or fry in the fires of hell!"

A few heads turned.

"I've already been there and I'm well done on both sides," Michael said.

335

The hand dropped. "Then you saw God!"

"Sorry, preacher," Michael said, shaking his head. "God abandons ship at the one hundred eightieth meridian. You're on your own from there west."

"Blasphemy!"

Bryan laughed. "The Japs bring their gods and they outnumber ours. We only have one."

"Those heathens are only fit to die," the old man said.

"Said like a Christian," Bryan noted.

Some dancers stopped, stared curiously.

A big marine sergeant who worked as a bouncer materialized behind the preacher. "This way to the pearly gates, Salvador," the marine said, grasping the old man's arm and pointing at the door.

"Sinners," Salvador hissed, spraying the word over the table and into the drinks. "You stand on the edge of the pit. Look inward!"

A score of heads turned. There was a scattering of giggles and the music faltered.

"Repent!" cracked like a whip.

Cobra Phillips stared over his horn, a pained look on his face. Then the music stopped altogether in a sputter of half-finished notes and the dancers stood motionless. All eyes turned to the corner.

The marine tugged. Soul Saver stood fast. With a grunt, the big service man jerked the old man back and away from the table. Applauding and cheering, the crowd parted and the old man was dragged backward across the floor, his worn black heels tracing streaks across the waxed hardwood.

"The Red Sea parted for the children of Israel, too," the old man shrieked. "Repent! Repent!" he screamed hoarsely as he was pushed through the

336

door.

"Thank God I'm an atheist," Michael heard Bryan mutter into his highball.

The music resumed and the dancers picked up their rhythms.

"You leave in two weeks?" Marilyn asked suddenly, breaking the mood.

"How do you know?" Bryan said with surprise.

"I'm a spy," the girl said, quiet humor playing in her eyes.

"Let's dance," Kohler said, pulling the girl to her feet.

"Good idea," Algernon agreed, rising. "Let's cut a rug."

After the two couples left, Michael sat motionless, drinking and staring into the dim light and blue smoke. Was the Soul Saver right? Who really knew? No man could ever answer that question. Then Kristie crowded the preacher out. Her look was hard, filled with uncharacteristic malevolence. He had earned it—deserved it. And Vicki, too, was there, searching frantically for something she could never find.

Michael smiled. Vicki had not been mentioned by anyone at the table. And Don Lindsay's name, too, had remained quiescent. Not a word of the war, damage, or casualties. Yet the lists had lengthened. Savage fighting in the Pacific and a stalemate in Europe had provided thousands of new names for the papers, thousands of crosses and stars of David. Would it ever end? Perhaps the war would continue on its own momentum forever, consuming everyone and everything until nothing but a sterile planet was left fit only for rats and cockroaches. That's it. The winners. Rats and cockroaches.

Michael tossed off the rest of his drink. There was the flash of satin, and the rustle of taffeta, and he clutched a fresh drink. Again he felt the deep heat as he watched the trim hips and black hose vanish into the crowd. He looked at his watch. Two more hours. The hands of the Bulova seemed stuck in time. He cursed.

The dancers returned, and there was more conversation carefully structured to humorous situations, funny movies, and radio programs. And time became unstuck.

Michael knew Bryan, Marilyn, Algernon, and Thelma were growing restless. Months of separation, liquor, and close dancing would inevitably fan the flames. The looks became longer and deeper, hands restless and daring. By eleven, Michael sat at the table alone.

He stopped drinking and nursed his highball while watching the dancers and Cobra Phillips. Finally, Vivian returned, a knee-length blue coat concealing her uniform and her marvelous legs. She extended her hand.

Wordlessly, Michael rose, enveloping the tiny hand with his. They walked to the door.

"How did Don Lindsay die?"

"Quickly," he said, hunched on the Murphy bed in the middle of Vivian's small studio. Staring at his drink, he added, "Is that enough?"

"Of course," she said. After hanging her coat in a closet, she seated herself in a chintz covered overstuffed chair opposite him. "I didn't mean to bring back . . ."

He interrupted with a wave, "It's not that. It's just that he's gone and no amount of talking can

338

ever bring him back. And a lot of others, too."

"I'm sorry. Sorry."

"Please don't pity me," he said, abruptly. Then looking at the empty mantel. "Your husband's picture is gone. You've had your losses."

"Craig ran off. He's AWOL in England with some Englishwoman."

"I heard."

"I'm suing for divorce." Then leaning forward, "You're in love, aren't you, Michael."

He finished his drink with a quick toss of his head. "I was, but I've lost her."

"She ran off with a drama teacher."

"Bryan told you?"

"Yes."

"It was my fault." He handed her his glass. Taking the glass, she walked to the icebox in the kitchen alcove while his eyes followed the cat-like, flowing movements of the remarkable body. Returning, she handed him his drink and sat down on the bed next to him, pulling her long legs up, staring with her wide-spaced hazel eyes like a very young girl contemplating a new toy.

"You've had malaria. You're not part of the crew."

He nodded.

"You'll never go to sea again."

"There are no absolutes in war except death."

"You'd have to volunteer."

He nodded.

"You wouldn't do that?"

He remained silent.

"Malaria can come back."

"True. I'll take quinine for the rest of my life." Elbows on knees, he leaned forward impatiently. "You wanted to see me?"

339

"Pepe's making trouble."

Michael shook his head, indicating a lack of memory. "What? Who . . ."

"Antonio's friend. Remember that night in the alley?"

Michael sagged back. "Of course. The bums." He narrowed his eyes, "They assaulted you—raped you." He punched the mattress. "You should've reported them."

"My God, Michael. I told you that was impossible—I told you what the cops do to women."

"Stinkin' world."

She raised her glass and touched his. "Amen." They drank and then he kissed her cheek, but her mind was somewhere else. She did not turn to him. Instead, she talked to a cheap throw rug at her feet, "Michael, you know Antonio died."

"I know."

"They're still looking for his killer. There's no statute of limitations on murder."

"Murder!" Rocking back and forth, he laughed so raucously a tear ran down his cheek. The girl stared in alarm.

She grabbed his arm. "Please, Michael—please."

Slowly, he regained control, wiped the tear with his sleeve. "Sorry, Vivian, but after Guadalcanal and Saipan, that word has no meaning." He drank. "Please go on."

"You know there were only two witnesses, Michael. Pepe and me."

"We've been over this. You know it was self-defense and so does that bum."

"You wouldn't expect him to tell the truth."

The sailor nodded agreement. "He didn't go to the police—not that scum."

"No. He's afraid of the cops. He's been in on a

half-dozen misdemeanors and he's on parole for armed robbery."

"Then I'm safe."

"Not really."

"Not really?" he repeated, staring at the girl.

She hurried on, "We made a deal. He'd keep his mouth shut if I didn't report him and break his parole. He could go up to San Quentin."

"Sounds great. How come he wants to deal?"

"He's going to be drafted."

"My God. The army can't be that hard up. We'll never win the war."

"I'm afraid they are. If I report him, he's going to tell them all about you. He heard me call your name in the alley and has a damned good idea of who you are and I think he knows you're back. They'd haul me in, put me on the stand, and . . ." Her voice broke.

Michael slid his arm around the girl's slender shoulders. "All right, Vivian, I understand." He took a drink. "But Vivian, you're my witness — saw it all."

The girl took several deep breaths. "True. But you'd be arrested, arraigned, called to a preliminary hearing, and probably tried. I asked a lawyer friend about it."

"But we'd beat him."

She shrugged. "Probably. But it would take time and money."

He clutched the bedspread and crushed a handful into a hard knot. "Damn! Damn! I don't understand. Just don't understand." And then staring at his glass: "I don't belong here." He emptied it.

Rising quickly, the girl moved to the alcove and then returned with a full glass. She sat so close to him, her thigh was against his. "Michael," she said

341

softly, "we'll beat him."

Looking into the soft warm eyes, he felt her hand on his. "I think we could do anything together, Vivian."

"You're going back to sea, aren't you Michael?"

"Not to run from that bum."

"It's the guys—Algernon, Bryan, and the rest."

"You're beginning to sound like my mother, Vivian."

She laughed. "Michael"—her voice was very soft and her eyes on the wall—"I'll wait for you, if you want me to."

He felt a sudden warm glow of happiness he had not felt in an eternity. "I wouldn't want to do that to you."

"I know how."

He felt her breath on his cheek. They both placed their highball on a night stand. Then, turning, his lips brushed the warm ivory skin of her cheek, not stopping until he covered her lips. The kiss was hungry, hot and lasting.

"Michael," she finally managed breathlessly. "Remember that night we spent together?"

"How could I forget?" he said, feeling the firm flesh of her back under the satin, kissing her cheek, her eyes, her forehead.

"We didn't touch each other." She ran a hand over the muscles of his arm, his back.

"God damned fools, weren't we?"

"I'm never foolish twice in a row, Michael."

"Neither am I," he said, pushing her back on the bed.

Groaning, she sank into the mattress, her arms tight around him. Her hair was so fine and silky it formed an amber halo, like watered satin that flowed over the pillow and down to her shoulders.

342

Their kisses were savage, his hands running over the hard breasts, nip-in waist, flare of hips, long legs. He reveled in the smoothness and warmth of the hot flesh he found beneath her satin blouse, the elegant curves of her breasts, the discovery of sculpted angularity precisely where angularity should have been, the taut muscles, her fluid movements, squirming to his caresses.

With an effort, she pushed him away. "Your clothes—your clothes, darling. I want you nude."

They stood and tore at their own clothes and each other's with trembling hands. He pulled off his jumper, clawed at her blouse, ripping buttons. Finally, they stood naked. She pulled him back on the bed, parting her knees and raising them high. He settled between them and felt her curl her spine like a cat, inclining her pelvis toward him. He seized one of her buttocks in each hand and pulled her to him. She took him and guided him. In a moment, he was deep in her, and the butting, thrashing, gasping and moaning began.

The horror was gone, death was gone. This was life, the beginning of life, the beginning of everything. He luxuriated and rejoiced in it.

Dawn crept into the room like a bright, playful spirit, prying the lovers out of their deep sleep. Michael was on his back, Vivian snuggled against him, face in the hollow of his neck, arm flung across his chest. "You were marvelous," she whispered.

"You're the best, Vivian." He kissed her forehead and the folds of her hair.

"You can go all night," she said, awed. "I've never known that before. Craig used to get it over

343

with and roll over and go to sleep. But you think of the girl—bring her to what she really wants, really needs."

He smiled. "I've been at sea for seven months. I've had a lot of time to think about it."

"It's been two years for me, Michael."

He kissed her and she pushed her body against his. "Stay with me, Michael. We could love each other . . . I—I could fall for you. I think I already have."

He stared into the warm depths of the striking hazel eyes. The color was heightened by a film of moisture. "I care for you, Vivian," he said, kissing her cheek, her long gazelle neck.

"Do you love me?"

"I don't know."

"If there were no war?"

"Then I'd love you, Vivian—want to stay with you."

"You're going back to sea. I know it, I can feel it."

He turned his lower lip under and bit down on it hard. Someone else seemed to speak. "I must."

"Back to those murdering Japs."

And then he said something that surprised himself. An insight he had never felt before or sensed before. The words seemed to come from a hidden place in his subconscious. "Japs are honest. They're not like Antonio and Pepe. They hate you, want to kill you, and do their damnedest to do it. No friendly faces and then a knife in the back, no smart-assed talk in an alley, no hypocrisy."

"You like them," she said, astonished.

"I hate them."

"Then you respect them."

344

He thought for a moment, jarred by the girl's perceptiveness. "Maybe I do. I never thought of it that way, but maybe I do. They're tough little shits."

"I told you once I'd wait for you."

"I remember. But you waited for Craig and what did it get you?"

"You're different. I love you, Michael."

"Didn't you love him?"

"At first. But now I hate him."

He turned to her and ran his hand over her breasts and down her back, feeling every plane. Finding her spine, he traced his fingertips downward. The ridge of her spine felt like polished beads beneath silk, and he followed it down until it disappeared into the divide of her small, solid bottom. He pulled her pelvis against his arousal, pushed against the warm mound of her womanhood. She wrapped her arms around his neck and kissed him fiercely. "Come back to me, darling," she whispered.

"I'll come back to you."

"Promise?"

"Promise." He pushed her onto her back and slid his body over hers.

She sighed and moaned, "I love you. I love you." In a moment she was incapable of speaking.

"Why? Why, Michael?" Maria asked from the battered sofa, voice filled with anguish. "You were assigned here. You had good duty and you aren't well."

Michael knew he could never justify his decision to return to sea. Even the assignments officer had been shocked when Michael requested the 2404

345

that morning. Looking at his mother's face, he realized no rationale would work; not duty, not patriotism, not Antonio and Pepe or anything else.

"I belong there, Mom," he declared simply. "I can give you no other reason."

"I can," she said with frightening candor.

He remained silent.

"It's the crew. It's always been that way since the beginning. You died with the subchaser but found new life with the PCS. Now it's Kohler and Schultz and the rest that give you a reason . . ."

"I don't know, Mom."

"Well I do. It's your world. A place where you belong. I failed—I couldn't do that for you." Her eyes filled. She looked away.

"I belong to you, Mother."

"Don't patronize me, Michael."

He stared at the floor silently.

"You're miserable here. You belong to them." She waved a hand.

"Maybe."

"Maybe, hah! And it's the Japs, too."

"The Japs?"

"Yes. If you didn't have them, you'd have to invent them. They've given you something I could never give you."

"What, Mom?" he asked, avoiding her eyes.

"An excuse for killing which gives you a reason to live. It's as old as men and will go on forever."

Holding her small shoulders, he moved his eyes to hers and the intelligence gleaming in the dark depths like smokey lamps. "I've got to report aboard." Rising slowly, he moved to the door. The wide, moist eyes followed him from the couch.

"What will you do when it's over, Michael?"

"What do you mean, Mom?"

346

"The war. It'll be over some day. What will you do then—find another one?"

Silently, the young man turned and left the room.

Epilogue

Standing on the lip of the crater, Keiko Yokoi could smell the acrid odor of sulphur. Leaning over the edge, she could see the incandescent pool of lava and hear the bubbles boil to the surface like a devil's brew.

She had taken the ferry from Shingu that morning, feeling a deep sense of joy and contentment, knowing she would soon experience the ultimate consummation of her love for Takeo Nakamura. For the entire journey she could see Oshima's smouldering peak beckoning like a beacon in a storm.

Now she stood on the brink of eternity, clutching the large white envelope.

There were voices behind her. "Young woman. Back. Back, it's dangerous. Wait. Don't go out there by yourself."

Turning, she saw a bent old man in the black uniform of a park caretaker approaching, while a dozen curious tourists stood behind him on the dirt path, staring.

She held up the envelope. "I'm not alone. We go together."

The old man nodded, understanding. "There can be a better way, young woman. The gods would understand." He moved closer.

Keiko smiled slowly. "No. There is no other way."

Stepping to the brink, she looked skyward, clutching the envelope to her breast.

349

"Beloved, we shall be together again for eternity," she cried.

"No, young lady!"

She stepped from the brink and plummeted into the lava.

Author's Note

Lieutenant General Yoshitsugu Saito and Admiral Chuichi Nagumo died during the invasion of Saipan. Because there were so few Japanese survivors, there have been conflicting reports as to just how both men died. I was careful to treat both officers in a manner consistent with their traditions and the circumstances of battle.

THE ONLY ALTERNATIVE IS ANNIHILATION . . .

RICHARD P. HENRICK

BENEATH THE SILENT SEA   (3167, $4.50)
The Red Dragon, Communist China's advanced ballistic missile-carrying submarine embarks on the most sinister mission in human history: to attack the U.S. and Soviet Union simultaneously. Soon, the Russian *Barkal,* with its planned attack on a single U.S. submarine is about unwittingly to aid in the destruction of all mankind!

COUNTERFORCE   (3025, $4.50)
In the silent deep, the chase is on to save a world from destruction. A single Russian submarine moves on a silent and sinister course for American shores. The men aboard the U.S.S. *Triton* must search for and destroy the Soviet killer submarine as an unsuspecting world races for the apocalypse.

THE GOLDEN U-BOAT   (3386, $4.95)
In the closing hours of World War II, a German U-boat sank below the North Sea carrying the Nazis' last hope to win the war. Now, a fugitive SS officer has salvaged the deadly cargo in an attempt to resurrect the Third Reich. As the USS *Cheyenne* passed through, its sonar picked up the hostile presence and another threat in the form of a Russian sub!

THE PHOENIX ODYSSEY   (2858, $4.50)
All communications to the USS *Phoenix* suddenly and mysteriously vanish. Even the urgent message from the president cancelling the War Alert is not received and in six short hours the *Phoenix* will unleash its nuclear arsenal against the Russian mainland. . . .

SILENT WARRIORS   (3026, $4.50)
The Red Star, Russia's newest, most technologically advanced submarine, outclasses anything in the U.S. fleet. But when the captain opens his sealed orders 24 hours early, he's staggered to read that he's to spearhead a massive nuclear first strike against the Americans!

Available wherever paperbacks are sold, or order direct from the Publisher. Send cover price plus 50¢ per copy for mailing and handling to Zebra Books, Dept. 3904, 475 Park Avenue South, New York, N.Y. 10016. Residents of New York and Tennessee must include sales tax. DO NOT SEND CASH. For a free Zebra/ Pinnacle catalog please write to the above address.